LENORA WORTH
I'll Be Home for Christmas

One Golden Christmas

Steeple
Hill®

Published by Steeple Hill Books™

STEEPLE HILL BOOKS

Steeple
Hill®

Recycling programs
for this product may
not exist in your area.

ISBN-13: 978-0-373-65134-4

I'LL BE HOME FOR CHRISTMAS AND
ONE GOLDEN CHRISTMAS

I'LL BE HOME FOR CHRISTMAS
Copyright © 1998 by Lenora H. Nazworth

ONE GOLDEN CHRISTMAS
Copyright © 2000 by Lenora H. Nazworth

Printed in U.S.A.

CONTENTS

Books by Lenora Worth

Steeple Hill

After the Storm
Echoes of Danger
Once Upon a Christmas
"'Twas the Week
   Before Christmas"

Love Inspired Suspense

Fatal Image
Secret Agent Minister
Deadly Texas Rose
A Face in the Shadows
Heart of the Night
Code of Honor

Love Inspired

The Wedding Quilt
Logan's Child
I'll Be Home for Christmas
Wedding at Wildwood
His Brother's Wife
Ben's Bundle of Joy
The Reluctant Hero
One Golden Christmas
*When Love Came to Town
*Something Beautiful
*Lacey's Retreat
Easter Blessings
   "The Lily Field"
**The Carpenter's Wife
**Heart of Stone

**A Tender Touch
Blessed Bouquets
   "The Dream Man"
†A Certain Hope
†A Perfect Love
†A Leap of Faith
Christmas Homecoming
Mountain Sanctuary
Lone Star Secret
Gift of Wonder
The Perfect Gift

*In the Garden
**Sunset Island
†Texas Hearts

LENORA WORTH

has written more than thirty books, most of those for Steeple Hill. She also works freelance for a local magazine, where she had written monthly opinion columns, feature articles and social commentaries. She also wrote for the local paper for five years. Married to her high school sweetheart for thirty-three years, Lenora lives in Louisiana and has two grown children and a cat. She loves to read, take long walks and sit in her garden.

I'LL BE HOME FOR CHRISTMAS

And now abide faith, hope, love, these three;
but the greatest of these is love.

—*1 Corinthians* 13:13

To Jean Price and Dee Pace,
for taking a chance on me,
and
To my mother, Myla Brinson Humphries,
who's in heaven with the angels.

Chapter One

He was tired.

He was hungry.

He wanted a big roast beef sandwich from that roast Henny had baked early in the week, and then he wanted to go to bed and sleep for at least fourteen hours.

Nick Rudolph shifted against the supple leather seat of his Jaguar sedan, his impatient foot pressing the accelerator further toward Shreveport, Louisiana, the interstate's slippery surface spewing icy rain out around the sleek black car.

He was also late. Very late. Carolyn would be fuming; he'd have to smooth things over with her. Right about now, he was supposed to be escorting her to the mayor's Christmas party. Instead, he was making his way along a treacherous stretch of icy road, on the coldest night of the year.

His mind went back to the meetings in Dallas he'd had to endure to cut another deal for Rudolph Oil. After all the hours of endless negotiations, he still wasn't sure if he'd closed the deal. They wanted to think about it some more.

That he wasn't coming home victorious grated against his ego like the ice grating against his windshield wipers. Over the last few years, work had always come first with Nick Rudolph. It was an unspoken promise to his late father, a man Nick hadn't understood until after his death. Now, because he'd seen a side of his father that still left him unsettled, Nick preferred to concentrate on tangible endeavors, like making money.

Nick Rudolph wasn't used to losing. He'd been blessed with a good life, with all the comforts of old money, and he didn't take kindly to being shut out. He'd win them over; he always did. He might have given up every ounce of his self-worth, but he wasn't about to let go of his net worth.

As the car neared the exit for Kelly's Truck Stop, he allowed himself a moment to relax. Almost home. Soon, he'd be sitting by his fire, the cold December rain held at bay outside the sturdy walls of his Georgian-style mansion. Soon.

Nick looked up just in time to see the dark shapes moving in front of his car, his headlights flashing across the darting figures rushing out onto the road in front of him.

Automatically slamming on his brakes, he held the leather-covered steering wheel with tight fingers. His mind screamed an alert warning as the car barely missed hitting a small figure standing in the rain before it skidded to a groaning halt.

"What in the world!" Nick cut the engine to a fast stop, then hopped out of the car, his mind still reeling with the sure knowledge that he'd almost hit a child. Coming around the car, his expensive loafers crunching against patches of ice, he looked down at the three people huddled together on the side of the interstate. Tired and shaken, he squinted against the beam of his car's headlights.

The sight he saw made him sag with relief. He hadn't hit anyone. Immediately following the relief came a strong curiosity. Why would anyone be standing in the middle of the interstate on a night like this?

The woman stood tall, her chin lifted in proud defiance, her long hair flowing out in the icy wind, her hands pulled tight against the shoulders of the two freezing children cloistered against the protection of her worn wool jacket.

The two children, a small boy and a taller, skinny girl, looked up at Nick with wide, frightened eyes, their lips trembling, whether from fear or cold, he couldn't be sure.

He inched closer to the haphazard trio. "Are you people all right?"

The woman pushed thick dark hair away from her face, shifting slightly to see Nick better. "We're all okay. I'm sorry. We were trying to cross over to the truck stop. We…you…I didn't realize how fast you were going."

Nick let out a long, shuddering sigh, small aftershocks rippling through his body. "I almost hit you!"

The woman stiffened. "I said we're all okay." Then as if realizing the harshness of her words, she repeated, "I'm sorry."

Something in her tone caught at Nick, holding him. It was as if she'd had a lot of experience saying those words.

"Me, too," he said by way of his own apology. He'd never been good with "I'm sorry", because he'd never felt the need to apologize for his actions. But he had been driving way too fast for these icy roads. What if he'd hit that little boy?

He ran his hand through his damp dark hair, then shoved both hands into the deep pockets of his wool trench coat. "Where…where's your car? Do you need a ride?"

The woman moved her head slightly, motioning toward the west. "We broke down back there. We were headed to the truck stop for help."

"I'll drop you off," Nick offered, eager to get on his way. Turning, he headed back to his car. When the woman didn't immediately follow, he whirled, his eyes centering on her. "I said I'd give you a lift."

"We don't know you," she reasoned. "It's not that far. We can walk."

"And risk getting hit again?" Regretting his brusque tone, Nick stepped closer to her, the cold rain chilling him to his bones. "Look, I'm perfectly safe. I'll take you to the truck stop. Maybe they can call a wrecker for your car."

"I can't afford a wrecker," the woman said, almost to herself.

"We're broke," the little boy supplied, his eyes big and solemn, their depths aged beyond his five or so years.

"Patrick, please hush," the woman said gently, holding him tight against her jeans-clad leg. Gazing up at Nick, she shot him that proud look again. "I'd appreciate a ride, mister."

"It's Nick," he supplied. "Nick Rudolph. I live in Shreveport." As he talked, he guided them toward his car, wondering where they were from and where they were headed, and why they'd broken down on such an awful night. "I'm on my way back from Dallas," he explained, opening doors and moving his briefcase and clothes bag out of the way.

"We used to live near Dallas," the little boy said as he scooted onto the beige-colored leather seat. "Wow! This is a really cool car, ain't it, Mom?"

"It's *isn't*," his sister corrected, her voice sounding hoarse and weak.

The boy gave her an exaggerated shrug.

Nick stepped aside as the woman slid into the front seat. Her eyes lifted to Nick's, and from the overhead light, he got his first really good glimpse of her.

And lost his sense of control in the process.

Green eyes, forest green, evergreen, shined underneath arched brows that dared him to question her. An angular face, almost gaunt in its slenderness, a long nose over a wide, full mouth. Her lips were chapped; she nibbled at the corner of her bottom lip. But she tossed back her long auburn hair like a queen, looking regal in spite of her threadbare, scrappy clothes.

Nick lost track of time as he stared down at her, then catching himself, he shut the door firmly, his body cold from the December wind blowing across the roadway. Running around the car, he hurried inside, closing the nasty night out with a slam.

"Mom?" the little boy said again, "don't you like Nick's car?"

"It's very nice," the woman replied, her eyes sliding over the car's interior. "And it's Mr. Rudolph, Patrick. Remember your manners."

The expensive sedan cranked on cue, and Nick pulled it back onto the highway, careful of the slippery road. "What's your name?" he asked the woman beside him.

"Myla." She let one slender hand rest on the dashboard for support as the car moved along. "Myla Howell." Nodding toward the back of the car, she added, "And these are my children, Patrick and Jessica."

The little girl started coughing, the hacking sounds ragged and raspy. "Mama, I'm thirsty," she croaked.

"They'll have drinks at the truck stop," Nick said, concern filtering through his need to get on home.

"We don't got no money for drinks," Patrick piped up, leaning forward toward Nick.

"Patrick!" Myla whirled around, her green eyes flashing. "Honey, sit back and be quiet." Her tone going from stern to gentle, she added, "Jesse, we'll get a drink of water in the bathroom, okay?"

Nick pulled the car into the busy truck stop, deciding he couldn't leave them stranded here, cold and hungry. He'd at least feed them before he figured out what to do about their car. Turning to Myla, he asked, "Is everything all right? Can I call somebody for you? A relative maybe?"

She looked straight ahead, watching as a fancy eighteen-wheeler groaned its way toward the highway. "We don't have any relatives here." A telling silence filled the car. Outside, the icy rain picked up, turning into full-fledged sleet.

"Where were you headed?" Nick knew he was past late, and that he probably wasn't going anywhere soon.

"To Shreveport." Myla sat still, looking straight ahead.

"Mom's found a job," Patrick explained, eager to fill Nick in on the details. "And she said we'll probably find a place to live soon—it'd sure beat the car—"

"Patrick!" Myla turned then, her gaze slamming into Nick's, a full load of pain mixed with the pride he saw so clearly through the fluorescent glow of the truck stop's blinding lights.

His mouth dropping open, Nick gave her an incredulous look. "What's going on here?"

"Nothing." Her chin lifted a notch. "Thank you for the ride, Mr. Rudolph. We'll be fine now."

The car door clicked open, but Nick's hand shot out, grabbing her arm. "Hey, wait!"

Her gaze lifted from his hand on her arm to the urgent expression on his face. "Let me go."

"I can't do that." Nick surprised himself more than he surprised her. "If you don't have any place to go—"

"It's not your problem," she interrupted. "If I can just make it into town, I've got a good chance of still getting the job I called about yesterday. Once I find steady work, we'll be fine."

"I can help," he said, almost afraid of the worn wisdom he read in her eyes. "I can call a wrecker, at least. And find a place for you to stay."

From the back seat, Jessica went into another fit

of coughing, the hacking sound reminding Nick of memories he'd tried to suppress for too long.

"That does it." He reached across Myla to slam her door shut. The action brought them face-to-face for a split second, but it was long enough for Nick to get lost in those beautiful eyes again, long enough for him to forget his regrets and his promises and wish for things he knew he'd never have. And it was long enough for him to make a decision that he somehow knew was about to change his life. "You're coming with me," he said, his tone firm. "I won't leave a sick child out in this mess!"

The woman looked over at him, her eyes pooling into two misty depths. "I…I don't know how to thank you."

Nick heard the catch in her throat, knew she was on the verge of tears. The thought of those beautiful eyes crying tore through him, but he told himself he'd only help the family find a safe place to spend the night. He wasn't ready to get any further involved in whatever problems they were having.

"You need help," he said. "If you're worried about going off with a stranger, I'll call someone to verify my identity." A new thought calculating in his taxed brain, he added, "In fact, my sister is a volunteer counselor for Magnolia House. I'll call her. She's always helping people." Having found a way to get out of this sticky predicament, Nick breathed a sigh of relief.

Myla turned back, her eyes wary. "What's Magnolia House?"

He waved a hand. "It's this place downtown, a homeless shelter, but a bit nicer. According to my sister it has private rooms where families can stay until…until they get back on their feet." He really didn't know that much about his sister's latest mission project, except that he'd written a huge check to help fund it.

Giving him a hopeful look, she asked, "And we don't have to pay to live there?"

"No, not with money. You do assigned tasks at the home, and attend classes to help you find work, things like that. My sister helped set the place up and she's on the board of directors. She'll explain how it works."

"Can you get us in tonight?"

Putting all thoughts of a roast beef sandwich or a quiet evening with Carolyn out of his mind, Nick nodded hesitantly. "I'll do my best. And I'll send a wrecker for your car, too."

She relaxed, letting out a long breath. Then she gave him a direct, studying stare, as if she were trying to decide whether to trust him or not. Clearing her throat, she said, "Thank you."

Admiration surfaced in the murky depths of Nick's impassive soul. He knew how much pride those two words had cost this woman. He admired pride. It had certainly sustained him all these years.

Debating his next question, he decided there was no way to dance around this situation. Starting the car again, he carefully maneuvered through the truck stop traffic.

"How'd you wind up…?"

"Homeless, living in my car?"

Her directness surprised him, but then this whole night has been full of surprises.

"If you don't mind talking about it."

"My husband died about a year ago." She hesitated, then added, "Afterward, I found out we didn't have any money left. No insurance, no savings, nothing. I lost everything."

Nick glanced over at her as the car cruised farther up the interstate, leaving downtown Shreveport at Line Avenue to head for the secluded privacy of the historic Highland District. Taking her quiet reluctance as a sign of mourning, he cleared his throat slightly, unable to sympathize with her need to mourn; he'd never quite learned how himself. So instead, he concentrated on the fact that she was a single mother. All his protective instincts, something he usually reserved for his sister, surfaced, surprising him. *Must be the Christmas spirit. Could I possibly have some redeemable qualities left after all?*

"What did you do?" he asked, mystified.

Lifting her head, Myla sighed. "I left Dallas and looked for work. I got a job in Marshall, but the company I worked for closed down. I ran out of money, so we got evicted from our apartment."

Nick could hear the shame in her voice.

"After that, we just drove around. I looked for work. We stayed in hotels until the little bit of cash I had ran out. That was two weeks ago. We've been sleeping in the car, stopping at rest areas to bathe and eat. The kids played or slept while I called about jobs."

She slumped down in her seat, the defeat covering her body like the cold, hard sleet covering the road.

Then she lifted her head and her shoulders. "I don't want to resort to going on welfare, but I'll do it for my children. We might be destitute right now, but this is only temporary. I intend to find work as soon as I can."

It was Nick's turn to feel ashamed. He was more than willing to write her a fat check, but he had the funny feeling she'd throw it back in his face. She had enough pride to choke a horse, but how long could she survive on pride? And why should he be so worried that she'd try?

Nick didn't have time to ponder that question. Minutes later, he pulled the car up a winding drive to a redbrick Georgian-style mansion that shimmered and sparkled with all the connotations of a Norman Rockwell Christmas. Suddenly, the wreaths and candles in the massive windows seemed garish and mocking. He'd told Henny not to put out any Christmas decorations, anyway. Obviously, the elderly housekeeper hadn't listened to him, not that she ever did.

Now, seeing his opulent home through the eyes of a person who didn't have a home scared him silly, and caused him to take a good, long hard look at his life-style.

"Man!" Patrick jumped up to lean forward. Straining at his seat belt, he tugged his sleeping sister up. "Look, Jesse. Can you believe this? Santa's sure to find us here. Mr. Nick, you must be the richest man in the world."

The woman sitting next to him lowered her head, but she didn't reprimand her son. Nick saw the pain shattering her face like fragments of ice.

Nick Rudolph, the man some called ruthless and relentless, sat silently looking up at the house he'd lived in all his life. He'd always taken it for granted, his way of life. His parents had provided him and Lydia with the best. And even in death, they'd bequeathed an affluent life-style to their children.

Nick had accepted the life-style, but he hadn't accepted the obligations and expectations his stern father had pressed on him. When he could no longer live up to those expectations, he'd acted like a rebel without a cause—until he'd seen the truth in his dying father's eyes.

Everything his father had drilled into him had

become a sham. And Joseph, overcome with emotion because he loved his Ruthie too much, had tried to tell Nick it was okay to be vulnerable when it involved someone you loved.

But it had been too late for Nick. He'd learned his lessons well. Now, he guarded his heart much in the same way he watched over Rudolph Oil—with a steely determination that allowed no room for weakness.

Maybe that was why he'd felt so restless lately. Maybe his guilt was starting to wear thin. Though he had it all, something was missing still. Nick had never wanted for anything, until now. All his money couldn't buy back this woman's pride or settle her losses. All his wealth seemed a dishonest display compared to her honest humility.

"No, Patrick," he began, his voice strangely husky, "I'm not the richest man in the world, not by a long shot."

"Well, you ain't hurtin' any," Patrick noted.

"No, I suppose I'm not," Nick replied, his eyes seeking those of the woman beside him. "Let's go inside where it's warm."

Opening the car door, he vented his frustration on the expensive machine. He *was* hurting. And he didn't understand why. How had the night become a study in contradiction and longing? How had he fallen into such a blue mood? Well, he'd just had an incredibly bad day, that was all. Or was it?

No. It was her—Myla. Myla Howell and her two needy children. He couldn't solve all the problems of the world, could he? He'd make sure they had a decent place to stay, maybe help her find a job, then go on with his merry life. Things would go back to the way they'd been up until about an hour ago.

And how were things before, Nick? an inner voice questioned.

Normal. Settled. Content.

And lonely.

And that was the gist of the matter.

These three ragamuffins had brought out the loneliness he'd tried to hide for so long. Denying it had been pretty easy up until tonight. But they'd sprung a trap for him, an innocent but clever trap. They'd nabbed him with their earnest needs and unfortunate situation. He'd help them, sure. He certainly wasn't a coldhearted man.

But he wouldn't get involved. At all. His formidable father had drilled the rules of business into Nick—no distractions, show no emotions. In the end, however, Joseph Rudolph had forgotten all his own rules. In the end, his own emotions had taken control of his life. Nick had learned from Joseph's mistake. So now, he let Lydia do the good deeds while he took care of business. It was a nice setup. One he didn't intend to change.

"I'll call Lydia. She'll know what to do," Nick said minutes later as he flipped on lights and guided them through the house from the three-car garage. A large, well-lit kitchen greeted them as the buzz of the automatic garage door opener shut them snugly in for the night. Nick headed to the cordless phone, intent on finding his sister fast. Then he'd have to call Carolyn and make his excuses. When he only connected with Lydia's perky answering machine, he left a brief, panicked message. "Lydia, it's your brother. Call me—soon. I'm at home and I could really use your help."

We make him uncomfortable, Myla Howell reasoned as she watched the handsome, well-dressed man talking on the phone. She knew she and her children were an inconvenience. When you didn't have money, or a place to sleep, you became that way.

She'd learned that lesson over the last few months. People who'd called themselves her friends had suddenly turned away. She wasn't good enough for them now. They didn't have time for her now. They couldn't be seen associating with a homeless person.

This man was the same. He couldn't wait to be rid of them. But, he had saved them tonight. She'd give him credit for that. She watched him moving about the kitchen, taking in his dark, chocolate-colored hair, remembering his gold-tinged tiger eyes. Golden brown, but missing that spark of warmth. Calculating eyes? She'd seen that kind of eyes before; still bore the scars from trusting someone who could be so ruthless. Would this man be any different?

She hoped so, she prayed so, for the sake of getting her children to a safe place. Refusing to give in to her fears or her humiliation, she focused on her surroundings instead. What a joy it would be to cook in a kitchen like this! She missed having a kitchen. Cooking was one of her pleasures and with hard work and lots of prayer, it could soon be her livelihood, too.

The gleaming industrial-size aluminum stove shouted at her while the matching refrigerator-freezer told her there was lots of bounty here to explore. The long butcher block island centered in the middle of the wide room spoke of fresh vegetables and homemade breads and pastries. Myla closed her eyes briefly, almost smelling the aroma of a lovely, home-cooked holiday meal. She'd miss that this Christmas. But next year…

Nick watched her in amazement. Under the surreal lights of the truck stop, she'd looked pale and drawn. But here in the bright track lights, Myla seemed to glow. She was tall, almost gaunt in her thinness. Her hair was long and thick, a mass of red, endearing curls that clung to her neck and shoulders. Even in her plain clothes, this woman exuded a grace and charm that few women would possess dressed in furs and diamonds. Obviously, she hadn't always been homeless. Her clothes and the children's looked to be of good quality and in fair shape. Not too threadbare; wrinkled, but clean.

Mentally shaking himself out of his curious stupor, Nick watched her closely, noticing the dreamy expression falling across her freckled face. Then it hit him. "You're probably hungry."

His statement changed Myla's dreamy expression to a blushing halt. "I'm sorry…this is such a beautiful kitchen…I got carried away looking at it." Nodding at the expectant faces of her children, she pushed them forward. "The children need something to eat. We had breakfast at a rest stop— donuts and milk."

The implication that they hadn't eaten since this morning caused Nick to lift his head, but he turned away before she could see the sympathy in his eyes. "Well, don't worry. Our housekeeper, Henrietta Clark, has been with the family for most of my life. She always stays with a friend down the street when I'm away, so she's not here tonight. But she cooks a lot, way too much for my sister and me. We usually wind up giving half of it away—"

"It's all right, Mr. Rudolph," Myla said to ease his discomfort. "We'll be glad to take some of your leftovers off your hands, right, kids?"

She was being cheerful for the children's sake, Nick realized. Relaxing a little, he dashed over to the gleaming refrigerator. "Let's just see what we've got. We'll have ourselves a feast."

Patrick hopped up on a wooden stool, yanking his fleece jacket off with a flourish. "My mom's the best cook, Mr. Nick. She can make just about anything, but her bestest is bread—and cookies."

"Oh, really?" Nick glanced over at Myla. "Well, come on over here, Mom. I could use an expert hand. I'm not very good in the kitchen."

Eyeing Jesse and unsure what to do with her, he lifted the quiet little girl up on the stool next to Patrick. With an unsteady smile, he registered that she felt warm, almost too warm, but then he wasn't a doctor or a daddy. What did he know about little girls?

Myla stepped forward, then took off her thread-bare wool coat. "Anything I can do to help?"

Nick watched as she hovered beside him, as if waiting for him to issue an order. Tired and unsure what to do himself, he unceremoniously loosened the red-patterned tie at his neck, then yanked off the tailored wool suit jacket he'd worn all day. Tossing the jacket across a chair, he watched as Myla straightened it and hung it over the back of the chair, her hands automatically smoothing the wrinkles out.

"Thank you," he said.

He watched as a flush bathed her cheeks. "I'm sorry," she said. "Force of habit. My husband liked everything in its place."

Nick nodded, then wondered about her marriage. Had it been a happy one? Not that it was any of his business, but the sad, almost evasive look in her eyes made him curious. Did she miss her husband? Of course, she probably did, especially now when she was struggling so much.

"How about a roast beef sandwich?" he asked as he lifted the heavy pan of meat out of the refrigerator. "Henny cooked this for Sunday supper, but I didn't get back into town to enjoy it."

"That's a shame."

"No, that's the life of an oilman. Lots of trips, lots of leftovers." Searching through a drawer, he found a large carving knife. "I say, let's cut into this thing."

"Yeah, let's cut into that thing," Patrick echoed, clapping his hands. "My mouth's watering."

Jesse smiled, then coughed.

"Are you hungry, Jesse?" Worry darkened Myla's eyes. "She has allergies and she's fighting a nasty cold."

A spark of warmth curled in Nick's heart. "Maybe some good food will perk her up." He offered Jesse a glass of orange juice.

Nick found the bread, then poured huge glasses of milk for the children. Myla located the coffeemaker and started a fresh brew. She sliced tomato and lettuce, then made some thick roast beef sandwiches. Soon all four of them were sitting around the butcher block counter. Nick picked up his sandwich for a hefty bite, but held it in midair as

Myla and her children clasped hands and bowed their heads.

Seeing his openmouthed pose, Myla said quietly, "We always say grace before our meals. I hope you don't mind."

Nick dropped his sandwich as if it were on fire. "No, of course not."

When Myla extended her hand to his, something went all soft and quiet in his ninety-mile-an-hour mind. When was the last time he'd said a prayer of any kind? He listened now to Myla's soft, caressing voice.

"Thank you, Lord, for this day and this food. Thank you for our safety and for the warmth you have provided. Thank you for sending us help when we needed it most. We ask that you bless each of us, and this house. Amen."

Stunned, Nick wasn't so sure he wanted his house blessed. He felt awkward as he lifted his hand away from the warmth of Myla's. To hide his discomfort, he said, "Let's eat."

Patrick didn't have to be told twice. He attacked one half of his sandwich with gusto. Nick flipped on a nearby television to entertain the children, but mostly to stifle the awkward tension permeating the room.

He watched them eat, hoping Lydia would call soon. Patrick wolfed his food down in record time, while Jesse nibbled at hers between fits of dry coughing. Their mother broke off little bits of her sandwich, as if forcing herself to eat, her eyes darting here and there in worry.

Finally, out of frustration more than anything else, Nick said, "That hit the spot. I was starved."

"Me, too," Jesse said, speaking up at last.

Nick's eyes met her mother's over her head. It didn't help to know that Jesse probably had been really hungry, when to Nick the words were just a figure of speech. Myla only gave him a blank stare, though, so to hide his confusion he munched on a chocolate chip cookie while he watched the children, and their mother when she wasn't looking.

The baggy teal sweater brought out the green in her expressive eyes. Worn jeans tugged over scuffed red Roper boots encased her slim hips and long legs. Couldn't be more than thirty, just a few years younger than him, yet she carried a lot of responsibility on her slim shoulders.

"You've got a pretty name," he said to stop the flow of his own erratic thoughts.

"I was named after my grandmother," she said. "She hated her name because people would always call her Mi-lee. My mother named me after her to make her feel better about it."

"Where's your family?" he asked, hoping to learn more about her situation.

She shot him that luminous stare before answering. "My parents passed away several years ago—

a year and a half apart. First my mother, from a stroke. Then Daddy. The doctors said his heart gave out, and I think that's true. He died of loneliness. They'd been married forty years."

Nick felt a coldness in the center of his heart, a coldness that reminded him of his firm commitment to keep that part of himself closed away. "Same with my parents. My mother died of cancer, and my father was never really the same after her death." He looked down at his half-eaten sandwich. "He...he depended on his Ruthie, and her death destroyed him. It was as if he changed right before my eyes." Not wanting to reveal more, he asked her, "Do you have any brothers or sisters?"

She nodded. "A brother in Texas—he's got five kids. And a sister in Georgia. She just got married a few months ago." She sat silent for a minute, then finished. "They don't need me and my problems right now."

"Do they know...about what's happened to you?"

Her flushed face gave him his answer. She jumped up to clean away their dishes. "No, they don't. Not yet." Turning toward the sink, she added, "I really appreciate your help, but I don't intend to live on handouts. If my job hunt pays off—"

"What sort of work are you looking for?"

"A waitress, maybe, for now. I love to cook. One day, I'd like to run my own restaurant."

Nick wanted to touch her face for some strange

reason. She had that dreamy look about her again, and it endeared her to him. He felt an overwhelming need to buy a building and turn it into a restaurant.

But he didn't touch her, and he didn't offer to fund her venture. Instead, he looked down, as embarrassed by being wealthy as she obviously was by being destitute.

Myla's touch on his arm brought his head up. "I want to thank you, Mr. Rudolph, for helping us. All day, I prayed for help, and then you came along. You offered us shelter, and that's something I'll never forget. So thank you, for your kindness and your understanding."

Nick looked in her eyes and felt himself falling, falling, as if in slow motion. Moving away abruptly, he said, "Call me Nick, please. And you don't have to thank me."

The confused look she gave him only added to his woes. He couldn't tell her that he rarely let people get close enough to touch him, either physically or emotionally. He couldn't erase the hurt look in her eyes.

When a special news bulletin interrupted the noisy cartoon on the nearby television, Nick was thankful for the distraction until he heard the report.

The familiar face of the local weatherman filled the screen, and after going over the progress of the ice storm covering the city, the newscaster suggested everyone stay put for the night. "The roads are becoming treacherous and travel may be hazardous until this storm passes. We should be able to resume normal activities by midmorning when higher temperatures and sunshine clear this system out."

Nick eyed the television, willing the man to say it wasn't so. When that didn't happen, he looked toward the silent phone, all hopes of Lydia's much-needed help freezing up like his winding driveway outside. With three pairs of questioning eyes centered on him, he could only give a gracious but shaky smile.

Thoroughly at odds, he wanted to ask Myla Howell why him? Why'd she have to pick him? And what was he supposed to do with her now? Instead, he took her hand. "Well, that settles it. You heard the man. You can stay here tonight."

"What?" Myla gave him a stunned look. "But what about your sister? What about Magnolia House?"

"It can wait," Nick stated firmly, silently wishing Lydia would call and rescue him before he drowned in those questioning green eyes. Or was he silently hoping she wouldn't call? To counter his treacherous thoughts, he added, "It's late and Magnolia House is downtown. It's too dangerous a trip in these icy roads. You'll have to stay here tonight."

"Are you sure?"

"Very sure." His tone was firmer than his confidence. Right now, he wasn't very sure of anything—except that he couldn't send this family back out into that cold, dark night.

Chapter Two

"Henrietta, please don't cry."

Nick ran a hand through his tousled hair, then gratefully accepted the cup of coffee the whimpering housekeeper handed him before she burst into tears again.

"Ah, Henny, don't do that. It's too early in the morning for theatrics. I didn't know my Christmas present would move you to tears."

"But, Nicky," the older woman began, her shimmering gray curls not moving a centimeter even though she bobbed her head with each word, "it's the sweetest thing anyone's ever done for me. God bless you. You're a good man…a good one…" Her words trailed off as her watery eyes centered on something beyond Nick's head.

Nick turned to find Myla Howell standing in the

doorway, wearing the same clothes she'd had on the night before.

"I'm sorry," Myla said, sensing she'd interrupted something important. "I heard voices…."

"Nicky?"

Myla looked from the old woman who stood with her hands on her hips to the man sitting like a king at the head of the long Queen Anne dining table. He was trying to read the newspaper, and judging from the frown marring his handsome face, he was losing patience with the woman standing before him.

"Who's this?" the woman asked, smiling kindly over at Myla.

Nick looked up. Myla didn't miss the surprise or the grimace on his face. "Oh, hello. Henny, this is Myla Howell. Due to the bad weather, Myla and her children were forced to spend the night in one of the guest rooms." He extended a hand toward the woman. "Myla, this is Henrietta Clark, my house-keeper and best friend."

Myla was thankful when the woman didn't ask any questions. "Nice to meet you."

Henny smiled and waved a hand. "Did I wake you up with my wailing, honey? I'm sorry, but I'm so excited. Nicky gave me the best Christmas present before he left for Dallas the other day—a trip to see my daughter and her children in Arkansas."

"And she's wailing because she's so touched," Nick added on a droll note. "She's leaving today."

"That's wonderful," Myla said. "I know you'll have a great time."

"I plan to," Henrietta said, "if I don't spend the whole time worrying about Nicky and Lydia."

"We'll be fine," Nick said, his attention already back on his paper. Then he asked Myla, "Would you like some breakfast, a cup of coffee, maybe?"

Myla took the cup of coffee Henny pressed into her hand, but she didn't sit down. "Actually, I came down to ask for some medicine. Jesse's had a bad night. She's running a fever."

Nick scowled. "Is she all right?"

Afraid that he wasn't pleased at this added problem, Myla nodded. "I think she'll be okay. I just need to bring her fever down."

"Your child?" Henny asked.

"Yes. My oldest. I'm not sure about her temperature, but she feels awfully hot."

Henny whirled around. "There's a thermometer around here somewhere. Nicky won't let me use it on him anymore."

A smile slipped across Myla's face. In spite of her concern for Jesse, she couldn't resist the mental image of the stout Henrietta chasing a snarling Nick around with a thermometer.

Nick's scowl went a few grooves deeper. "She still thinks of Lydia and me as her babies." He gestured for Myla to sit down. "Does Jesse need anything else?"

Myla appreciated the warmth in his words, even if it didn't quite reach his eyes. "I don't think so. Just rest and good food. If you don't mind, I'll feed them breakfast before we leave."

He looked down at the table. "I put in another call to my sister. You can't take chances with this weather."

"No, I wouldn't do that to Jesse. I appreciate your letting us stay here, Mr. Rudolph."

"Call me Nick."

"Okay." Myla sensed, knew, he couldn't wait to be rid of them. "I'm sorry we've disrupted your life."

"It's no problem," he said. "Did you sleep all right?"

"Yes, we all did until Jesse started coughing."

Myla wouldn't tell him that she'd tossed and turned in spite of the warm, cozy room and the enormous bed. She felt so alone, so out of place in this grand old house. But she was certainly thankful that they hadn't had to spend the night in the car.

When she looked up, Nick's gaze softened. "Don't worry about your daughter. If she's sick, we'll get her to a doctor."

"Thank you."

Henrietta burst through the swinging door from the kitchen, a bottle of pills in one hand and a thermometer in the other. "How old's the child?"

"Eight."

"Half a tablet, then. And I'll fix her up some of

my special hot lemonade with honey to help get that down. The lemons—good for a cold." She turned to strut back to the kitchen, then whirled to face Nick. "Oh, Nicky, I almost forgot. Are you sure you and Lydia can handle things tonight?"

Nick looked confused, his gaze moving from Myla to his housekeeper. "Tonight? What's going on tonight?"

"Your dinner party," Henny said with arms akimbo. "Don't tell me you forgot to call the temp service. You told me not to worry about a thing, that you and Lydia would take care of calling someone to fill in for me."

Nick sat up, realization hitting him. "You mean my sister and I are in charge of…kitchen duty?"

Henrietta shook her head. "I knew you weren't listening to me the other day." She shot Myla a knowing look. "A one-track mind, that one. If it don't have to do with oil, he don't want to deal with it."

"I guess I *wasn't* listening," Nick agreed. "And I think we'd better round up someone to take care of that. We both know Lydia's as useless in the kitchen as I am."

The housekeeper mumbled something about pre-occupied executives, then explained, "It's too late to call the temp service. They're booked through Christmas, I imagine." Looking disappointed, she asked, "You want me to stay?"

Myla listened, then squeaked, "I can do it."

When both Nick and Henrietta looked at her as if she'd gone daft, she wanted to drop through the tapestry rug underneath her feet. But this would be a good way to pay Nick back for his help, and it would make her feel a whole lot better about things. "I can cook. I can do whatever needs to be done." When Nick kept staring at her, she rushed on. "Well, if I'm going to stay here all day anyway, I can't just sit around twiddling my thumbs. I'd like to help, to pay you back for your kindness."

Henny smiled from ear to ear. "Well, now, isn't that a nice gesture on your part, honey."

"I'll pay her, of course." Nick gave Henny a sharp look, then turned a questioning glance at Myla. "Do you have experience with this sort of thing?"

Myla didn't tell him that she'd once been considered the best hostess in her neighborhood. That had been one of her husband's demands, along with all his other demands. Instead she said, "I've been in charge of dinner parties before, yes. Henrietta can show me where everything is." Lifting her chin, she added, "And I could use the money."

She watched as Nick weighed his options, hoping for this reprieve, this time out of the cold. Finally, he spoke.

"Well, I certainly don't have time to find anybody else. Okay, you've got the job. But I expect everything to run smoothly—and that means making sure your children—"

"They'll stay out of your way," Myla said. "I promise."

"Good." He turned to Henny. "After breakfast, you can get things settled up between you."

"You're the boss," Henrietta said, smiling to herself as she ambled into the kitchen.

Nick watched her, and Myla saw the doubt clouding his features. Wanting to reassure him, she said, "Don't worry. I can do whatever needs to be done. I want to help and I won't let you down."

"That's good," he contended, "since I'm trusting you alone in my house."

Not liking his tone, she retorted, "I'm a Christian, Mr. Rudolph. I won't steal anything if that's what you're implying."

"I wasn't implying anything. And I certainly didn't mean to insult you."

Seizing the opportunity, Myla rushed on. "Then you might consider letting me fill in for Henrietta. I could work for you until she gets back from her trip."

That got his attention. "I hadn't planned on a long-term replacement. I don't go all out for the holidays."

"That's a shame," she countered. "Christmas is such a beautiful, blessed time of year."

"I don't like Christmas," he insisted. "In fact, this dinner party tonight is more of an obligation to my clients than a celebration."

"Why wouldn't you want to celebrate?" she had

to wonder out loud. "The birth of the Savior is a joyous time."

He didn't give her the answer she wanted. Instead, he said, "Henny's planning to be gone until the first of the year. Are you willing to work through Christmas?"

Myla was glad, but surprised that he wanted her to stay that long. She needed a job, but hadn't counted on this becoming a long-term arrangement. This would give her some time, though, and a safe place for her children. "A month? That would help us get a good start on the new year."

Nick's next words were dusted with doubt. "And, it would solve both of our predicaments—you need a job, I need a good worker."

"What about my children? You obviously don't want them underfoot."

"We'll get them enrolled in school. You were planning on doing that, weren't you?"

Resenting his superior attitude, she retorted, "I hadn't thought past getting them to a warm bed."

Nick countered. "Hey, it was your idea. After Christmas you can take the money you've earned here and do whatever you like. This is a sensible solution for everyone concerned."

Myla had to agree. "So you're asking me to stay here and work for you for the next few weeks?"

He almost grinned. "I don't remember doing any asking, but yes, I guess I am."

She held out her hand. "Deal, unless that other job I came here for is still open. Then, I'll help you only until I can start there."

"Deal," he said, shaking her hand. "I'm glad you understand that this is only temporary."

"Oh, I understand. And I'll need to get my car. We've got a few belongings left in the trunk."

"I'll take care of that. You take care of your daughter, then get together with Henny so she can explain how everything's run around here." He started toward the long, central hallway, then turned. "We'll put you in Henny's apartment off the kitchen. It's more private."

"That's fine," Myla said. At least it would be a roof over her head for a while, and it would be much more suitable than the spare guest room, since this was a strictly business arrangement. "I'd better get back up to the children. Jesse needs this medicine."

"Don't forget Henny's hot lemonade with honey," he reminded her. "Works wonders. I've got to get to work. Oh, and one other thing. I always do a background check on my employees. Any problem with that?"

Hesitating, Myla stammered, embarrassed. "No, but I think you should know a few things. I haven't held a job since high school. I was…I chose to stay at home after my children were born. And my credit is shot because…I had to file bankruptcy."

He gave her a sympathetic look that hid his own doubts as to the wisdom of this arrangement. "Anything else?"

"Isn't that enough?" she replied with a small smile. "I'll do a good job, I promise," she added sincerely.

Nick stared down at her a moment, nodded briefly, then turned to go.

She watched Nick walk away, then she sent up a silent prayer. *Don't let me mess this up, the way I've messed up my life.*

She'd be so ashamed if he knew the whole truth.

"This is so exciting!"

Lydia Rudolph stood at the window of her brother's downtown Shreveport office, gazing out at the Red River some twenty floors below. "I mean, I'm twenty-five years old, big brother, and this is one of the few times I've actually seen you do something almost human." She fluffed her shining blond bob and beamed brighter than the lighted Christmas stars twinkling insistently on the building across from them. "This only goes to show what I've tried to tell you all along—doing something good for someone brings out the best in people, even an old Scrooge like you."

"I am not a Scrooge," Nick said in protest. "I can't help it if I don't feel the same strong sense of religion that you do, Lydia. I'm quite happy with my life the way it is, thank you. In fact, I'm just a happy-go-lucky kind of guy."

Lydia snorted, causing her bright red hoop earrings to jingle. "Right. You're a great faker, Nick, and we both know it. But this is a start. I'm glad to see you involved with something besides this oil company."

"Yes," Nick responded dryly from his perch on the massive teakwood desk. "Having two rambunctious children and their pretty mother in my house for the holidays is about the most exciting thing I can imagine. And here I was hoping you'd help me out of this mess."

"They're people, Nick, not a mess." Lydia swung around, the fringe on her red suede jacket almost hitting her brother on the head. "I think you needed this. You couldn't wait to tell me all about it when you got here this morning."

"I told you all about it because what I need is your help, little sister. *They* need your help. This is a very temporary situation."

Nick wished he'd just kept his mouth shut. This whole business was starting to get to him. Still amazed that he'd hired Myla to run his house, he had to wonder at his own sanity. He was reeling from the strange turn of events in his life. In the span of less than twelve hours, he'd committed himself to saving a homeless mother and her two waifs. Not involved? Hah! He was involved up to his eyeballs.

Resolving to get this situation cleared up—
another of his father's rules: no loose ends—Nick
gave his sister a pleading look. "This dinner party
is important, Lydia. I need to reassure some of our
local stockholders. We've pulled through our
slump, but I've still got people jumping ship. Are
you going to help me?"

"I'm thinking," Lydia said, settling herself down
in the comfortable black leather swivel chair behind
Nick's desk. "If I help you with this woman and her
children and your precious party, will you go to
church with me on Christmas Eve?"

Nick gulped his coffee too fast and burned his
tongue. "That's blackmail," he said, spurting out hot
coffee in the process. "You know how I feel about
that."

Lydia's knowing smile didn't help his bad mood.
"What happened to that almost-human I was just
talking to?"

He scowled, rubbing his burned tongue against
his top teeth. "I'm the same as ever. And I refuse to
be pushed into a situation about which I feel uncomfortable. If you can't agree to help me, please
leave. I've got work to do."

Lydia jumped up to come around the desk. "Oh,
Nick, remember when we were little? Remember
Mother taking us to the Christmas Eve service?
You in your Christmas suit, me in my velvet dress?
You cared then, Nick. You loved Christmas."

"Well, I don't love it now," he said, his mood getting darker by the minute. "And I have work to do."

Lydia stood staring at him. "And I thought helping someone out of a jam would make you less grumpy. When are you going to stop being mad at God, Nick?"

"Probably never," he said, tired of this argument. Thinking back about last night, he remembered Myla's prayer. She'd thanked God for simple things. Basic things. Things most people took for granted every day. Arrh, there he went again, daydreaming about a woman he'd just met last night. "Look, Lydia," he said, "I won't kick them out. You know that. But we do need to help them. And since this sort of thing is your department…"

Lydia nodded. "Of course I'll help. But you made the right decision, Nick. Giving her a job was the best thing you could do."

"I didn't have much choice. She was available on the spot and I needed someone immediately. Now I hope I don't live to regret it."

"You won't," Lydia assured him as she headed toward the door, her long black wool skirt swishing around her matching boots. "You did need someone immediately, and I don't think you'll regret it at all."

"Hey, you're the bleeding heart, remember?" he replied. "While you've been out trying to save the world, I've been breaking my back to save this company."

"And you've done a good job," his sister acknowledged. "The latest stock report shows we're up forty cents per share. We haven't had to dip into that old pile of money Daddy left us, so why don't you relax?"

Nick's eyes grew dark. "I promised him—"

"No, you swore on his grave," she reminded him. "Nick, when are you going to forgive and forget? Yes, he was harsh, but he was only human. It's just that we didn't see his human side until it was too late. I don't want it to be too late for you, Nick. But you're already headed down the same road he took—giving orders and doling out cash, never getting your hands dirty, never facing reality. It's not too late for you yet, not if you realize that money isn't everything."

Nick eyed his little sister curiously, still amazed that she'd escaped their father's ironhanded approach to life. Lydia was so like their mother, good, kindhearted, openly loving. And, Nick reminded himself bitterly, he was his father's son. "Look, Lydia, doling out cash is what I do best. Money, I've got."

"Uh-huh. And that's about all you've got."

Defending himself, he said, "Well, I haven't heard any complaints. We've both got everything we need."

She shook her head. "Except faith, Nick. That's the one thing I've got that you lack." With that, she shut the door and left.

She was wrong, of course. He didn't need the added assurance of some higher power watching over him, which she insisted on believing. He had everything he needed. Didn't he? Head of a successful company, owner of one of the finest homes in Shreveport, possessor of a social book that rivaled anybody's in Louisiana. His list of attributes spoke volumes about his life.

But that's about all you've got. Lydia's words taunted him again. Oh, all this Christmas sentiment was affecting his better judgement. It was normal to feel at odds with so much Christmas hype being shoved down his throat.

Remembering other, happier Christmases, Nick stared out the window, mindless of the crawling traffic below. His father had taught him to keep his emotions at bay, and had set a firm example by never showing any sort of affection or compassion himself. Until Ruth died. Watching his proud, self-sufficient father crumble had only reinforced Nick's own need to stay in control.

Now, he was trapped, so trapped, in a firmly encased persona that gave him a ruthless outlook on life. He'd get through Christmas the same way he had each year since his parents' deaths, by celebrating with a detached kind of fascination, like the cynical kid who didn't believe in Santa anymore.

Except this year, he reminded himself, he'd be doing it with a lovely widow and her two noisy kids. "Why do I have a bad feeling about this whole thing?" he asked himself.

"The whole thing is going to be a disaster," Myla mumbled to herself as she once again checked preparations for the dinner party that loomed less than two hours away. Henrietta had gone over all the details with her. The food was ready; it only needed to be heated when the guests arrived. But Myla wasn't so sure about herself.

She wore a white long-sleeved blouse and black trousers, courtesy of Lydia's closet. Henrietta had insisted Lydia wouldn't mind or even miss the functional outfit.

"All you have to do is keep the food coming," the older woman had explained. "Nicky likes everything to run smoothly—these people are clients and stockholders, but this is a casual dinner. Just put it out on the buffet, real nice and hot, and keep your eyes open for seconds. The bar's fully stocked, and Nicky'll mix what drinks are needed."

Since she didn't condone drinking, Myla was glad she didn't have to play bartender. The rest sounded simple enough. After all, she'd done this hundreds of times before. Smoothing the knot of hair coiled at the nape of her neck, she took a deep, calming breath. The children were tucked away in Henny's small sitting room, armed with books to look over, coloring pads and crayons, and various other things Henny stockpiled for her grandchildren. They could watch a little television before they were to go on to bed. Surely, nothing could go wrong.

The kitchen door swung open. Nick marched in, whistling to himself. He'd saved the Dallas deal, another coup for Rudolph Oil, and a nice nibble to share with his fidgety stockholders. Stopping in midwhistle, he looked around the kitchen, and then into the set of exotic eyes watching him.

"Who did all of this?" he asked in a deadly calm voice as his gaze trailed over the fresh ivy and holly berry greenery adorning every available corner. The scent of bayberry candles lifted through the air, giving the room a cozy holiday effect.

Seeing the scowl on his face, Myla said, "I…I did. I found the decorations in the garage. I thought it would look nice for the party."

"I don't care for a lot of frivolous decorations," he said, noting that she looked right at home. "I just wanted a simple, quiet evening with no fuss. Did the cake I ordered come?"

She nodded, swallowing back her embarrassment. "Yes, your coconut cake is right here on the counter."

So it was. To avoid lashing out at her for her innocent assumptions, he concentrated instead on the rich cake he'd had a local restaurant prepare for tonight.

Before he could speak, she spoke to him. "I'm sorry about the decorations. I didn't realize—"

"Never mind," he said on a tired sigh. "It is Christmas, after all, and I do need to appear all jolly-holly for these people."

Myla leaned against the counter to steady her nerves. "Everything's in order. The table's set. The food's ready. I really didn't have that much to take care of."

"Plenty to drink?" he asked as he scanned the mail lying on the countertop.

She lifted her shoulders. "Yes, but I must tell you, I don't drink and I'd prefer not to have to mix drinks for your guests."

He shrugged. To each his own. "I'll take care of that, then. But don't worry. I don't expect this stoic crowd to get too wild."

Relieved to hear that, Myla relaxed a little. "Henny told me how important this is to you."

He moved into the room, throwing his briefcase on a desk in the corner before heading to the refrigerator. "Henny's very efficient. She knows how these functions work. The old-boy networking system never slows down."

Myla noticed the lines of fatigue around his eyes. He seemed so cool and in charge that she found it hard to believe he could be worried. "Can I get you anything?" she asked.

"Nah, I'll just have some juice." Spying a tray of

appetizers in the refrigerator, he picked up a cracker covered with a shrimp mixture and popped it into his mouth. "That's good," he said between chews.

"I found the shrimp in the freezer," she explained. "I know the recipe by heart."

"You're in charge of the kitchen," he said by way of appreciation. "Do you need anything?"

I need to have my head examined, she thought. She was terrified of being here, but she needed this job. She wouldn't allow her children to be homeless again.

"No, Henny went over the schedule with me."

"Good." Nick placed the empty juice glass in the sink. "Guess I'll head up to get a shower." Turning back on his tasseled loafers, he asked, "How's Jesse?"

"Much better." Touched that he'd bothered to ask, Myla guessed he was just being polite. "Her fever is down." At his questioning look, she added, "They're in Henny's room, all settled in."

He nodded, wondering why he'd become so tongue-tied all of a sudden. "By the way, your car's in the auto shop. It should be fixed in a couple of days. Your belongings will be delivered tomorrow."

"But…" Myla began, not knowing how to ever thank him. He'd taken care of everything in such a businesslike manner. She supposed he was used to taking matters into his own hands, while she was just beginning to learn how to deal with everyday problems on her own. "Thank you," she said, her voice tapping down the tad of resentment she couldn't deny.

He raised a hand to ward off her gratitude. "It was no trouble and besides, I'm depending on you to run my house. You can't do that if you're out trying to get your car fixed."

"Good point," she reluctantly agreed. He didn't take compliments or praise very well. "I'm sorry for all this trouble."

Nick shrugged. "Don't worry. If it'll make you feel better, I'll send you the bill."

"I insist," she said as she watched him plow through the swinging door to the hallway. Somehow, she'd pay him back for his kindness, but she couldn't say if it would make her feel better or not.

Nick's bellowing call from the den brought her head up. Rushing through the swinging door, she flew down the hall to the other room to find him standing in front of the tree she and the children had put up that afternoon.

"What's this?" he asked, his hands on his hips, his chin jutting out as he stared at the eight-foot-tall evergreen.

"It's a Christmas tree, of course," she said, wondering why the fresh-cut tree seemed to be bothering him so much. "Henny called a nursery and had it delivered."

Nick ran a hand through his hair and gave

another long sigh. "I told her in no uncertain terms, that I did not want a tree in this house."

"She never mentioned that to me."

"No, I don't suppose she would have. Well, too late to take it down now."

Finding her courage, Myla stepped closer to the tree to touch one of the brilliant ornaments she'd found in a huge box in the garage. "The children had such a great time decorating it, I'd appreciate it if you would try to enjoy it."

Nick's gaze moved from the tree to the woman at his side. Her eyes were almost the same shade as the lush branches reaching out toward him. And they sparkled every bit as brightly. He couldn't deny her this one concession to his rigid holiday rules.

"Okay. The tree can stay up, but no more decorating without consulting me first, no matter what Henny tells you."

"All right."

He didn't like her tone or the hurt look in her eyes. "What are you thinking?"

She smiled then, but her eyes still held a certain sadness. "That you have a beautiful house. Six bedrooms, is it? And four baths? And those sunrooms. I've always loved having lots of live plants in a sunny room."

Nick hadn't really noticed the plants. He shrugged, his gaze sweeping casually over his surroundings. "It's almost too big for a bachelor and his baby sister, but it's home."

"Is it?" she couldn't help but ask.

"Is it what?"

"Home?"

"I live here, don't I?"

"Yes, but...oh, never mind. This place is like something out of a dream, but it just seems as if something is missing in this great, old house."

She'd sensed it, when she'd gone through the rooms earlier, dusting and gawking at the same time. The house was as reserved and cool as the man who lived in it, and just like him, it cast out a false sense of contentment.

Nick sighed, then turned to go. "Don't try to analyze me, Myla. There's nothing missing here. Everything is as it should be."

"If you say so."

She watched as he left the room and stalked up the curving staircase. How sad that he couldn't enjoy the holidays. Myla wondered what had made him this way. She turned back to the tree, her gaze fixed on the gold and white angel watching her from the top of the sturdy blue spruce. "I think Nick Rudolph needs your help," she whispered.

An hour later, the house was filled with the sound of laughter tinkling on the air as crystal glasses tinkled with ice. The aroma of mulling cider wafted through the night while the fire in the massive marble fireplace located across one wall of the den crackled and popped. Myla viewed the cluster of people scattered around the tree, making sure each guest had plenty to eat and drink, while she listened to the carefully selected group's conversation.

"Nick, I love the house this year," a stout woman covered in diamonds said between bites of puffed pastry stuffed with artichoke filling. "I haven't seen it this festive and bright in a long time."

Nick's smile was all calculated charm. "Glad you approve, Dottie. I'm not much on the holidays, but my new housekeeper insisted I put up a tree, at least." He guided Dottie away from the tree, then said, "Remind me to show you Rudolph Oil's fourth-quarter report. I'd love to have you serve on the board again. We could use your input."

Clearly enthralled, the woman practically preened. "You know, I've been telling Jacob we need to reconsider that decision."

Jacob, a tall gray-haired man, listened diligently. "Whatever you say, dear."

Nick grinned, then caught Myla's eye. He saw the disapproving look she cast his way and wondered what he'd done to offend her. Excusing himself from Dottie, he cornered Myla by the buffet.

"Is everything all right?"

"Fine," she replied, her gaze scanning the crowd. "Would you like another glass of soda?"

He finished off the cool liquid left in the bottom of his glass, then shook his head. "No, but I'd like to know why you were glaring at me earlier."

"No reason," she said, busying herself by putting out more cans of soda for his guests. "I was just watching you work the crowd."

"And you disapprove?"

Myla gave him a direct stare. "No, I'm just surprised. One minute you're acting like a regular grizzly bear and the next you're turning on the charm."

Recalling their earlier encounter right here in this room, Nick replied, "Look, I'm sorry I got angry about the decorations and the tree. You were smart to spruce this place up…and it looks wonderful. Perfect."

"Glad you approve," she said, not at all convinced of his sincerity.

Sensing that she didn't exactly trust his motives, Nick smiled over at her. "I do approve. So far, everything's going according to schedule. And I owe that to you."

Before she could respond, he turned away to greet some more guests, leaving her with the memory of his aftershave. She'd smelled it earlier when he'd entered the kitchen. He was a handsome man. A self-reliant man, who liked to rule over his domain.

This was his world, not hers. She'd had a similar life with her husband, but now…now, she intended to make her own way, with her faith to shield and guide her. She wouldn't put her trust in another ruthless man. And Nick Rudolph was exactly that.

She watched him play host to the hilt as he mixed business with pleasure and made her feel like an out-of-place Cinderella watching the prince dance with all the other girls at the ball.

"Bill, you rascal," Nick said, laughing as he playfully slapped the tall, blond-headed man on the back. "How are things looking for your re-election to the Senate? Can I depend on you down in Baton Rouge?"

"Can I depend on your donation to my next campaign?" Bill countered with a hearty laugh, thus beginning a rather long and detailed account of his political aspirations. His wife, a slender brunette in a pricey red pantsuit gave a bored smile as her eyes fell across Myla, then moved on.

The look of dismissal galled Myla, but she knew her place. She'd been poor before she married Sonny Howell. And now, she'd come full circle. She could afford to be gracious to the woman; she'd once been so like her.

Once again, Nick excused himself from his guest to head toward Myla with a purposeful stride. Afraid that she'd done something wrong again, she moved to meet him.

"Everyone's here except—" Nick stopped in mid-sentence when a loud screeching noise, followed by a bellowing bark and the crash of dishes, rose from the back of the huge house. "What was that?"

The doors of the kitchen burst open as a tall woman with flowing blond hair ran into the room, her black dress clinging to her slender curves.

"Carolyn?" Nick looked surprised, then laughed in relief. "Leave it to you to make a grand entrance."

The lovely Carolyn fumed with indignation. "Nick Rudolph, how dare you laugh at me? It's bad enough that you stood me up last night, but now this. You've got to do something!"

"Do what?" Nick looked confused. "What's the matter?"

The other guests had gathered around now, each waiting and watching as Carolyn pulled at a torn spot in her black hose. "It's Pooky," she said on a low moan. "He's in the kitchen—"

Another wailing scream rose from the kitchen, followed by a growl and another scream, this one human. Several loud crashes joined in with the screams.

Nick plopped his glass down on a walnut table. "What's going on in there?"

Carolyn moaned again and tugged at her hair. "That's what I'm trying to tell you, Nick. I brought Pooky along with me to ward off muggers and when I went to put him in Henny's room, a...a cat ran out and now Pooky's chasing the crazed creature around the kitchen and when I tried to stop him, well…that cat lurched into my leg and well, look, a fifteen-dollar pair of nylons ruined." Tossing her evening bag and black velvet cape into Nick's face, she added, "And I'm bleeding. You know I'm allergic to cats!"

The uproar in the kitchen increased now, the crowd moving in closer, each guest hovering near the swinging doors, afraid to go in and see what Pooky and the mysterious cat were doing to each other.

"Cat?" Nick shook his head. "I don't have a cat."

Another scream brought Myla into action. Pushing through the dazed spectators, she called to Nick, "The children!"

"Children?" Carolyn eyed Nick suspiciously. "I thought I saw something unusual hiding behind Henny's couch. Nick, what's going on here?"

Nick looked over at Carolyn, prepared to explain everything until he heard Myla's low agony-filled moan. That moan did not bode well, not at all. Giving Carolyn's things to the skinny brunette in red, he dashed toward the kitchen. The sight that greeted him caused him to echo the same low-pitched moan.

A tabby cat, scrawny and hissing, sat on a blade of the still ceiling fan, one paw extended in the attack position while a howling, barking Saint Bernard sat underneath, his tongue fairly hanging out of his big, toothy mouth as he waited for the next chase to begin.

Patrick sat in the middle of the counter, surrounded by what had once been the carefully arranged entrees for the dinner party. Now those entrees were not only arranged all over the counter, but also all over Patrick and all over the once white tile floor. Jesse hovered in the doorway leading to Henny's apartment, her wails matching pitch with the cat's. The Saint Bernard, tired of playing chase with the pitiful cat, turned and started lapping up what remained of the platter of roast that Myla had carved so lovingly and garnished with parsley and star-burst carved cherry tomatoes.

Myla's eyes met Nick's. Of their own accord, her hands came up to cover her face. He's going to send all of us packing, she thought.

Nick's face burned with a rage born of shock. "What happened here?" His voice grew deeper and more deadly with each word. "Would someone like to tell me what in blazes happened in here?"

The room, filled with twelve warm, curious bodies, remained silent, except for the occasional hissing from the ceiling fan and the melodious lapping on the tile floor.

"I'm waiting." Nick circled the carnage, his eyes brown with a fire of rage. "I want some answers, now!"

Finally, a feeble voice rallied from the direction of Henny's room. Jesse stepped forward, shivering with fear, her eyes bright with freshly shed tears.

"Mamma, we forgot to tell you about the cat," she said before she burst into another round of high-pitched sobs

Chapter Three

The door leading from the garage burst open. Lydia bounced into the room, wearing a black crepe dressy pantsuit, her blond bob shining as brightly as her diamond earrings.

Myla recognized her from the many pictures of Nick and Lydia hanging around the house. But Carolyn...was she Nick's girlfriend? Nick had been busy doing a good deed last night and now look what it had caused him. Even Lydia's upbeat mood didn't help the situation.

"Sorry I'm late," she began, her earrings twinkling like twin stars, "but I had to stop by—" Her eyes registered shock for a split second before she burst out in a fit of uncontrollable laughter. "Food fight? Nick, why didn't you tell me? You know how I love to throw my food at you!"

"Not now, Lydia," Nick said, his growl more

pronounced than the drooling Pooky's. "We've had a bit of an accident and I was just trying to get to the bottom of it."

"Looks like Pooky here beat you to it," Lydia countered, rushing forward to pet the massive Saint Bernard. "Hey, boy, what did you get into this time?"

"It's not Pooky's fault," Carolyn said as she side-stepped a pile of shrimp dip to comfort the hyper dog. "I walked over for the party, so I brought Pooky with me. I had no idea that a cat and two strange children would attack us when we entered the back door."

"Next time, try using the front door like the other guests," Lydia replied sweetly, though her eyes indicated she felt anything but sweet.

"Ladies, please," Nick said, raking a hand through his crisp dark curls. Turning to Myla, he watched as she knelt to comfort her sobbing daughter. Instantly, he regretted his anger from before. "Jesse, how'd we manage to acquire a cat?" he asked, his tone deceptively soft, his eyes centered on Myla as if to say *this is your fault.*

Jesse looked up to her mother for reassurance. Myla, stung by Nick's anger and by Carolyn's high-handed attitude toward her children, shot him a defiant look. Thinking she could kiss this new job goodbye, she patted Jesse on the shoulder. "Just tell the truth, honey."

Jesse took a deep breath to clear away another

round of sobs. "Mr. Nick, I'm sorry. But today when Momma was getting stuff ready for your party, me and Patrick went for a walk out in the backyard. We weren't supposed to, 'cause I'm sick and Patrick gets into stuff, but we snuck out.... Anyway, we heard a cat meowing behind that big building by the pool. Patrick came back in the house when Momma wasn't looking and got some food for the cat. It was real hungry." Sniffing, she looked up at Nick. "We wanted to help it so it wouldn't freeze to death, like you helped us, Mr. Nick." She wiped her nose again with her hand, her big blue-green eyes wide with the importance of her confession.

Nick looked uncomfortable, but Myla saw the touch of warmth Jesse's innocent words had provoked in his eyes.

"Why didn't you tell me about the cat, sweetie?" she asked her daughter, her heart breaking. Jesse loved animals. She'd never let one starve or stay out in the cold, in spite of her allergies around certain animals. Hunger wasn't pretty—in animals or humans.

"We were afraid you'd make us let it go," Jesse said, dropping her eyes to the floor.

"Yeah, and we didn't want Mr. Nick to kick us out," Patrick piped up as he held out his dip-covered fingers. "I tried to catch it, Mamma, but it was too fast. And besides, I'm scared of that big dog."

"Pooky wouldn't hurt a flea," Carolyn protested,

looking from one child to the other accusingly. Then she turned to glare up at Nick. "You told me you helped some people out last night; you didn't tell me they were staying in your home."

Bristling, Myla shot Carolyn a proud look. "I'm *working* for Mr. Rudolph while his housekeeper is on vacation."

"Working for Nick?" Carolyn whirled around. "Is that true—even after what you told me last night?"

Nick's look warned her to drop it. "Things have changed since then. I'll explain later."

Myla's eyes met his. He was embarrassed, but she saw the hint of an apology. He was too much of a gentleman to make a scene. Obviously though, he'd avoided telling Carolyn everything. Wondering if he was ashamed of her being here, Myla felt like a circus sideshow.

Deciding she'd really give them all something to talk about and try to save Nick's reputation and her much needed job in the process, she pinned Carolyn with a level look. "Yes, it's true. Mr. Rudolph was kind enough to help us out last night. You see, we've had a rough time lately. We've been living in our car." That statement caused an audible rumbling through the room, but it didn't stop Myla. "He found us stranded on the interstate during the ice storm, and he brought us here. Knowing I needed a job, he asked me to work for him while his regular housekeeper, Henrietta, is on vacation. And as long as he doesn't have a problem with that, I don't, either. I'm just very thankful that he was kind enough to care about my children and me.

"The Bible says, 'Blessed are ye that hunger now: for ye shall be filled. Blessed are ye that weep now: for ye shall laugh.' Yesterday, I was hungry and weeping. Today, thanks to Mr. Rudolph's kindness, I'm warm and full and laughing, in spite of all of this mess." Dismissing Carolyn's surprised, cynical look, she turned to Nick. "Isn't this the true spirit of Christmas? You took us in, when there was no room at the inn. You did something entirely unselfish. It's the best Christmas present I could ask for, and I thank you. And I take full responsibility for my children's actions."

Nick stood still, in shock. He should be angry that she'd turned his party into a sermon on the mount. Instead, he felt a great rush of warmth moving through his body. Ashamed, he blinked to hold back the blur of tears forming in his eyes. He'd never seen a woman as brave as Myla Howell. She had more courage among this crowd of cutthroats than he'd ever possessed, ruthless as he was supposed to be.

Of course, her courage was one thing. Being called a pushover was quite another. Glancing around, he waited for the looks and whispers that were sure to come. But to his surprise, his guests didn't condemn him or laugh at him. They came, one by one, to pat him on the back.

The senator was the first in line. "Perfect, my friend. Helping the homeless is one of my campaign pledges. I'll hold you up as an example."

That comment was followed by Dottie's tear-filled pledge. "How could I ever doubt your sincerity again, Nick? Jacob and I will be happy to serve on the board of Rudolph Oil, and I intend to call our broker first thing tomorrow and instruct her to buy a substantial amount of Rudolph Oil shares." Then, glancing at Myla, she whispered, "And I'll leave a check for your housekeeper, too. A little Christmas gift. Such a tragedy."

"But..." Nick didn't know what to say. Myla had single-handedly turned a disaster into a public relations dream. Now, after giving her eloquent speech, she went on to introduce herself to the group and assure them that they would have a decent meal, after all.

Sending Nick a daring look, she called, "Pizza, anyone?" Then, turning to him with a gracious smile, she whispered, "You can't fire me now."

"I wouldn't dream of it," he whispered back, his eyes full of a grudging admiration, and his heart full of something warm and unfamiliar.

All the guests started talking and laughing, except Carolyn. Myla saw the blonde throw Nick a scrutinizing look.

Carolyn stood, then smiled sweetly at Nick. "Since when did you find religion, Nicky?"

Nick didn't answer. Instead, he said, "Carolyn, why don't you wait for me in the den?"

"I'll order the pizza," Lydia said, jumping over broken dishes to find the phone. "How about three vegetarians and three with pepperoni and sausage, all large with extra cheese?"

Everyone clapped their approval. Lydia herded the humans and Pooky toward the den. "Just make yourselves at home while I dial the emergency pizza number."

Carolyn gave Myla a cold look, then pranced into the den with the rest of the crowd. As she walked past Nick, she said, "We really need to talk."

Nick watched her go, then turned to stare at his wrecked kitchen, before settling his gaze on Myla and her daughter. Lifting Patrick down, he sent the little boy scooting toward his mother. A long sigh escaped from deep within Nick's lungs as he watched Patrick hug Myla's neck and smear her with shrimp dip. How could he be mad at them when they stood huddled together as if he were about to issue an order for their execution?

"I'll clean it up immediately," Myla said, her voice firm while her hands shook. "I'm so sorry, Nick."

He held up a hand to ward off her apology. She'd put up a good front for his guests, but he could see she was visibly upset. She'd said she'd handled a few dinner parties, but never one such as this, he'd wager.

"It's okay," he said, pushing away his questions for now. Swallowing the lump of pride caught in his throat, he added, "Thanks. You sure handled that better than I did. You made me sound like a saint."

"Saint Nick," Patrick said, giggling as he wiped a glob of dip on his pajamas.

"Not a saint, Patrick," his mother corrected, "just a very kind and understanding man."

"Flattery will get you everywhere," Nick retorted, smiling in spite of himself. "You obviously have me confused with someone else."

She wouldn't let him get away so easily. "Oh, no. I know what I'm talking about. You're uncomfortable in this role, being heroic, I mean. What happened to make you so afraid of reaching out to others, Nick?"

Lydia hung up the phone, interrupting before he could answer. "I can't believe Carolyn. She knows that dog doesn't belong at a dinner party. She should have left the big brute at home to run around on that two-acre lot she calls a backyard."

"She brought him along for protection," Nick said, glad to change the subject.

Lydia snorted. "I've never know Carolyn to need protection."

"Careful, sis."

Lydia turned to Myla and the children. "He's right. I have to remember not to judge too harshly. It's so nice to meet you. Nick's told me all about you."

Myla looked at Nick. Yes, she was sure he'd called Lydia first thing this morning, telling her how much he regretted being a Good Samaritan. "Well, he apparently didn't tell *Carolyn* all about us."

Getting back to the immediate problem, Nick said, "I'm not worried about Carolyn or her dog right now." Motioning toward the fan, he said, "What about that?"

The cat still sat on guard, its bright yellow eyes narrowing suspiciously each time anyone made a move.

"We'll get it down and clean it up, don't worry," Lydia said. "How about we call it Shredder, kids?"

"Yeah, Shredder," Patrick agreed, clapping his sticky hands together.

"Who said we were going to keep it?" Nick asked, his hands on his hips.

"The worst is over." Myla turned to Lydia. "Would you mind getting Shredder out of the way so I can clean this up?"

"Sure." Lydia called softly to the frightened animal. "We'll take him to Henny's sitting room and teach him some manners while you two straighten things out." The meaningful gaze she shot her brother told him she was referring to much more than the mess on the floor.

"Gee, thanks." Nick pulled off his navy-and-burgundy patterned wool sweater, then rolled up his blue shirtsleeves so he could get down to work.

"Lydia, you just want to see me get my hands dirty, right?"

Lydia bobbed her head and grinned.

Myla stepped forward as Lydia bribed the cat down with a piece of roast beef. "Nick, you don't have to help."

The animal refused to come into Lydia's arms, but did jump down and run into the safety of Henny's apartment. Lydia and the giggling children followed, discussing the now famous battle with animation.

Left alone, Nick and Myla could only stand and stare around them. Everything was ruined. Nick moaned softly when his eyes lit on the mashed remains of his prized coconut cake.

"You have guests," Myla stated, picking up the cake plate to remove the source of Nick's woes. "Go ahead. I'm sure Carolyn needs comforting after her horrid ordeal."

Nick heard the sarcasm in her words and saw the twitch of a smile pulling at her lips. He relaxed and smiled back, his eyes meeting hers. "Carolyn Parker and I grew up together," he explained. "She's divorced and rich, and expects me to jump when she calls. We escort each other around town on various occasions. And about last night—"

"You don't have to explain anything to me." Myla sidestepped a pile of spinach salad. "Your social life is your business. But why didn't you tell her everything…about me?"

"Because I didn't think I owed her an explanation. I didn't feel the need to go into detail about your situation."

"That was considerate," she said, thinking he was one of the most gentlemanly men she'd ever met. Then again, maybe he used his impeccable manners as a shield.

Nick tried to take the flattened cake from her. He wanted a little taste of that wonderful cake before she threw it out. "I'm glad you understand."

"Oh, I understand." She turned, looking for the trash can. "And I'm really sorry the children ruined your party." He tried to pry the cake out of her hand, but she pulled it away. "Nick, I've got it. Why don't you get a mop from the—"

Nick made one last-ditch effort to reach for the cake, leaning forward from the waist so he wouldn't have to step in the pile of spinach salad. But just as he lunged forward, Myla turned to dump the cake in the trash.

Nick came crashing against her, knocking Myla completely off balance. The cake sailed up as she whirled around. He got a taste of his cake, all right, in the face, as he slipped in salad dressing, with cake and Myla sliding right into his arms. By the time the impact was complete, Myla had cake all over her face and shoulders, too. Unable to move or breath, she watched as Nick licked creamy almond-colored icing off his lips.

His arms holding her, and the remains of the mushed cake, against him, he asked, "Are you all right?" When she nodded, he licked his lips again, causing something like kindling wood to spark and curl in Myla's jittery stomach. "Ah, that's so good," he said, lifting his hands to dump the ruined cake into the trash. "I could have handled anything but losing my coconut cake. I think I'm going to cry."

Myla huffed a breath, then turned to find a towel. "Please, if you do, don't mess up the floor."

"Very funny."

Nick raised a hand to take the towel from her, his fingers gripping her wrist. Lifting her head, she saw a set of bronze-colored eyes lazily assessing her. Gone was the cold indifference, the quiet reserve, and in its place, a heated brilliance that took her breath away.

"Let me go, Nick," she said on a soft whisper.

"Wait, you have a big glob of cake on your right cheek."

Reaching up, she touched her face. "I'll get it off. Now, let me go so we can clean up this mess."

"Let's start right now."

Before she could move or protest, he began wiping her face, his fingers gently lifting icing and cake filling off her cheek, his amused gaze causing sparks to ignite again in her stomach. She tried to pull away, but he held her steady.

"Right there." He took the towel and wiped it

across her jaw. "Yep, that's it." He held her away to inspect his handiwork. "All clean now."

Myla could only stare at him. What on earth was the man trying to do to her? Here she was, covered with cake and shrimp dip, in the middle of his kitchen, with her children and his sister in one room and a pack of hungry guests as well as a jealous girl-friend in the other. Everything was ruined, and Nick should be angry with her. Instead, he was treating her with such intense concern that she thought she might cry from the sheer sweetness of his gesture. She could have handled his anger; his kindness was much harder to bear.

"Are you finished?" she managed to ask as she gritted her teeth to keep the lump in her throat from choking her.

Nick, seeing the torment in her eyes, stood back, then carefully wiped bacon-and-mustard salad dressing from his khaki trousers. Thinking he'd made her uncomfortable, he said, "I'm sorry. I didn't mean to offend you, Myla."

To calm her own wayward feelings, Myla turned to the sink. "It's all right. I…I'm just surprised that you didn't…that you aren't—"

"What?" Confused, Nick tugged her around again.

Myla sighed, then took the towel from his hands. "You should be mad—I promised you everything would work out fine tonight, and now I've ruined your party. Why didn't you just get mad at me?"

A bit amused, Nick lifted a brow. "So, you're upset because I'm not upset?"

She bobbed her head. "Yes. No! I mean, I could have handled you shouting and ranting. Why did you have to be so nice to me?"

Nick watched as she frantically tried to wipe the counter, not knowing how to comfort her. "I am so sorry," he repeated, a mock glare coloring his face. "What was I thinking?"

"Exactly," Myla agreed, unaware that he was smiling behind her back. "You don't have to be nice!"

Nick understood that she wasn't used to any tenderness and that realization bothered him. What had she suffered, to make her so wary of a kind gesture? He wanted to ask her, but decided she'd just clam up if he tried. So instead, he teased her. "I promise, if this happens again, I'll try to be justifiably angry."

She whirled around just in time to see the sparkle in his eyes. Hiding a smile, Myla relaxed a little. "Guess you miss Henny, huh?"

He laughed. "Yeah, but her dinner parties were never this exciting, I have to admit." Pivoting, he said, "I'll go get the mop."

Her hand shot out to stop him. "Wash your face first."

Lydia stuck her head around the corner from Henny's apartment. "By the way, Nick, I thought you both should know—I stopped by Magnolia

House on my way over here. They're full, probably will be until well after the first of the year. But Myla, I did put your name on the waiting list."

Myla looked up at the man who'd saved her, praying he'd let her stay until she could find somewhere else to go.

Nick didn't say anything, but she could tell by his blank expression that he wasn't too pleased with the news. Together, they silently cleaned the kitchen while Lydia got the children and Shredder off to sleep.

Finally, when they'd finished and the whole room had been restored to order, Nick turned to Myla. "Well, at least you can stay here until the first of the year."

"Yes, and I'm thankful that the good Lord led me to you."

He gave her a puzzled look, then said, "Maybe it's the other way around, Myla."

Myla's heart soared. Maybe he was beginning to feel differently about Christmas and helping others. She followed him into the den where Pooky lay fast asleep in front of the roaring fire. The guests were playing a game that involved telling the truth regarding scruples.

Carolyn turned to Nick. "Your turn, darling. Are you willing to test your scruples?"

"Scruples?" Nick laughed, his shrug indifferent. "Why, you all know I don't have any. None at all."

Myla sat watching him. He had deliberately

downplayed his good side, the side she'd seen first-hand. *You're wrong, Mr. Rudolph. You have scruples—you just haven't used them in a while.*

Again, she had to wonder what had caused Nick to turn into himself. As she watched him, his eyes touched on her and she saw the warmth shining there. She said a silent prayer. *Dear Father, help Nick to find his way back to you. And thank you for leading me to him.*

The next night when Nick came home from work, he found a freshly baked pound cake sitting on the counter, its buttery aroma filling the house. The kitchen sparkled and gleamed. Holly branches from the garden decorated the counters, giving the room a homey effect.

The back door opened and Myla, Patrick and Jesse all rushed into the room, giggling and chattering. All three held arms full of firewood. Myla looked up, a hesitant smile cresting her lips.

Patrick said, "Hey, Mr. Nick. We're gonna start a fire."

"So I see."

He nodded toward the boy's mother, noticing the way the December wind had brightened her cheeks and pinkened her lips, giving her fair skin a perfect contrast to her fiery wind-tossed copper-colored hair. As was his nature, Nick watched and waited as she ordered the children to place the wood in the den.

"And don't try to light a fire. I wouldn't want you two to burn down the Christmas tree." Turning back to Nick, she said, "Dinner will be ready in an hour."

"That's fine." He gazed at the fat cake sitting on the counter. "That smells wonderful."

"Want a slice?" She headed toward the refrigerator to pull out the milk. "Milk or coffee?"

"Milk." Nick slid out of his khaki trench coat. "This looks good."

"Well, it's not coconut cake, but I wanted to make up for last night. I hate seeing grown men cry."

He chuckled, then took the glass of milk and a generous slice of the still-warm cake, his eyes following her as he bit into the flaky lemon-flavored mound. Myla waited as he chewed it with glee, a little moan of appreciation escaping as he swallowed.

"I think I'm in love," he murmured as he closed his eyes. After another hefty bite, he said, "Oh, you wouldn't believe the phone calls I've been getting all day."

Concerned, she asked, "About what?"

"About you. About the pizza party. We really impressed the stockholders. They're throwing their support toward Rudolph Oil, and you."

"Me?"

"They want to help you out."

Myla had to turn away to keep him from seeing

the tears welling in her eyes. Maybe there was hope, after all. Of course, these people didn't know her background. She wondered how they'd feel about her if they knew the whole story. "I can't take any charity, Nick," she said to hide her fears.

"Of course you can," he reasoned. "They admire your strength, Myla. Last night, you showed them something they've taken for granted."

She shrugged, her back still turned away. "I only told the truth according to my beliefs. It's what I live by."

Thinking she was about to launch into another sermon, Nick cleared his throat. "I have some checks here. Will you take them? You can use the money after…after you leave here."

"Charity," she said, dreading the thought of not being self-reliant.

Nick came to stand beside her. "Yes, charity, but given with the best of intentions. And besides, they can write it off on their income tax, so take the money, Myla."

She stopped stirring the steaming pot of vegetables. "The Lord loves a cheerful giver."

"That's the spirit. You can always pay them back."

She smiled then. "Did they write checks?"

"Yes, why?"

"I'll record their names and addresses and offer them my services. I want to start my own catering business."

He stared over at her. "Catering…you'd be good at that." Shaking his head, he added, "I admire your ingenuity. You'll do just fine in life, Myla." With that declaration, he finished the last bite of his cake.

Myla turned back to her cooking. She had to stop watching this man eat. She wanted to cook him hearty meals and take care of him. He needed more than a housekeeper; he needed a spiritual partner. And after ten years of marriage to Sonny Howell, she wasn't sure she was ready for that yet.

Answering him finally, she said, "I have to do this, Nick. I have to provide for my children."

Nick put his empty plate and glass in the sink. "I believe you will. Patrick was right. You are a good cook."

"Thank you. Cooking's about all I have to offer." She faced him at last. "I need to tell you— the other job I came here to see about—it was a cook in a restaurant. I called today…and they've already hired someone."

Nick put a hand on her shoulder. "You found this job, Myla. Maybe…maybe you'll be better off here, for now." Not sure how to comfort her, he added, "And hey, if you keep this up, I'll be as fat as Santa by Christmas."

She laughed then. "You can work it off by starting that fire Patrick and Jesse want."

"Good idea. I rarely build a fire for just myself."

He headed toward the swinging doors, then whirled. "By the way, how's Shredder doing?"

"He won't come out of Henny's apartment."

She waited, but when he just stood staring over at her, she asked, "Is there anything else, Nick?"

"Yes," he said, lowering his head a bit. "You're wrong, you know."

"About what?"

"Cooking isn't the only thing you have to offer, Myla."

He turned to go, leaving her to wonder what he'd meant by that statement. *Careful, Myla,* an inner voice warned. Nick was just being polite, trying to boost her ego. He didn't know anything about her, and right now, she didn't have the nerve to tell him the truth.

An hour later, Nick looked at the place set for one in the formal dining room. In spite of the Christmas centerpiece sitting in the middle of the long, shining Queen Anne table, the room still seemed empty and vast. In spite of the plate of steaming vegetables and hot-buttered noodles, the baked chicken and delicate dinner rolls, he couldn't seem to get excited about eating.

Too much cake, he reasoned, plopping down on an antique chair to try to enjoy Myla's marvelous efforts. "At last, peace and quiet."

With his first bite, he heard Myla's soft voice lifted in prayer. She was blessing their food in the other room. Sheepishly, Nick closed his eyes and listened. Glad when she'd finished, he whispered his own animated "Amen," then straightened his linen dinner napkin to get on with his meal.

Before he got a bite of succulent chicken between his teeth, he heard giggles from the kitchen, followed by voices all talking at once. They were a close trio, his little pack of strays. Myla seemed very protective of her children. Nick had to wonder what kind of man would leave her and her two children with nothing.

It's not your problem, Nick, he reminded himself. Sit up straight and eat your dinner.

With his first bite of the flaky roll, he remembered holding Myla the night before. Somehow, he'd managed to lose all decorum right there in his own kitchen. Carolyn would just love to have the details of that.

Of course, he didn't owe Carolyn or anyone else any explanations. He liked having no strings attached, and no obligations to anyone. Memories of his loving parents moved through the room like ghosts, haunting Nick with a poignancy he refused to acknowledge. He couldn't deal with the responsibilities of that kind of devoted love. He had other obligations—to Lydia and Rudolph Oil. Wishing Lydia didn't always work so late, he tried once again to eat his dinner.

By his third bite, Nick could stand it no longer.

Used to his house being quiet, he hopped up on the pretense of telling them to keep it down so he could eat. Making a beeline for the swinging door, he opened it to find three sets of surprised eyes looking at him as if he were the abominable snowman.

"Are we bothering you?" Myla asked, jumping up to take the glass he had in his hand. "Can I get you anything?"

Nick threw up his hands. "Yeah, a chair. You all are having entirely too much fun in here. I decided I'd better eat in here with you, just so we could avoid anymore surprises like last night's."

"Sure!" Patrick patted the stool nearest him. "Come on in, Mr. Nick. We don't mind him eating with us, do we, Mom?"

"Of course not," Myla replied softly. "After all, this is his house. He can eat in any room he chooses."

Nick's smile spread across his face like cream over strawberries. "I'll go get my food."

In a few minutes, he was settled in, packing away Myla's dinner like a man starved. Between bites, he regaled the children with tales of the adventures of Lydia and Nick as they were growing up.

"See this scar?" He showed Jesse a faint white dent right in the middle of his forehead. "Lydia gave me that with a roller skate. Had to have seven stitches. Mother made both of us go to bed early for a month."

"Why'd she hit you with a roller skate?" Jesse asked, her hoarseness making her voice soft-pitched.

"I chased her with a granddaddy long-legs," he explained, a grin encasing his face. "She hates spiders."

"I'm not scared of bugs," Jesse stated. "We lived in the country. I played with bugs all the time."

"Yeah, but we don't have that house no more, Jesse," Patrick reminded his sister. "It was repo—repur—"

"Repossessed," Myla finished, the flush on her cheeks indicating her discomfort. "Hush up now, and finish your dinner. We have to get up early tomorrow to get you both enrolled in school."

Nick steered the conversation away from the house they'd lost. "School? You two are too smart for that, aren't you?"

"Lydia's helping me get them straightened out," Myla said over the children's giggles. "She's been such a help—she's even looking into low-cost housing in this district, in case I don't get into Magnolia House."

"Trust good ol' Lydia," Nick replied.

Wondering why he sounded so sarcastic, Myla said, "You don't share the same strong faith as your sister, do you?"

Shocked by her directness, Nick became defensive. "I've learned to rely on myself. I don't need to turn to a higher being to help me through life."

Myla leaned forward on her stool, her voice quiet. "Being self-reliant is good. After all, the Lord gave us brains. But sometimes, Nick, we can't do it all by ourselves. We need His help. And it's all right to ask for it."

She could see the anger sparking through his eyes.

"I don't need His help." Waving his arms, he spanned the room. "As you can see, I'm doing okay on my own."

She nodded. "Oh, yes, you're doing great material-wise. But what about spiritually? You don't like Christmas. Why is that, Nick?"

"That's none of your business," he said, getting up to stomp to the sink. "Your job is to run this house efficiently, not delve into my personal life."

She followed him. "Of course. You make perfect sense." She started stacking the dishes he absently handed her. "But then, you're in charge, right?"

"And what does that mean?" They stood shoulder to shoulder, heads up, eyes flashing.

"I know what's expected of me here, Nick. I work for you and I intend to do a thorough job. But I can't help but notice you don't have a strong sense of faith. That bothers me."

Wanting to turn the tables on her, he said, "Yeah, well, you need to be more concerned with your own problems. After all, you're the one without a home!"

Hurt, she said, "I'll find one. And I'll find a good job, too."

He groaned as she almost sliced his palm with a knife in her haste to load the dishwasher. "You'll barely make ends meet, Myla. It's going to be a struggle."

"I'll manage," she retorted. "I have a higher help than you'll ever know."

"Oh, that's right. Your faith. Well, faith won't get you through a cold winter night, now will it?"

"It did," she replied calmly. "I prayed for help and the Lord sent it." She gave him a meaningful look.

"Fine," he said, sighing in defeat. "So, why can't you just do the job you were hired to do, instead of wasting your time trying to save me?"

"I just thought you could use a friend."

"I don't need a friend, and you need to concentrate on getting your own life back in order."

"I will, but in the meantime, if you need to talk…"

"I don't need anything, Myla." Trying to change the focus back to her, he added, "I'm willing to help you in any way I can, though. And I'm worried about you moving into that homeless shelter too soon. Having faith is one thing, but surviving is quite another."

"I would think you'd want me to move out," she replied. "You spout all this encouragement, then hand me a few checks to cover your own embarrassment. I'm trying to start over—on my own, and while I appreciate everything you and Lydia and your friends are doing, I have to do this for myself. If that means giving myself over to blind faith, if that means putting my trust in the Lord, then I can do it. I won't let anyone ever make me question my faith again." She stopped loading dishes to stare across the room at her two suddenly quiet children.

"What do you mean?" Nick asked, his hand on her arm. "What happened between you and your husband, Myla?"

"I…we'll talk later, maybe." Pulling away, she called to the children. "Jesse, Patrick, time for bed."

Patrick immediately followed Myla to Henny's room, but Jesse held back. Running up to Nick, she tugged on his jeans. "Daddy wasn't a bad man, Mr. Nick. Momma told us to always remember that. My Daddy wasn't a bad man. He just had some problems, is all."

"Jesse!" Myla's voice echoed through the house.

The little girl ran away before Nick could question her further. What did all this mean? Up until now, he'd believed Myla to be a grieving widow, but there was obviously more to this.

"Who are you really protecting, Myla?" he whispered. "Yourself and your children? Or your dead husband?"

Chapter Four

The next week passed in a busy rush for Myla. After getting the children back in school, and finding a church nearby to attend while she was working for Nick, she fell into the daily routine of cleaning and cooking, and learning more about Nick's life. Each detail drew her closer to the man who'd reluctantly saved her from the streets, and each detail showed her that Nick needed to find his own faith again. He'd refused her invitation to attend church.

"I send them a hefty check each month," he informed her. "I catch up on paperwork on Sundays."

"You should rest, and spend the day in worship," she replied. And have some fun, she wanted to add.

He'd shot her one of his famous scowls, but his words hadn't been as harsh as he'd have her believe. "You should mind your own business."

"Yes, sir." She certainly knew her place, and she needed the money. She'd have to be more cautious in her resolve to help him spiritually. And more cautious about her growing feelings for her employer.

But how could she resist being drawn to this intriguing man? She watched him leaving the house in a hurry each morning at the crack of dawn. He hardly bothered to stop and sip the coffee and orange juice she had waiting. She watched him come dragging in at night to wolf down the dinners she prepared before he went straight into his spacious office and clicked on the computer. Nick often worked long into the night. She knew, because she couldn't sleep very well in her new surroundings and she'd seen the light on in his office many times.

Myla had had an instinctive urge to go and check on Nick in the middle of the night, the way she used to do with her late husband. But that wasn't part of her official duties. And neither was being so attracted to him.

Her duties this morning involved cleaning the master bedroom. As she stood in the wide upper hallway, she prayed for guidance.

Dear Lord, give me the strength to get my work done, and not think about the man who's helped me so much.

But the minute she entered the big masculine room decorated with tasteful plaids and subtle stripes, Nick's presence shouted out at her. His suit from yesterday was draped across the standing valet. Out of habit, she brushed it out and hung it up, so he could wear it once more before she took it to the cleaners.

His shoes were shelved in the long, well-lit closet off the dressing room. He had several pairs, some black and brown leather, some gleaming white athletics, all expensive and classic in design, just like their owner. His shirt, impeccably white, was tossed on a chair, waiting to be laundered and pressed at the cleaners, along with all his other tailored shirts.

So much about Nick's habits reminded her of Sonny. Sonny had been a perfectionist, almost fanatical in his demands. Nick wasn't quite that bad, as far as she could tell. He demanded loyalty, hard work, and the best in everything—but he demanded those things in himself first and foremost.

Myla picked up the shirt, catching the scent of his spicy, crisp aftershave. The shirt spoke of the man. Solid, honest, clean. And lost. He was a good man, but he was a lonely, sad man. His quiet, aloof nature drew her to him, then his rare burst through smiles and dry humor held her.

She couldn't fight her feelings, but she reminded herself she'd been on the bottom for so long, coming up for air was scary. She couldn't read anything into Nick's smiles and concerned gestures.

He was just being kind. And he was used to having someone wait on him hand and foot. He was selfish and stubborn at times, and other times, he was caring and compassionate. Just his nature. She didn't think she was ready to deal with another domineering male just yet, though.

"Come on, Myla," she told herself as she hastily cleaned the large, elegant room. "You work for him. He gave you a job and a place to stay and food for your children. Nothing more. He owes you nothing."

Since she was alone in a twenty-room mansion, she could talk out loud. "And I owe him everything."

Silently, she thanked the Lord for giving her this reprieve and remembered that she'd promised to do things differently this time.

Moving into the bathroom, she cleaned the large garden tub with a new vigor, putting images of Nick Rudolph's handsome face out of her mind. Then she hurried out of the room, determined to stick to business.

And ran right smack into the arms of the very man she was trying to escape.

Myla's dust rag and cleaning supplies went in one direction and her armful of laundry went in the other as she plowed into Nick, sending him back against the sturdy oak railing on the second floor landing.

Catching her just as his back hit the banister,

Nick gripped her shoulders to keep both of them from toppling down the stairs. "Goodness, is there a fire in there?"

She leaned against him in relief. "Nick, you scared me!"

"I'll say. Are you all right?"

Myla glanced up at him, embarrassed and acutely aware of his arms holding her. She had to learn not to be so clumsy! "I'm fine. What are you doing home so early?"

Nick hesitated, his smile as wry as ever. Then she noticed with a mother's keen eye, he looked flushed and his dark eyes were glazed over with a red-rimmed heat.

Concerned, she automatically put a palm to his forehead. "Why, you're burning up with fever!"

He pushed her away with a gentle shove. "Tell me something I don't know. Don't get too close. According to my friend and racquetball partner, Dr. Loeffler, I've got the flu. That's the only way he'd ever beat me and he knows it."

Myla kicked her scattered cleaning supplies out of the way and steered him toward his room. "You went to work like this, and played racquetball! Honestly, don't you ever know when to quit?"

He drew his brows together, amused at her righteous indignation and her bossy nature. "I felt kind of tired this morning, but things got progressively worse as the day wore on. Dr. Loeffler checked me over after our game and told me to get home. Guess he couldn't believe he'd actually beaten me."

Myla clucked over him with all the vigor of a mother hen. "Will you stop making jokes and get into bed? I'll make you some chicken soup and get you some medicine for that fever. What did the doctor tell you to do?"

Nick gave her a lopsided grin. "He told me to let a beautiful woman serve me chicken soup and give me something for my fever."

Laughter bubbled in her throat, but she managed to keep her tone stern. "You're impossible. You'd better be all tucked in when I come back."

"Yes, ma'am, Nurse Myla."

She put both hands on her hips. "And don't expect me to baby you. I'm busy and you need to rest. I know you must really feel horrible. You never come home early."

He sent her a mock scowl. "No, I don't, but I still intend to get some work done. So, hand me my briefcase before you head down to concoct your flu survival kit."

Hissing her disapproval, she picked up the heavy leather satchel he'd left on a chair. Shoving it at his midsection, she said, "You do love your work, that's for sure."

Nick watched as she pranced out of the room, then he dropped like a lead weight onto the big bed. Holding his hands around the stuffed briefcase, he nodded to himself. He did love his work, but right now it was the last thing on his mind.

He fell back in a heap against the fluffy plaid pillows. Well, if a man's gotta be sick, he reflected with a grin, at least it helps to have a spunky red-headed nurse waiting on him hand and foot. This might turn out to be a good thing. He could actually enjoy being here, that is, if his body would just stop hurting all over.

A few minutes later, Myla was back with the promised soup and medicine, glad to see he was dressed in a blue sweat suit. He sat propped against pillows with paperwork scattered all around him, and a laptop computer centered in front of him on the bed.

"Are you going to eat and then rest?" she questioned as she set the bed tray down in front of him, then pulled the laptop away.

Giving her a mock angry glare, he brought the laptop back beside him. "Can you spoon-feed me?" he teased, enjoying the way her denim skirt whirled around her boots as she fussed with his discarded clothes.

"I don't think so," she retorted, a smile creasing her lips in spite of her reprimanding look. "You don't seem that weak to me."

"Gee, such a caring nurse."

"I'm sorry," she finally said, taking his droll

humor seriously. "I'm just not used to you being home during the day. You've thrown me completely off schedule."

Nick knew his smile was awfully smug. He'd also brought a becoming blush to her apple cheeks. He liked knowing that his presence distracted her. That meant she was interested. Although, he reassured himself as he watched the winter sun dancing off her radiant auburn hair, he really didn't have time to indulge in a relationship. And he had no earthly idea where this one was going.

He put the laptop aside, then sampled the soup before sitting back to stare up at her. "I think you're just not used to me, period. But I'd say, all in all, this arrangement is working out okay. Other than that one unfortunate incident with Shredder and that overgrown puppy of Carolyn's, you and the children haven't been any trouble, if that's what you're worried about."

"I'm not," she said, backing away, memories of being in his arms in the middle of the kitchen floor reminding her that she needed to concentrate on her job. "I'd better get back to work."

"Myla, wait." He gave her a questioning look. "Tell me how you do it?"

A look of confusion colored her green eyes. "Do what?"

"Keep that serene expression on your face. After

everything you've been through, including putting up with my demands, you seem so at peace."

She looked up then, her not-so-serene gaze meeting his. "I found my strength again," she said simply. "I found my faith again, after I thought I'd lost it forever."

Uncomfortable with this turn in the conversation, he said, "How'd you manage a thing like that?"

She lifted her chin. "Prayer. You know, Nick, when you have nothing left, you always have prayer."

No, he didn't know that. It had been a very long time since he'd relied on prayer. "Why...how did you lose your strength?"

She backed farther away, like a frightened bird about to take flight. "I don't want to discuss that."

"I'd really like to know...and to understand."

When she didn't answer immediately, he said, "Look, I'll take my medicine, and I promise I'll eat my soup. Sit down in that chair over there and talk to me."

Myla hesitated only a minute. Wanting him to see that he, too, could find his strength in faith, she sat down and watched as he diligently took two pills with a glass of juice; then, his eyes on her, he dutifully ate his soup.

Satisfied that he'd finish the soup, she leaned back for a minute. "You see, at one time, I thought God had abandoned me."

Surprised, he stopped eating. Funny, he'd thought that very thing himself, right after burying his father. "Why would you think that? You seem so sure about all this religious stuff."

She lowered her head, her hands wringing together, her eyes misty with memories. "I wasn't so sure for a while. Because of something I did, or rather, something I didn't do—and I'd rather not talk about it. It took me a long time to see that God hadn't abandoned me. It was the other way around."

"You mean, you abandoned Him?"

She nodded. "I gave up on Him. I didn't think I was worthy of His love."

"Why would you think a thing like that?"

"I had it drummed into me enough," she said, then gasped. "Oh, never mind. I shouldn't have said that."

"Well, you did. What do you mean?"

When she didn't speak, Nick sat up to stare across at her. "Does this have something to do with your husband?"

Her silence told him everything he needed to know. And brought out all the protective instincts he'd tried so hard to ignore. "Myla, did your husband do something to hurt you?"

Myla didn't want to cry. She'd learned not to cry. But now, after she'd heard Nick voice the truth, her worst secrets floated up to the surface of her consciousness, causing the tears to roll down her cheeks like a torrent of rain coming from a black cloud. Holding her eyes tightly shut, she tried to block out the painful memories. She couldn't let him see her like this. Lifting out of the chair, she said, "I need to get back to work."

Nick moved his tray away with a clatter and stood up. "Myla, did you and he…was it a good marriage?"

She bit her bottom lip, then gave him a soul-weary look. "In the beginning, yes. But, it turned ugly after a few years."

Nick closed his eyes, then opened them to look at her with dread. "Did he…did he abuse you?"

She brought her hands up to her face and cried softly.

Nick pulled her hands away, his eyes searching her face. "Did he?"

"No, not physically," she said, her hands automatically gripping his. "Nick, please don't make me talk about this now." She didn't want the bond they had developed to be destroyed, not yet.

"I want…I need to know," he said, his voice husky, his words gentle. "I won't judge you, Myla."

But she was afraid he would, just as so many others had. "I'm…not ready to tell you everything."

The pain in her green eyes stopped Nick from pushing her any further. Instead, he said, "What can I do, to help you?"

She looked up at him, unable to ask for his help, unable to ask for his understanding.

But Nick knew instinctively that she needed both.

So before she could bolt, he tugged her into his arms and rocked her gently, as if she were a child who needed reassuring. "No more questions," he promised. "But if you want to cry, you go right ahead."

Myla did cry. Shutting her eyes tightly closed, she let him hold her for a while, thankful that he didn't press her any further about her marriage. Just to be held, unconditionally, that was comfort enough for now.

"All right," he said after a while, letting go to pat her shoulder. "Feel better now?" At her silent nod, he added, "You can't keep this inside. Lydia knows people, therapists and counselors, who can help you. And…I want to help, too."

She lifted her head, then wiped her eyes with the back of her hand, resolve settling back over her like a protective winter cloak. With a shaky smile, she said, "You're a fine one to be giving me advice. I am a lot better now, though, really."

He looked doubtful. "How can you say that?"

"I told you, I found my faith again—alone, on a dark cold night. I was huddled in the car with the children, with nothing left…nothing. In the moonlight, I saw my worn Bible lying on the dashboard. I hadn't read it in months. I did that night, though, with a flashlight. While my children slept in the cold, I found my faith again in that single beam of light, and I cried long and hard, and I prayed, really prayed, for the first time in a very long time."

Nick swallowed back the lump forming in his throat. "What did you find there in that light, that helped you?"

She sniffed, then lifted her head. "He said He would not leave me comfortless, but I had forgotten that promise. In First Corinthians, chapter thirteen, verse thirteen, the Bible says, 'And now abideth faith, hope, love, these three: but the greatest of these is love'."

Nick stood there, his heart trembling. Love. The one thing he'd been so afraid of since his father's breakdown and death. "How did that verse sustain you?"

She smiled then. "I knew that no matter what, I had my children with me and I loved them above all else, except the Lord. They were my gift, and no matter what kind of life I'd had with their father, they were my responsibility. Love, Nick. Love is the greatest gift of all. It gives us our strength. It gives us a reason to go on living, even when we'd rather curl up and sleep. I realized that God gave us unconditional love when He sent His son to save us from our sins. I realized that God hadn't abandoned me. He was reaching out to me on that dark night."

Nick sighed, his own fears cresting in the midst of her eloquent story. "But…unconditional love is so hard to give and so very hard to expect. To love so completely, you have to give up so much control.

How can you trust something that abstract, something that can make you seem so weak?"

"That's the whole point," she said, her expression changing from sorrowful to hopeful. "Love doesn't make us weak, Nick. Love gives us the strength to go on. That night, alone and afraid, I remembered God's unconditional love for me. I'd lost that, as well as my trust. I'd been emotionally stripped of that love and that trust, by a man who didn't know how to give either."

"Your husband."

She nodded, then stepped back. "I'm all right now. I won't be afraid of the dark, ever again. I made a promise to take care of my children. They don't deserve to have to live like this—they didn't do anything wrong."

"Neither did you. You seem so brave. Is that for your children's sake?"

"I have to be strong, for them."

Nick felt his heart melting in half. He'd never seen such a fierce defense of love, or heard such a strong testimony. She had come to him with nothing, yet she had more to give than any woman he'd ever known. "Is there anything I can do?"

Unable to look at him, Myla couldn't speak about her pain. Leaning close, she whispered, "Just hold me again."

He did, for a long while, his arms wrapping her in what little protection he could offer. Finally, he brought a hand up to her chin so he could wipe her tears away. Gazing down at her, Nick wanted badly to kiss her.

But Myla stood back, her voice clear once again. "You'd better rest. And I'd better get away from you. I don't have time to get the flu."

He laughed at that. "Always the practical one." Leaning back down on the bed, he added, "I am feeling a little wobbly. Are you sure you're all right?"

"I'm fine now," she said as she lifted his tray away, her eyes downcast. "Do you need anything else?"

He looked up at her, thinking how right it seemed to have her here with him, thinking he needed her strength. "No, thanks. You've spoiled me quite enough, I believe."

His words soothed Myla like a balm. "Nick?" she called from the door.

"Hmmm?"

"Thank you, for understanding."

He wanted to tell her he didn't understand, really. But the weight of sleep blocked out his reply. He didn't understand how one minute he could be so sure, so secure in his firm, smug convictions, then the next, begin to doubt everything he stood for.

He wasn't as fearful as he should be. He wasn't so much afraid of reaching out for love now. Myla had done that for him. She'd opened up her heart and told him a story of faith that left him humbled and ashamed. For so long now, he'd been afraid of the power of love. He'd believed loving someone could make a person weak, just as his grieving, dying father had become. But he'd been so very wrong. Nick needed to hold Myla again, just to be held himself.

Instead, he reached for his pillow and buried his dreams and his doubts in a deep, troubled sleep.

Nick woke hours later to find his room dark, except for the flickering light from the fire someone had lit in the sitting area fireplace. The room was cozy, but a flash of thunder and lightning told of the wintry chill settling over the city. He shuddered to think Myla and her children could have been out there, alone, in that cold night. And he wondered how many people were cold and shivering and afraid this night.

Groaning, Nick rolled over, acutely aware of his own discomfort. This was a mean flu bug, that was for sure.

His throat felt like he'd swallowed a jalapeño pepper and his head throbbed with each beat of his pulse. Craving a long, hot shower, he rose to calculate the distance to the bathroom. A bold knock hit the bedroom door before he could attempt the trip, causing a ricocheting rumble in his head.

"Come in," he called in a raspy voice.

Lydia popped her head in the door. "Well, big

brother, sleeping the day away won't get your Christmas shopping done."

He moaned, rolling over to face the fire. "Go away."

"Glad you're feeling better," she replied as she tossed him a bag of prescription medicines. "Dr. Loeffler sent you these—antibiotics and a decongestant. He said to take all of it."

"He's just trying to poison me so I won't beat him at racquetball again." Giving her a false smile, he added, "I don't like being sick."

Lydia handed him two drawings. "Maybe these will cheer you up."

Nick grinned. Jesse had reproduced the kitchen disaster, complete with Shredder sitting on the ceiling fan and Pooky lapping away amidst a pile of food. Patrick had drawn a Christmas tree loaded with colorful gifts.

"Your two biggest fans send their regards. Aren't those two adorable?"

Nick laid the pictures on the nightstand. "Yeah, and very well-behaved, as far as children go. Lydia, has Myla told you anything about their past?"

"A little. Why?"

"We had a long talk today. She's had a rough time, but she won't tell me exactly what happened in her marriage."

Lydia sat down to stare at her brother. "Well, don't press her. I introduced her to Reverend

Hillard. I'm sure he can give her some spiritual guidance."

"Maybe," Nick said, remembering the story Myla had told him. "But I think her faith's intact. It's her self-esteem I'm worried about."

Lydia sat up, her eyes squinting toward him. "You're worse off than I thought. Did I hear you say something good about someone's faith? And that you're actually aware of another person's mental stability?"

He nodded, then shot her a wry smile. "Yes, you did. I want to help her, Lydia. She's a good woman."

"Well, praise the Lord." Lydia hopped up to give her brother a breath-stopping hug. "Oh, Nicky, I knew you'd come around. You really want to help, really, really?"

"Yes, really, really," he said, laughing. "I'd be a real Scrooge if I didn't see how much Myla and her children have been through. But don't make more out of this than it is. I think this flu's gone to my head."

"Or maybe Myla's gone to your heart," Lydia said softly. "After all, it is Christmas. A time for miracles."

He patted her on the back. "I'd forgotten what a joyous time it can be. And I'm sorry, really sorry, for being so hard to live with since Father's death."

She kissed him on the temple. "No need to apologize. Welcome back, Nick."

* * *

When Nick came out of the bathroom, his food was sitting on a tray in front of the leather armchair by the fireplace. Glancing around, he was disappointed that Myla wasn't there to make sure he ate everything on his plate. He still had a lot of questions to ask her.

Lydia was right. He did have a soft spot in his heart for Myla and her two children. And the spot was opening to include other possibilities such as attending church and opening the Bible he'd tossed aside years ago.

He should be scared, yet when he searched for the old fear, he only found a new, growing strength. Now, he was beginning to dread the time when Myla would have to leave.

Two weeks until Christmas. Usually, this old house was hushed and quiet around this time of year, haunted by the memory of his parents. Not this year. This year, things were going to be different.

A soft knock at the door caused him to put down the spoonful of beef stew he'd been about to eat. Two reddish blond heads bobbed just above the ornate door handle. Patrick and Jesse eyed him curiously.

"You two going to stand out in the hall all night, or are you going to get in here before your mother catches you?"

"We ain't supposed to be here," Patrick said in a small whisper. "But we wanted to say hi."

"It's *aren't*—we *aren't* supposed to be here," Jesse corrected as she pushed Patrick into the room.

Patrick made a face at his sister's redundancy. "I know that. That's what I just said."

"Where's your mother?" Nick asked, smiling at them.

Jesse tossed her ponytail. "Talking to Miss Lydia. Mama's gonna go to school at night and she's looking for another job, for when Miss Henny comes home. We'll just have to live in the shelter for a while, that's all."

Nick didn't want to think about that, so he changed the subject to more pleasant things. "Well, Santa'll be coming soon," he said, hoping to find two worthy allies in the children. "What do you want him to bring you?"

Both children rushed to his side, talking at once. Nick heard it all, registered each request and vowed to travel to the North Pole if he had to, just to get them all the loot they wanted.

"And what about your mom?"

"Oh, that's kinda hard," Jesse said, giggling. "Mama wants stuff you can't find in the mall."

"Yeah, like what?"

Jesse settled down on the floor, wiping her nose with her hand. "She wants a house, of course. She talks about having a home of her own again. And she wants a job. She doesn't like not having any money. Oh, and once, she told us she'd like a long soak in a tub of hot water, then get dressed up in a pretty green dress for a special Christmas dinner. She loves to cook, you know."

Nick once again marveled at the simple things he'd taken for granted. Clearing his suddenly clogged throat, he said, "Are you sure that's all she wants?"

Thinking for a minute, her nose scrunched, Jesse held her hands wide. "Oh, and roses. She loves yellow roses."

Patrick nodded. "Yeah, and one day, Daddy got real mad and mowed all of hers down."

Nick went still inside. Trying to keep his tone light and casual, he asked, "Why would he do a thing like that?"

"'Cause she didn't have dinner ready on time," Jesse said in a matter-of-fact voice. "She cried when he wasn't looking."

Dinner. No wonder she'd tried so hard to make his dinner party a success. No wonder she'd been so shaken when it had gone bad. She was used to fixing things up, hiding her fear behind a false bravado.

Patrick pulled on Nick's sleeve, bringing him out of his numbed state. "I don't want much, Mr. Nick. I just wish we didn't have to leave here, ever."

Nick was beginning to wish that very same thing.

Before Nick could reply, however, the door swung open and Myla stomped into the room, a mother's wrath apparent in her expression. "What in the world! You two are supposed to be in bed! How'd you get up here?"

"We snuck by you," Patrick blurted out in spite of his sister's glaring look.

"That's obvious enough." Myla pointed a finger toward the door. "Get back downstairs with Miss Lydia. Do you both want to catch the flu?"

"I didn't breathe on them," Nick said, glad to find a light moment in the children's misdeeds. "And I'm glad they came by for a visit. I was getting downright lonely."

"Want us to stay awhile?" Patrick offered hopefully.

"No, he doesn't," his mother interjected. "Go on down. I'll come and read to you and help you with your prayers in a little while."

Nick managed a chuckle as he watched the children scoot out of the room. "Well, you certainly got rid of those two varmints."

She looked at his half-eaten food. "Why didn't you eat your supper?"

"I wasn't very hungry."

"Are you feeling better?"

"A little. I heard you and Lydia were plotting down there."

"Planning," she corrected. "There's a difference."

"I've never looked at it that way."

She started to take the tray, but his hand shot out to stop her. "Myla, could we talk some more?"

"No," she said, not daring to look at him. "I'd rather not."

"I won't press you about your life before," he said. "I just have some questions, about…this unconditional love about which you speak so highly."

She glanced up then, her eyes wide. "You want to discuss…religion?"

"Yes," he said, smiling slightly. "I think I'd like that."

And so they talked. She told him the stories of the Bible that he'd forgotten. As she talked, memories washed over him; memories of his mother, telling him these very same stories, her faith as strong and as shining as Myla's. How could he have forgotten the beauty in that? How could he have let it slip so far away?

After Myla said a gentle prayer for him to feel better, both physically and spiritually, he sat in the darkness alone, watching the fire. And realized he was tired of being alone in the dark.

Then it hit him—Myla had said something earlier about being afraid of the darkness. They were so alike, he and his Myla. They'd both been out in the cold for too long. Together, maybe they could find the warmth of that unconditional love she'd told him about. Together, with the help of a higher being watching over them.

Outside, the rain fell in cold, indiscriminate sheets and Nick shuddered, thinking again that she might have been out there tonight, all alone and frightened.

But she wasn't out there. For some strange reason, God had sent her to him instead. He wouldn't take that obligation lightly.

"Not again, Myla," he whispered to the fire. "Not ever again, if I can help it."

Then he did something he hadn't done in a very long time. He folded his hands and he prayed.

Chapter Five

It was well past midnight. Myla tiptoed into the kitchen, careful not to wake the children sleeping in the bedroom just down the narrow back hallway. With Nick being home sick the last couple of days, her mind was in turmoil. Sleep was impossible.

She didn't want to admit that she'd enjoyed playing nurse to him. The first morning, they'd talked and laughed together, sitting on the sunporch off the second-story hallway. Nick had insisted she sit with him while he had breakfast. It had been a comfortable, cozy distraction, complete with frolicking squirrels putting on a show in the great oaks lining the sloping backyard. Then, later in the day when he'd woken up feeling better, he'd come downstairs to eat a sandwich in the kitchen, reading the paper in silence while she went about her work. So domestic, so homey. So *wrong,* Myla reminded herself.

Setting the bags she carried on the counter, she pulled out the small treasures her first paycheck from Nick had allowed her to buy for her children. This would take her mind off of dreaming about a man she shouldn't be thinking about.

A sweater set for Jesse—pink-and-blue striped with little white bows on the Peter Pan collar. An inexpensive fashion doll with two sets of clothes. Some new jeans and an action toy for Patrick, along with a set of army men with tanks and jeeps. It wasn't much, but they'd have something under the tree. This year especially, it was important to her that her children understand the real Christmas celebration, so she didn't want to make a big deal out of gift giving. Yet she couldn't help but breathe a sigh of relief tonight.

She'd had horrible visions of them spending Christmas out in the cold, or in a shelter. Now, thanks to Nick's kindness, they were going to be celebrating Christmas in this beautiful, rambling house. Thinking of how lucky they were to be safe and warm, she stood there letting the tears fall freely.

And that's how Nick found her.

Her back was turned toward him and she was wearing a worn, thick flannel robe, pink with blue faded flowers and small red heart-shaped designs which, in the moon's soft spotlight, reminded him of aged paper valentines. He felt as if he could watch her forever, but when he heard her soft intake of breath and saw her wipe at a tear, he went to her, touching her lightly on the arm.

"Are you all right?"

Myla jumped at his touch, surprise widening her eyes. "Nick! What are you doing up?"

"Shredder woke me. That sneaky cat's taken a liking to me, I believe. He's also taken a liking to the foot of my bed, where I left him fast asleep."

She laughed then, but the laughter turned back to tears. "I'm sorry. I've been so emotional lately. Christmas always does that to me, but this year…well, I have a lot to be thankful for."

Nick once again felt the sharp contrast in her world and his own. "I can't imagine what it must have been like for you, out there. You're very courageous."

She sniffed back her tears. "Hardly. When it comes to survival, you just do what you've got to do."

"You're starting over," he said, careful of how he worded his next request. "Don't you think it's time you really left the past behind? Tell me everything about your marriage, Myla."

She looked up, deciding there in the darkness she could trust him with the truth. "Yes, I think it's time to move on, and I guess talking about it would help." Then she gave him one last chance. "Are you sure you want me to burden you with the sordid details, though?"

"Burden away," he replied, his voice quiet and encouraging. "I won't be able to sleep if you don't tell me what's made you so sad."

She took a deep breath, then brought a hand up to play with one of the buttons on the front of her robe. "My husband deceived all of us. Sonny was a big fake, in complete control. And he had me trained as his robot. He even had the children trained, too. Only I didn't see it until it was too late."

"Tell me why."

She leaned back against the counter, her eyes shining. "I wish I knew why. Why I let him do the things he did, why I let him make me feel so small and helpless. Looking back, I think it was my need to please—my family, his family, our friends, him. I wanted to be a good wife, a good mother. That was my only ambition in life, because that's all Sonny wanted me to be. He'd convinced me that I wasn't very good at anything, but I thought at least I could be good at that. As it turned out, I didn't do such a hot job."

Nick took one of her hands. "Hey, who's doubting now? I can't believe you'd let anyone make you doubt yourself like that. You seem so capable, so strong."

"I wasn't always so surefooted," she said in a whisper. "I did have doubts, and I'm so ashamed of what I let happen."

He shook his head. "It can't be that bad."

Pulling away, she headed to the refrigerator to pour two glasses of juice. Then she found the cookie jar and placed two fresh oatmeal cookies on a napkin for Nick. "It's so bad, I'm still ashamed to talk about it. Nick, Sonny embezzled funds from the bank he managed, and when the authorities found out…he committed suicide in his fancy car."

Nick could only stand there staring at her. The background check had only listed her as a bankrupt widow, just as she'd told him. "Myla, I had no idea."

"No, how could you? No one did. We went to church every Sunday, we had a nice ranch house in the country. We had everything. But it was all a sham. Sonny only played at being a Christian. He used church for networking and finding new clients. And when that didn't bring in enough money, he turned to crime.

"He had this obsessive need to always have more. More money, more power, all of the latest things—cellular phones, computers, any kind of gadget that would make him look successful. He never spent much time with the children—he had very little patience with them—but then he'd buy them all sorts of expensive toys to win their affection after he'd treated them badly. And I…I was so blind, so convinced that I had to work harder, try harder to be the perfect little wife, I didn't see that he was suffering, until it was too late. I never wanted more money or things. I wanted more of him, emotionally. But he couldn't give me that. And I didn't do anything to save him."

"But it's not your fault—"

"Yes," she said, bobbing her head. "Yes, it is. And I've been running ever since. From my family, because they blame me. From my so-called friends, because they can't be seen with me anymore. From myself, because I can't stand to look in the mirror each day. I had to protect my children, and that's the only thing that kept me going, until that night when I realized I wasn't alone." Looking up at him, she said, "Then, not too long after that night, I found you."

He turned to stand beside her as they both stared out into the bleak winter night. "So you've been struggling with this, all this time?"

She took a sip of juice, then set the glass down. "I kept thinking I should have done something to help Sonny."

"Help him? What could you have done?"

She turned, both hands braced on the counter. "I should have followed my instincts when I suspected something was wrong. But Sonny was hard to deal with even on a good day. He'd threaten me by telling me that I wasn't a good wife, and that it was my fault he felt so much pressure. Then he'd tell me he'd leave and take the children. I...I began to doubt my own Christianity. I mean, here I'd lived with this man for years and I'd believed he truly felt the same way I did, but he didn't. He put up this big front, but it was all an act. And I was too afraid to do anything about it, so I did what I had to, to protect my children."

"Why did you marry him?"

"I loved him, and I wanted a family. Sonny promised me we'd have a good life. He came from a wealthy family—his parents always overindulged him—and I'd never had very much. It seemed like a dream. And turned into a nightmare. After he… after he died, I found out there was no money, no insurance, and most of the expensive things he'd bought got repossessed, right along with my house."

She faced him squarely now, her pride gone right along with all the fancy possessions and high hopes she'd once had. "I will always remember the day they came and locked up my house. The bank officer had been a friend of ours. He kept telling me how sorry he was, but he didn't really offer to make things any better. He was just doing his job."

"You don't forget that feeling, you don't forget the scorn and pity you see on people's faces. Ever. That's why, this time I intend to do things my way, with the help of the Lord. I won't ever let anyone make me doubt myself or my faith again."

Nick leaned close, his gaze sweeping her face. Unable to see his expression completely in the muted light, Myla waited, wondering if he, too, would turn away in disgust. But he didn't. Instead, he placed his hands on her face, his touch as soft as the moonlight, and then he kissed her.

The touch of his lips on hers was gentle, yet powerful. No one had reached out to her like this in a very long time. A soft, secure warmth spread through her, blocking out the cold night and the bad memories. As much as she needed this, Myla was still afraid to give in to the myriad feelings coursing through her system. She couldn't let herself become too dependent on this man's kindness.

Nick felt her tense up, heard the defeat in her soft sigh. Cupping his hands on her shoulders, he stared down at her. "You don't have to doubt me, Myla. I know I was completely indifferent when we met, but I've changed a lot since then. I want to help you through this."

She touched his face with her hand, hope warring with despair in her mind. "I know you do. And you can, with your money, with your connections, but don't you see—that's the kind of help Sonny provided. He took care of me materially, but he was never there with me spiritually. I won't be a burden to anyone again. And I won't commit to anyone who can't go the distance with me. Right now, I'm still too battered to take things any further, Nick."

Nick stood there holding her, wondering if he,

too, was afraid to take things any further. He'd certainly done a complete turnaround. But from the moment he'd looked into those luminous green eyes, he'd been hopelessly lost. Or maybe hopefully found.

Still struggling, still amazed, he said, "What about feelings? What about need?"

She gave him an imploring look. "Do you need me, Nick?"

"I think so," he said honestly. "But I'm moving into dangerous territory here. I've got to learn *how* to need someone."

Myla took their juice glasses to the sink, then turned to face him across the kitchen. "Maybe we both should step back and consider the consequences of our feelings. You've got everything a human could possibly need, but you've lost your faith. I've lost everything—all the comforts of home—but I've found my faith again. I won't have it stripped away, and I won't let you step in and take control the way Sonny always did."

"You think I'd do that to you?"

"No, you're not like him, but you're still fighting against your own feelings, and that could cause the same sort of resentment Sonny felt toward me. He teased me about my church work and my beliefs, then pretended he felt the same way when others were around. That hurt more than anything. I won't get into a battle of that kind with you. I won't make you choose. That has to be your own decision. And, needing me has to come from your heart, not from some sense of obligation or sympathy."

He moved across the kitchen to take her back into his arms. "I'm not so sure what I'm feeling right now, but I do know that it's not just an obligation to ease my hardened soul. I want to take care of you, but I understand how important it is for you to pull yourself out of this, both emotionally and financially. I should know—I've been doing that same thing since my father died."

"We've both been lost," Myla said, her gaze holding his.

Nick tugged her close then lifted a hand to touch her face again. "Right now, I don't feel so lost anymore." After a tender kiss, he told her, "But I do think I'm losing the battle, with you and with your mighty God."

"We have to be sure," she reminded him. "No matter how we feel about each other, there has to be a commitment to a third being in this relationship. That's the only way it can work."

Nick didn't reply. He knew she was right. She wouldn't live a lie again. This time, she wanted a commitment that meant turning control over to God, instead of letting another human being control her. It was a tall order, and one he'd have to give careful consideration and prayer.

"We'll make it work," he assured her. "We'll

take it slow. I'm not a very patient man, but...I think I can learn to be."

Myla's heart soared as she gave him a chaste kiss on the cheek. "Thank you, for listening. And for not judging."

As he watched her walk down the hall, her long red hair trailing around her neck, Nick realized she might be the one without a place to live, but he was the one without a home.

"Mama, Mama, can we get up now?"

Myla rolled over, opening her eyes slowly to find her children sitting up in bed, watching her as if she knew all the secrets to life. Moaning, she sat up to wipe hair out of her eyes. "What time is it?"

"Six o'clock," Jesse said, reaching out to hug Myla tightly. "Can we please see what Santa brought?"

Christmas morning. Myla hugged Jesse against her. "Sure, honey. Just let me get the sleep out of my eyes."

As the children jumped up and down in glee, Myla thought about the Christmas Eve service they'd all attended last night, including Nick.

"It's his first time in ten years," Lydia had explained, tears in her eyes. "Oh, Myla, this is the happiest Christmas we've had in a long time."

It had been happy for Myla, too. Reverend Hillard was a wonderful, compassionate preacher and a good listener. He'd helped her deal with her past through prayer and positive discussions. Then, to relive the Christmas miracle, to see the shining faces of faith in the muted light of hundreds of candles, had only renewed her own faith and strength. She'd come so far with God's help, and now, Nick, too, seemed to be finding a new strength. Could it be possible that God had brought them together to help each other heal?

But she had to remind herself, she was still fearful of depending too much on anyone else to help her back on her feet. Especially Nick, since he still seemed so unsure himself.

After church, he'd dropped them off back at the house, then after making some excuse about putting in an obligatory appearance, had headed out to a party at Carolyn's. Myla had never felt so lonely, sitting there watching her children sleep. Was Nick still fighting his feelings? Did seeing Carolyn only reinforce his need to stay in control?

But, Myla groggily reminded herself this morning, she had no hold over Nick, and soon, she'd be moving out anyway. God had a purpose for her, but maybe that purpose wasn't for Nick and her to be together. She'd have to leave that in God's hands.

"Mom, hurry," Patrick whined from his perch at the foot of the bed, his cartoon character pajamas as bright as the glow in his eyes.

"Hold on, sweetie." As she washed her face and

tugged on her clothes, Myla said a prayer for guidance.

Help me to do Your will, and guide me in my feelings for Nick. If You want us to be together, give Nick the strength to learn to love. Show me the way, Lord, and give me the courage to walk away from him if I have to make that choice.

"Get up, Nick!"

Lydia yanked the covers back, sending a cold rush of air into Nick's warm, sleep-covered world.

"Why do you always have to stalk into my bedroom and bother me?" he asked, groping for the blankets as he took in her bright red flannel pajamas. "And do you have to look so jolly?"

Lydia held the blankets away. "I heard the pitter-patter of little feet downstairs. You wanted to be awake and alert for the big event, remember?"

"I remember."

"Well, get moving. I want to see them when they find all that loot you bought for them."

He'd only meant to buy the children a few toys, not a truckload. "Did I go overboard?"

"That's an understatement, big brother. But I seriously doubt the local toy store is complaining. You made them go over the top in sales, I'm sure."

Nick sat up, then gave his sister a sleepy stare. "Lydia, I've been meaning to ask you—has Myla talked to you any more about her marriage?"

Lydia's usually perky face became guarded. "What do you mean?"

"She has, hasn't she? Lydia, I want to know what's going on with her. I mean, she told me what happened, with her husband's suicide and all. But, I need to know—is she healing now? Or does she still feel guilty?"

He didn't want to scare Myla away, but he had to know if she was really feeling better about things, because his own patience was wearing thin. He wanted to nurture her and protect her, yet he held back, waiting, hoping.

"That's very personal, Nick. And you know I can't discuss that with you." Sitting down on the bed, she said, "Please, don't press her on this. Women who've been through that kind of pain…it takes a while for them to trust again." Maneuvering him back to the task at hand, she added, "But, at least she's been receiving counseling from Reverend Hillard. That's so important for her state of mind." Then, changing the subject with expert ease, she added, "And at least she can't fault *you* in the gift-giving department. Now, hurry up!"

Nick went into the bathroom to wash his face and toss on his clothes. Minutes later, he came back, dressed in khakis and a sweater, and worried that he'd made a big mistake. "I just wanted them to have a good Christmas. Think Myla will mind?"

Lydia extended a hand to him as he emerged.

"Only one way to find out." Hugging him close, she said, "Merry Christmas, Nick."

The sound of squealing children greeted Nick and Lydia as they entered the double doors to the den. The room was in total chaos. Wrapping paper and toys decorated its usually sedate interior.

Lydia patted her brother's neck, then pushed him into the room. "My, my, sure looks like Santa came here."

Patrick looked up from the gigantic toy train that whistled as it sped around the Christmas tree. "Look, Mr. Nick. Santa brought me a train and some boots and a farm set. How'd he know we used to live on a farm, anyway?"

"Santa's very smart," Nick said, his eyes meeting Myla's. She stood in the corner by the window, her expression tight-lipped, her face pale.

"He gave me a mermaid doll that sings," Jesse shouted, running up to Nick and Lydia to proudly display the beautiful doll. "And a dollhouse."

Lydia fell to the floor, exploring the treasures as if she were only eight years old herself. Holding up the less expensive doll Myla had bought for Jesse, she asked, "Who's this?"

"I don't know her name," Jesse replied, her attention on the other toys surrounding her.

"She's very pretty," Lydia coaxed, her gaze flying up to meet Nick's.

He looked from her to Myla, his heart sinking. Uh-huh, he'd blown this one, big-time. What had he been thinking?

Myla pivoted to head for the kitchen. "I'll go make some coffee."

Nick followed, ready to apologize for his excessiveness. He winced as she yanked the refrigerator door open and pulled out a huge can of coffee. Taking a deep breath, he stopped her before she could bring the scoop to the filter cup. "I'm sorry, Myla."

Myla set the scoop full of coffee down with a shaking hand. "How could you, Nick? After I told you how I felt…after I told you how Sonny used to try and buy our affection."

"I…I got carried away," he tried to explain. "Christmas around here is usually so gloomy, and I wanted to do something special for the children."

Some of the anger left Myla. How could she be mad when he'd been so generous? Although she knew his motives were completely different from Sonny's, it still worried her that he had some of the same traits. "I know you meant well, Nick, but I can't have them thinking this is the way it's going to be from now on. A lot of expensive toys can't prepare them for the tough time we've got ahead of us. I want them to be children, to enjoy the wonder of Christmas morning, but I also want them to understand that Christmas is about more than getting toys."

"Of course," he agreed, helping her to finish making the coffee. "And I truly wasn't thinking. I never meant to overshadow what you'd already bought for them."

Myla turned on the oven and shoved in the coffee cake she'd made the day before. "I'm very grateful to you," she admitted, "but you have to understand how important this is to me."

"I do understand," he said, following her to the cabinet. "But it's important that you understand me, too. I'm trying to change, Myla. I've...I've been bitter and self-centered, and so preoccupied with work since my father's death, and you know how I am. I'm used to taking charge and telling everyone what to do."

At her knowing I-couldn't-agree-with-you-more glance, he hurried on. "This was a big step for me, to celebrate Christmas in any way at all. And to be able to give to someone, freely and with sincerity...well, it's been a long time since I've felt like this. Maybe I never knew what Christmas was all about myself, until now."

Myla had to swallow the lump in her throat. His admission reinforced what she already knew about him. Behind that indifferent exterior lay a heart of gold. A hurting heart. He had so much to give, much more than a pile of money. And he was trying hard to show her that, even if he had gone about it too excessively.

She stopped her busywork and turned to stare up at him, her eyes wide. "Oh, Nick, it was wonderful, watching their eyes light up when they ran into that room. What you did…it was so sweet, and I shouldn't be mad. But what am I supposed to do with all those wonderful gifts when we move into Magnolia House?"

"You've got awhile," he said, not wanting to think about that. "And you can let them keep their things here and come back here anytime to play with the stuff until you get settled in your own place."

She placed her hand on his. "Christmas is here, Nick. In a few days, Henny will be back from Arkansas. We're on the list to move into the shelter. Lydia says we can move in soon, and after a few months, I should be able to find a low-income house with Lydia's help. I've still got a lot of hard work ahead of me."

He lowered his head, then held her hand tight against his. He couldn't tell her that he had no intention of letting her move into a homeless shelter. "I know—we agreed from the beginning this situation couldn't last. I guess I'd just conveniently forgotten about it."

No, that wasn't exactly true. He'd thought of nothing else, but he had to tread lightly here.

"Yes, we agreed this was only a temporary arrangement," she reminded him. "Don't make it any harder for me, please?"

He saw the pain in her eyes, saw the plea to let her go peacefully, without a big fuss. How could he do that now, when she'd opened up his heart and staked a claim on him? But her firm resolve told him he didn't have any control here, none at all. "If you need any advice—"

She pulled her hand away, trying to ignore the little sensations coursing through her body. "Sonny always advised me. It's time I did things on my own."

That angered him. His voice deepening with each word, he said, "I'm not Sonny."

Lydia peeked in the swinging doors before Myla could reply. "Hey, everything all right in here?"

"Fine," Nick said, waving her away. "We'll be back in soon with some coffee cake."

That reminded Myla of the hot oven. With a wail, she hurried to check the cake. Smoke poured from the stove as she pulled the door open. "Oh, I forgot about it. It's ruined!"

Lydia stepped inside the kitchen, her eyes wide with disbelief. "Have you ever noticed when you two get together in the kitchen, something always goes wrong?"

Myla pulled the charred cake out of the oven, then rolled her eyes. "Too many cooks spoil the broth."

Patrick and Jesse came running. Patrick held up a bright green laser gun and aimed straight for the blackened cake, firing a noisy round of pretend lasers. "Got it," he said with a grin. "Gee, Mom, you used to know how to cook."

Myla looked at Nick, a smile twitching at the corner of her mouth in spite of her earlier concerns. He laughed, too, relaxing as the tension between them eased.

"Anyone for pizza?" Lydia asked, her eyes lifting skyward.

"Dinner was wonderful."

Nick's eyes met Myla's across the expanse of the Queen Anne dining table. He liked this. He liked having Lydia and the children here to share a big Christmas dinner. He didn't know when exactly he'd started liking it, but his mood was more in line with the holiday spirit because of Myla and her two children. Now if he could just convince her to stay here, with him.

"Thank you," Myla said in a hushed tone. Her mind kept going back to what Nick had said in the kitchen. He was changing. She could tell that. He'd even said grace before he carved the turkey for dinner. Still, she was reluctant to trust him completely. Yet when she sat here, looking at him, exchanging warm smiles at some cute comment from one of the children or just noticing how handsome he looked in his sweater and casual slacks, she knew it wouldn't take much for her to fall for him. Oh, this was so hard!

Lydia cleared her throat loudly, bringing Myla's head up. "And the dressing…I love oyster dressing, don't you, Nick?"

"Yes, love it."

"Can I have a piece of pecan pie?" Patrick asked.

"You've barely touched your meal," Myla said, her eyes still on the man at the head of the table. "Considering we had a light breakfast, I'd say you'd better eat as much as you can."

"I did eat," Patrick whined. "I'm ready for pie."

"In a few minutes, Patrick."

Jesse tried. "I'm ready for pie, too, Mama."

Myla's gaze shifted from one child to the other. She couldn't help but smile. Jesse was almost completely well from her cold, and her children were well fed and warm. In many ways, this Christmas had been one of their best together. "Oh, all right. I guess you can have dessert now." Looking down the table, she saw Nick's grinning expression. "I suppose you want some pie, too?"

"Yes, Mom," he said, bursting out in laughter, then quickly clearing his throat to look serious. "If that's all right with you?"

Myla rose to get the requested goodies. "Of course. I didn't bake it for it to just sit there looking pretty."

After the children hopped up to follow their mother, Lydia gave her brother a curious look. "What's going on?"

"Nothing. Everything's great." He changed the

subject. "Remember when you mentioned taking the children to see the Christmas lights at the American Rose Center?" At her confused nod, he added, "I think tonight would be a perfect time."

"What are you up to, big brother?"

He leaned forward with a conspiring look. "I want to give Myla her Christmas present, is all. Oh, and take Shredder with you. I don't want any children, dogs, cats, old girlfriends, or sisters around when I do it."

Myla sat on Henny's bed, reading a how-to book on opening a small business that Lydia had given her for Christmas. A cup of lemon-mint tea steamed nearby, while Shredder snoozed in a curled ball at her feet. Dusk played across the back gardens, coloring them in a golden brilliance that reminded her of the paper Jesse's mermaid doll had been wrapped in. Shaking her head, she wondered if Nick had wrapped it himself, or paid a department store a pretty penny to do the job.

Placing the book on a nearby table, she rose to watch the cold December dusk entice the waning sun behind the trees. It had been a good Christmas, but it was almost over. This would soon only be a memory. Nick would soon be a memory. Would he think about her after she'd moved on with her life?

She sighed, then settled into a wing chair to read some more of her new book. This quiet time was much needed and appreciated. Lydia was such a help with the children and they loved her. They'd miss that attention when they had to leave.

Where was Nick? He'd mysteriously disappeared right after the meal. Was he at Carolyn's house, begging her to understand why he'd been late yet again?

A tapping on the partially opened door caused Myla to glance up. Nick poked his head in, a hesitant smile cresting his features. "May I come in?"

She slapped the book shut, rising up out of the chair to greet him. At the sight of him in a tuxedo with his dark hair glistening, she had to hold her breath. How she envied Carolyn right now.

"Going out?"

He walked into the room, stopping inches from her. "No, I'm dining in tonight."

"But I...after our late dinner, I thought—" She tried to hurry around him. "I'll go warm things up right now."

"Myla, you don't have to rush into the kitchen and cook."

The look in his eyes caught her, holding her with its secretive warmth. It was a look of knowing, a look of wonderment, a look of pure pleasure.

"Okay. What's going on?"

"We're going to spend some time alone," he explained. "And I've instructed Lydia to take good care of the children, so don't worry."

Wary of his motives, she asked, "Is this some sort of scheme to make up for your extravagance?"

"Are you still mad about that?"

"No, I'm not so mad now."

"Good. I want you to put everything out of your mind. Don't worry about the children, or this house, or the future. Can you do that for a little while, Myla?"

"But Nick—"

"No questions. Trust me."

He reached out a hand, and she took it, the beat of her heart following his lead. Trust. That was the one thing standing between them. She hadn't quite learned how to trust again.

As if sensing her reluctance, Nick smiled down at her. "Come on, Myla. It's Christmas. Let's enjoy it together."

Christmas. A time of love and miracles. Was it so selfish to want a little of the joy for herself?

The sight that greeted her was indeed full of magic.

Nick took her to the glass-enclosed sunroom off the den, where a table was set for two, complete with candlelight and two steaming mugs of hot chocolate. And all around the room were roses, dozens and dozens of yellow roses, sitting amid the scented candles and the ficus trees. She'd never seen so many shades of the color yellow. The fat, buttery petals ranged in shades from pale cream to deep, bright lemon, and the fragrance reminded her of her own long-lost rose garden.

Tears misted her eyes as one word escaped her throat. "How?"

He looked pleased as punch. "My secret. But before we eat, I've got a few other surprises for you."

She couldn't speak. When she held back, he said, "Trust me, remember?"

Then he handed her a basket full of scented soaps and colorful bottles of bubble bath, along with her mug of hot chocolate.

"Thank you," she said, pleased with his thoughtfulness. "It's been a very long time since I've indulged in a bubble bath."

"And this," he added, handing her a large, colorfully wrapped box.

Gushing, she set her other goodies down, then opened the box to find a full-skirted, round-necked dress with long, tight-fitting sleeves. The fabric was a flowing, vivid Christmas green brocade. "Oh, Nick, it's beautiful, but I can't accept this."

"Yes, you can. I want you to go back to your room and enjoy your soaps and bubbles, soak for as long as you want. Then put on your new frock. We'll eat when you're ready."

Surprised, she shook her head. "I can't. The children, the kitchen needs cleaning. I've got a million things to do."

"Not right now. Now, go. I'm still the boss around here, remember?"

She saw the teasing light in his eyes and sighed.

"You're spoiling me just as much as you tried to spoil my children."

"Let me, for just a little while?" he asked in a quiet tone. A request, not an order, Myla noticed.

She looked up at him, seeing the need in his eyes. He wanted to do this, needed to be able to give. But this was more than showering her with gifts, this was a gift from his heart. Her own heart answered, beating tightly against her chest.

She turned to go, but stopped at the door to glance back. "How did you know, about the roses?"

He lifted a finger to his lips and smiled. "My secret."

She went into her room and ran a long, bubbly bath and enjoyed reliving each of his gifts. A bubble bath. A new dress. Yellow roses.

Then suddenly it hit her how he'd figured it all out.

The children! Now she knew. Her children had told him her fondest desires. Overcome with joy, she tried not to cry. Not now. Maybe tomorrow, or the next week, when she was alone and struggling again, but not now. But she wouldn't cry tears of pity; her tears would be full of joy for a man who'd tried to make her dreams come true, for a man who'd seemed so distant until he'd touched her, physically and spiritually. A man she'd fallen in love with.

I love him, she thought. Maybe she'd loved him

from the first time she'd seen him there on the road. But would she ever be able to admit to that love?

Trust me, he'd said. Could she?

"Just for tonight, Nick," she whispered as she relaxed in the scented bubbles. "Just for tonight."

Chapter Six

A little while later, Myla entered the sunroom with an expectant feeling of hope, her eyes meeting Nick's in shy anticipation.

Nick swallowed hard, then extended his hand, his heart beating against the tucking of his shirt. He'd wanted everything to be perfect, but he'd never dreamed a woman could look so lovely, so radiant. "You look wonderful. The dress becomes you."

She patted her upswept red hair and lowered her head. "You did a great job of guessing my size."

"The children helped out there."

"Ah, would that be the same children who told you about my silly daydreams?"

"The very same. Did I leave anything out?"

She took the glass of mineral water he offered her. "No, not a thing." Then reaching out to touch one of the roses, she said, "Thank you for the flowers. It means a lot to me."

He guided her toward the table. "Well, if I have it my way, you'll never be without yellow roses again."

His firm declaration touched Myla, making her love him even more. "Sonny hated them," she said quietly.

"I could never hate anything that made you happy," he replied steadily. Then, "Hungry?" He lifted the top off a silver server.

Myla relaxed then, bursting out in a fit of laughter. "Turkey sandwiches?"

He grinned. "My specialty. I'm not as proficient in the kitchen as you. I did, however, bring a bag of chips and the rest of the pecan pie."

"Oh, that reminds me," she said, sitting down, "I've got a surprise for you. I'll give it to you after we eat."

Nick helped her with her chair. "I thought I was the one full of surprises."

She watched him sit down. "You certainly are, and I really appreciate all of this."

Reaching out, she took his hand to say grace. "Thank You, for bringing Nick and me together to heal each other. Thank You for finding me a place to feel safe when there was no room in the inn. In the same way You protected Your Son, Jesus Christ, on the night of His birth, I ask You to now protect us on this holiest of holidays. Amen."

Nick looked up at her, his hand still holding hers. "I want to tell you something."

"All right."

"I saw Carolyn on Christmas Eve."

Myla's heart sank. Had he done all of this just to let her down easily? Swallowing her pride, she said, "I know. You don't have to explain."

"Yes, I do. I told her I can't see her anymore. We both knew it wasn't going anywhere. Carolyn has a lot of things she needs to work through, but I'm not the one she needs to make her happy. I'd rather be here, with you."

Myla's eyes brimmed with fresh tears. "Do you mean that?"

"Yes, I certainly do. I understand we also have a lot to deal with, a lot of things to get cleared up between us. But I'm willing to try. I'm willing to work toward that commitment you need."

"Meaning, you're ready to make a commitment to Christ?"

He nodded, then bowed his head. "Yes, I am. But I'll need your help."

"I'll be here."

Lifting his head, he said, "What about Magnolia House? What about finding your own place?"

"I can do all that, and we can still get to know each other. It can work, Nick. All I ask for is some time."

It wasn't the answer he'd hoped for, but he didn't

intend to give up. Not at all. "Okay. I've been told patience is a virtue. Eat your sandwich."

He smiled, content for now to sit and watch the play of candlelight on her face. Later, he'd figure out how to keep her by his side.

Myla smiled back, then lowered her head, the action causing a tendril of hair to slip over her brow in a looping curl.

Nick Rudolph, ruthless oil millionaire and man of action, was left breathless and speechless—immobilized by an endearing smile and a wayward curl.

Myla Howell, the no-nonsense, pragmatic woman, felt like a princess—captivated by a set of golden brown eyes and the scent of yellow roses.

The meal was wonderful, Myla decided. She could see the change in Nick, from the glow in his dark eyes to the sincerity of his smile. And she loved him because he'd been willing to change, for her. Tonight, she refused to think about her doubts or how she'd ever be able to leave this lovely house—and this lovable man.

They finished the meal, then Nick held out his hand to her to dance to the soft Christmas music playing from the stereo. Bing Crosby sang about being home for Christmas.

Confused, Myla sank into his arms. "I...I haven't danced in a very long time."

Nick snuggled closer to her. "You should dance. You should enjoy life to the fullest."

"Sonny didn't like dancing."

He frowned, then spoke into her ear. "Well, I do."

His nearness left her feeling lightweight and listless. Breathless. "You're very good at it, too."

He lifted his head, his gaze slipping over her face like brown velvet. "It helps to have a lovely woman in my arms."

"Nick, I—"

He held a finger to her parted lips. "No doubts. Not tonight, Myla, remember. It's Christmas."

"So it is," she said, her face inches from his, her eyes shining.

He lowered his head to hers, kissing her with all the warmth he felt in his heart. She accepted his touch, his need, as her own. His gentleness moved her beyond doubt.

And so, they danced, slowly, quietly, softly, while the winter wind lifted up to the glowing stars outside.

When the song ended, Myla took him by the hand, pulling him into the kitchen. "Want your surprise now?"

Not wanting the moment to end, Nick held back. "Hey, I set the rules. Who said you could start bringing out surprises?"

"How about, together we make a new set of rules?"

"Sounds good to me. My father taught me the old set, and I don't think they worked so very good."

"Sit down," she instructed, shoving him into a chair, "and close your eyes."

"I like this game," he teased, his eyes tightly shut.

The smell of pound cake wafted through the warm kitchen. "Ah, now I know this has been the best Christmas ever."

"Okay, open your eyes."

The cake sat whole and fat before him, waiting for him to take the first slice. He didn't remember having ever received a better present.

"You carve, and I'll make coffee," she called over her shoulder.

"Hey, just a minute." He stood up to pull her into his arms. Giving her a thorough kiss, he said, "Merry Christmas, Myla."

"Merry Christmas, Nick."

"Now, let's eat some of that cake before something happens to destroy it!"

Three a.m. Nick stood by the fireplace in his bedroom, watching the dying embers with unseeing eyes.

It had started out innocently enough. All he'd wanted to do was show Myla a good time. Give her something special for Christmas. An evening she'd always remember.

Instead, she'd given him an evening he'd never be able to forget. She'd looked so very beautiful in her new dress that was the exact shade of her exotic green eyes.

Nick had realized two things this Christmas evening. One, he'd been lost in this big house, and he'd been lost in life. He wanted to be found. And two, he had fallen in love with Myla Howell, maybe from the first time he'd seen her. It didn't matter. What did matter was that he loved her and wanted to make a life with her.

Now, he had to be very sure and very careful. Wisely, she'd seen things in him he hadn't even seen himself. He wanted to take care of her, to love her and cherish her. But in order to do that, he might have to make one of the hardest choices in his life. He might have to let her go, in order to gain her love.

And, he'd never been very good at letting go.

Thinking about her need to be independent and self-sufficient, he said a prayer for courage and patience. Then it occurred to him, his father had neglected to teach him the most important rule of all.

Follow your heart.

Myla groaned, stopping on the busy street corner to rest for a minute, her thoughts rushing by like the lunch-time traffic. The last few days since she, Nick and the children had spent a quiet New Year's Eve together had been busy and tiring. With the new year had come the realization that she needed to hunt for a new job, and prepare herself for the move into Magnolia House. This morning, she'd driven into the city to do just that, but something had happened that had left her shaken and confused, and more determined than ever to improve her standard of living.

Checking the digital clock on a nearby bank building, she reasoned she'd have enough time to meet Lydia and Nick for lunch and make it by Magnolia House to fill out some forms, before it was time for the children to get home from school. Even as she stood there, her empty stomach rumbled an urgent message, and her head felt light from lack of sustenance.

The sign over her head announced the Milam Street Coffeehouse. Lydia had said to meet them here. Pushing the dark-tinted heavy door open, Myla looked up to find a familiar face watching her from the other side.

Nick. He looked as wonderful as the coffee smelled. She didn't know if her stomach lurched from hunger, or from the sight of him waiting there for her. Every bit the successful business tycoon, he was dressed in a dark wool suit and cream-colored shirt, the browns and blues in his tie picking up on his dark good looks.

Myla's heart thudded, causing her next words to rumble much like her empty stomach. "Well, hello there. Where's Lydia?"

Nick grinned, then stood to greet her. "She got tied up with a phone call. Sent me on ahead to meet you." Glancing around with disapproval, he added, "Although this place wouldn't have been my first choice." Guiding her to a chair, he said, "You look tired."

She couldn't yet bring herself to tell him what had happened to her today, so she just said, "Job hunting is hard work."

He waved to a nearby waiter. "You'll feel better after you eat something. And, I have a bit of good news, I think."

"Oh, and what's that?"

"Lydia said something about knowing the man who owns this restaurant. He's looking for help, and that's why she wanted you to meet us here."

Myla glanced around at the eclectic style of the new eatery, her eyes scanning the paintings by local artists and the other forms of artwork decorating the two-storied open-air building. "It's different, but I like it."

Nick didn't look so sure. "Well, I don't. This place doesn't look as classy as Lydia described. Hope the food is good, at least."

"Hope I get hired," Myla said in a weary voice.

Nick didn't like the idea of her working in an eclectic restaurant centered in a run-down building, but he didn't think she'd listen to him. "Are you interested?"

Her eyes lit up. "Of course. I got really down this morning, kind of depressed." Shrugging, she decided not to tell him just how down she'd been. "But I'm better now."

"Good." Taking her hand, Nick waited while she told the waiter she'd have a chicken salad sandwich, then he reluctantly ordered himself a hamburger. "You know, even though Henny's due back any day now, you don't have to move out immediately, and you don't have to take the first job that comes along."

"Thanks," she said, taking a sip of much-needed coffee. Her empty stomach rejected it, though, so she pushed it away. "But I don't want to miss my spot on the list at Magnolia House. It's hard to get in, with so many people needing temporary shelter."

He tapped his fingers on the glass-topped bistro table. "Well, don't overdo things. Lydia tells me you've already enrolled in a business class and a cake-decorating course for the spring."

"Yes, I need both to get me started and give me some experience."

Finally, his patience sorely tried, Nick said, "Look, you don't have to move into the shelter at all. I have guest rooms. You can stay as long as you want."

Both hands on her coffee cup, Myla said, "Nick, we agreed that I'd leave after Christmas. I'm not your responsibility, and technically, it wouldn't be right."

"But I feel responsible…I want to be responsible

for you, and technically, we wouldn't be doing anything wrong. I'd be a perfect gentleman."

Touched by his thoughtfulness, she said, "That means a lot to me, because I know you are a gentleman, and if I get in a pinch, I'll call you. But I need this time, if for nothing else, to prove to myself that I'm capable. I depended on Sonny for so much…it's time I learned how to deal with things on my own."

He ran a hand through his hair, frustrated with her stubborn determination. "Yes, and I promised I'd give you some time to do just that. I'm sorry."

Sitting back in her chair, she said, "I'm going to Magnolia House after we eat. You're welcome to come along and see the place for yourself."

"I just might," he replied. "Lydia's been after me to take a tour ever since the place opened. Of course, I'll probably take one look at it and tell you not to leave me."

The way he'd said that spoke much more than mere words. They sat looking at each other for a minute, then Myla said, "I'm not leaving you, Nick. I'm just doing what I have to do. We can still see each other."

"Right. You think you have to do this, to prove something to yourself and the world. I'm trying very hard to accept that and understand."

"And I appreciate your efforts. If we still…feel the same about our relationship after a few months, we'll see what happens next."

He continued tapping on the glass tabletop. "I know, I know. Patience is a virtue."

She shot him a broad smile. "Hebrews, chapter 10, verse 36—'For ye have need of patience, that, after ye have done the will of God, ye might receive the promise.'"

Nick shook his head. "That's all great, but what about my will?"

"You have to give that over to Him, for now."

"It's hard."

"But you'll receive the promise."

"Which is?"

"A good life, the life you desire."

When she looked up, Nick's eyes were centered on her. "I hope the life I desire turns out to be with you."

His reply overwhelmed her. What was he saying? Had he really come to care for her as much as she cared for him? Afraid she'd cave in, she asked, "Have you heard from Henny?"

He leaned back in his chair to loosen his tie a notch. "Only to say she'd be here any day now. She sounded odd, not herself, kind of distant and tired. I'm worried about her," he added with concern. "Her health isn't good at all these days but she's far too stubborn to let anyone know if she's not feeling well."

"Maybe she misses fussing over you. And me, I've got to continue this job search. I'll talk to the owner here, to see what he has to offer, then fill out a few more applications."

Nick did not want her to work in this fledgling establishment. It was just like Lydia to go for the underdog, even in her choice of restaurants, but that didn't mean Myla had to work here.

"Can you type?" he asked, his tone light and hopeful.

"Barely. I haven't since high school."

"I don't suppose you've ever worked on an oil rig?"

Myla looked skeptical until she saw the laugh crinkles surrounding his eyes. "No, but thanks for the offer. So far, I've been turned away at six restaurants, two offices, three fast-food joints, and a half-dozen retail stores. I've offered to cook, clean, type and file, and just about anything else I can think of. The job market is slim for a woman without a college degree who's fast approaching her thirties. But I'm not the only one." She looked down at the marble design on their table. "Today, I saw several people worse off than me."

Nick stopped his tapping. "I can't imagine not having a job. My grandfather did all the scraping and clawing in my family."

His words reminded Myla of Sonny. "You know, Sonny's parents gave him everything. They spoiled him, then when he got out on his own, he couldn't handle the responsibility." She glanced up at Nick, a deep sorrow filling her soul. "Money really can't solve our problems, no matter how much we think it can. So just be glad you've done a good, honest job of holding on to what your grandfather built."

He looked sheepish. "I'm not so proud. I'm an overachiever, and unlike Sonny, I am responsible— my parents taught both of us that lesson—and a lot of people depend on me."

Myla knew he was right there. Nick had a strong sense of responsibility. And now, he had taken her on as his own responsibility, too. "Does it get to you, knowing people's livelihoods depend on your daily decisions?"

"Sometimes, yes, but I've never had time to dwell on it too much. My father had bad timing." A dark look twisted his features. "He died right in the middle of the oil crisis, and I've been trying to keep my head above water ever since. So far, I've done a passable job…Rudolph Oil is still intact."

"But what about its leader? It's important to take care of your spiritual side, too." Sensing his need to talk, she said, "Tell me about your father."

Running a finger over his coffee mug, Nick looked away. "He died of a broken heart. He loved his company and my mother. Watching her die from cancer wasn't easy for any of us, and then when he thought he was going to lose Rudolph Oil, too…" He shrugged, then turned quiet again.

Myla saw him in a new light, understanding why he'd tried so hard to stay detached and distant. Pain did that to people. Touching his hand, she said,

"Haven't you done enough scraping and clawing yourself? You do work hard, but you need to work on that chip on your shoulder, too."

"I can't be weak," he said, telling her his worst fear. "I can't become the man my father became. You talk about living a sham—he did. He thought he was so in control, then he crumbled right before my eyes. I can't let that happen to me."

"God won't let that happen, Nick. Not if you use Him as your strength and your guidance. He won't leave you. If you crumble, He will be there to catch you."

"Maybe. That still doesn't explain my mother's death and my father's heartbreak."

Now she understood completely. He blamed God for making his life miserable. "No, God didn't want you or your parents to suffer. But he can't stop a person from dying when that person's time has come. Sure, the circumstances aren't always pleasant, but that's part of life. God is our guide, but it's up to us to make the first steps toward our journey. That's called free will."

"Free will. The will to make our own choices. But you just quoted me scripture about doing God's will."

"God's will, yes, but based on the right choices," she explained. "We can't blame God for all the bad, and then turn around and expect Him to take care of all the good we want in life. We have to trust in Him, pray for His guidance, then go out and make our own choices, based on an educated, gospel-backed decision. We use the scriptures, past traditions, our own experiences, and our own reasoning, to decide what to do. And sometimes, we have to face great grief and bitter sadness, but we go on, using God's love as our strength."

All around them, the restaurant flowed and ebbed with people. The sound of the cash register computing tabs blended with the burr of a coffee grinder, while the laughter and whispered words of the few patrons filtered up to the high ceilings.

"Life goes on," Nick said, his gaze settling on hers. "How'd you get to be so wise?"

"Not me, the Bible," she replied, hoping she'd helped him feel better about things. And herself as well.

Just then a tall man with sandy blond hair and horn-rimmed glasses brought their food to the table. Nick immediately gave the grinning man a get-lost look.

But the lanky man continued to stare. "Hey, I'm Grant Lewis. I own this place. Lydia told me to look for you today—she described a tall woman with long red hair and uh…an uptight executive."

Myla giggled while Nick frowned. "That's us," she said.

Nick had no choice but to shake the man's hand, then watch with jealous politeness as Grant smiled down on Myla.

"So, this must be the great cook Lydia's been hounding me to hire."

Myla shook his hand, then asked, "Do you need someone?"

"Sure do," Grant replied as he pushed at his glasses, his blue eyes bright with hope. "One of my best waitresses quit last week. She's a college student and her course load was too heavy. Said she had to crack the books or lose her scholarship."

Myla nodded her understanding, then said, "Well, I can start right away, but only part-time for now."

Nick shot her a warning look. "Don't be so hasty. You don't even know what he's paying."

"Minimum wage plus tips," Grant replied, his hands on his hips. "We're not in the black yet, but we're getting there, so hopefully I'll be able to offer you better pay one day."

"One day? She needs a stable job right now," Nick said, his scowl deepening. "And she has one, with me."

Myla watched Nick's brow furrow. So much for being patient. "Nick, I need a *permanent* job," she reminded him gently.

Grant obviously hadn't missed the friction between them. "Is there a problem?"

"Yes," Nick retorted.

"No," Myla insisted. Giving Nick a meaningful glare, she added, "Mr. Rudolph is afraid of letting me make my own choices, but I'd be happy to work for you, Grant. After all, we did agree that I'd need to find another job soon, right, Nick?"

Nick shrugged, frowned, then sighed long and hard. Just to show Grant that he wasn't as uptight as his sister had implied, he said, "Oh, all right. It's your decision."

Myla smiled appreciatively. "I can start today, if you need me. But until I can find adequate child care, I can only work the early shifts—I have two children. And right now, I have to fill in for Nick's housekeeper, but she's due home any day now."

Grant waved both arms. "That sure would help. As you can see, we stay pretty busy with the lunch crowd. Lydia tells me you can cook, but do you have a problem with waiting tables?"

"No, of course not," Myla replied. "I'll do whatever needs to be done. I really need a job. I'll be moving into Magnolia House in a few days."

Grant adjusted the salt and pepper shakers, then shook her hand again. "Lydia explained your situation, and I understand completely. When you're done with your meal, come to the counter and fill out some paperwork. I've got to get back to the kitchen."

After Grant left, Myla looked over at Nick. He didn't look as happy about this as she felt. Wanting reassurance, and wanting him to know that she appreciated his help, she said, "What do you think?"

"I think I'm going to be very jealous of Grant Lewis," he admitted. "You'll be working closely with him every day."

"Nick—that's very flattering, but I'll be fine. I only have eyes for men who buy me yellow roses."

That made him smile. "I'll keep you in a fresh supply to remind you—and him."

Lydia fluttered onto a chair just then, collapsing in an elegant pile against the table. "Nourishment, please?"

Grant was back, Nick noticed. Johnny on the spot.

"Hey, Lydia." Grant said, beaming like a street lamp.

There went that puppy-dog grin again.

"Grant!" Lydia sat straight up, causing her silk floral print scarf to do a fast float. "Nice to see you again." Smiling over at her brother and Myla, she said, "Did Grant tell you he writes poetry? He's a very good writer," she added emphatically.

Grant looked sheepish, then lifted a hand in explanation. "We have open mike night sometimes. People can share their work."

Not liking the way Grant was ogling his sister, Nick said, "How very generous of you."

Myla caught Nick's blazing gaze, her look warning him to back off. It was obvious Grant was smitten with Lydia. And vice versa.

Leaning close while Grant and Lydia flirted tactfully with each other, she said, "Well, at least you don't have to be jealous of Grant with *me*. Not with Lydia around."

Nick glared at the man who'd just ruined his day completely. "No, I just have to worry about some smooth-talking artistic type hoodwinking my baby sister."

"He's not trying to hoodwink anybody," Myla whispered as Lydia's sharp ears perked up. "Now, be nice."

"I don't want to be nice. And I intend to have a private conversation with Lydia later. She's far too gullible and naive when it comes to these matters." Concentrating on Myla again, he said, "You haven't eaten much."

Myla's stomach did a revolt as she eyed her half-eaten sandwich. "I guess I'm too keyed up to eat." She stood up, turning to Grant. "Could you give me that application? I can fill it out while we finish."

Grant managed to tear his eyes away from Lydia. "Sure, just come on back to the kitchen." Then to Lydia he said, "Stay here. I'll be right back."

Whirling around, Myla started to follow Grant. The room began to spin, making her feel as if she were being sucked into a huge black vortex.

"Myla?" Nick saw her go pale, watched as she stumbled, then crumpled into a heap. He reached out to catch her as she went limp.

Grant came rushing over to pull her chair out,

while Lydia took her hand. "She doesn't look too great," he said, his eyes meeting Nick's.

"Myla, can you hear me?" Nick asked softly, concern evident in his words. "What's wrong?"

"Blood," she managed to whisper.

"Blood?" Nick looked down, searching for any signs of red. "Did you hurt yourself?"

She raised an arm to show him the wide bandage running across the fold inside her elbow joint. "I gave blood this morning. It always makes me queasy."

Lydia's worried gaze flew to Nick's face. "We need to get her home."

Grant took her arm, then shook his head. "Ah, man, they do it all the time."

"Do what?" Nick screamed, all sorts of horrible thoughts rushing through his head.

"Homeless people," Grant explained. "They give plasma to get money. It doesn't pay much, but when you're out of work, it will buy food."

Shocked, Nick looked down at the woman in his arms. "Myla, do you need money that badly?"

Slowly, Myla opened her eyes to focus on his face. "No, I don't need money too much now, thanks to you. But…someone I met today did. So I gave some blood. I had to do it, Nick. Please try to understand."

Chapter Seven

"You're right, Lydia. I don't understand."

Nick paced the length of the kitchen, his eyes dark with a rage he couldn't even begin to contain. "Giving plasma for money! I've never heard of such a thing. I give blood…I donate regularly at the Red Cross, but she did it out of some sort of desperation. And she didn't even take the time to eat properly before or after she did it. She's barely above the required weight, to begin with!"

"Nick, calm down," Lydia said, her gaze shifting to the array of voices coming from the den. "Myla will be back in here soon. It won't do for her to see you so upset."

"Oh, she knows I'm upset."

He glanced toward the den where Jesse and Patrick were playing with Shredder and their Christmas toys. Myla was in Henny's room, washing her face.

"Yes, I imagine she does, since you practically carried her all the way to your car—after causing a scene with your ranting. Thank goodness Grant was able to stay calm, at least."

Pulling his hands through his hair, Nick grimaced. Now he was being compared to a poet! "Yes, Grant Lewis is a very understanding man. He did settle me down. And he got Myla to nibble on a cracker and drink some juice."

Lydia smiled slightly, relief washing over her youthful face. "Yeah, Grant is so sweet, I've gotten to know him better since approaching him about this job for Myla. In fact, we have a date tonight."

Nick looked at his little sister as if she'd lost her head. "A date? You hardly know the man!"

"I'm getting to know him," Lydia stated. "And don't you start with me. You never approve of anybody I date."

Nick cringed at that accusation. "That's not true. I liked Ralph Pimperton."

"Ralph Pimperton is a pompous...snob."

"Well, yes, he is that, but he really liked you, and he comes from a fine family."

"I didn't like *him,* Nick. Now, please promise me you won't try to intimidate Grant. He's really shy, you know."

Nick glowered at her. "This day is going from bad to worse. First Myla takes a job that I think is unsuitable, then she faints, and now you're telling me you're smitten with a coffeehouse poet."

Lydia stood nose to nose with her brother. "He's more than that. He's a good, decent man and I'm glad to know him. And his place of business is very suitable."

Nick gave his sister a quizzical look, his protective instincts surfacing all over again. "Well, get to know him even a little more before you get all mushy about him."

Lydia stuck her tongue out at him, contradicting her words. "I'm a grown woman, Nick. I know how to handle my own social life, thank you very much. And Myla knows how to find a job. You'd better just stay out of all of this."

Heaving a heavy sigh, Nick tried to relax a little as he listened to the noise coming from the den. He didn't like having to second-guess women. He did, however, like the noise that children could make, he decided. He especially liked knowing they were all here, safe and happy. And he guessed his sister deserved to be happy, too. But what was so wrong with wanting to protect the people he cared about?

But Lydia was right. He couldn't control her life forever. And he certainly couldn't control Myla's, not when he'd promised her he wouldn't interfere.

"Oh, all right. Invite him over for dinner sometime," he suggested, defeat pulling him down. "That way, *I* can get to know him, too."

Lydia grabbed him by the head, then gave him a wet, sisterly kiss. "That's the spirit. I think you'll be pleasantly surprised."

"Well, I've had enough surprises for one day," he said in a low growl.

The sound of a door shutting brought his head up. Myla came in, her walk not nearly as wobbly as it'd been earlier. Nick gave his sister an imploring look.

"I'll go play with the other kids," Lydia said, winking at her brother.

Nick shot her a mock nasty glare, then turned to the auburn-haired woman who'd caused him no small amount of worry, and joy, over the last few weeks. "Are you all right?"

"Much better," she said quietly. "I'll start dinner."

He reached out a hand to stop her. "Forget dinner. Lydia's taking care of that. We need to talk."

Myla placed both hands on the sparkling clean counter, avoiding the accusation in his eyes. She really didn't want to talk about her reasons for doing what she'd done. In spite of her calm front, she was still shaken.

Nick stood across from her, his own hands braced tightly against the same counter. "Myla, if you need more money—"

"I don't. That's not why I gave the plasma."

"Then, please, explain it to me."

She brought her hands together, then clasped them in front of her, closing her eyes for a minute. "I was out job hunting, walking the streets from door to door, and I passed a plasma center. I was tired, worried, frustrated, and there was this line of people blocking my way. Then I saw the sign that said the center would pay for plasma. I looked around at the people—they were waiting to give blood."

She stopped, taking a long swallow as tears welled in her eyes. "That's when I saw this old man, dressed in ragged clothes, sitting on the curb. He looked so gaunt and frail, and when he saw me coming, he held up a hand and asked me if I had a few dollars so he could buy food. He explained that he wanted to give plasma, to get some money. But he wasn't in very good shape. The nurses had turned him away."

She looked up at Nick, her expression grim. "So I offered to go in and give my own plasma. When I came out, I gave him the fifteen dollars I'd earned. It upset me so badly, I gave him the money, then I ran away, down the street." Lowering her head, she covered her face with both hands. "I didn't want to wind up like that, but I had this horrible vision of my children standing in the street begging for food. I sat on a bench and…after a few minutes, I was okay. Just a moment of self-pity. I was so ashamed of how I'd reacted, I tried to forget all about it. But I can't get that old man's face out of my mind."

She looked up, seeing the compassion in Nick's

eyes, hoping he could understand how profound seeing the homeless man had been for her, that she'd had no choice but to help him in some way.

"Myla." He came around the counter to take her in his arms. "You're not so very tough, after all, are you?"

Myla leaned against him, allowing herself this simple luxury. "No, I'm not tough. I'm scared to death of being a failure. I can't let my children down, though."

Nick patted her back, then lifted her chin so he could see her face. "You won't let them down. I know that in my heart. What you did was a sweet and noble thing, but you don't have to worry. I won't allow that to happen to you and your children."

"But what about that old man? What about all the children lost out there in the cold and the dark? Somebody has to do something. We can't just keep running away from people who need our help."

He couldn't answer that. "I know they're out there. And we can try to help, but we can't save all of them."

She looked up then, a new light of hope cresting in her eyes. "But you will help me, right? You'll help me to find a way to save some of these people. I have to do it, Nick. I know how they feel."

A strange thudding began deep inside Nick's

chest. Was this his calling then, to help those who couldn't help themselves? Was this a way to bring him closer to God, and his beloved Myla? Was this a way to redeem himself at last?

"We'll do it," he said. "Whatever we can, we'll do it, together. I promise."

Myla hugged him close, a new warmth flowing through her tired body. "That was worth fainting over," she said, her worry turning to happiness.

He stroked her hair, then said, "Well, just promise me you'll take care of yourself. You gave me a bad scare back there."

"I'll be fine now."

The back doorbell rang, bringing Patrick bounding through the kitchen. "Pizza man's here. He sure got here quick."

Nick took Myla by the hand to head for the door. "He knows the address well," he said dryly.

"Another week." Myla's attention shifted from Nick's worried expression to Lydia's pleased one. "I'm next on the list. I can move into Magnolia House this weekend. With my new job, and now this, my life is beginning to take shape again. I won't have to resort to welfare."

Nick wished he could be as happy about this as the two women sitting across from him in his kitchen. Lydia was positively giddy over the poet fellow, the noble Mr. Grant Lewis, and now Myla was happily working two jobs and in sheer joy about moving into a homeless shelter of all places. He really, truly, would never understand women.

Glancing up from his apple strudel, he gave Myla an encouraging look in spite of his mixed feelings about her leaving. "How long will you be able to stay there?"

Seeing the worry in his eyes, she tried to reassure him. "We can stay up to a year, but I don't intend to let it drag out that long. I'm saving as much money as I can to find a low-rent place."

Still concerned, Nick said, "Now explain how this place works to me again. I want to understand the whole process."

Lydia piped up. "I've been explaining it to you, but you never listen." At her brother's wince of disapproval, she said, "Grant was interested, so I gave him a tour. He's more than willing to help out with the homeless situation in this city."

"Very honorable," Nick said. "Is there anything the wonderful Grant Lewis isn't willing to do for you—or to you—for that matter?"

"Nick!" Hurt, Lydia implored Myla. "Will you please ask my overbearing brother if he could possibly put a little faith and trust in me."

Myla glanced at Nick, her brows lifting in a question. When Nick only pouted, she said, "Look, I work with Grant every day. He's a very nice man."

"His company isn't very stable," Nick argued.

"The restaurant business is fickle and unpredictable. He might have to shut down any day now."

"You know that for a fact?" Lydia asked, anger slicing through her words.

Nick looked smug. "No, but I know enough about business to predict such things."

"We're getting rave reviews," Myla stated. "In fact…Grant and I are considering opening up a catering business just as soon as I can get back on my feet."

"What?" Nick gave her a surprised look. "Myla, don't overextend yourself."

"I won't," she said, a wary tone in her words. "Grant's already allowed me to do some extra cooking. We're trying out new recipes on the customers. And just as soon as Henny's able to come back to work, I intend to expand on that."

Nick threw up his hands. "Can we concentrate on one change at a time? Let's get back to talking about Magnolia House. If I hear one more word of praise for Grant Lewis, I think I'll lose my lunch."

"Poor Nick, he never handled change very well," Lydia explained to Myla, before launching into a thorough speech on how the homeless shelter was set up. "Magnolia House is a transitional place, not just a homeless shelter. It's more like an apartment building, and since this is a new program to help the homeless, it's in high demand. It's always full—a sign that this problem is growing."

Myla offered Nick some more strudel, hoping to soothe his temper and his concern, but put the lid back on the pan when he silently refused with a shake of his head. Taking a bite of her own dessert, she said, "Which is why I'm anxious to learn all I can about it and help others."

"We're behind you all the way. Grant's willing to help and we know big brother wants in on the action. Right, Nick?" Lydia gave her brooding brother a hearty shake.

Nick moaned, then sighed long and hard before glancing over at Myla. "Don't you just love eternally perky people?"

Myla gave him a serious glance. "Do you want to help us with this, or not?"

Turning serious himself, he nodded. "Absolutely. I'm already looking into it. I've talked to several other prominent businessmen in the area, and they've pledged their support, too."

"Thank you." Myla started clearing the dessert dishes away. "I'll bring home some more information next time I go in."

The phone rang nearby, and Lydia hopped up to get it, giving Nick an opportunity to talk to Myla alone. "I guess this is it, then. You'll be leaving soon."

"Yes," she said, her heart fluttering at the thought of having to leave the safety of this wonderful old house. "I don't want you to worry about me, though. I'm tough and I have a strong sense that this is what the Lord wants me to do."

Nick wanted to tell her he had his own strong sense about what she needed to do, but he held back. "You and my baby sister," he said, shaking his head in wonder. "You both seem so sure, so confident. Me, I'm still floundering around, afraid."

Myla smiled at his endearing self-doubt. "Lydia will be all right, Nick. Grant is really a decent man."

Nick nodded, his eyes on his sister. "I guess I hadn't realized she's all grown-up."

"And very capable of taking care of herself," Myla reminded him. "You should be very proud of her."

Lydia's concerned call to Nick stopped his reply.

"It's Henny's daughter. They had to rush Henny to the hospital. Nick, they think it's her heart."

Myla heard the fear in Lydia's voice and saw that same fear shooting through Nick's dark eyes. She listened as Nick took the phone, then placed her arm around Lydia's shaking shoulders.

"I see," he said into the receiver. "Keep us posted. Call day or night, collect. And we'll be on the first plane up there—I don't care what Henny says—I'm coming."

Hanging up the phone, he turned in shock to his sister. She fell into his arms, her muffled cries absorbed into his shirt.

"It'll be okay, honey," he said, kissing Lydia's

fluffy bob. "We'll go up there to be with her, make sure she takes care of herself." He looked over her head at Myla, his expression dark and grim.

The pain Myla saw in his eyes ripped her heart apart. She'd seen Nick struggle to downplay his emotions, but this pain was too fresh and too much of a shock to hide.

"Nick, what can I do?" she asked, wanting to comfort him.

Gently extracting Lydia from his arms, Nick handed his sister a tissue.

Lydia rushed away, a new batch of tears welling in her usually bright eyes. "I'll go call the airline and book us a flight."

Nick waited until his sister had left the room, then turned back to Myla. "Lydia's been warning me about Henny's health. But I was always too busy, too absorbed in myself, to notice."

Myla knew he was telling the truth. And she also knew he'd changed a great deal in the last month. She watched as he tried to shut himself down, as he struggled against the old pains and resentments. Giving him some time alone, she began clearing the dinner dishes away, but Nick's hand on her arm stopped her.

With a gentle tug, he pulled her close, burying his face against her hair. "Stay. Stay here. I need you to be here when I get back, in case…"

He left the statement hanging, but Myla understood what he was asking. If she stayed, though, she'd risk losing her spot at Magnolia House and a chance at a fresh start. But she knew in her heart she couldn't desert him now.

"Of course I'll stay, Nick. Henny might need help once she gets back."

He lifted his head then, to look into her eyes. "If she doesn't make it back—"

"We have to pray that that doesn't happen," she gently reminded him. "But if it does, we'll get through it, together."

"Together," he repeated, his eyes dark and somber. "God sent you to me just in time, didn't He, Myla?"

She patted his cheek. "Go check on your sister."

A few days later, Myla answered the phone at the coffeehouse, expecting it to be an order for a late lunch.

"Myla?"

Nick's voice cut across her midafternoon tiredness, making her snap to attention. She'd been waiting to hear about Henny's condition since Nick and Lydia had left for Little Rock. "Nick, how is she?"

"She made it through the bypass surgery," he said over the wire, his tone hopeful. "The doctors assure us she'll have a full recovery."

Relief flooded through Myla. "That's wonderful. When will she be able to come home?"

He hesitated, then plunged right in. "That's the other reason I'm calling. Her daughter wants her to recuperate here in Little Rock, with her family and the doctors nearby."

"Well, that's understandable." She waited as silence echoed through the line. "Do you want me to stay awhile longer, to help out?"

He let out a long sigh. "You know I'd like nothing better than that, but you'll lose your spot on the list at Magnolia House. I can't ask you to do that, but on the other hand, there's really no need for you to rush now."

Giving up her place at the shelter wouldn't be half as hard if it didn't involve living under the same roof with him, she reasoned. Sending up a prayer for strength and guidance, she swallowed back her concerns. She could do this. She had to do it, for Henny's sake, and to show Nick that she believed in him. She wouldn't run out on him when he needed her the most.

"I'll be here, Nick."

That simple statement seemed to reassure him. "Thank you. I know how much I'm asking, Myla, but I won't forget this. I'll make it up to you, somehow."

Hanging up, Myla looked up from the order pad she'd been doodling on to find Carolyn Parker coming toward her. What on earth was the tall blonde doing here? And why now, of all times, when Myla's doubts were foaming over like the cappuccino she watched Grant mix for a customer.

"Hello," Carolyn said as she dropped down on a stool at the long lunch counter. "How are you, Myla?"

Myla didn't like the appraising look the other woman was giving her, but she managed a polite smile. "I'm fine. It's good to see you again, Carolyn. I'm sorry about what happened with my children and the cat."

"No problem." Carolyn tossed her long hair away from her face and placed her black leather purse on the counter in front of her. "Guess you're wondering what I'm doing here."

"Well, yes, I am," Myla admitted. "Would you like something to drink?"

"Oh, no. I just wanted to talk to you, about Nick."

"I see."

Carolyn's luminous eyes softened then. "He's changed so much, I guess I'm just trying to understand what's happened to him."

Confused, Myla studied the other woman's face. She looked sincere, and sad. "I don't know if I can help you out, Carolyn. I don't understand Nick too well myself."

"Oh, but you do," Carolyn insisted. "He's different since he met you. And I've been stewing about it for weeks now. You see, I had this silly idea that

Nick would ask me to marry him. We've been kind of dating for so long, but I guess in my heart I knew it was more of a convenience than anything else. Still, I never gave up. Until you came along."

"I'm sorry," Myla said, embarrassed at the woman's directness. "I didn't mean to come between you and Nick."

"Maybe not," Carolyn replied, her eyes cool. "But I can't compete with you and your Bible."

That statement left Myla unsettled. She didn't like the implications of the other woman's words. "What do you mean?"

"I mean, I've seen a lot of come-on lines in my time, but spouting Bible verses is a new one. You have Nick's attention now, but I don't know if you can hold him with that demure little self-righteous act for long."

Shocked, Myla lifted her chin, then gave Carolyn a direct look. "It's not an act. My beliefs are sincere, but I'd never use them to try to win a man. I care about Nick because he took the time to care about me. Maybe you never got any closer to him because you can't see beyond his money or his status."

Carolyn snorted. "And you can?"

Myla bristled, but stood her ground. "Yes, I've seen Nick's gentle side, his caring, giving side. He's a good man, and I'm glad he's changing for the better. You should be, too."

Carolyn rose, her eyes now full of hostility. "Not if it means I have to give him up."

Myla felt sorry for the beautiful blonde. "Maybe you never really had him to begin with."

That caused Carolyn to pause. "Maybe not. But it's not over yet. You're just a housekeeper, after all. He feels sorry for you. He'll get tired of playing this new game and he'll come back to me. He always does."

Hiding the pain of the put-down and Carolyn's smug assumption behind a serene smile, Myla could only hope that didn't happen. But she wouldn't give Carolyn the satisfaction of seeing her doubt. "If you really love Nick," she said as Carolyn turned to leave, "you'll be glad that he's finally getting over his bitterness and pain. Or were you even aware that he's been suffering all these years?"

Carolyn rolled her eyes and laughed. "Funny, he always seemed happy when he was with me."

"Then you really don't know him at all," Myla said softly.

Carolyn lifted her arched brows. "I know him well enough to warn him away from you. You're living in his house. How does that fit in with your holier-than-thou attitude? Or had you stopped to think what any hint of scandal could do to Nick's reputation and his business?"

With that, Carolyn lowered her head and walked out the door, leaving Myla blushing and angry.

Grant came to stand beside Myla, his eyes on the woman leaving the restaurant. "Wow, who was that?"

"A friend of Nick's," Myla said absently, trying

to hide the embarrassment Carolyn's words had inflicted. "And a very lonely woman, apparently."

"That's a shame," Grant replied, his mind already back on business as he greeted a customer across the room.

"Yes, it certainly is," Myla said to herself, her own doubts working their way through her mind in the same steady pace as the lunch crowd had worked its way through the diner earlier. "She's worried about competing with me, but I know I don't stand a chance against her. Especially if she decides to make trouble for Nick."

Just one more thing to add to her list of worries.

Grant came back then. Tapping Myla on the arm, he said, "Hey, where'd you go?"

"Sorry, boss. Just woolgathering. Did you need to talk to me?"

Grant lowered his head, his shy eyes studying the counter. "About our catering business—"

"Don't tell me you've changed your mind?"

"Oh, no." He shook his head. "I want to start it, right away. It will mean lots of long hours, though."

"I can handle it."

"What about your children?"

Myla traced an invisible pattern on the rich mahogany of the counter. "Well, Lydia has offered to help out. And once I move into Magnolia House, I'll have trained counselors there to help with the children."

"A built-in day care?"

"Something like that." She swallowed the dread back. "I don't have much choice. I have to work. And, I am very interested in this, Grant."

"Enough to form a partnership?"

Surprised, Myla looked over at him, her smile beaming. "Partners? I just thought I'd be working for you."

"I think partners would be better," Grant said. "You have a lot of fresh ideas, and hey, the customers keep coming back for your muffins and cookies."

"They seem to like them," she agreed. Extending a hand to him, she said, "Thank you, Grant. This is like a dream come true."

"Well, don't get too dreamy," he replied. "First, we have to work out a plan and set some goals."

"I'm ready," Myla said. Somehow, she'd make it all work. For her children's sake. She had to remember that their needs would always come first. Even if that meant giving up being with Nick.

Myla's new routine kept her busy, which kept her mind off Carolyn's dire warnings about Nick. She worked the breakfast and lunch shifts at the coffeehouse, then rushed home to do her work at the mansion while waiting for the children to come home on the school bus. She was tired, but content. With two jobs, she was steadily saving money. Of course, when Henny recovered, one of her jobs would end.

Myla was almost glad Nick had been called away. It would be much easier to leave his home, to leave him, now that she'd had a few days without him in her life. But he was never far from her thoughts. She'd missed him terribly.

Right now, she remembered Nick's knock on her door late last night when he and Lydia returned from Little Rock. He didn't say a whole lot, but she could tell he needed to see a friendly face.

"Thank you for staying," he whispered so as not to wake the sleeping children. With that, he gave her a quick hug before heading upstairs with his tired sister. This morning, he was up and gone before she could get breakfast started. So she came to work wondering if he was really all right, and wondering if he was having second thoughts about their budding relationship.

Just to keep herself busy, she'd baked a blueberry cobbler, and smiling, was happily serving it up to the few customers who'd come in for a late lunch.

"I'll have a double helping, if you don't mind," a deep male voice said into her ear.

Whirling, Myla laughed, her heart skipping a beat as Nick grinned down at her.

"Nick! It's good to have you home."

"It's good to be home," he said, settling onto a bar stool, his expression as carefree as a school-boy's. "We got back so late last night, we didn't really get a chance to talk. I missed you."

"I missed you, too. How's Henny?"

He took the cobbler Myla automatically scooped up for him, his eyes lighting up at the sight of it. "Doing great. She insisted I come back to check on you. She thinks we were made for each other."

"Were we?"

"I'm beginning to believe that, yes."

Remembering Carolyn's declaration that Nick would soon get bored with her, Myla turned away to finish filling the sugar containers. The sooner she could move out of his house, the better, no matter how much she cared about him. Then she'd be able to think this through and get a clear grasp on reality.

Nick stopped nibbling his cobbler, his eyes locking with hers in the mirror behind the counter. "What's wrong?"

Should she tell him? Deciding to keep things light, she only said, "I saw Carolyn the other day."

That got his attention. "Really. I haven't talked to her in a while. How's she doing?"

"She seemed confused," Myla admitted. "I think she misses you, too."

"Did she say something to you, to upset you?"

Because she cared for him, she didn't tell him about Carolyn's other threats. "No, not really. Nothing I can't deal with. Maybe you should check on her, though."

Giving her a curious look, he said, "All right. But I have to admit, I'm not accustomed to the woman in my life telling me to call my ex-girlfriend."

"I'm not like other women," she told him in a curt little tone.

"No, you're not. For one thing, you make such an incredible blueberry cobbler, that it makes me want to weep with sheer joy."

She smiled in spite of herself.

He leaned over the counter, his hand touching her face. "And for another, you're much too smart to let anything my ex-girlfriend might say upset you. Right?"

"Right," she said, touched that he'd worded it in a way that didn't force her to admit to anything. "Just see about her for me, all right?"

"All right."

She sat down beside him to drink a quick cup of coffee while he finished his dessert. When he rose to leave, she said, "I'll see you at dinner. I've got a meat loaf ready to pop in the oven."

"Okay." He headed toward the door, thinking how comforting it was to have someone to come home to. He'd rounded the corner, heading the short distance back to Rudolph Oil when Myla's frantic call stopped him.

"Nick!"

Myla's shouts echoed through the skyscrapers. Nick pivoted to find her running toward him, a look of panic draining the color from her face. Hurrying to meet her, he said, "What's the matter?"

"It's Jesse. Her school called. She's got a fever and she's having trouble breathing. I've got to go and get her, but Grant borrowed my car to make a delivery. Can you give me a lift?"

"Of course." Taking her by the arm, he guided her across Milam Street. "My car's parked at the office. It's just around the corner."

"Good. I got one of the other waitresses to cover for me. I really appreciate this. I know you've got a lot of work to catch up on."

"Don't worry about that. I don't mind. I'll call the office from the car and let my secretary know I won't be back today."

They reached his car in record time. As Nick leaned down to unlock her door, Myla put a hand on his arm, her eyes full of gratitude. "I owe you so much."

Nick wanted much more than just gratitude, but he couldn't tell her that. "Stop worrying," he said in a reassuring tone. "Now, let's go take care of Jesse."

Chapter Eight

"It's not your fault," Nick said softly as he handed Myla the cup of icy soda. All around them, hospital personnel whizzed by, taking care of the business of healing the sick.

Myla looked around, a concerned expression darkening her face. "I've been so busy lately. I should have seen this coming. I've always been able to gauge her allergies before, but I just thought she'd caught another cold."

"You had no way of knowing it would turn into pneumonia," he told her as he urged her to sit down on the mauve floral couch in the pediatric waiting room of Schumpert Medical Center. "This stuff is very tricky."

"But I should have been more careful," Myla said, holding her head against one hand. "She's been so sick all winter, and I just kept pumping her full of medicine and sending her to school. I can't believe I didn't catch this in time."

Nick put an arm around her, then squeezed her shoulder for reassurance. "You've had a lot on your mind."

A burly, gray-haired doctor came marching up the hall from the pediatric ward. Spotting Myla and Nick, he halted in front of them. "Ms. Howell, I'm Dr. Redmond." After giving Myla a brisk handshake, he spoke to her in a hushed tone. "You've got one very sick little girl on your hands. We'll need to keep her a few days. She's very congested."

Myla put down her cup of soda with shaky hands. "Will she be all right?"

"I think we can help her," the doctor said. "We've already started administering antibiotics, but it's hard to pinpoint whether this was brought on by a bacterial infection or her allergies. We'll run tests to be sure. We've got her under oxygen until she can breath a little better on her own."

"Whatever it takes, Dr. Redmond," Nick said, his arm around Myla's waist. "I'll cover all the costs."

"Of course, Mr. Rudolph. Anything for the son of Joseph and Ruth Rudolph. Your mother was a special woman. We all miss her very much."

"Me, too," Nick replied. Then, "Just take care of Jesse for me, okay?"

"That we can do." Giving Myla another pat of

assurance, the doctor said, "You can see her now, Ms. Howell."

After the doctor told them he'd check back with them later, Myla looked up at Nick. She was already feeling tremendous guilt because of Jesse's illness. Now, she had the added burden of owing Nick yet again. Maybe if she hadn't been so distracted these past few weeks, if she'd kept her mind on her children's welfare instead of obsessing about Nick, this wouldn't have happened.

Her tone firm, she said, "I can't let you pay for this. I'll use the money I've been saving."

"Myla…" Nick pulled her out of the hallway, away from prying eyes and ears. "Don't think about all of that right now. Your little girl is sick and you don't have insurance. I can help you."

In spite of his good intentions, Myla felt ashamed for having to rely on him, and even more ashamed that she'd let Jesse get so sick. "And what about the next time, and the time after that? Nick, don't you see, you're stepping in to take care of me." Her voice cracking, she added, "Which means, I can't even take care of my daughter on my own!"

The frustration in her eyes only made Nick want to protect her even more. She blamed herself for this, no doubt. And, she probably wanted to blame him, too. "Listen," he said in a gentle tone, "this isn't your fault. And I don't mind whatever comes our way. I want to take care of you."

"I've got to learn to handle things on my own," she retorted, a desperation in her words. "I've got to be more careful from now on." Giving him an imploring look, she grabbed his arm. "Nick, she's so sick."

Nick pulled her close in spite of her resistance. "All the more reason to let me help—this time. Stop worrying about being so self-reliant and concentrate on your daughter." Pushing her hair away from her temple, he looked down at her. "And would you please stop apologizing and thanking me for my generosity. I'm not a saint or a martyr, Myla, but I refuse to let you do this on your own. End of discussion."

"Why?" she had to ask, the humiliation of being needy fighting with her love for him. "Why do you insist on being my knight in shining armor?"

Hearing her ask that question, Nick wondered why himself. Maybe because he *needed* to do something. He couldn't stand by any longer and watch her struggle. Not because she was a widow with two children; not because she didn't have a decent place to live or a good job; but because…he was in love with her. The urge to tell her so hit him with the force of the wind whipping outside the hospital windows. He stared at her, wanted to tell her, but her look of dread and defeat stopped him. "Because you need me," he said.

Myla couldn't deny that. Just having him here made this easier. Sonny had always insisted Jesse didn't have allergies and that Myla was just babying the little girl. Nick hadn't even questioned it. Yes, she needed him. But she wasn't willing to admit just how much. Not yet.

"I'll pay you back, a little each week," she declared, her tone stubborn.

He reached for her, gently urging her back into his arms. "Okay. We'll work out the details later."

"I want to see my daughter now," she whispered. Then, "Nick, I am really grateful to you. Thanks, again."

Gratitude. Nick had never had much time for that kind of mushy sentiment. Now, as he stood staring out the window of Jesse's room, he thought how ironic it was that he'd fallen in love with a woman who thanked him almost daily for his generosity. He'd dated lots of women and they'd all had some sort of pedigree attached: old money, new money, star quality, socialite connections, snobbish attitudes, but never had one of them given him any gratitude.

Myla was different. Stubborn. Determined. Firm in her beliefs. And bound to show the world she could handle things on her own. Would she resent him for always rushing to her rescue?

Jesse stirred under the oxygen tent, bringing Myla up out of her chair and Nick back from the window.

"Mama?" A small hand reached out in the darkened room, and Myla was immediately there to take it.

"I'm right here, honey. It's all right. Try to go back to sleep."

She patted Jesse's hand, her eyes meeting Nick's over the bed. He seemed so distant, so far away in his thoughts as he stood there by the window, watching the sun set. Now he moved to stare down at her daughter, concern evident in his dark eyes.

"She's drifted off again," he whispered. "Want to step out and get some fresh air?"

"Maybe in a minute." She walked around the bed to join him. "She looks so tiny and helpless, lying there like that. I'm afraid to leave her."

He wrapped an arm around her waist to tug her close. "Then we'll stay."

Myla leaned against him, glad for the support. "It's so late. Why don't you go back home? You've been at one hospital with Henny, and now this with Jesse. You need to go home and get some rest."

"I don't mind. I don't want to leave you."

Touched, she asked, "Does being here make you think about your mother?"

"Yes, but it's better now." He kissed the top of her head, then said, "You know, after Mother died, my father donated a huge sum of money to help build a new cancer wing. But he never set foot in this hospital again, and neither did I, until today."

Myla lifted her head to gaze into his eyes, her heart going out to him. "Nick, why didn't you say something? You didn't have to stay."

"Yes, I did. You were right, Myla. I can't blame the doctors or God for my mother's illness. I know miracles happen everyday, but sometimes there's just no way to save someone you love. When I think of all the time I wasted, blaming others, wallowing in my misery, I wonder sometimes how I got through each day. Now, after having been around you, I'm finding it easier to accept. Why was it so hard before?"

She held her arms on his shoulders, smiling up at him. "Maybe because your grief was getting in the way. You weren't open or willing to listen then. Now, you are."

He threw his head back, lifting his eyes to the sky. "It sure takes a heavy load off my back."

"That's the beauty of having someone higher to turn to. We don't have to waste our energy worrying about things we can't change."

"But we can concentrate on the things we can change."

"Exactly."

"Well, then, Ms. Howell, take some of your own advice, and stop worrying about your daughter. I predict she's going to be just fine."

Myla shot Jesse a loving look. "I certainly hope so."

"Would you feel better if we said a little prayer?"

"I've been praying," she admitted, "but, yes, I'd appreciate it if you'd pray along with me."

He did, asking for Jesse's quick recovery and asking for the courage to go out and help others who might be worse off. Because, it would take courage and strength to make a visible change within himself. But he intended to do it.

Jesse's harsh cough broke into his thoughts. Myla wasted little time slipping out of his embrace to rush to her daughter's side. Nick watched helplessly as Myla soothed the little girl with a few gentle words.

The tender scene shattered his heart into a million pieces, reminding him of how his father had held his mother, trying in vain to ease her horrible pain. Had his father been weak then, or had he simply been overcome by love and grief? Maybe his love for Ruthie had been his strength. Bitterly, Nick wondered if he'd misjudged his father, after all. Was it possible to be vulnerable and still remain strong?

If this was a test, he was certainly going to try to live up to it. Walking to the bed, he leaned over Jesse. "We're both right here, honey. Do you need anything?"

The little girl reached out her hand, taking Nick's stronger one. He wrapped his fingers around her frail little bones, his heart bursting with such a protective warmth that he wondered how anyone ever managed to get through fatherhood at all.

"I'm scared," she whispered, her big blue-green eyes wide and misty.

Nick gripped the tiny fingers clinging to his hand. "We all get scared sometimes, Jesse. But you're going to be all right. I won't let anything bad happen to you."

Myla looked at the man holding her daughter's hand, her own tears mirroring the moisture she saw gathering in the depths of his eyes. He didn't know it, but he'd just given her the one thing all his money couldn't buy. He'd given her that part of himself he'd been hiding from the world. By admitting his own fears, Nick Rudolph had shown just exactly how much courage he had.

And, he'd given her the ability to trust again.

Later, when dawn colored the trees outside a vivid newborn pink, Myla roused Nick out of his cramped position on a nearby chair. "I'm worried about Patrick. Will you go and check on Lydia and him before he goes to school? And get some rest while you're there."

Half asleep, Nick smiled at her bossy nature, feeling warm and content with the new intimacy that had developed between them during these past few hours. "How's the patient?"

"She's breathing better."

He got up to stretch long and hard. "Ah, we made it through the night."

Myla's warm gaze touched on his face. "Yes, we did."

He shook the creaks out of his neck. "Okay, then, I'll check on our other wards, then I guess I'll see you for lunch, maybe." With that, he headed for the darkened door.

Myla handed him his coat. "Nick?"

He turned, an expectant look on his face.

"Give Patrick a kiss for me."

With that, he took the two steps to reach her. "I'll do better than that. I'll take him one from his mother."

Surprised, Myla lifted on tiptoe as he kissed her solidly on the lips. When he reluctantly let her go, she managed to say, "Well, thank you, I think."

Nick's wide grin cut through the darkened room. "Now that's the kind of thanks I can live with."

"She's much better."

Myla held her daughter's hand, rubbing her fingers back and forth over the soft skin as she waited for Dr. Redmond to give them an update. Nick sat nearby, his relief evident as he smiled over at Jesse.

After three days in the hospital, the little girl was getting restless. "Can I go home? I miss Shredder."

Dr. Redmond held his hands together, absently pivoting on his tennis shoes, his eyes fixed on Jesse. "The antibiotics have kicked in," he said, his gray brows knotted together. "She showed all the signs of having bacterial pneumonia, but based on her history with allergies…I'd say this was more an allergic reaction than a case of pneumonia. This dry heat we use to stay warm, coupled with her not being able to get out in the fresh air, probably triggered all of this. But we still need to pinpoint exactly what caused her to have such an adverse reaction."

"What should we do?" Nick asked, his own gaze centered on Jesse. "What do you think caused this?"

"Oh, could be several things." The doctor eased over to Jesse, his smile reassuring. "I'm sure regular old dust and mold contributed a lot to it. Pine straw, dry leaves, and as I said, dry heat—a humidifier would help there."

"She does have a hard time with mold," Myla said. "I always kept our house as clean as possible to avoid provoking her allergies."

"Yeah," Jesse added hoarsely. "Mama wouldn't let me play in the barn back home." Then giving Myla a sheepish look, she added, "But I did help Lydia rake pine straw the other day. Me and Patrick and Shredder played in it."

Myla shot her daughter a reprimanding look, then quickly amended her feelings to reprimand herself instead. "I'm sorry, honey. I should have told Lydia, but I never thought about all those pine trees in the backyard."

"Hey," Nick interjected, "it's okay. Now that we

know, we'll all be more careful. And we'll go out and buy a humidifier right now."

The doctor flexed his shoulders, then smiled down at Jesse. "Who's this Shredder I keep hearing about?"

"My cat," Jesse piped up, beaming.

The doctor stopped smiling. "You have a cat?"

Myla nodded. "Yes, a stray. We kind of adopted him." Seeing the doctor's disapproving look, she asked, "Do you think she's allergic to the cat?"

Carefully wording his statement so as not to upset Jesse, the doctor told them, "No one can predict these things. She picked up a bug and her allergies collided with it. It's that simple. We'll send her home with some medicine for the symptoms, but I'd like to do a new set of allergy tests and start her on shots once we find the culprits. But even then, you'll need to keep her away from dust, and that tempting pine straw." Pulling Myla aside, he whispered, "And I'd advise getting rid of the cat."

Later, as they zoomed away from the hospital to take Jesse home, Nick turned to Myla. "What if she's allergic to Shredder? We'll have to give him to someone else."

"She'll be devastated," Myla whispered, glancing over her shoulder to make sure Jesse wasn't listening. "But if it's dangerous to her health, we won't have a choice."

"Of course, I can keep the cat after you move out," he offered, thinking the tiny animal would help ease his own loneliness. "Maybe by the time you get a new place, we'll know one way or the other."

"That would make Jesse feel better, I'm sure." Giving him a meaningful look, she added, "Now I'm worried about moving at all. If we do go to Magnolia House…well, it's very old and not in the best of condition. I hope the move won't provoke another allergy attack."

"That is something to consider," he said, feeling a wave of hope rise in his heart. "And wouldn't it be a shame now, if you just had to go on living at my big, old house?"

Myla stared ahead, acutely aware of how Nick had talked to the doctor as if Jesse were his own child. But the reality of this was that Jesse was her responsibility. "I can't do that, Nick. And you know why."

He maneuvered the car through a busy intersection, then gave her his full attention. "Why? You'd still be my employee and we have plenty of chaperons."

"It's not that. You've been very understanding about our relationship."

"Yes, I've learned extreme patience. You know you can count on that. So, what's the problem?"

"It's just not right, Nick. I need to get my own place for my own peace of mind, as well as your standing in the community."

Taking one hand away from the steering wheel,

he gave her a sharp look. "My standing? What are you talking about?"

Gritting her teeth, she plunged right in. "Carolyn could make trouble for us. She hinted at it the other day. She said people would talk if they knew we were…living together, so to speak, especially if they found out we had feelings for each other. I can't put you through that, and I certainly won't expose my children to that kind of ridicule."

Stopping for a red light, Nick banged the wheel of the car. "Well, you're right about one thing. I do need to pay Carolyn a little visit. And when I'm finished, I think she'll be straight on a lot of things."

"Don't…don't say anything you'll regret," she cautioned. "I don't want Carolyn to think I'm telling you things about her that aren't true."

"I know what to say," he assured her. "You taught me patience. And I'll sure need it with Carolyn."

True to his word, Nick did have a long talk with Carolyn Parker. But to Myla's dismay, instead of making it clear that he was ending things with Carolyn, Nick invited the blonde to serve on the grass-roots committee he was forming to help the homeless.

"If she sees that I've changed for the better and that I still care for her as a good friend, maybe she'll leave us alone," he explained to Myla. "Besides, we've done nothing wrong, so we have nothing to hide."

Myla wasn't so sure, but she did agree that they had

nothing to be ashamed of. She was working for Nick, nothing more. No matter that she loved him dearly. She'd do the right thing, for her children's sake.

Tonight, she stood in the kitchen preparing a hearty dinner for the ad hoc committee Nick was heading up. The team included Nick and Lydia, a reporter from one of the television stations to bring in publicity, Carolyn because of her connections within the society of Shreveport, and Grant— because Lydia had insisted he was sensitive to the needs of the homeless.

Now, Carolyn came into the kitchen, her cool gaze slipping over Myla to settle on the pot of gumbo Myla had stewing on the stove.

"Have you heard the news?" Carolyn asked, flipping on the nearby television set. "I thought you'd like to know."

"Know what?" Myla asked warily.

To her surprise, the reporter who was due here any minute was on the early news, covering a story on Magnolia House. The sound of hammering echoed behind the smiling dark-haired newswoman as she explained how a group of local companies had banded together to donate a new heating and cooling unit to the transitional shelter.

"These men are installing the new unit while we have this mild break in the winter weather. And they're cleaning and renovating the ancient air ducts, too," the reporter, a lady named Brooke Alexander, explained.

"A new unit?" Myla's eyes widened. Thinking about the mold and dust that would be cleared away, she remembered Dr. Redmond's warning. That wouldn't be a problem for Jesse now.

"This gesture of kindness is costing a small fortune," the reporter continued, "but these companies banded together to pay all the expenses."

Suspicious, Myla leaned over the counter. A thought popped into her head, but she couldn't quite put it to words. Anxious to hear more, she turned up the volume.

"The leader of this project has asked to remain anonymous," Ms. Alexander said, "but sources tell us he runs one of the most successful oil companies in Louisiana."

No doubt who that was, Myla mused, her gaze locking with Carolyn's. "Nick did this, didn't he?"

Carolyn nodded slowly, no hostility in her eyes. "Yes, I believe he did. He'd mentioned it to me when he asked me to serve on this committee, and I guess he couldn't wait to get started on things. You must be very proud of him."

"I am," Myla admitted. "And you should be, too."

Carolyn came around the counter to sample the gumbo. Taking a spoon, she dipped a helping, then held it away to cool for a minute. "I am. And Myla, I want to apologize for the way I acted the other day. I've always been a sore loser."

Myla searched Carolyn's face, then, seeing the sincerity in the other woman's eyes, went back to her task of slicing French bread. "You're not a loser, Carolyn. You're a lovely woman and I know Nick cares about you. I'm just sorry if I've caused you any heartache."

"You didn't. Nick did. But I'm over it now. You see, I've never seen Nick like this. He really has changed. And when he took the time to come and really talk to me, in a way we haven't talked in years…well, I knew I'd never win him back. All he could talk about was you and how he was going to form this corporation to help the homeless."

Myla chuckled softly. "He's pretty determined, once he sets his mind to something."

Carolyn grabbed a slice of bread and dipped it into the gumbo for one more taste. "Yes, and you'd better remember that."

"Oh, I'm well aware of it," Myla answered. "But thanks for the warning."

Carolyn lifted one brow. "You know, I thought Nick was married to his work. Maybe I was wrong. Maybe I just wasn't the right person to pry him away from Rudolph Oil. I think you might succeed, though."

"If anything happens," Myla said, stressing the *if,* "we will have to take it slow. I have to be very sure."

"Just don't hurt him," Carolyn warned. "That would devastate him at this point."

Myla watched as Carolyn pranced out of the room. Maybe she should consider her feelings for Nick long and hard. After all, she'd spouted platitudes to him, talked to him, helped him to find his faith again. If she let him down, he might lose all the trust he'd gained over the last few weeks, and never regain it again.

Had Carolyn really been trying to understand, or was this warning just another way for her to fuel Myla's own doubts?

"Trust in God," Myla said as she absently stirred the thick gumbo. "And put a little trust in Nick, too."

Now, if she could just learn to trust herself.

Chapter Nine

After Myla served coffee and dessert, everyone gathered around the empty dining table with pads and pens. Nick stole away and found her in the kitchen, busy loading the dishwasher. Stopping in the arched doorway, he remembered watching her like this before. How natural she looked, so domestic and womanly, so beautiful. She was the type of woman who loved having a home to call her own.

Yet she didn't have any place to call her own.

"Need some help there?" he called, lifting his shoulder off the doorway to push toward her.

Myla pivoted at the sound of his voice. Noting how attractive he looked in his old jeans and faded red polo shirt, she calmed her tap-dancing nerves to a slow waltz. "How's the planning committee going?"

"For the moment, it's going without me."

Handing her a glass, he added, "We were hoping you'd join us."

She shook her head. "I...I used to serve on committees, too many of them. Sonny resented it, but he couldn't tell me to stop—all part of his carefully constructed public image. I've already told Lydia I'll be glad to work behind the scenes, but I don't want to be on the committee. It's nice to just do my job now."

She didn't tell him that since Jesse's illness, she'd made a firm commitment to sticking strictly to business—just until she could get out on her own and get a proper perspective on her feelings for Nick.

Nick didn't let her get away so easily. "But isn't this part of your job? I mean, aren't you the one who told me we had to do something, make some changes?"

She lifted her brows, stopping her busywork to stare up at him. "I intend to do something. I'll stamp and fold mail-outs. I'll make copies and run errands. I'll even cook for the volunteers."

"And stay hidden away, just like you once accused me of doing?"

"That sounds like a challenge."

"It is a challenge. None of us know what we're doing in there. But you, you've been there. You could be a big help, and I want you...because you have firsthand experience."

Placing one hand on her hip, she teased him to

hide the warm feelings his words provoked. "Oh, and since you're the boss, I guess that's an order?"

He smiled when he saw the twinkle in her eyes. "Yes, I guess it is. But I'm asking, not demanding. And I'm not asking to enhance my public image, but because I care."

"You have changed."

"Okay, okay. I get the point. Are you going to help us or not?"

She turned on the dishwasher, then took one more look around the spotless kitchen "Okay. Guess it wouldn't hurt to just sit in and listen. Let me check on the children, and then I'll be right in."

He waited for her, watching as she kissed her sleeping children, his heart helplessly opening another fraction because of the sweetness of her nurturing strength. Then when Jesse opened her eyes and called out to her mother, he stopped at the door.

"Mama, where's Shredder? I want him to sleep with me."

Myla leaned over her daughter, placing a hand on Jesse's face. "You know Shredder is off-limits in here until we're sure you're completely well, honey. He's just fine in his little bed out in the garage, and during the day he gets to roam around the rest of the house."

Jesse looked so sad, Nick couldn't help it. He stepped back into the room. "Your mother's right, sweetie. You might be allergic to that crazy cat."

Jesse sat up, her big eyes imploring Nick. "But

I love Shredder. You aren't going to make us get rid of him, are you, Mr. Nick?"

Nick squatted by the bed, so he could see Jesse better. "Of course not. He just has to stay out of Henny's rooms for a while, until we're sure you're not allergic."

That seemed to calm the little girl. "Okay. That's all I was worried about. Mr. Nick, please take care of Shredder for me—after we move into the shelter."

Nick glanced up at Myla, then looked back down at Jesse. Swallowing the tightness in his throat, he said, "I will. Shredder will always have a home here."

"Even if I can't come to visit?"

"Even if you can't come to visit."

Jesse lay back down then, her voice so soft, Nick had to strain to hear her words. "'Cause Shredder was just like us, wasn't he? He didn't have any other place to go."

Myla sat down on the bed then to gather her daughter close. Her words were husky, but Nick heard the tremor in her voice. "That's right, honey. Mr. Nick took us in when we didn't have a place to stay, and I know he'll take care of Shredder for us. You don't have to worry about that."

"I promise," Nick said, his eyes on the woman holding the little girl. "Always."

Myla tucked Jessica back in, then pulled the door partly closed before turning to Nick. "Nick, I—"

"Don't say thank you, please," he whispered. "You don't owe me anything. Can't you see, you and your children have redeemed me. I was so lonely, so alone, so bitter. Now, I have something to fight for. And I will fight for you, Myla. Oh, I know you're holding off on any decisions and I know you have to do things your way, such as writing me those checks for the doctor's bill. But I won't give up. I don't give up too easily."

"I have noticed that about you," she said, stopping him in the alcove just outside the door to the dining room. "Nick, I'm really proud of what you did for Magnolia House."

Shrugging, he said, "I don't know what you're talking about."

"Yes, you do. You went in there and overhauled their heating and cooling system. It was a very unselfish thing to do."

He lowered his head, not used to being heralded for doing good deeds. "I did it for Jesse."

"I know that," she said softly, "and you helped all those other people in the process."

"That's me, just an all-around good guy."

"You are a good guy. Jesse obviously thinks you hung the moon."

He shook his head, then grinned. "No, I just hired someone to do it for me." Then turning serious, he said, "Your daughter and I have grown closer in our efforts to keep Shredder from being booted out of the house."

Myla had noticed that bond between her daughter and this man, especially tonight. It would be so hard to pull her children out of the safe environment Nick had provided for them. "It was very sweet of you to talk to her about Shredder."

"I talked to her because I care about her—and that wild cat. And like I said, I don't give up easily. Not even on a woman who thinks she has to do everything her way."

No, he wasn't one to give up, Myla thought. She had to make him see her fears, though. Make him understand that this wasn't so simple. "But *I* don't have anything to offer you, Nick. I'm so afraid I'll make the same mistake twice."

He held her, his hands firm on her arms. "Look at me, Myla. I'm not like Sonny. I'd never treat you the way he did. I'd never hurt you."

"I want to believe that," she said, hoping to make him understand. "I do. And really, it's not you I'm worried about. It's me. I don't want to let you down."

Amazed at her self-doubt, Nick said, "You haven't let me down so far. You don't give yourself enough credit, Myla."

Voicing her worst fears, she said, "But what if Carolyn is right? What if you're just intrigued with me because I'm your new cause? What if these feelings aren't strong enough to carry us through in the long run?"

He hissed a bitter laugh. "Do you think I feel sorry for you? Is that it? Do you think I'm doing all of this out of pity?"

She dropped her head. "Maybe. I don't know."

He gently tugged her close, then wrapped his arms around her waist. "Myla, Myla, sometimes I *envy* you. I envy your strength and your courage and your convictions. I've wanted to help you all along, but…I don't feel sorry for you. You don't allow that."

She lifted her head, her eyes searching his. "You've changed so much since that first night. I just have to be sure, Nick. Very sure."

He touched a hand to her hair. "Well, I am sure. I was lost the night I saw you standing in the middle of that road." Seeing the stubborn glint in her eyes, he plunged on. "I'd always heard Lydia talking about Magnolia House, but I never had the time or the inclination to go to the place myself. Well, the other day, after what the doctor told us about Jesse's condition, I did go. I had to check the place out before I could bring myself to let you move in there."

He stopped, taking a long breath, his eyes going dark. "When I saw the other children—the ones I don't even know, living in those cramped apartments, wearing clothes donated by other people and eating food provided by someone else—I understood why Lydia does the things she does, and why you gave that old man your plasma money.

"It broke my heart to see those families, but they

all had one thing in common. They were all fighting this thing together, and they seemed secure and happy. And I kept remembering that Bible verse from Proverbs about those who are rich yet have nothing, and those who are poor, yet have great riches."

"I know the verse," Myla said, thinking of how many times she'd counted her blessings, even when she had nothing worldly in her possession. "It's hard to grasp, though, when you see homeless people on the street."

He nodded. "Yes, especially when you live in a mansion and have a fat bank account, yet still manage to gripe your way through each day. I'm ashamed to think I never really cared about what was going on around me before."

She patted him on the arm. "Well, now you do care. And that's what's so important." If nothing else, she and Nick would have that bond to share. And she'd be remiss to turn him down now, when *he* was asking for her help. Smiling up at him, she said, "I'll serve on your committee, Nick. I'll do whatever I can."

He gave her a quick, reassuring kiss, then took her into the long dining room. Lifting a hand to the others at the table, he announced, "We have a new recruit. Myla has agreed to serve with us—and not just behind the scenes."

Lydia clapped, her smile broad. "Oh, good.

We've got the preliminary plans for the charity ball laid out and we've registered our incorporation papers with the state—we're calling our organization Hope, Faith and Love, Incorporated. But Myla, we need to ask you something."

Eyeing her warily, Myla said, "Sure, I think."

Brooke Alexander, the reporter who'd joined up to promote her television station's charitable image, said, "We've come into some property, a house in the old Highland District, and we're going to recruit people to remodel it for a deserving family From everything Lydia and Nick have told us tonight, you're eligible to apply for it."

Her interest growing, Myla sat down. "I've been trying to find out more about how to qualify for one of those low-cost houses. Are you saying I could possibly get this house?"

"We think so," Grant said, tapping his ink pen on his notepad. "The house has already been donated, free and clear. All you need to do is fill out the application and wait for the board's approval. But, whether you get the house or not, we'd like you to give a speech at the charity ball—telling about your situation."

Lydia gave Grant a look of total adoration. Nick, however, didn't have time tonight to fume at his little sister's obvious infatuation. He was too busy studying Myla's reaction to the news of the house. Would she be pleased?

Too astonished to notice anything else, Myla asked, "How many people will be at this event?"

Lydia leaned forward. "If all goes as planned, about two to three hundred."

"Three hundred people!" Myla shook her head. "I couldn't possibly."

Carolyn gave her a level stare. "Nick thinks you have a story to tell."

"He would." Myla sighed, then ran a shaking hand through her long tresses. Could she really face all those people with her humiliating story? "I'll...I'll have to think about this."

Lydia jotted down some more notes. "Well, we don't have much time. We've already formed a solid board of directors, and we're setting up the bylaws now. We're shooting for mid-April for the membership kickoff, with the ball as our first fund-raiser."

Myla shook her head. "That's only a couple of months. No, I can't. I'm not ready to talk about everything that's happened to me."

Nick spoke softly from the doorway behind her. "Think of all the people you'll be helping."

His dark eyes washed her with a warmth that left her mystified. This new Nick was even more intriguing than the old reserved one. And rather than making her into a charity case, he was working toward helping her in a positive way. He was willing to let her make it on her own, without any pressure about their relationship. This would be a risk, but it would also give her the freedom to make her own choices. And she'd have a home again.

"Hope, Faith and Love," she said, her eyes meeting Nick's. "These three."

"And the greatest of these is love," he reminded her gently.

Biting her bottom lip, she nodded slowly. "I'll be so nervous, and we don't even know if I'll get the house."

"You'll win the house and every heart at the ball," Nick said. And he'd see to it personally, if it would make her regain her self-confidence.

"Looks like she's already won one," Brooke teased, her keen eyes lighting on Nick. "Maybe that's the real story."

"Yeah," Carolyn added, getting up to leave. "And if you can win ruthless Nick Rudolph over, you don't need to worry about anyone else in this town."

Myla didn't miss the sarcasm or the hint of regret in the other woman's parting words. And apparently from the interested look in her eyes, neither did Brooke Alexander.

"I don't want to make a big deal out of this," Nick warned the reporter. "Let's keep my involvement low-key, okay?"

"Sure, Nick." The woman's smile was practiced and precise. "Just the facts, I promise."

Myla waited until the others had left, then turned

to Nick. "Did you plan this—getting me involved, I mean—just to shift the spotlight from yourself?"

He gave her a level look. "No. Actually it was Carolyn's idea to have you speak at the fund-raiser. You've managed to win her over, too. Quite a coup."

Myla looked skeptical. "Well, if I get my own place, I'll be away from you. Probably why she suggested this."

"Whoa, I hadn't thought about it that way. Carolyn's pretty crafty, but I do believe she's sincere about this. She didn't flirt with me once tonight. In fact, I think she's found a new catch— my friend from the city council. He's single and up- and-coming, just her type, and Lydia had the good sense to seat them next to each other at some stuffy social event the other night."

Myla laughed in spite of her worries, then said, "I appreciate your board's considering me for the house, and of course I understand I might not qualify. I just hope you didn't bully anybody into doing this—"

He shook his head. "I'm doing what I thought you wanted most in the world—I'm helping you to find a place to live."

Realizing he was right, she didn't argue with him any further. This had been her goal, her dream all along. This was her chance to prove herself. And maybe, this was Nick's chance to prove himself, too.

"I'll be at your fancy ball," she said at last.

He gave her a look that told her everything, yet revealed nothing. Did she see regret in his eyes, or relief, or maybe both?

"You can wear the green dress."

Gripping her hands together, Myla looked away, sweet memories of that special Christmas night coloring her mind. "Yes, that is the only elegant thing I own."

"Wear it for me," he whispered, reaching out to draw her into his arms. "And we'll come home and have a turkey sandwich and pound cake, and we'll dance underneath the stars."

"Sounds perfect," she said as she leaned into his kiss.

Except by that time, she might be living in a different home.

"I'm getting a house," Myla told Grant a few weeks later as they cleaned up after the breakfast rush at the coffeehouse.

"That's great, isn't it?" he asked, giving her a questioning look. "I mean, this is all you've talked about since you started working here. Now you won't have to live in the homeless shelter, right?"

"Right." Myla finished making a fresh pot of French vanilla decaf. "At least I can bypass that part of the transition. I wasn't looking forward to shifting my children around."

Grant stopped stacking dishes to stare over at her. "So, things are working out for you. Then why do you look like you've just lost your best friend?"

Myla started doodling on an order pad lying by the cash register. Grant was very astute and sensitive. And right on target about her mood today. She had been down since learning that the board of directors for Hope, Faith and Love had voted for her to be the recipient of their first house.

She didn't know why she was reacting this way, but something just didn't feel right about this. Maybe it had all been too easy, and she surely wasn't used to getting things the easy way. Or maybe, the truth be told, she didn't really want to leave Nick, after all.

Deciding she could trust Grant, she said, "Oh, who am I kidding? It's because I love working for Nick, and I love cleaning that big old house of his, and cooking and pretending I'm a housewife again."

Grant nodded, his poetic eyes gazing over at her with a too knowing expression. "Oh, I see. You've found a home and you don't want to leave it, because you have feelings for the owner. Does he know how you feel?"

Embarrassed, Myla placed a bundle of clean forks in a nearby holder. "*I* don't know how I feel. On the one hand, I think I love Nick and could be completely happy with him. But on the other hand,

I still don't know how he really feels about me. And I have to be sure, not only of him, but of myself. So, I figure the only way I can do that is to go ahead and move out on my own and see if we can hold on to what we think we have."

Grant rolled his eyes. "This is complicated, huh?"

"Very." Turning to a customer, Myla handed him his espresso, then took his dollar. "And I don't want to burden you with the details."

"Hey, that's what friends are for," Grant said, his gentle blue eyes touching hers. "You'll find your way, Myla. After all, you've come this far."

"Yes, I have," she reminded herself. "And I am excited about the house. It's so cute. It needs work, of course, and I'm required to put in five hundred hours of sweat equity to help fix it up, but I can't wait. I get a twenty-year, interest-free loan, so it's really going to be mine."

"That sounds fair," Grant remarked, straining as he reached for some clean coffee cups. "Need any help?"

"Yes. We rely on volunteers to help do most of the work. Nick has set this corporation up so that everything is donated, including time."

"I'll be there," Grant said, pushing his glasses up on his long nose. "Especially if it means I'll get to see Lydia more."

Smiling at last, Myla nudged him with her elbow. "How's that relationship going, Romeo?"

Grant sighed, then shook his head. "Let's just say, I know what you mean about Nick Rudolph. That man's hard to get to know." He waved his hands. "One minute he's teasing me, the next, he's glaring at me."

Myla could picture Nick doing exactly that; he'd certainly shifted moods on her enough. "So, in other words, things could be great between you and Lydia if Nick would just back off?"

"Something like that," Grant replied. "Her big brother thinks I have less than honorable intentions toward Lydia, but I really like her, you know."

"I do know," Myla said as she took the money for a customer's cookie and coffee. "Lydia has a kind heart and she's very serious about helping other people."

"She sure is," Grant agreed readily. "I'll admit I didn't believe that at first. I thought she was just some bored rich kid out to appease her sense of social duty. But now that I've spent some time with her, I can tell she's really sincere. Did you know she's thinking of going back to college to become a bona fide counselor? She wants to do more than just volunteer a few hours a week."

Surprised, Myla gave him a wide-eyed look. "Does Nick know that? No, of course, he couldn't, or I'm sure I would have heard all about it."

"No, not yet," Grant said, his voice low and worried. "She's been trying to figure out a way to spring the news on him."

"That should be interesting." Then, wanting to reassure her friend, she said, "Nick means well, Grant. It's just…he's been both Lydia's brother and surrogate parent for so long, he's forgotten how to let go. I think he's turned all his pain into some sort of overprotective focus on his sister."

"Yeah, I know," Grant replied. "And Lydia sure sees it. That's why she's afraid to tell him about her plans. She doesn't want him to lash out at me, or think I put her up to this—which he'll do, I guarantee."

"Maybe I can talk to him," Myla offered. "Smooth the way once Lydia breaks the news?"

"You've got enough to deal with."

"I can handle Nick," Myla said, although she dreaded the tirade once Nick found out about Lydia's plans. "Let me take care of him, and you concentrate on Lydia, okay?"

"Okay," Grant said, "but I can fight my own battles. I'm not afraid of Nick Rudolph."

"Very noble," Myla teased, "but…Nick's really an old softy underneath all that bluster. We both need to remember that."

Grant nodded, then patted Myla on the shoulder. "Well, now that we've discussed both our personal lives, how about we discuss something else that's been on my mind?"

"What's that?" Myla asked, confused by the intense look on his face.

"Adding more to the menu," Grant said. Waving his hand again, he added, "After all, we've made a good team so far."

Relieved, Myla grabbed the computer printout of their profits and losses. "Oh, that reminds me—"

Grant wiped his hands on his white apron, a frown marring his boyish face. "You're not going to quit on me, are you?"

"No, nothing like that." She tapped the ledger with her finger. "I got a call about a catering job—they'd like us to cater a sit-down dinner for about twenty-five people and I'm anxious to test the waters." Before he could answer, she continued, "It's going to be hectic, but I think this is a good opportunity. We'd get lots of publicity."

Grant's eyes lit up. "Are you serious?"

She gave him a playful punch on the arm. "Well, as you just pointed out, we've made great progress so far and this would give us exactly what we'd hoped for, even though it is earlier than we'd planned. We can start building a strong base for our catering company. That is—if you think we're ready?"

Rubbing a hand across his swarthy chin, Grant thought about it for about a minute. "You do have a point, and from the smell of that garlic bread baking, I'd be crazy to let our first catering customers get away without sampling it. After our first hundred thousand or so, we can branch out."

Grinning, he extended his hand. "I think it's a good idea. Tell them we accept."

"What's a good idea?"

Myla looked up to find Nick staring across the counter at her, with Lydia right beside him, smiling shyly at Grant. Grant glanced over at Myla, panic in his eyes.

Lydia hopped up on a bar stool, spinning around before she stopped, breathless and giggling. "Hi, Grant."

Nick sat down in a more dignified manner, his curious look moving from Myla to Grant. "You two look as if you've just committed a felony. What's with the guilty faces?"

Before Myla could answer his question, Lydia spoke to Grant again. "How's it been going?"

"Great. It's good…uh, real good. We were just—" He shot Myla a beseeching look.

"We were just going over the books," Myla interjected to stop Grant from stuttering. "Business is picking up."

"That's wonderful," Lydia said, her eyes on Grant. "By the way, I really enjoyed that movie the other night."

Grant pushed his bifocals up on his nose. "Me, too. Uh…can I get you a cup of coffee?"

Myla glanced at Nick. He was glaring, his dark eyes flashing such a protective fire for his sister, she was surprised he didn't come across the counter to grab poor Grant by the collar.

To waylay any such action, she said, "We've been making plans to branch out, and start our catering services right here from the coffeehouse."

"Really?" Nick spoke at last, a look of disbelief plastered across his face. "Are you sure you're ready to take on more work?"

Trying not to get too defensive, Myla placed a hand on her hip. "With Grant's help, yes, and only after Henny's completely well and back home, of course." There, that should reassure him that she wouldn't slack up on her responsibilities to him. "We've been offered a small catering job, and we just now this very minute decided to go for it."

"Sure did. That's what we were doing when you two showed up." Grant handed Lydia her coffee, then managed to ramble on. "Myla's a real treasure. Since she's started working here, we're becoming famous for our cookies and pastries."

Lydia bobbed her blond head. "Yep, Nick and I have put on a few pounds ourselves since Christmas."

"Speak for yourself," Nick said, his expression relaxing as he patted his tummy. "And pass the double chocolate chip cookies and a cup of that New Orleans blend coffee, please."

Lydia grabbed a cookie as Myla held out the basket. "Grant, you've done a wonderful job with this old building. This is fast becoming one of downtown's most popular spots."

Grant lowered his head and smiled, his face flushing red. "Like I told you, I needed a place to read my incredibly bad poetry."

Lydia looked pleased as punch. "A poet *and* a smart businessman. I like that."

Grant blushed, then offered to show Lydia a new display of paintings they'd hung that very morning.

Nick rolled his eyes as his sister practically skipped away with Grant, then said under his breath, "I think my sister's about to make a conquest. She's been stringing him along for weeks now, in spite of my warnings for her to be careful. I don't think I can bear to watch this anymore."

"Well, don't worry," Myla said, hoping to calm his brotherly concern. "Grant is a good man. He goes to church every Sunday and plays his guitar with the choir at times. And his poetry is very spiritual. He wouldn't hurt a fly."

"Great. My sister falls for the Lord Byron of Coffeeshops."

Myla glanced over at Lydia and Grant. They were deep into their own conversation, both with stars in their eyes. Deciding now wasn't the best time to tell Nick about his sister's plans—in fact, it might be best to let Lydia handle that herself—she told him, "She'll be fine." Then, she added, "What brings you two in this early in the day, anyway?"

"Wrapping up plans for the benefit ball," he explained. "Can we still count on you to make that speech?"

Her stomach twisted into a bowknot, but she quickly calmed it down. "I'll be there, but I'll be busy over the next few weeks working on the house. I got a call today, telling me I passed the application process."

He sat perfectly still, his pride shining in his golden brown eyes. "I knew you would. Need help with the renovations?"

She didn't miss his smug expression. Challenging him, she said, "I expect you to be the first in line."

"You can count on it," he replied, his tone casual. "I need to do something to make up for causing you to miss your spot at Magnolia House."

"Yes, but you've already worked hard to make up for that. Setting up this corporation will help so much, Nick. You're going to make a big difference in this community."

"That's a switch," he said, a look of humility on his face. "But you're right. This is different from just writing a check. I've never worked harder."

"And I'll bet you're enjoying every minute of it."

He gave her a wide smile. "That I am."

Lydia's hands clapping together brought both Myla and Nick's heads around. "Grant has agreed to come to our benefit ball. He can sit at our table, since I just talked him into making a sizable contribution to our cause."

"Lucky Grant," Nick teased, his eyes settling on his bubbly sister. "You never stood a chance, you know," he said to Grant.

Grant's laugh was more from nerves than humor. "I can live with that."

Nick turned back to Myla, his expression blank. "Now if I only can."

"You're doing great," Myla said in an encouraging voice, thinking he was as hard to read as the abstract art hanging on the high walls around them.

He feigned a look of innocence. "Far be it from me to interfere with my sister's social life, even though she's accused me of doing just that. I've got enough problems trying to deal with my own."

Just then, a customer called to Myla. She hurried to get the man his bagel and latte, waving to Nick. "I've got work to do."

"So do I," he said, rising up off his stool. "See you at home?"

"Okay." Myla watched him leave, all the while wondering where exactly her own home was supposed to be.

Dear Lord, show me the way. Do I belong with Nick, or should I make this move out on my own? I leave it in Your hands.

Out on the sidewalk, Nick said a similar prayer of his own. He hoped he'd done the right thing this time. He only knew he was letting the woman he loved go in order to win her back fair and square.

The little voice inside his head reminded him that he hadn't been so fair and square.

He told the little voice to be quiet.

Chapter Ten

"Well, it's finished."

Nick stood back to admire the cottage they'd renovated for the first recipient of the Hope, Faith and Love, Incorporated, Housing for the Homeless. "My neck aches," he added as he rubbed the sore muscles at his shoulders.

Myla saw the pride shining in his eyes. That same pride shined within her heart. "It's beautiful, Nick."

He glanced over at her, one paint-dusted hand still on his neck. "And it's yours. All yours."

Weeks had passed—long weeks of hard work and dedicated hours of remodeling the little house. All the volunteers had left after they'd celebrated with pizza and soft drinks. Jesse and Patrick were running around in the backyard, happy to be in their own home. Shredder had opted to live with Nick and Lydia at the mansion, and Jesse hadn't argued. She planned to visit the cat often. Her allergies were all clear now, but Myla was watching her closely with spring coming up.

Now, Myla walked up onto the tiny front porch, admiring the fresh coat of white paint and the blue-colored shutters. "I'm going to plant azaleas," she told him over her shoulder.

"And don't forget the yellow roses."

"Lots of them."

"I'll help you."

She whirled to lean over the new spindle railing. "You have helped me, from the very beginning. I'll never be able to repay you, Nick."

"You already have," he said, coming up to sit on the gray-painted wooden steps. "You gave me something I never dreamed I could find again—my faith."

"I didn't do it," she explained, lowering herself down beside him. "God did."

"He sent you to me."

"He knows how to deal with ruthless executives."

"Yes, He certainly dealt me a curveball. And not just with you—now I've got that Grant fellow to contend with, also."

"How are things with Lydia and Grant?" she asked, careful that she didn't put her nose into their business without being asked.

Nick gave her a knowing glance. "Don't pretend you don't know a thing about them. I know Lydia confides in you almost daily."

Myla tossed her ponytail off her neck. "Okay, yes, I know a little. But I want to know how *you* feel."

He fell back against a square porch column. "Like I'm losing my baby sister…like I'm losing control."

"Or gaining a brother-in-law?"

Nick held up a hand. "Don't! I'm not ready to hear that yet."

"She could do worse," Myla offered, taking his hand in hers. "And I'm proud of you for staying so *in control.* Lydia has to be able to make her own decisions, good or bad."

"Oh, I'm trying hard to stay sane. Especially since she also informed me she's thinking about becoming a social worker. What's gotten into my sister?"

"How long have you known about that?" Myla questioned, surprised that he hadn't ranted and raved about it.

"She told me last night." At Myla's questioning look, he added, "Don't worry. I handled it with brotherly concern and complete calm. You've taught me patience, see? And as you just pointed out, the good Lord has dealt me a whole new set of challenges."

Myla couldn't help but love him all over again. He looked so completely, utterly confused. And so adorable. "But you took what He dealt you and did something positive. And now look."

He lifted his head to look around the peaceful, tree-shaded neighborhood, refusing to feel guilty about her happiness. Spring was just around the corner; already the dogwoods and crape myrtles were starting to bud. He shouldn't feel so lousy— he'd only given the woman he loved the very thing she wanted most in the world.

To hide his overactive conscience, he said, "This is only the beginning. We have two other houses lined up for this summer and fall."

Myla leaned back to take a long breath of the clear, crisp air. "Everything's so beautiful today. So green and fresh. The air smells so rich."

"All is right with the world," Nick said, his tone light in spite of the great sadness coloring his heart. "My sister's changing right before my eyes. Henny's glad to be home, and she's taking things easy. You have a good job with Grant and your catering business. And I've just lost…a wonderful housekeeper."

Myla's heart shifted into an erratic beat. She wanted to thank him for keeping this light, but she didn't think she could voice the words. So instead, she said, "I left you a pound cake in the pantry."

His eyes went all warm and misty. "I'll savor each bite."

Myla sat still, the awkward silence surrounding

her. This was it; this was the moment she'd dreamed about since that cold, dark night in her car. She had her own home again, but it was a bittersweet victory.

How could she say goodbye to Nick? She should be happy; she had a place to call her own, at last. Was it wrong to want to be with him?

As if sensing her doubts, Nick looked across at her, his dark eyes holding hers. "I'll miss you so much."

Now, why did he have to go and say that? Swallowing back the tears threatening her eyes, she said, "I know. But we agreed we'd see each other a lot. At church, at the HFL meetings, and you can come over for pizza anytime."

His laugh was stilted. "I'll probably be over a lot. Henny won't be able to cook those elaborate meals anymore. We're both on a low-fat diet now."

"I'll come and help out," she offered, her heart melting. She wanted to run to him and hold him in her arms forever. But…he needed time and so did she. At least, that's what she kept telling herself.

He got up to leave. "I expect you to, but not tonight. Right now, you need to enjoy your first night in your new house."

"Nick?" she called. "Your parents would be so proud of what you've done."

That statement brought his head around. "Do you really think so?"

"Yes, I do."

He came back to lift one foot up onto the steps, his gaze searching her face. "I want to tell you something—something I haven't told anyone, not even Lydia."

"Okay," she said, patting the place he'd just vacated. "I'm listening."

He sat back down, his hands clasped. "I told you my father died during the oil crisis, but I didn't tell you how he died. He loved my mother so much, but he wasn't much of a church-goer. Mother and Lydia went to church, while Father and I concentrated on the business, always the business. Anyway, when Mother was diagnosed with cancer, well…he literally fell to pieces. And it got much worse after her death.

"I couldn't deal with that—seeing him so weak, so lost. It confused me because he'd always been so strong and firm, so distant and hard to understand. I turned away from him, refusing to help him through the worst time in his life. I couldn't deal with his grief, or mine."

Myla grasped his arm. "Go on. Tell me everything."

"I caused my father's death, Myla."

She gasped, her heart filling with compassion. "What do you mean?"

He continued to look down at the shiny new steps. "We had a terrible argument. He had changed so much, I was only trying to pull him back, to snap him back to reality. I needed him to be strong again. I shouted at him, reminding him of all the things he'd taught me—show no weakness, be a man, don't let anybody get the best of you.

"I think he realized he'd created a monster. I saw the disappointment in his eyes, watched him grip his chest. He died before the paramedics could get there. A massive heart attack. But even after his death, I was still that monster. I became even more cold and uncaring. I didn't have Lydia's strength, or the ability to open my heart."

"Nick, Nick, that's just not true." She brought his head around, pulling him down on her shoulder. "Inside, you were a caring person. You were just still grieving, and no wonder. Your father taught you about business, but he didn't teach you about what's really important in life."

He buried his face in her hair, his words muffled and raw with pain. "I can't do it anymore, Myla. I can't be that person. None of us can go through life without experiencing love. And for such a long time, I was afraid to love because I didn't want to wind up hurt and broken, like my father."

Myla didn't speak. She stroked his hair, understanding he'd carried this burden for so long. He cried softly, draining all the bitterness and the coldness out of his soul, then he lifted his head to look at her.

"I didn't know how to help him. I equated love and need with weakness." Taking her face in his hands, he said, "But you taught me that it's okay to be weak sometimes. You taught me that love is our strength."

"It is, it is," she said, closing her eyes to the overwhelming love inside her heart. "God has forgiven you, Nick. And so has your father. Isn't it about time you forgive yourself?"

He wiped the single tear from her face. "Isn't it about time we both forgive ourselves?"

He was right. She'd blamed herself for Sonny's misdeeds and his death. Nick had been through a similar pain. Maybe that was why God had brought them together.

"Let's forgive each other, right here, right now," she said, tears trailing down her face.

"Amen."

Together, they asked for God's forgiveness, and together, they prayed for a new hope and a new beginning. Then they sealed it with a kiss.

And somewhere, high up in a tree, a gentle dove cooed softly, her sweet call echoing their prayer and lifting it up toward heaven.

"Momma, you look so pretty," Patrick said, a baseball glove in one hand and a Popsicle in the other.

Jesse nodded her agreement, her mouth opening with a squeal of glee. "It's the dress you dreamed about!"

Myla smiled down at her children. "Yes, it certainly is."

The green brocade dress brought back all the memories she'd stored up like a hidden treasure in her mind. It was a beautiful dress, but the real treasure was in the man who'd given it to her. Yet she'd chosen to leave him.

And he'd honored her choice by biding his time, learning patience, doing things that made her more and more proud of him each day.

He'd helped her realize her dream. She now had her own home. Glancing around the white walls of her small living room, Myla again felt the pride of being here, safe and in control, self-sufficient. That she'd gotten the house on her own merit helped to ease her loneliness. Maybe that should be enough.

But lately, other dreams had been filtering into her mind. What was stopping her from rushing into Nick's arms? What was holding her back from being with the man she loved with all her heart?

Knowing Nick had suffered a pain so similar to her own had made Myla see she'd been unfair to him right from the beginning. Nick was a self-made man, fashioned after his father's skewed idea of the perfect son. When he'd realized his father's stipulations were really a sham, that there was no foundation holding up his father's firm declarations, Nick had turned bitter. But Myla had seen that bitterness melt into a warmth that promised a new beginning for Nick. He was the best of his father, and his mother.

Tonight, she'd tell Nick that she loved him. She was out here on her own now, secure and confident that she could handle any situation. Although Nick had helped her along the way, she'd earned her catering reputation with her hard work and her determination, and she'd earned this house through her own efforts and the backing of a group dedicated to helping others. She wouldn't let any of them down.

Especially Nick.

Car lights illuminated the front yard, shining through the screen door like a spotlight. A neighbor's teenage daughter, a sweet girl named Lily, came into the room with popcorn, all set to stay with the children and enjoy a movie on television.

"Looks like your date's here," Lily said, her expression dreamy. "Wow, he's nice-looking."

"Yes, he is," Myla had to agree.

"Isn't he the one that planted that big yellow rose out by the front steps?"

"The very one," Myla replied, remembering the morning she'd awakened to find the beautiful rose planted underneath her bedroom window. She'd fallen for him all over again.

Nick stepped onto the porch, his gaze settling on Myla as she opened the screen door. "You look great," he said, his eyes sweeping over her. "I'm as nervous as a teenager at his first prom."

"You don't look nervous," she said with a breathless laugh. "Black tie becomes you, Mr. Rudolph."

He tugged at his bow tie. "Thank you. Green brocade becomes you. Are you ready?"

"Ah…yes." She grabbed the small black purse she'd found at a secondhand store. Turning to the children, she said, "Behave for Lily, okay? And go to bed on time."

"I'll stay as long as you need me," Lily offered.

"Thanks," Myla said. She leaned down to kiss Patrick and then Jesse. "I love you," she whispered.

Her words tore through Nick. He wanted her to say those words to him. But he was fast losing hope. He'd watched her walk out of his home; he'd let her go, hoping against hope that she'd come back. He couldn't bear to have her out of his life, but he'd planted her a yellow rose as a symbol of her new freedom. When would she come back home to him?

He guided her down the steps, silent and serious, then helped her into the car, his heart now a hopeless mess, his mind tortured with loneliness.

Myla noticed his silence and tried to relax, but her nerves were strung tight. Thinking of how she'd changed since her first ride in this car, she looked out the window, watching the cottages and apartments give way to businesses and skyscrapers as they headed downtown to the Expo Hall located on the Red River.

"Are you all right?" Nick asked, his eyes on the road.

"Fine." She chanced a glance at him, wanting to ask him the same thing. "I just hope I don't embarrass myself or you."

"You won't. You probably gave the hardest speech of your life that night in my kitchen when you first told me about Sonny."

They reached the parking lot, which was already packed. Nick concentrated on finding a spot close to the building. Pulling the car into place, he switched off the ignition, then turned to Myla. "Before we go in, I just wanted to tell you—" With a groan, he reached for her, kissing her firmly on the lips. Then he let her go to stare at her. "Good luck."

"Thanks," she said, breathless. "I'll need a little luck to survive this speech." Especially after that kiss.

"Oh, you'll survive. That's what you do best."

Stopping him, she said, "Nick, I couldn't have survived these past few months, not without you."

She wanted to say more, but his continuing dark mood only added to her anxiety. Was he having doubts of his own?

As Nick helped her out of the car, then quietly and firmly guided her toward the doors of the big building, her heart sank. He seemed so distant tonight, more like the old Nick. Yet his kiss had been so real, so stirring. Maybe she was just imagining things because of her jittery nerves.

After the speech, then, she'd tell him she loved him. If it wasn't too late.

Inside, the glittering crowd of some of the city's richest patrons contrasted sharply with their purpose of being here. Lydia had estimated they'd be raising over one hundred thousand dollars to help build and remodel low-cost housing.

The minute they entered the massive hall, people began to stop Nick, shaking his hand, patting him on the back, congratulating him for being the steering force behind this ad hoc organization. He introduced Myla as they went along, but the glamorous faces started to merge in her mind.

Then the reporter who'd been in on the first committee meeting walked up to greet them. "Hello, Nick," Brooke Alexander said, her smile beaming as brightly as her simple diamond pendant.

Nick shook her hand. "Hi, Brooke, how are things at KTAS?"

"Great." Turning to Myla, the petite brunette said, "Good to see you again, Mrs. Howell. I understand you'll be giving testimony to HFL, Incorporated's good work here tonight."

Myla nodded. "Yes, as you know, I'm one of the recipients of that good work. The Rudolphs have helped me tremendously over the past few months."

Brooke stuck her microphone in Nick's face. "What do you have to say about that, Nick? You used to be called ruthless. You always wanted to remain anonymous, sort of a silent backer. Since serving on this undertaking with you, I've seen a different Nick Rudolph. Care to tell our viewers what's changed?"

Nick looked at the woman in green beside him, his eyes locking with hers. "A lot of things, but mostly, my attitude. Now, if you'll excuse us—"

With that, he urged Myla to keep moving. "I've had enough of reporters for one night."

Myla glanced back at him, thinking maybe she'd figured out the reason for his dark mood. "She's right, though, isn't she? You did want to remain anonymous before."

Nick shot her a frustrated look, tugging her close in the crowded room. "Yeah, right. Well, not anymore. I'm right here in the spotlight tonight, and involved in every aspect of this new organization."

Aggravated with his sarcasm, she said, "Well, why do you look so miserable?"

"Because I'd rather be somewhere else, alone with you." His eyes blazing, he said, "I miss you, Myla. I prayed for patience, but it isn't working."

She couldn't help her smile, and the wave of relief that washed over her. "I can tell."

"I want you back," he said just as the crowd shifted, pushing them together. He stared down at her, longing to tell her what was in his heart. But he'd promised to give her time. So he could only hold her close, taking in the fresh scent of her upswept hair, taking in the emerald green of her shining eyes as he fell in love with her all over again. "I want…to kiss you again."

Before Myla could tell him that she wanted to be back with him, and that she wanted him to kiss her again, Brooke Alexander appeared by his side. "Oh, Nick, I had one more question."

Groaning, Nick tried to be polite to the smug woman. "Look, Brooke, I don't have any comments to contribute to your newscast. I just want to enjoy this evening."

"Oh, don't be so modest," Brooke insisted. "Everyone knows you spearheaded this organization, but do they know the real story?"

"What story?" he asked warily, his gaze shifting from Myla to the jeering reporter.

The reporter leaned forward, her tone conspiring as she covered her mike. "From what my sources tell me, you had a lot more to do with Mrs. Howell getting this first house than anyone is aware of. Rumor has it your relationship with her involves more than just a neighborly concern."

Nick tried to pry Myla away, but she stood watching the reporter's face expectantly. The woman was obviously implying she knew about their relationship, Myla decided. Well, she wouldn't let Nick take the heat, and she certainly wouldn't let this woman turn their relationship into something other than what it was, just for the sake of sensationalism.

"It does involve more," she said, deciding honesty would be the best policy. She'd tell this nosy newshound the facts about what a good man Nick Rudolph really was. "It involves people caring about the community; it involves a kind, decent man helping someone in need. I think your viewers should know that, Brooke."

Sensing she had a story, Brooke Alexander pressed closer. "Anything else you'd like my viewers to know, Mrs. Howell?"

Nick tried to shove Myla away from the pesky woman. "No, she doesn't have anything else to say. As you know from serving on this committee, Mrs. Howell had to be approved by the *entire* board of directors in order to receive her house. I actually had very little to do with their decision to finance her house."

That didn't stop the reporter. "But shouldn't she know *who* donated the house she's living in?"

That stopped Myla in her tracks. "What do you mean?"

Her expression triumphant, Brooke continued, "We all know about the volunteers who've worked on remodeling the house, but we don't have the whole story on the person who actually gave the house to Hope, Faith and Love, Incorporated."

Shoving the mike back at Myla, she asked,

"Wouldn't you like to know who that person is, Mrs. Howell, so you could thank *him* personally and publicly?"

Myla's heart raced as fast as her mind. It didn't take much to figure out what the reporter was hinting at. Nick had bought her house for her. That's why this had been too easy. Why hadn't she seen it before? Maybe because she hadn't wanted to?

Before she could comment, Nick tugged her through the crowd. "Just keep walking."

"What was that all about?" she asked. "Or should I tell you? When he didn't turn around, she said, "You *gave* me that house, didn't you?"

Nick looked at her as if she'd gone daft, but she saw the truth in his eyes.

"You did. You bought me a house!" Anger spilling forth, she added, "After all that talk about the board's approval and other people being screened, you hand-picked a house for me, then you just gave it to me. I didn't get it on my own, after all."

Dragging her close, Nick decided it was time to put all of his thoughts into action. "All right, yes! I bought the house—to remodel for you—because I love you."

That declaration stopped her. "Love? You love me?" Even as her heart swelled, she relived the dread that being married to Sonny had brought her. "But you deceived me, Nick. This is downright unethical, just like something Sonny would have pulled."

"I am *not* Sonny," he said, drawing a weary

breath. "And for months now, I've been trying to prove that to you. I wanted you to be happy, Myla, and if that meant letting you go, then—"

"Happy?" She snapped the one word back at him. "How can I be happy knowing the man I love lied to me about something so important?"

Through his embarrassment, Nick saw a ray of hope. She'd said *the man I love*. He'd heard her, and so had half the city. He had witnesses.

All around them, people were staring and whispering, some with smiles on their faces, others with shock registered in their eyes.

"I wasn't deceitful," he insisted. "I didn't lie to you. I just never exactly spelled out the stipulations. All I did was buy a piece of run-down property. As a matter of fact, I bought several. Then I backed off and let the board decide the rest." Wanting to convince her, he said, "There were several applicants, too, but you had the best record. You had two jobs, and you were trying to find a place to live. A lot of the board members remembered you from our famous Christmas party, so they knew you were working on improving your situation.

"The other applicants, while needy, didn't seem as determined as you. One complained about having to work on the house, and the other, well, he took off to another state with some hefty donations he'd stolen from Magnolia House. I'm learning that not everyone is as trustworthy as you, Myla."

"So am I," she retorted, tapping her foot in agitation, her green eyes blazing fire.

"Just try to understand," he said lamely, wishing hard that he'd been honest with her all along. "I just wanted you to have a chance."

"*Everyone* who applied for that house deserved the same chance," she said, her anger calming to a slow boil. "But you bypassed that and gave the house to me."

"No, I did not," he said in defense of his actions. "I simply donated a house to the cause. The board picked you. And me, well…yes, I wanted to help you. I'd already cost you your place at Magnolia House, so I wanted you to have what you most desired."

"I won't live there, not knowing you practically gave it to me."

"I did not give it to you. You still have to pay off the loan," he reminded her, hoping to encourage her to be reasonable. When she kept heading for the door, he added, "I only did it because I love you, Myla. You see, I learned another lesson my father forgot to teach me—the one about having to let something go, in order to prove your love."

"You have a funny way of interpreting that," she said over her shoulder.

Determined, he called after her in a loud booming voice, "Myla, let's stop fighting. We love each other. I need you. And you need me."

Embarrassed and aware of their growing audience, she gave him a scathing look. "No, I don't."

Nick waved a hand in the air, scattering curious, elegantly dressed people left and right. "Yes, you do. I know it. You know it. And now, everyone in Shreveport knows it."

Looking across the room at him, she said, "And they also know that you're still as ruthless as ever. How could I have ever trusted you?"

"Because we love each other."

She ran out the door. Behind him, Nick heard someone clapping. The entire mob chimed in with a hearty round of applause. Turning, he saw Lydia and Grant watching him, along with everybody else in town.

"Bravo!" Lydia called out. "Glad you two finally saw the light. Now go after her. She's still got to make her speech!"

Growling at his sister's unsinkable optimism, he called back, "I think she just did!"

He caught up with her out on the steps facing the river, where a spring breeze teased at her billowing skirt. Inside, the Shreveport Symphony launched into Mozart, while Nick's head buzzed with adrenalin and aggravation.

"Leave me alone," Myla said, her hair whipping in the wind. "I need to think."

Groaning, he jabbed a hand toward her face.

"Myla, think about this—buying the property was the only way I could get things started. Someone had to donate the first house to be renovated. I had the funds to do it, but I knew you'd never agree to me just handing it over to you."

"Yes, you knew!" She faced him squarely, her eyes blazing. "But you did it anyway. Can't you see, Nick, I've lived with deceit and lies and hypocrisy for so long, I just can't tolerate it, even for a good reason, even for someone I—"

"Someone you love?" Nick reached out, pulling a sprig of burnished hair away from her face. "It's scary, isn't it?"

Her eyes widened with wonder. "You're scared, too, right? You've practically told me how scared you are. But you shouldn't have lied to me, Nick. We're supposed to trust each other, remember?"

His heart soaring, he tugged her around. "Of course, I'm scared, and of course, I trust you. It's myself I couldn't trust. Why do you think it took me so long to tell you how I feel? I'm so used to taking action, I forgot to just tell you with words."

She thought about how he'd opened up to her, sitting there on the porch that day. "You told me about your father. Why didn't you tell me what you'd done with the house?"

He shrugged, then looked away, out at the churning waters of the Red River. "You wanted the house. I wanted you to be happy. I guess I'm still working on the part about putting things into God's hands. This wouldn't have backfired on me, if I'd only placed more trust in Him."

"And if I'd put more trust in you," she admitted. Searching his face, Myla took a long, shuddering breath to control her skittish emotions. "We've both been busy trying to control *my* life. I've been as bad as you, not willing to give an inch because I felt I had to show everyone I could do it."

Laughing softly, he urged her to him. "Myla, sweet Myla. I don't want to control you. I just want to spend the rest of my life with you. We can have fun working out the details."

But she still wasn't so sure. "What do you see in me?"

Cupping her face between his hands, Nick searched her eyes. "I'll tell you what I see. I see a strong, beautiful woman who's worked hard to bring herself up out of poverty. I see hope, faith, love…and my own salvation."

She started to cry, then—tears of joy, mixed with tears of pain, as her heart let go of its pride. "Oh, Nick. You planted me a rosebush. That was the sweetest thing. You planted me a rosebush at a house you managed to get for me—just so you could give me the freedom to make my own choice. There is no greater sacrifice than that."

Loving her logic, Nick said, "I had to let you go,

in order to win you back. It was the hardest thing I've ever tried to do. Please tell me I didn't fail completely."

Watching his face, seeing the sincerity and fear playing through his eyes, Myla was touched in that distant, secret spot where she'd stored up her love for him. Nick had the same doubts, had known the same pain and hopelessness she'd once known. But in spite of it all, he'd stood by her and her children. She realized with a burst of joy that neither of them had had a choice in the matter.

It had been in God's hands all along.

As if reading her thoughts, Nick said, "Myla, if I didn't have a dime to offer you, I'd still want to help you, to give you anything to make you happy and secure. I'd never desert you or try to control you. I just want to love you, to spend my life with you, whether it's at my house or yours. Wherever you are—that's my home, Myla. And that's the honest truth."

With that, Myla threw herself in his arms. "We both had something to prove."

Nick hugged her close, relief washing over him. He'd never make the same mistake twice. From here on out, he'd be completely honest with her, and with himself. Starting now.

Letting her go, he bent down on one knee. With the Red River flowing by a few feet away from them, he took her hand in his. "Now that we've settled all of that, I have something to ask you."

Myla's eyes widened while her heart fluttered like the flags flapping in the wind above their heads. "Yes?"

"Okay, I was only going to ask if I could have your cheesecake at dinner."

With both hands, she playfully slapped him on the shoulders. "Oh, you!"

Lifting his head, Nick asked her the real question on his mind. "Will you marry me?"

Tears fell down her cheeks. "Will you stop doing things behind my back in the name of love?"

"Hey, I'm doing the asking here, but yes, I promise to be completely up front with you— always. Now, I repeat, will you marry me?"

"Yes, I'll marry you."

"Do you love me?"

"I do love you."

"That's good, because I love you, too. Let's have pizza at the wedding reception. And a huge, fattening pound cake."

"Okay." She waited for him to stand, then threw herself into his arms for that other kiss they had both been wanting.

Nick enjoyed the kiss, then looked at his watch. "Come on, you have a speech to make."

"Wait." She reached into her clutch purse to pull out her dog-eared copy of the speech she'd prepared. "I don't need any pointers. I know exactly what I want to say."

"And what's that?"

Myla stopped, looking up at him, her eyes filled with tenderness. "I couldn't have done it without hope, faith, and…love."

Nick looked up at the stars twinkling over their heads. "And the greatest of these is love."

"That's right," Myla said, moving up the steps toward the ballroom. "It's all a matter of knowing whom to trust."

Epilogue

"Quite a crowd today," Nick said, his arm wrapped around his wife's slender waist.

"Yes, but we expected that with the holidays so near." Leaning against him, Myla watched as people came and went, Christmas packages tucked underneath their arms, the smell of fresh-baked bread and homemade vegetable soup wafting around them.

"Well, you should be proud. I am." Nick kissed the top of her head, then patted the soft rounding bulge just beginning to show in her stomach. "We have a lot to be thankful for this Christmas."

"Uh-huh." Myla grimaced. "If I can just get through morning sickness."

"Feel bad?"

"No, I feel marvelous, happy and in the Christmas spirit. I can handle a little nausea."

"Yeah, I believe you can handle just about anything. Guess that's why I love you so much." He gave her another peck on the cheek, then let her go. "I've got to get moving. The next group of volunteers is waiting for me to teach them how to build houses. Come on, walk me to the truck."

Myla followed him through the glass double doors of the modest brick building, squinting at the noonday sun running down Line Avenue. After eight months of marriage, she was still very much in love.

And amazed at how blessed her life was now. She'd become partners with Grant, her soon-to-be brother-in-law. Then, keeping that partnership intact, and with Nick's encouragement, she'd opened up this place.

Bread of Life was more than a restaurant, though. It was a unique place where people who didn't have money for food could eat a good hot meal, along with some of the most influential people in the city, who paid donations to keep the nonprofit restaurant open. So far, the response had been tremendous.

Homeless people found hope here, in the form of job offers or assistance with education, or medical needs.

Nick liked to tell people it offered more than a meal, it offered solutions. And he was now a vital part of those solutions, a devout advocate for homeless rights and ways of getting people off the streets and back to productive lives.

He and Myla had even toned down their own lives, remodeling the mansion to make it more childproof and homey, and putting a needy family in the house he'd originally donated for Myla.

Reaching his used work truck where Jessica and Patrick sat waiting, Nick turned now, pulling Myla into the circle of his arms. "Don't work too hard, Mrs. Rudolph. We've got a lot to celebrate this year."

Myla nuzzled his neck, savoring the warmth and security he always offered. "Yes, we certainly do."

"Hey, Mama," Patrick called through the partially open window, "are you sure you're gonna be done here by Christmas?"

"Of course she will," Jessica replied in her proper, big-sister tone. "She's just doing her job first."

Giving her children that endearing look Nick loved so much, Myla nodded to her family. "I promise, I'll be home for Christmas."

Nick looked up to the shimmering winter sky, then smiled at his wife. "This year, we'll *all* be home for Christmas."

* * * * *

Dear Reader,

Homelessness has always been a problem the world over, yet we can never give up hope that it will eventually be solved.

This book has special meaning to me because I've worked with homeless people. I've visited homeless shelters and helped to feed people coming through a soup line. And the one thing I've noticed about homeless human beings is that they don't always know that someone cares about them. Sometimes, they just want to give up.

While Myla's story is part fairy tale and part reality, I know there are women out there who can achieve the same successes she achieves, and there are organizations willing to help these women every step of the way.

It's not easy, but there is a way to break the cycle. I hope my story will inspire some of you to work toward helping the homeless and, in doing so, find nourishment for your own soul.

Until next time, may angels watch over you while you sleep.

Lenora Worth

ONE GOLDEN CHRISTMAS

A man's heart plans his way,
but the Lord directs his steps.

—*Proverbs* 16:9

To my nieces—
Layla Baker and Brittney Smith
With Love Always

Chapter One

Leandra Flanagan didn't know how her life could have changed so completely in just a few days. One day, she'd been a top advertising executive at a major Houston firm, making more money than she'd ever dreamed possible, and the next day, she was back in her hometown of Marshall, Texas, applying for the job of Christmas Pageant Coordinator for the city of Marshall.

She'd come full circle.

And she wasn't too happy about it.

"Ah, now, honey, don't look so glum," her mother, Colleen, told her, a hand on her arm.

That gentle hand was dusted with flour and cinnamon from the batch of Thanksgiving cookies Colleen was making for the church. That gentle hand brought some measure of comfort to Leandra, in spite of her own misgivings.

"Sorry, I was just thinking about the strange turn of events in my life," Leandra said, pivoting away from the kitchen window to help her mother with the leaf and turkey shaped cookies. "I'm just worried, Mama. I never thought I'd wind up back here in Marshall. I still can't believe I let you talk me into coming home."

"'The Lord will give grace and glory,'" Colleen quoted, her smile giving enough grace and glory to make any gloomy soul feel better.

"Mama, I appreciate that, but what I need along with any grace or glory is a good job. I had a good job and I guess I messed up, big time."

Colleen huffed a breath, causing her gray-tinged bob of hair to flutter around her face. "Sounds like you made the right decision to me, a decision based on your own values and not what your boss at that fancy advertising firm expected you to do."

In spite of the pride shining in her mother's eyes, Leandra didn't feel as if she'd made the right choice. But in the end, it had been the only choice she could make. She'd quit a week ago, and at her mother's insistence, had come home for an extended holiday, hoping to work through her turmoil before going back to Houston after the new year.

And now, her mother had gone and gotten the idea that Leandra could "fill in" down at city hall, just for a few short weeks.

"Well, no sense in worrying about it now," she said, spinning away from the long counter where her mother had baked so many batches of cookies over the years. "I guess I'll just go and see what this pageant job is all about, at least earn some money through the holidays and keep myself busy."

"That's my girl," Colleen said, a bright smile centered on her round, rosy face. "Then come on back for lunch. Your brothers will be here and they're all anxious to see you."

"I suppose they are, at that," Leandra replied, grabbing her wool coat and her purse. "They probably can't wait to rub it in—about how I had to come home with my head down—"

"I'll hear none of that kind of talk," Colleen retorted, her words gentle as always, but firm all the same. "Your brothers are proud of you, and glad to have you home, where you belong."

"Oh, all right," Leandra said. "I'll try to pretend that I planned it this way."

Colleen beamed another motherly smile at her. "Maybe you *didn't,* but maybe God *did.*"

As she drove the few blocks to city hall, Leandra had to wonder what her mother had meant by that remark. Why would God in all of His wisdom bring her back to the small-town life she'd always wanted to get away from? Why would God want Leandra Flanagan to wind up back in Marshall?

Her mother would tell her to wait for the answer, that it would come soon enough.

But Leandra was impatient. She didn't want to wait.

"I can't wait for you to get started on this," Chet Reynolds told her an hour later as he shoved a stack of folders in her arms and directed her to a small, cluttered office in the corner of the building. "And first thing, ride out to Nathan Welby's place—it's the big Victorian-style house just out on Highway 80— and hire him on to build the set. He's the best carpenter in town—a single father of three. He works full-time in construction, but he's off for Thanksgiving this week, and he needs the extra cash. Only he's kinda stubborn and prideful, hard to pin down. Can you get right on that for me, Leandra?"

"Am I hired?" Leandra asked, still in a daze. They'd barely conducted a proper interview, mainly because Chet Reynolds had never been one to talk in complete sentences. He just rambled on and on, merging everything together.

"Why, sure." Chet, a tall man who wore sneakers and a Tabasco sauce embossed polo shirt, in spite of the cool temperatures, bobbed his balding head over a skinny neck. "Known your mama and daddy all my life, watched you grow up into a fine, up-standing young woman—that's all the credentials I need. That, and the fact that my last coordinator had her baby three weeks early—won't be able to come back to work until well after Christmas—if she comes back at all. I'm trusting you to do a good job on this, Leandra."

So, just like that, Leandra had a new job. A temporary job, but a job all the same, based solely on her parents' good name and a little baby's early birth. The hiring process had sure been different from all the interviews and questionnaires she'd had to endure to land her position back in Houston. And the salary—well, that was almost nonexistent, compared to what she'd been making in the big city.

Good thing she had a substantial savings account and some stocks and bonds to fall back on. Listening to her father's advice, she'd built herself quite a little nest egg. And a good life as a *happily* single city woman who'd enjoyed pouring all of herself into her work. That is, until she'd gotten involved with the wrong man.

But that life is over now, she told herself as she squeezed behind the battered oak desk in the pint-size office.

"Must have been a closet in another life," she mumbled to herself. Dropping the folders on the dusty desk, she sank down in the mismatched squeaky wooden swivel chair. She hadn't seen furniture such as this since—

Since she'd left Marshall five years ago.

Putting the size and spaciousness of her plush, modern office in a high-rise building in downtown Houston out of her mind, Leandra spent the next two hours organizing the haphazard plans for the pageant. It was going to be a combination of songs and stories that would tell the miracle of Christ's birth, complete with a live manger scene—which meant that someone had to start building the elaborate set right away.

She couldn't put together a Christmas pageant without a proper set, and the entire production was already weeks behind schedule, and now with just a short month until Christmas, too. Well, first things first. She called her mother to say she'd have to miss lunch after all.

She was back at work and she aimed to get the job done. Her parents had taught her that no matter your job, you did the work with enthusiasm and integrity, and she needed this distraction right now to take her mind off her own worries. She would put on the best Christmas pageant this city had ever seen.

With that thought in mind, she hopped up to go find Nathan Welby.

It was the biggest, most run-down house she'd ever seen. And Nathan Welby was one of the tallest, most intriguing men she'd ever seen.

The house must have been lovely at one time, a

real Victorian treasure. But now, it looked more like a gingerbread house that had been half-eaten by hungry children, a total wreck of broken shingles and torn shutters and peeling paint. An adorable wreck that begged to be restored to its former beauty.

And the man—was this the best carpenter in town? Someone who lived in such a sad place as this? He was sure enough a big man, a giant who right now was wielding a very big ax and using it to slice thick chunks of wood into kindling.

"Chet, you've sent me to find Paul Bunyan," Leandra muttered to herself. "Hello," she called for the third time.

The big man chopping wood in the backyard had to have heard her. But he did have his back— a broad, muscled back—turned away from her. And there was lots of noise coming from inside the dilapidated house.

Leandra had shuddered at all that noise. It sounded too familiar. Being the baby and only girl of a large family had taught her that she didn't want a repeat in her own adult life. She had no desire to have a large family and she certainly had no desire to stay at home and bake cookies and cart kids around to various events the way her mother had.

That was why her relationship with William Myers had seemed so perfect. No commitments beyond companionship, no demands about marriage and a family. William hadn't wanted any of those things, either. But he'd certainly asked for a lot more than she'd been willing to give in the end.

But she refused to dwell on *that* mistake now.

No, Leandra thought as she waited impatiently for the man to turn around and acknowledge her. She only wanted to get back to her own plans, back to her civil, peaceful, *working* life in the big city, minus William's domineering influence.

And yet, here she stood, out in the middle of nowhere, about to hire a man she'd never met as carpenter for a one-month project.

Why had she ever let her mother talk her into taking this job?

She'd knocked on the heavy double doors at the front of the house several times before working her way around back. Music, giggles, screams, dogs barking, cats screeching—had she only imagined this house of horrors, or was it real?

Was he a real man?

He turned then, as if just now realizing someone was calling to him, and Leandra saw that he was very real, indeed.

Real from his golden blond wavy hair to the blue-and-red-plaid flannel shirt he wore, to the faded, torn jeans covering his athletic legs to the muddy hiking boots on his feet.

Real from the intense, wary look centered in his hazel, catlike eyes, eyes that spoke a lot more than any of the other noises coming from this carnival fun-house.

"Hello," she said again on a much more level voice, now that she was standing about ten feet away from him. "I'm Leandra Flanagan, from city hall—"

"I paid the light bill, lady," he said in a distinct East Texas drawl that sounded almost lazy. Dismissing her with a frown, he turned to center the ax over a wide log.

Leandra watched as he lifted his arms in an arc over his head, the ax aimed with calculated precision at its target, and in a flash of muscle and steel, went about his work.

The log split in two like a paper box folding up on itself. A clean split, with hardly any splinters falling from either side.

There was nothing lazy about this man, except that enticing accent.

Leandra swallowed back the shocked awe and justified fear rolling into a lump that felt as dry as that split log in her throat. "No, I'm not here about the light bill," she said, stepping over an old tractor part to get closer. "I'm here because—"

"I paid the gas bill, too." He turned away again, his head down, then reached to heave another log up on the big stump.

Off in the fenced pasture behind him, a beautiful palomino gelding neighed and whinnied, tossing its almond-colored mane and pawing at the dirt, its big eyes following Leandra.

Well, at least the horse had acknowledged her presence.

In spite of her frustration at being ignored, Leandra had to marvel at the sheer strength of the man. And the sheer brawny force surrounding him like an aura. He practically glowed with it, standing there in the fall leaves with the sunshine falling like glistening gold across his face. He was real, all right. A real woodsman, yet he was like someone who'd just stepped out of a fairy tale.

If only she believed in fairy tales.

He's only a man, she reminded herself. But so different from all the men she'd had to deal with in Houston. Refusing to dwell on *that,* she also reminded herself why she was here.

"Mr. Welby? I'm not here for any bill collecting." She waited, extended her hand, saw that he wasn't going to shake it, then dropped it by her side.

From inside the house, a crash sounded, followed by shouting and more dog barking. This caused the horse to prance closer to the fence, obviously hoping to get in on the action.

"'Scuse me," the man said as he dropped the ax and moved to brush past her. Then in his haste, he politely shifted her up out of the way as if she were a twig or a hanging branch.

He stomped up on the porch, opened the paint-chipped back door and bellowed like a lion. "Hush up in there. We've got company out here. Mind your manners, or you'll all three be washing supper dishes well into next week."

Miraculously, the music—a melancholy country tune—stopped in midwhine, the dog stopped barking and the screams tapered off to a few last whimpers of "leave me alone."

Even the big horse stopped his pawing and stood staring, almost as if he were posing for a perfect autumn picture, complete with a weathered gray barn in the background.

Then silence.

Silence over the golden, leaf-scattered woods surrounding the house. Silence as the November sunshine sent a warming ray down on Leandra's already hot cheeks. Silence as Nathan Welby turned around and stared down at her, his eyes still that wary shade of brown-green, his mouth—such an interesting mouth—twisted in a wry, questioning tightness that almost passed for a smile.

Silence.

"You were saying?"

Leandra realized she'd been staring. "Oh, I'm sorry," she began, then because she was at a disadvantage, having to look up at him, she took a step up onto the long, wraparound porch.

Only to fall through a rotted floorboard.

Only to be caught up by two strong hands, brought up by two strong arms, like a rag doll being lifted by a giant.

Only to find herself face-to-face—when she lifted her head about three inches—with those incredible ever-changing eyes again.

He settled her onto a rickety old wicker chair on the porch beside him, then kneeled down in front of her, his expression etched with a sweet concern, his long straight nose and wide full mouth giving him a princely quality. "I've been meaning to fix that. Are you hurt?"

Leandra brushed at her dark tights and pencil straight wool skirt. "No, I'm fine. Just a scratch, maybe."

His eyes followed the length of her leg, then he leaned over for a closer look. "Did it snag your hose?"

Clearly flustered, Leandra rubbed the burning spot on her calf muscle again. "No, really. I'm fine. Old. I mean the tights are old. It doesn't matter."

"Okay," he said, his gaze still on her leg. Then his glance shifted to her face and the lazy, easy-moving accent was back, along with the wry smile. "Now, what can I do for you?"

She at least now had his full attention. It was very disconcerting, the way he stared straight into her eyes, like a great cat about to pounce on its prey.

She brushed her suddenly sweaty palms across

the tail of her tailored suit jacket, pushed at her chin-length curly brown tresses. "Well, I've just been hired as the Christmas pageant coordinator— for the city, you know—to coincide with the Marshall Christmas Festival. The pageant will be held at the civic center right across from the First Church—the big one downtown. The church sponsors the event."

Nathan Welby stood up then, crossed his arms over his broad chest and rocked back on the heels of his worn boots as he stared down at her. "Okay, and what's that got to do with me?"

She was at a disadvantage again, having to look up at him. And with the rich autumn sunshine streaming behind him like that—

She squinted, swallowed again. "I want—that is—the city wants *you* to build a new set. I've been told you're the best carpenter around here. I mean, I know you're busy, but if you could find the time, we'd pay you."

He kept rocking, his eyes never leaving her face, his whole countenance still and watchful, as if he were on full alert.

At first, Leandra thought maybe he didn't understand. She was about to explain all over again when a little girl with blond hair falling in ripples down to her waist came rushing out onto the porch, her eyes bright, her hands held together as if in prayer as she gazed up at Leandra.

"Are you gonna be my new mommy?"

Completely confused, Leandra could only form a smile and stare down at the beautiful, chocolate-milk-stained child. "I—"

"Brittney," Nathan said, taking the child up in his arms to wipe her face with his flannel sleeve, "this nice lady is Miss Flanagan from city hall, and she came to offer me a job. I don't think she's in the market for any mommying."

He gave Leandra an apologetic, embarrassed look, a kind of sadness coloring his eyes to deep bronze. As he held his daughter with one strong arm, he tugged at the gathered skirts of her blue denim jumper with his free hand.

The child, as if sensing that sadness, kissed her father on the cheek then laid her head against the curve of his neck, causing something inside Leandra's heart to shift and melt.

Then the little girl's next words, whispered with such an innocent hope, made that shift grow into a big hole of longing in Leandra's soul.

"But, I've been praying each and every night since Mamma went away and only just now, Daddy, I asked God to please send me a new mommy, so you wouldn't be sad and grumpy anymore, and so Matt and Layla would quit picking on me so much."

She turned to Leandra then, her big blue eyes, so different from her father's, so open and honest, so sweet and beseeching. "And now, here *you* are. And you're so pretty, too. Isn't she, Daddy?"

Leandra watched as this lumberjack of a man swallowed back the obvious pain she'd seen in his eyes. Giving her a shaky smile, he said in a husky voice, "As pretty as a little lamb, pumpkin."

Leandra's utter confusion and nervous energy turned as golden and warm as the sun at her back. If that statement had come from any other man, she'd have laughed at the hokey, down-home line. But coming from Nathan Welby, said in that lazy drawl and said with such sweet natural sincerity, the remark became something entirely different, and took on an intimate meaning.

A meaning that Leandra did not want to misinterpret.

It was a compliment, said in daddy fashion to appease his daughter. Nothing more.

Apparently pleased with that answer, however, Brittney placed her plump little hands on her father's cheeks and touched her forehead to his, a wide grin on her rounded face. "Isn't she perfect for the job, Daddy?"

Chapter Two

Nathan looked down at his daughter's big blue eyes, so like her mother's, and wished he could feel good about all the hope centered there. Alicia's eyes had always reminded him of the sky over Texas, big and vast and deeply blue. Now, both his Brittney and her older sister, Layla, looked so much like Alicia it hurt him each time he came face-to-face with either of them. And he hated turning away from his own children, but that's exactly what he did sometimes—to hide his pain.

His gaze moved from his daughter to the woman standing in front of him. Leandra Flanagan's bewildered look caused her features to scatter and change like leaves floating through a forest. Yes, that was it. This woman reminded him of autumn—all golden and cool—whereas his Alicia had always reminded him of springtime—refreshing, colorful, blossoming.

Stop it, Nate, he told himself as he shifted his tiny daughter in his arms. Why did he always have to compare every woman who came along to his deceased wife?

Yet, there was something about this particular woman that made her stand out from the crowd. Only, Nate hadn't quite figured out just what it was, exactly.

"I'm sorry," he said now to Leandra. Placing Brittney down on the porch, he rubbed a hand across her wheat-colored curls. "Sugar, go on in the house now and let Daddy talk to the nice lady. I'll be in in a little while to help you with those leaf place mats you're making for next week's Thanksgiving dinner."

"Okay, Daddy, but don't forget what I said." Brittney gave Leandra another pleasant, gap-toothed smile. "You wanna stay for supper?"

The woman's expression went from baffled to downright panic-stricken. Nate watched as her big pecan-colored eyes widened. He could see by the way she was squirming and shifting, she felt uncomfortable with this whole situation. She'd come out here to offer him some much needed extra work, and instead had been asked on the spot to become a mommy to his children.

Something she obviously hadn't expected, or wanted, and probably something she didn't run into every time she conducted business.

Well, he couldn't blame her for being a bit put off. Leandra Flanagan was clearly *all* business, from her spiffy wool tailored suit, to her dark tights to the expensive loafers covering her tiny feet.

But in spite of that aloof, sophisticated air, he liked her hair. It was a curly, chin-length golden-brown that changed color and direction each time she ran a hand through it.

And he kinda liked her lips, too. They were a pure pink and rounded. They fit her square, angular face perfectly.

Too bad she wasn't mommy material. Not that he was looking, anyway.

Wanting, needing to explain, he waited, his heart hurting for his child, for Leandra to answer his daughter's question. To her credit, she handled the embarrassing moment with savvy.

"That's awfully nice of you to ask," she told Brittney. "But I've already missed lunch with my four brothers. I think I'd better go on home for supper."

"You got four brothers?" Brittney held up her hand, showing four fingers. "That's this many."

Leandra laughed then, a genuine laugh that filled the afternoon with a lilting melody. "Yes, that's this many." She raised her own four fingers. "And I'm the baby of the bunch."

"I'm a baby, too," Brittney admitted. "Not a real baby. Just the baby of my family. And I get tired of it, sometimes."

Leandra bent down, her dark hair falling forward in a perfectly even wedge of curls as she came face-to-face with Brittney. "I get tired of it, too. My brothers love to pick on me."

Brittney rolled her big eyes and bobbed her head. "That's 'xactly why I need a new mommy. I get picked on, 'cause I'm the youngest and all. You could…proteck me."

"It's pro*tect*," Nathan corrected, "and I don't think we need to discuss this with Miss Flanagan any more today. Now, scoot. I'll be in in a little while, okay?"

"Oh, okay," Brittney said on an exaggerated breath. "Bye, Miss Flan-again."

Nathan saw the amused expression on Leandra's face, and relaxed a little himself.

"Well, Miss *Flan-again,* bet you weren't expecting all this when you made the drive out here today."

"No, not really," Leandra said, rising to face him, that curtain of hair covering one eye. "Your daughter is precious, Mr. Welby. And I'm flattered that she thinks I'm a good candidate…but—"

"But you aren't the one needing extra work, right? And call me Nate."

She laughed again. "Call me Leandra, and yes, as a matter of fact, I took this job because I did need work."

Her smile was self-deprecating. She looked uncomfortable again, standing there shifting her tiny weight on those fancy leather shoes.

Nathan noticed her lips, her smile all over again. While he enjoyed the attraction, the feeling also brought him a measure of guilt. He hadn't really noticed another woman this much, in this way, since Alicia had died. He couldn't do that to her memory.

Deciding to end this interesting diversion, he indicated the steps. "Care to sit a spell?"

"Sure." She joined him there, her hands pulling at her tight skirt for modesty's sake.

It didn't stop Nathan from admiring her shapely legs, though.

"Leandra, I appreciate the offer, but I'm afraid I'm going to have to turn you down on this job."

"Why?"

Her gaze locked with his, and again, he felt as if he were lost in a November forest full of sunshine and leaves and cool waters.

Before he could answer, three blond-haired children and a reddish-blond-coated, shaggy dog came crashing out of the door to fall all around them on the old, rickety steps.

"'Cause Daddy swore he'd never set foot in a church again after Mama died."

"Matt, that's enough."

Leandra heard the pain and anger in Nathan Welby's words, but she also heard the gentleness in the reprimand to his son, too.

Watching as the beautiful Irish setter roamed the

backyard and barked with joy at falling leaves, she wondered what she had walked in on.

This family had obviously suffered a great loss. His wife. Their mother. No wonder a sense of gloominess shadowed this old house.

"I'm sorry…about your wife," she said, hoping she wouldn't add to their discomfort.

Nathan glanced at the children. "You three go finish raking those leaves by the big oak, all right?"

"But Daddy—"

"Go on, Matt. And don't throw leaves at your sisters."

Reluctantly, the three overly-interested children trudged down the steps.

Nathan turned back to Leandra, his voice low. "Thank you." He looked away then. "She died three years ago, in a plane crash." His shrug said it all. "I guess I've got some reckoning to do. I haven't quite gotten over it."

Leandra's heart slammed against her chest and the gasp was out of her mouth before she could stop it. "How awful."

Then, the silence again.

But not for long. The three little ones were back in a flash, chasing the big dog right back up onto the porch, their eyes and ears set on listening.

Nathan didn't fuss at them this time. He seemed lost somewhere else, completely unaware his children had stopped their chores.

Not knowing what to say, Leandra got up to leave. "Well, I guess I'd better be going. I'm so sorry I bothered you—"

"Wait," Nathan said, his big hand on her arm. "I'd like to clarify that statement, if you don't mind." Sending a fatherly glare to his three children, he added, "And if certain among us could remain quiet and use their manners and quit eavesdropping, I'd highly appreciate it."

"But we want you to take the job, Daddy," the older girl told him, her arms wrapped across her chest in classic teenage rebellion mode. "You need to get involved again."

"Yeah," Brittney added, hopping up to twirl around. "And we figured we could help out, too, so you won't be so scared about going back to church."

"How's that?" Nathan asked, a certain fear centered in his golden eyes.

Leandra knew his fear wasn't that of a coward, but of a father who was afraid to hear what his children might have decided behind his back, a man afraid of his own emotions, his own sense of unspeakable loss.

"I want to be the angel," Brittney said, flapping her arms. "Don't you think I'd make the bestest angel, Miz Flan-again?"

Her mind clicking, Leandra saw the opportunity presenting itself to her. If she hired on the children, the father was sure to follow, regardless of his aversion to churches.

And a child shall lead them.

"You know, we do happen to have an opening for an angel," she said. "But have you had any experience?"

Brittney scrunched up her pert nose. "Once, when it snowed, I made angels in the snow with my hands and legs. Does that count—'cause it hardly ever snows here—and I don't get much chance to do that."

Leandra made a point of placing a finger to her jaw, as if she were deep in thought, although there was no earthly way she could have turned down this little girl. "I do believe that counts. If you've made snow angels, then you know all about the importance of this job. When can you start practice?"

"You mean I'm hired?"

"You're hired," Leandra said, extending a hand to seal the agreement.

"I'll be there whenever you say," Brittney replied, her big eyes shining, her small, slightly sticky hand pumping Leandra's. "I'm going inside to practice angel stuff right now."

"Wait a minute—" Nate said, holding up a hand.

"But, Daddy, you can't say no," the older girl told him. "And I want to sing." She looked at Leandra with the same big blue eyes as Brittney's, although hers held that tad of attitude that just naturally came with being an adolescent. "I've sung some in the youth choir at church anyway, and they said they were looking for people for the Christmas pageant. I could help out there." She shrugged, just to show it was no big deal to her either way.

"Another experienced applicant," Leandra said, slapping a hand to her side. "We do need all the voices we can get for all those wonderful traditional Christmas songs. I'll let you know when we start rehearsal. And…I didn't get your name."

"Layla," the girl said, her eyes wary in spite of the tiny smile on her freckled face, her standoffish attitude breaking down a little.

"It's nice to meet you, Layla," Leandra said. "And I appreciate your offer to help."

"What about me?" Matt said.

He had white-blond hair and even bigger blue eyes than his sisters. And an impish quality that made Leandra think of her own brothers. He was probably walking trouble, but how could she refuse those big, questioning eyes and those cute dimples?

"What about *you?*" she asked, squinting as she leaned over to study him closely. "What do you think you're qualified to do?"

"I guess I could be a shepherd," he offered, his hands jutting out from his hips in a businesslike shift. "I helped Daddy round up some cows once that had strayed over onto our property from Mr. Tuttle's land. And I was only around seven at the time."

"How old are you now?" Leandra asked, caught up in wanting these children to be a part of her pageant.

"Ten. Is that old enough?" He asked it with such sweet conviction that Leandra knew she'd just lost her heart forever.

"As a matter of fact, I need a ten-year-old shepherd," she told him. Then she shook his hand, too. "You'll have an important job, you understand—watching your flock by night and all of that."

"I know," he replied. Then he rubbed the fingers of one hand with his other hand in a nervous gesture. "But I might need help with my costume. Our mom always made that kind of stuff."

Leandra swallowed back the sorrow she felt for this lovely family. "We'll find someone to help with that, I'm sure."

Having settled their immediate futures, Layla and Matt turned to go back in the house with Brittney. At the door, Layla whirled to her father, her long straight hair flying out behind her.

"Will you help, too, Daddy? Please?"

Nathan let loose a long sigh. "I need to talk to Miss Flanagan now, honey." When his daughter just stood there, her eyes sending him a beseeching look, he hastily added, "Oh, all right. I'll think about it."

That seemed to satisfy the teenager. She smiled and went inside the house. Then Leandra and Nathan heard a loud "Yes," followed by laughter and clapping.

"I didn't get to interview the dog," Leandra

said by way of cutting through the tension centered on the porch.

Nathan shot her a wry smile, then lifted his head toward the Irish setter pacing the yard again. "Oh, and I guess you just happen to have a spot for that big mutt, too. Maybe dress that setter up as a camel or a cow? Might as well throw in the horse—he'd fit right in in a stable."

"You're not pleased with this, are you?"

He dropped his hands down on his faded jeans. "Now what gave you that impression?"

"Oh, I guess the glare in your eyes and the dark, brooding frown creasing your forehead."

"Well, no man likes to be ambushed and side-swiped all at the same time."

"I didn't ambush you. I simply asked your children to be a part of the Christmas pageant."

He scoffed, held his hands to his hips, and looked out over the cluttered yard. "More like, they told you exactly what they wanted and you fell for it, right off the bat."

"Sounds like you've had experience in that area yourself."

He grinned then, and took her breath to a new level. She liked the way the skin around his eyes crinkled up when he smiled. He had a beautiful smile.

"I've had lots of experience being railroaded by those three, that's for sure." Then he turned serious. "It's just hard, saying no to them since—"

"Since their mother died. Nate, I'm so sorry. It must have—must still be—so hard for all of you."

"We have our good days and our bad days," he said. Then he motioned for her to follow him out into the yard.

"She loved this place. We'd just bought it, been here about three months, when she died."

"That's terrible."

"Yeah, terrible. Just like this place. I've been meaning to go ahead and fix it up, but my heart's just not in it."

"It's a lovely old house," Leandra said, her gaze shifting over the peeling paint and fancy fretwork. "It could be turned into a showplace."

"Maybe."

"Nate, if you don't mind me asking—how did it happen?"

"The plane crash, you mean?"

She nodded.

The silence stretched between them again in a slow-moving arc much like the sun stretching over the sky to the west. The air felt chilly after the wind picked up.

He looked out over the pasture, his gaze following the prancing horse as the animal chased along the fence beside the Irish setter. "She was going to visit her folks back in Kentucky. She hadn't been home since…since we got married."

Leandra sensed a deep regret in him, and a

need to have this burden lifted from his shoulders. But she wouldn't force him to talk about something so personal.

And yet, he did just that.

"They didn't want her to marry me. I was dirt-poor and from Texas, after all. She came from a rich family—money, horses, all that bluegrass class. That's how we met—she came here with her father to buy a horse from this rancher I was working for and—"

"You fell in love with her."

"Yeah, from the beginning. But I was beneath her and I knew it. So did her folks. They gave her an ultimatum—them or me." He stopped, sighed, ran a hand through his golden locks. "She chose me."

He said those words with awe, a catch in his throat that only brought a painful roughness to Leandra's own throat.

"She hadn't planned on ever going back there, but her mother got real sick. They kinda patched things up and she was so happy. Couldn't wait to get home and tell me all about how her parents finally wanted to meet their grandchildren."

Leandra wanted him to stop now. She didn't think she could bear to hear the rest of this tragic story.

But then, Nathan needed to tell it.

"They sent her home on their private plane—

can you believe that—and it crashed in a bad rainstorm just before landing at the Longview Airport. Killed her and the pilot. We waited and waited at that airport, me and the kids, but she never came home."

And he was still waiting, Leandra told herself as she clutched her arms to her chest to stop her own tears from forming.

"I am so sorry, Nate." She placed a hand on his arm. "I didn't mean to dredge up all this. I'm sure you have your reasons for not wanting to be involved in church, but I'd love to have you working on this project with me."

When he didn't answer, she turned to go. To leave him to his grief and his memories. She wished she'd never come here. But then, the children needed to be involved, needed to have the support and love of a church family.

Maybe that was why God had sent her. Not for Nate. But for the children.

"Hey, Leandra?"

She liked the way he said her name in that long, tall, Texas drawl.

She turned at the corner of the house. "Yes?"

"When do you want me to start?"

"You mean, you'll do it? You'll build the set for me?"

He nodded. "Yes, for you…and for my children."

She stood there, her heart breaking for him. He

didn't want to do this, but he loved his children enough to try.

"What was your wife's name?"

"Alicia," he said, again with that reverence.

"Alicia would be proud of you."

He nodded again, then dropped his head.

That beautiful golden silence moved between them, bonding them like a cord of silky threads.

"And what's the dog's name?"

"Mutt," he replied with a shrug and a lopsided grin.

She chuckled then. "I think I have a spot for Mutt, too."

"The horse is named Honeyboy," he told her. "I bought it for her."

She didn't have to ask to know he was referring to his wife.

"About this job—" he began.

Afraid he'd already changed his mind, she said, "You can start first thing in the morning, if that's okay."

"I'll be there."

And she knew he would.

Chapter Three

"I met the most incredible family today," Leandra announced at supper that night.

It was good to be sitting here, safe and warm in her parents' rambling home nestled in the heart of one of Marshall's oldest neighborhoods. This big oak dining table had been the center of many such family meals, and now with two of her brothers married and fathers themselves, more chairs had been added to the long table.

The noise level had increased through the years, too.

"What did you say, suga'?" Her father, Howard, asked, cupping a hand to his ear, the twinkle in his brown eyes belying the seriousness of his expression.

Leandra threw up her hands. How could anyone carry on a civilized conversation in such utter chaos? It had been this way all her life, that is until she had escaped to the quiet sanctuary of her own tiny apartment far away in the big city.

Looking around now, however, she realized she had actually missed the big family gatherings. She'd missed her brothers, in spite of their opinionated observations, and she'd especially missed her parents.

Her oldest brother, Jack, was busy cleaning up the spilled peas his two-year-old son, Corey, had just dumped on her mother's prized braided dining room rug. His wife, Margaret, was soothing their five-year-old Philip's hurt feelings at losing out on one of the drumsticks from the big batch of fried chicken her mother had prepared for the clan.

Michael, Leandra's next-to-the-oldest brother, was holding his six-month-old daughter Carissa, trying to burp her and eat his own meal at the same time, while his wife, Kim, passed food to their four-year-old, Cameron, and worked on crowd control so Colleen could rest for a few precious minutes.

Mark, the brooding professor who taught at Panola College and broke hearts on a regular basis, was actually reading a book and eating a chicken leg at the same time. No wonder the man was still single!

And Richard, only two years older than Leandra, was smiling over at her, his brown eyes assessing the entire situation much in the same way he watched over his customers at the old-fashioned general store he ran just outside of town.

Everyone seemed to be talking at once, except Richard.

"Tell us about this interesting family, Sis," he said now, his hand perched on a big, flaky biscuit.

Surprised that anyone had heard her, Leandra thankfully turned to her handsome brother. Richard had always looked out for her. "The Welby family," she said by way of an explanation. "I was out there today, and I hired Nathan Welby to build the set for the Christmas pageant."

"Oh, really," Colleen said, her gaze centered on one of Jack's noisy little sprites. Shoveling mashed potatoes onto little Philip's cartoon-character plastic plate, Leandra's mother didn't seem to be aware of anyone around her.

But Leandra knew her mother better than that. Colleen never missed a beat. She was almost super-human in her maternal instincts and her ability to keep everything organized and together, in spite of the chaos surrounding her large brood. Leandra could never understand how her mother did it, nor why Colleen seemed so content to be a homemaker.

"Yes," Leandra replied in a loud voice, so her mother, at least, could hear her. "Mr. Welby— Nate—agreed to build a whole new set, and I signed all three children up for parts in the actual program."

"You sure had a productive day," Howard said, his gentle gaze moving down the table toward his only daughter. "Nate is a good man. He's had some bad times, but he's a hard worker. I talk to him in the bank every time he comes in."

"Which is every time he needs to borrow more money," Jack, who was also a banker like his father, stated in his businesslike way. "I don't see how the man keeps up, what with the mortgage on that dilapidated house, those three kids, and with that huge animal to feed."

"Are you talking about the dog or the horse?" Leandra said, irritated at her brother's high-handed attitude.

Because he'd come from a good, comfortably blessed family, Jack had always held the notion that he was somebody special. And he looked down on those who didn't meet his own high standards.

"Both," he said, smug in his little corner of the dining table, his pert, pretty dark-haired wife smiling beside him. "The man needs to find a better-paying job and he needs to learn to control those three brats of his. Are you sure you should have invited them to be a part of the program, Lea? They can be very disruptive at times."

"Yes," Margaret, who always, always agreed with her husband, added, her nose lifted in the air. "I taught that middle one—Matt—in Sunday school last year—that is when he showed up. He was loud and unruly, not well-behaved at all. That man needs a firm hand with that little boy or there will be trouble down the road."

Leandra's guard went up. Bristling, she said in a level voice, "Matt seemed perfectly polite to me, considering the sad circumstances. I just think the Welby children need some positive attention. The little one, Brittney, is going to be an angel. Layla will be singing in the choir, and Matt will be a shepherd."

"You'll regret that choice, I'm sure," Margaret said through a sniff. "He'll knock down the entire set."

"I don't think I'll regret anything," Leandra snapped back. "I think I can control a ten-year-old." When Margaret gave her a look of doubt, she sweetly added, "I did grow up with these four, after all."

"But you aren't married, and you can't possibly know how to deal with children," Margaret stated, her smile of maternal wisdom extending across the table to her own precocious five-year-old who'd insisted he wanted to sit by his nana.

The cutting remark hurt Leandra, but only for a minute. She'd long ago learned to ignore her sister-in-law's pointed remarks regarding her own often-voiced choice to remain single and motherless for as long as possible.

"You're right there, Margaret," Leandra replied in a calm, firm tone. "But I've watched Jack and you with your own children and I think I can safely say I've learned so much from your…uh…parenting skills."

As if to help his aunt make her point, little Philip picked up his spoon and hurled it over the table like a boomerang. It landed, soggy mashed potatoes and all, right in his mother's lap.

Margaret instantly hopped up, an enraged expression causing her porcelain skin to turn a mottled pink. "Young man, that was totally uncalled for. Philip, that is unacceptable behavior. Do you hear me?"

Philip smiled, stuck out his tongue, then looked up at his grandmother with such an angelic expression that Colleen had to turn away to hide her own amused smile.

"Tell Mama you're sorry, sugarpie," Colleen coaxed in a grandmother voice. Then in a stern, firm tone, she added, "Philip, we don't throw spoons in Nana's house, okay?"

The boy looked sheepish, then bobbed his curly head. "'Kay, Nana. Sowee."

His sincerity was sorely questioned as he proceeded to mash his peas into a green, slimy blob with his balled-up fist.

Margaret turned to Jack. "Would you please talk to your son?"

Jack tried, really he did. "Philip, behave and eat your food, or I'll have to move you over here between your mother and me for a time-out."

That brought a pout and a gut-wrenching sob to Philip's upturned face.

"Now look," Margaret huffed. "You've made him cry."

Colleen soothed her grandson's feelings, and brought him under control, too. "Philip, we don't want a time-out, do we?"

"Nope."

"Then please finish your meal, so we can all have some apple pie."

The little sandy-haired boy turned demure as his grandmother smiled over at him.

"As you were saying," Mark called to Leandra, his book still open by his plate, his quiet, intelligent gaze falling across his sister's face.

Mark was so good at that, listening quietly, observing, taking everything in, even with his nose buried in a book.

"Oh, just that the Welby family is very interesting," Leandra continued, hoping Jack and Margaret would just stay quiet and let her enjoy what was left of her dinner. "And it's just so sad—about his wife, I mean."

Mark nodded, then pushed his tiny glasses up on his nose. "Alicia was a beautiful woman. And well-educated, too. We often talked about literature when I'd see her at church functions. She loved poetry."

Leandra let that tidbit of information settle in. So Nathan had married a beautiful—Leandra couldn't imagine her any other way—wealthy, educated woman who liked to read sonnets. Alicia was beginning to take saint status in Leandra's mind.

"How'd she ever hook up with the likes of Nate Welby, then?" Michael, who'd been quiet, finally asked.

"She loved him," Kim, his wife, said, poking him in the ribs. "It was a fairy-tale romance, from everything I've heard. She was lovely and he's sure a handsome man. They were a striking couple."

Yep, that's exactly the way I see it, Leandra thought. Only now, Nathan was suffering too much to see his own potential, or that of his children. He'd let everything come to a standstill. His faith was in ruins, just like his house. Leandra wondered how someone could ever get through that kind of grief.

"Well, it sure had a tragic ending," Jack said in his superior way. "They were ill-suited from the beginning. I knew that the day they moved to town."

Ignoring him and the hurt in her own heart, Leandra asked, "When exactly did they move here? I never knew them before and I don't recall running into any of them on visits home."

She certainly would have remembered Nate, at least.

Colleen pushed her plate away and leaned back in her chair. "They came here a little over three years ago, I guess. Apparently, from what I've heard at church, Alicia Welby took one look at that old house and had to have it."

"And Nate tried to move heaven and earth to get it for her," Howard added. "They came from Paris."

"Paris, France?" Margaret asked, her eyes brightening at the prospect. Margaret loved sophisticated people, and fancied herself one, from what Leandra could tell.

"No, silly," her husband retorted, rolling his eyes. "Paris, Texas."

"Oh." Margaret looked properly chastised, then shrugged. "Well, I didn't know."

"An honest mistake," Colleen said, amusement coloring her merry eyes. "Nate worked on a big ranch near Paris, dear. But he took a construction job here, hoping to make more money. That's when they bought the house."

"A few weeks after he started his job, though, Alicia was killed in a plane crash," Howard explained. "And then, to top things off, her mother died—whether from bad health or heartbreak over the loss of her daughter—who knows. But I hear Alicia's father doesn't have anything to do with Nate or the children." Howard shook his head, then glanced at Leandra. "Such a tragedy, but Nate put his nose to the grindstone and now he's made a name for himself around here. People respect Nathan Welby. They know they can count on him to get the job done."

"He told me about his wife's death," Leandra said in a quiet voice. "But he didn't mention Alicia's mother, or her death. I guess he and the grandfather don't get along, since he didn't say much about that either." She paused, then looked down at her plate. "I think he works so much to take his mind off his wife's death, maybe."

The whole room quieted after that. It was certainly a sad situation. Even Jack looked solemn for a minute.

"I'm glad you hired him, Lea," her father said as he got up from the table. "Nate is a proud man, he's just lost his way, can't shake his grief. Maybe having something spiritual to occupy him will help." Then Howard turned to Colleen, "Good dinner, honey. How 'bout me and these boys do the dishes?"

"Oh, how thoughtful," Colleen replied, her gaze locking with her husband's. "You don't mind, do you, boys?"

Amid groans and whines, came the reply, "No, Mama."

Leandra had to smile. The love her parents shared was so obvious and abiding, it practically glowed. She loved how with a sweet smile and a calm, level voice they got their children to do things. And she loved the way they still called their grown sons boys. It was an endearing trait that somehow brought tears to her eyes.

She had to wonder what was going on right now at the Welby household. Was little Brittney vying for her father's attention? Was beautiful Layla pouting in her room? Was Matt getting into trouble? Was Mutt curled up underneath the dining table?

Would they have someone to say their prayers with them, to hug them good-night and tuck them in to bed?

Leandra hoped so, and then promptly told herself to quit worrying about the Welbys.

Looking around, she realized in spite of the noise and disorganization of a Flanagan family dinner, she loved her family and enjoyed being home with them, even if it was for just a short time. After the holidays, she'd have to head back to Houston, hopefully with another high-paying job lined up, thanks to her contacts there who had supported her decision to leave Myers Advertising.

After Christmas.

After she'd organized this grand production.

After she'd spent well over a month working side by side with Nathan Welby and his three lovely, slightly manipulative children.

Well, at least her time here wouldn't be dull or boring. She'd been worried that it would be hard to get over what had happened with William, hard to settle into small-town life again. But today had been filled with excitement from the get-go. Now, she didn't think she'd have time to dwell on the mistakes of her recent past.

Being anywhere near Nate Welby would cure that particular malady, she was sure. The man caused her heart to jump and her palms to become sweaty, for some strange reason. And she had to admit, William had never done that for her. He'd been a comfortable convenience, at the most.

Nate was anything but comfortable or convenient.

Probably because he was just so very different from any man she'd ever encountered. And probably because she was feeling such a sweet sympathy for his plight.

Just thinking about him, however, made her kind of tingly inside. Even now, hours after she'd left him standing by the fence watching his beautiful horse, his big hand centered on Mutt's shaggy back, Leandra felt a soft, golden bond with Nathan Welby. The feeling wasn't unpleasant, not at all.

Leandra looked up then to find her mother regarding her with a calculated little smile.

And silently hoped that her all-knowing mother hadn't read anything into this new development, or the dreamy expression that Leandra was sure had been plastered across her face.

He wouldn't get his hopes up.

Nate sat in the overstuffed recliner in the darkened parlor of the rambling old house, Mutt sleeping peacefully at his feet, and wondered if his luck was about to change.

He had lots to do between now and Christmas, at least. An extra job would mean even more time away from the children, but then they were used to his long hours. But he liked to keep busy, he reminded himself. He had calls every week for carpentry work all over East Texas, and he was next in line to be promoted to construction foreman at work. He liked to work until he was too tired to think, so he'd hired on with a construction crew that sent him all over, sometimes here, sometimes over across the line in Louisiana. But he didn't like to leave the children for too long, so he didn't take anything farther than driving distance.

But there was never enough distance between him and the emptiness he felt as he sat here each night, remembering.

Yet, he didn't take any jobs that would cause him to have to move away from this house.

Because he felt so close to Alicia here.

And because his children loved their home.

Since Alicia's death, they'd settled into a routine of just getting through each day, making ends meet, making sure they took care of each other. Now, Nate knew that grief-dulled routine needed to change.

Layla helped him out with the younger ones, but she was at that age where a girl really needed a mother.

And Matt, bless his heart.

Matt still missed his mother, still cried out for her in his sleep, even though he tried so hard to be a little man.

And little Brittney always seemed lost in a child's world of make-believe, happy and chattering and content, too young to understand or notice her father's pain, or express her own.

Now, Brittney had announced that she'd been praying for God to send her a new mommy. And she'd decided Leandra Flanagan was the one for the job.

Why hadn't he noticed that his children were hurting just as much as he was?

Maybe because he'd made it a point to always find something to occupy his time. Maybe because he buried his own sorrows in his woodworking hobby out in the barn. Maybe because he just couldn't bring himself to think about it.

Nate felt the tears pricking at his tired eyes, and swiped a hand across the day-old beard stubble edging his face. He didn't know whether to laugh or cry.

Lord, he'd cried so many nights, sitting here in front of an empty fireplace, waiting, watching, silently screaming his wrath at God.

He was tired of the burden, the weight of his grief.

And yet, he couldn't let it go just yet. He was selfish that way. He wanted to blame God a little bit longer. It helped to ease his own guilt.

Thinking back over the day, he remembered Leandra. She was a pretty woman. Petite and tiny-framed, delicate, but so precise.

So different from Alicia.

Why did Brittney think a businesswoman, who obviously didn't have time for children, would possibly want to be her mommy?

Was the child just so lonely, so afraid, that she'd picked the first woman to come down the pike to be her mother? Were his children that desperate?

Or, had Leandra Flanagan come along for a reason?

Had God answered his baby daughter's prayers?

Nate sat there in the dark, wondering.

He didn't want to open up his heart to God again. He was still so mad at God, it hurt to even try to form a prayer in his head, let alone voice that prayer.

But, tonight, he somehow found the courage to do just that. For Brittney.

"Lord, help me. Help me to be a good father again."

Because today Nate had realized something so terrible, so tragic, that he felt sick to his stomach with knowing it.

He'd been ignoring his children, simply because they reminded him of their mother so much. He'd been a shell of a father, moving through each day with slow-motion efforts that sometimes took all his strength.

Until today.

Today, an autumn-hued angel had appeared on his doorstep and offered him a chance to find a little salvation. A no-nonsense, full-steam-ahead angel who'd somehow managed to be gentle and understanding with his forlorn, misunderstood children, in spite of her all-business exterior.

Which meant Leandra Flanagan wasn't always all business. The woman had a heart underneath all those layers of sophistication.

No one, since Alicia had died, had ever actually taken the time to just talk to his children. Not even their father.

But Leandra Flanagan had done just that, and had pulled them into something good and noble, simply by asking them to be a part of her show.

Nate wouldn't forget that kind gesture, ever.

"You don't have to hit me on the head, Lord," he said into the darkness. "I hear You loud and clear."

Leandra Flanagan might not be the answer to his prayers nor Brittney's, either, but the woman had sure made him see himself in a different light.

"I'm going to build the set for this pageant, Lord," he said. "And I'm going to do a good job, but I can't make any promises past that."

Nate didn't want God to win him back over. He still had a grudge to nurse, after all. He had to do this, though. He had to go back to church. To pay back Leandra for her kindness.

To make his children proud of him again.

And maybe, to bring a little Christmas spirit to his own grieving heart.

Chapter Four

"Okay, everybody, we need to show some real Christmas spirit here."

Leandra looked around at the group of people gathered in the civic hall to begin rehearsal for *One Golden Christmas*. While the event was being put on by the church, it would be held in the town civic hall to accommodate what they hoped would be a sold-out performance on Christmas Eve.

Smiling, she continued to explain how things would go. "I'm just here to oversee everything from rehearsals to ticket sales. You have a fabulous director. Mr. Crawford has the script all ready and you each have your assignments. If there are any concerns, please see me later. Now, I'm going to sit back and listen to Mr. Crawford's instructions right along with the rest of you."

Leandra took a seat, then turned toward the

doors at the back of the large building. Where was Nathan Welby?

Glancing at her watch again, she wondered if he'd changed his mind about building the set after all. If he didn't show up, she'd be in serious trouble. The set should have been built months ago, but it seemed as if everyone involved in spearheading this project had procrastinated until the last possible minute. She might wind up having to talk her brothers into helping out.

Well, at least Nathan's children had made it into town. All three were here, along with all the other children who were out of school for the week of Thanksgiving.

The Welby children had apparently hitched a ride with their neighbor, Mr. Tuttle, who was playing Santa Claus. And he looked the spitting image of Father Christmas with his white beard and rounded belly.

Right now, the children were being assigned to an adult coordinator who would oversee their costumes and rehearsal schedules.

Leandra groaned silently when she saw her sister-in-law Margaret taking the Welby children and several others over to one side of the center. Apparently, Margaret had volunteered to help out, since little Philip had a brief appearance in one of the production numbers. Well, she'd better be nice.

After making sure Mr. Crawford didn't need her,

Leandra got up to go outside. Maybe Nathan was already here somewhere. Had she remembered to tell him where to meet her? Since the church was practically across the street from the civic center, she didn't think he'd have a problem finding them.

It was a crisp, fall day. Cars moved down the street at a slow pace, contrasting sharply with the traffic snarls Leandra had sat through on a daily basis back in Houston.

The air smelled fresh and clear. Leandra inhaled deeply, more to calm herself than to enjoy the weather. She was afraid she'd made a terrible mistake in hiring Nathan Welby.

But he'd said he'd be here.

That's when she heard the sound.

It couldn't be possible, of course. But it sure sounded like the clippity-clop of a horse's hooves moving up the street. The sound echoed loudly off the historic old courthouse down the way, then grew louder.

Leandra strained her neck, looking around to see what was making all the noise.

Then she spotted him.

Nathan Welby, riding Honeyboy, coming up the street as if he rode a horse into town every day. Looking just like a cowboy, coming straight in off the range. Looking mighty fine in his battered brown suede cowboy hat and flannel shirt. Of course, he had on jeans and cowboy boots, too.

And there it was again, that golden aura that seemed to permeate everything about the man. Or was it just that each time she saw him, she saw him in streams of brilliant light?

Leandra had to swallow. For a minute, she wondered what it might be like to be swept up on that horse and carried away by Nathan Welby.

Since he was headed right for her, the feeling grew. To defend the sudden overwhelming daydreams whirling like flying leaves around her mind, Leandra wrapped her arms across her midsection and waited with what she hoped was a professional look of disapproval on her face.

Nathan rode right up to the steps, slid off the horse with a natural grace, then tethered Honeyboy to a nearby iron bench before tipping his hat to Leandra.

"Morning."

"Good morning," Leandra replied, amazement fluttering through her heart as she watched him remove his hat and shake out his golden locks. "Do you often ride your horse to work, Mr. Welby?"

"It's Nate, remember," he told her as he stepped forward, one long leg on the step just below her, his hat in his hand. "Sorry I'm late. My truck wouldn't crank. I called old man Tuttle to bring the kids while I tried to get the thing to work."

Leandra nodded, then smiled over at Honeyboy. "Obviously, the truck didn't cooperate."

Nate gave her a slow, lazy grin. "Obviously."

They stood there, silent, for what felt like a long time to Leandra. Since Nate didn't seem in any hurry to converse, she tried to get things rolling. "Well, let me just go in and tell someone where I'll be, and then I'll take you over to the city hall work area, so we can go over the plans for the set."

He nodded, leaned back on his boots, kept the lazy grin. Then he said, "I'm gonna walk on over to the church and ask Reverend Powell if I can let Honeyboy graze on the back lot. Want to meet me there?"

"Sure." She whirled to go up the steps, very much aware of his gaze following her. Telling herself to slow down before she tripped over her own feet, Leandra burst through the doors only to find Margaret standing there, waiting for her.

"This will never do, Lea," Margaret said, her hands on her hips. "We have to talk."

"What's wrong?" Leandra glanced down the aisle where Mr. Crawford was talking to the group, going over the script and songs. "Is there a problem already?"

"Yes," Margaret replied, taking Leandra by the arm to guide her out into the hallway off to the side. "It's about those Welby children. They're already proving to be quite a handful."

"Why? What happened?"

"Well, that little one—Brittney—she insists that you promised she could be an angel, and I've tried to explain to the child that my Philip wants to be an angel. Whatever you told her, you have to change it. Give her another part or something."

"I will not," Leandra countered, her tone firm. "I told you at dinner the other night that Brittney was going to be an angel. You didn't object then."

Margaret shrugged. "I didn't want to bring it up in front of everyone."

Meaning she knew better than to bring it up, Leandra figured. Colleen would have set her straight right away, and Margaret knew it. Well, Leandra was Colleen's only daughter, and just as assertive. But not nearly as sweet and patient.

"Margaret, listen to me. I promised that child she could be an angel in this pageant and that's exactly what she'd going to be. I won't break my promise."

Margaret gave her an indignant stare. "Not even for your own nephew. Philip will be heartbroken if he doesn't get to be an angel."

Leandra lifted her gaze heavenward to ask for patience. "I don't want to disappoint Philip, either." Trying to figure out what to do, she threw up her hands. "We can certainly have more than one little angel. We'll have a whole chorus of angels, with Philip and Brittney being the smallest ones. How's that?"

Margaret didn't seem too pleased. "Well, I wanted him to be the *only* little angel. I just thought he'd be so cute, you know?"

Leandra had to smile. "He is cute, Margaret, and I'm sure he'll be a wonderful asset to the pageant. But I promised Brittney. Remember, Philip has a large, loving family to support him. Brittney deserves that chance, too. We can be her church family, and support her efforts as well."

"Oh, all right." Margaret waved a hand as she pranced away. "But I'm warning you, I won't put up with any foolishness from those three country bumpkins."

Leandra had to check herself or she would have grabbed her sister-in-law to give the woman a good shake.

"Lord, grant me patience and understanding," she whispered as she pivoted to leave again. Then she remembered she was supposed to let someone know where she'd be, just in case any problems came up.

And with Margaret's attitude regarding the Welby children, Leandra knew there would surely be more to come.

Already, this little project was turning out to be more complicated than she'd ever imagined.

One of the main complications was waiting for her in the churchyard. Nathan stood talking quietly with Reverend Powell while Honeyboy enjoyed munching on the dry grass surrounding the prayer garden.

Why did her breath seem to leave her body every

time she was near Nate? Why did he look so natural standing there, that enticing grin on his handsome face, his trusty steed nearby? Why did it seem as if she'd been waiting for just such a man all her life?

Ridiculous, she told herself as she made her way down the meandering pathway leading to the tranquil gardens and church grounds. Towering oaks swayed in the morning breeze, loosening yet more fall leaves. They made a swishing sound as Leandra trudged through them.

At least she'd had the good sense to dress casually today. Her lace-up boots, jeans and long sweater fit right in with Nate's standard attire. And Reverend Powell never bothered to dress up, except for Sundays. He, too, was wearing a flannel shirt along with khaki pants.

I could get used to this casual atmosphere, Leandra thought as the two men glanced up and waved to her. When she'd first gone to the big city, all she'd wanted was to be sophisticated and elegant. She'd abandoned jeans and flannel and anything else that might appear casual and country.

But, it didn't seem half-bad now. It felt right, here in this beautiful old town.

And casual took on a whole new look on Nate Welby. He could easily pose for one of her ad campaigns.

That thought reminded her that she was no longer in advertising. She no longer had the sophistication and elegance of being in the big city. But she would go back soon, she promised herself. And this time, she'd be a little wiser and a whole lot smarter. And successful once again.

After everything that had happened, she didn't feel so successful right now, however.

"Why the frown?" Reverend Powell asked her as he held out his arms to greet Leandra with a bear hug. "It's too pretty a day for that stoic face, Leandra."

"Hello, Reverend," she said, smiling in spite of her worries. "I'm just working through some concerns, but it's so good to see you again."

"Good to have you back home with us," the Reverend replied. "And in charge of the big pageant, too. You always did like to stay busy. But don't forget to enjoy this time with your family, too."

"She's probably frowning because of me," Nate interjected, a puzzled look settling on his face. "I was late to work on my first day. And I don't think our Miss Leandra here fancies people who show up late."

"You had a good reason," Leandra said, hoping to convey her understanding. "But I do hope you can get that truck fixed."

"It's just the fan belt. I'll pick one up at the auto parts store," Nate countered. Then he shrugged. "Don't worry, Honeyboy needed the exercise, and Mr. Tuttle hauled my tools in his truck."

Leandra nodded, then lifted a brow. "Remind me to thank Mr. Tuttle later."

Reverend Powell gave them an astute grin. "Well, I sure am glad to see Nate back at church for a change—horse and all."

Nate acknowledged that comment with a slight nod. Then he gave Leandra his full attention, smiling sweetly at her. "Ready to get started?"

"Yes." She turned back to the Reverend. "I told Mr. Crawford I'd be over at city hall if anyone needed me. I have my cell phone, but in case I miss a call, or you hear—"

"Don't worry. I'll take a message," the Reverend said, turning to head back to his office. "You two kids have fun."

Fun was the farthest thing from Leandra's mind. She felt Nate's presence as surely as the wind and the sun.

Business, she told herself. This is business. And she'd learned not to ever again mix business with pleasure.

"So, here are the plans. I'm not sure who designed the original set but the props are old and need repairing and repainting, and some of them need to be done over from scratch. We're way behind, so feel free to change things to suit your own interpretation—that is as long as it fits in with the script."

Nathan leaned back against the long conference table, crossing his arms over his chest as he watched Leandra. She moved around like a little bird, flittering and fluttering, fussing and fixing.

"Hey, calm down. It'll get done."

"Will it?" she asked through a laugh that sounded more like a choking spell. "I'm beginning to have my doubts. I don't know why they waited until the last minute to get going on this, but—"

"But it will get done," he repeated, looking down at her. "That is, if you relax long enough for me to ask you a few questions."

She stopped then, bringing a hand up to push that irresistible hair away from her flushed face, her dark eyes dancing to a standstill. "Oh, I'm sorry. What questions do you have?"

"Are you married?"

She skidded like a cat caught in a paper box. "Mr. Welby, you know I'm not married. I mean, your daughter asked me to be her mommy the other day and I would have certainly mentioned it if I were already attached to someone." She stopped, looked down at her boots, pushed her hair back again. "Well…you understand what I mean, I'm sure."

"I'm sure," he repeated, grinning. "Didn't mean to upset you. It's just that you seem so…single."

Leandra looked up then, giving him a chance to see the little flash of fire in her eyes. "Single? I seem *single.*" She tossed her hair off her face. "And what's that supposed to mean?"

Nate turned to stare down at the plans spread out on the table. The nativity scene, the Christmas trees, the stars, the doves and angels—all meant to be cut out of plywood—lay there in a flat uncluttered pattern against the table, waiting to be created, to be shaped into something special, something with meaning.

"You're all business," he said, still looking over the patterns and shapes. "All energy and fire. All stressed-out and high-strung. Most people I know who act like that are workaholics, and usually they're single since they don't have time for any type of personal relationships." He wanted to tell her he knew firsthand about working all the time, but instead he stopped, pulled a hand down his jawline. "And it just seems this project needs a calming touch. It is all about peace and tranquillity, after all. Are you sure you're up to this?"

She was mad now. He could see it in the little pink spots underneath the bridge of freckles moving across her pert nose. He could see it in the tapping of her booted foot and in the way she let her hands slide down to her hips in a defiant stance.

"I think I can handle things, thank you," she said, her gaze moving over him then back to the plans. "Back in Houston, I was in charge of several very large advertising accounts, Mr. Welby. National accounts."

She stressed the *national* part. "It's Nate," he told her. "Call me Nate. And I didn't mean to offend you. But, lady, you're not in Houston anymore, and you need to take a deep breath and learn to enjoy yourself."

She huffed a deep breath. "*You're* telling me to enjoy myself. *You,* of all people? Don't you work a lot of long hours, too? Don't you have obligations, things that have to get done?"

"Yeah, I guess I do," he said, dropping his gaze back to the patterns. Well, she'd surely nailed him there. And he didn't have a quick comeback. Except to say, "But I don't get all flustered over every little thing. Mostly, I just go about my business, and I do take a minute here and there to enjoy life." Even as he said it, though, he knew that wasn't really the truth. And he knew he was picking on her to ease his own nagging guilt.

"That does it," Leandra told him, pointing a finger at the table. "I *am* enjoying myself, and my status, married or single, is none of your concern, and *if* I seem a little nervous, it's because I like having things in order and on time. And while we're standing here chewing the fat, things are not happening, Mr. Welby—"

"Nate."

"Nate. Nate! I need you to concentrate on making some sense out of this mess. Can you possibly do that for me? Can you actually get started on this—today?"

Nate lifted his hands, palms out, to ward off another tirade. "Sure. Sure. Just trying to help. Just wanted you to take it slow." He shrugged then. "I guess I just wanted you to know that it'll be all right. I'm here and I'll get my part done on time. And if you need help with any of the rest, just let me know. I thought after our talk yesterday, that we were friends, kinda."

She actually looked sheepish, then her skin blushed like a fresh pink rose. "Well, all right. Thank you...Nate. And I'm sorry if I seemed a bit snappish. We are friends, of course, and I do appreciate your willingness to help." Then she whirled like a little tornado. "I think I'd better go check on the children."

"Good idea. I'll round up the plywood and my tools and get these patterns cut, at least. Check back with me in a few hours and we'll see where things stand."

But he already knew exactly where things stood between his new boss and him. At an impasse, obviously.

She nodded, already heading for the exit.

Nate watched her stomping away, then moved a hand over the pattern of a dove lifting out toward the heavens. "Well, *Mr. Welby,* you sure have a fine way with the ladies. Scared that one right out the door."

Which was just fine with him, Nate told himself.

He surely didn't need someone as complicated and high-strung as Leandra Flanagan messing with his head.

And yet, the scent of her perfume lingering in the air did just that.

Three hours later Leandra returned to the work space that had been set up for Nate behind city hall. With worktables and extra, needed tools provided by Reverend Powell and the city, Nate had gone to work on cutting out the patterns for the backdrop of the pageant.

But Leandra didn't find him working.

Instead, he was in the churchyard, apparently giving all the children a ride on Honeyboy.

And little Philip was up on the big horse right now, laughing merrily as Nate guided the gentle gelding around in a wide circle.

Frustrated beyond measure, Leandra felt her blood pressure rising. Everyone said Nate was such a hard worker. But did the man ever do any work!

Before she could scream her wrath, she stopped to watch Nate with the children. He smiled that lazy smile and cooed softly to Honeyboy, all the while assuring little Philip that he was safe up on the big animal. Even Margaret seemed to be grudgingly captivated as she watched her son's beaming smile.

"Hey, Mommy," Philip shouted, waving as he

went round and round on the horse, Nate taking him through a slow canter.

"Hello, darlin'," Margaret called back. "I want to get a picture of you up there." She pulled a camera out of her big purse and snapped a couple of shots. Turning to Leandra, she said, "Isn't that just adorable?"

"Sure is," Leandra replied, her gaze scanning the crowd. "But Mr. Welby—Nate—is supposed to be working on the cutouts."

Margaret took another picture, then waved a hand. "Oh, he did. Look over there."

Leandra turned in the direction of the prayer garden, then let out a gasp. "Oh, my."

They were all there. The Santa kneeling over the baby Jesus, the angels, the doves, the Christmas trees, the squares that would become gift boxes. They had yet to be painted and decorated, but the patterns that had been flat and lifeless a couple of hours ago where now all cut out and ready to be finished. And Nate had them all lined up, as if waiting for her inspection.

"So the man can move fast when he has to."

Margaret lifted her brows. "What?"

"Oh, nothing," Leandra said, her gaze shifting back to Nate. "Just mumbling to myself."

Margaret watched Leandra as she watched Nate. "He's handsome, don't you think?"

"I didn't notice," Leandra replied with a shrug.

"Well, maybe you should," Margaret countered, an impish smile spreading across her porcelain complexion.

Before Leandra could find a retort, Philip called to her. "Aunt Lea, come ride with me."

"Oh, that's okay, baby," Leandra said, waving him on as she walked up closer. "You go ahead."

Nate turned then, his gaze sending her a definite challenge. "Oh, come on, Aunt Lea. You're not scared of horses, now are you?"

"Of course not," Leandra replied, acutely aware that all the children were watching her. And just to prove to the man that she could relax and actually enjoy herself, she strutted across the yard to pet Honeyboy. "I just don't feel like riding today, that's all."

"Nonsense," Nate said. Turning to Philip, he added, "Hold on now."

And before Leandra knew what was happening, Nate lifted her up in his arms and forced her up onto the horse, behind little Philip. She had no choice but to gracefully settle back in the saddle, the imprint of his big hands lifting her, and his face so close to her own clicking through her mind like one of Margaret's pictures.

While she glared down at him in shock, Nate leaned close, grinning up at her. "As pretty as a lamb and as light as a feather."

Leandra's mouth fell open, only to snap back

shut. Oh, this would never do. How could she work with this man over the next few weeks? He was a major distraction.

And she did not like distractions.

But as she held on to Philip and let Nate guide them around, with all the children and their parents clapping and laughing, and Margaret snapping pictures, she had to smile.

And Nate smiled right back up at her.

Well, at least she'd managed to accomplish one of her goals today. She'd told Nate she was enjoying herself, working on this project. At the time, however, she'd been too keyed up over being around him for that to be a true statement.

But he'd done his work, kept his part of the bargain and all in all, things had gone pretty smoothly with the rest of the rehearsals and the million other things that had needed her attention. It had been a productive day.

So right now, she had to admit in spite of how the man made her palms sweaty and her heart shaky, she *was* enjoying herself. Way too much.

Chapter Five

The Wednesday before Thanksgiving dawned dark and cloudy with the promise of rain, which didn't help the mood of Leandra's little band of actors, directors, stage hands and general all-around volunteers.

The production was going well, over all, however. They'd gotten through the first few rough rehearsals enough to iron out the kinks and get everyone accustomed to their parts. Since it was mostly singing and a few one-liners, Leandra felt good about things so far.

When she *could* concentrate on *things*.

Never one to daydream, for the last three days she found herself constantly wondering what Nate had been doing. Had he finished painting all the Christmas trees? She'd better go check, just to make sure he'd capped them off with the glistening gold-tipped snow like she'd suggested. Or maybe he hadn't understood her instructions about the huge gift boxes. Maybe he wouldn't remember that she wanted one gold-and-white striped and another red-and-green edged.

Any excuse to just be near the man.

"I've really got to stop this," she told herself as she headed around the corner to just get a peek at Nate's work area—just in case he needed her—just to see what he was doing today.

What he was doing was sitting on a bench, just sitting there staring at his finished products.

Leandra had to give the man credit. He'd worked hard, and in just three days, he'd finished most of his assignment. She knew he'd taken some of the pieces home with him to work on at night. Layla had told Leandra this in a huffy voice, claiming her daddy had stayed out in the barn until well past midnight all week, painting "those big Christmas things." And just when he'd finally taken a week off from work, too.

Those big Christmas things now represented a beautiful backdrop to the pageant. In Nate's talented hands, the shapes and figures had taken on a new life. He'd taken the basic patterns and turned them into art—his colors were brighter than Leandra had imagined them in her mind, his angels more holy, his doves more alive with bright white-and-gold flight, his trees almost touchable, close to smelling like real cedar.

Everything was perfect.

Except the expression on Nate's face.

"What's wrong?" Leandra asked as she came to sit down beside him on the stone bench.

"I'm finished," he said simply, his tone quick and resolved. "Nothing left for me to do here."

"And that's a bad thing?"

He didn't look at her. Made it a point not to look at her. "I like to keep busy."

"Now who's the workaholic?" she asked, nudging him with her elbow, a teasing edge in her voice.

When he looked up, however, any further teasing remarks vanished. Leandra had never seen such a tragic, sad look in a man's eyes. It frightened her, touched her.

"Nate?"

"I'll be okay," he said at last, his hands clutched together almost as if in prayer, his head bowed. "I get like this when I'm done with a project." He sat silently for a minute, then said, "Sometimes, when I'm working on a construction job and we're finished—say it's a new house, I stay after everyone else is gone, just to get the full image of that house in my mind. But I don't see the wood and beams, the new windows and fresh brick."

He looked up at her then, his amber-colored eyes reflecting the storm clouds rising above them. "I see children running in the grass. I see a woman planting flowers by the front door. I see a husband coming home to his family from a good day's work. Safe, warm, happy, together. That's what I see with each house. That's what I want for each house."

Leandra swallowed, but for the life of her, she couldn't tear her gaze from him. He'd just spoken of such beautiful things—the things most common people wanted in their lives—with such a great pain in his eyes, that it hurt physically to look at the man. And yet, she couldn't look away. And she didn't know what to say.

So she just sat there, her gaze locked with his. Then something passed between them on that stone bench, with all of Christmas spread out before them in golden bright colors.

Before she knew what was happening, she took his hand in hers. "Nate, I was wrong about you. I didn't think you'd get this done, but...it's absolutely beautiful. Everything is beautiful."

"And now I'm through," he said again, a trace of panic threading through his words. "Time on my hands."

And then she understood.

Most people who worked too much were working toward the future and success. But Nathan Welby was working against the past, and what he deemed his failure. Other people worked to brag, to validate what they'd accomplished, while Nate only worked to hide, and to forget what he'd lost.

And yet, out of that work, he created beauty. Only he couldn't see that. Or maybe he did; maybe it hurt him to see such beauty and know he'd lost part of his soul.

She had misjudged him. His slow and easy ways were an ingrained part of his nature, but he fought against that nature by staying busy with steady work that kept him from having any quiet time to remember.

Leandra longed to convince him that he had a future, a future bright with the promise and hope of his children, but she didn't know if she had that right, since she'd always put her career ahead of marrying and settling down. And she certainly wasn't the person to preach platitudes to him, since she'd made such a mess of her own life.

But she could pray for him, ask God to help this gentle giant, this sensitive, easygoing man, to find his way home again, for the sake of his children.

And she could quit looking at him as a distraction, and start looking toward him as a friend in need.

"Nate, I—"

Children, gold-hued children, laughing and shoving to reach their father, interrupted her next words. Layla, Brittney and Matt all scrambled around them like an explosion of bright burning sparklers.

"Daddy, I tried on my wings this morning," Brittney told him, hopping on his lap to give him a kiss. "They fit perfect-ity."

"They fit *perfectly*," Layla corrected, the old eye-roll exaggerating her words.

Matt clamored for his own bragging rights. "And my shepherd robe fit real good. Miss Leandra's mom made it for me. She's nice."

"That was nice of her," Nate said, a smile chasing the gloom away from his features. "And, Britt, I can't wait to see you as an angel, sugar."

"Can we go home now?" Layla asked, pushing long blond strands of hair out of her eyes. "You promised you'd cook a turkey on the grill for tomorrow, remember?"

"I do remember," Nate said, his gaze locking with Leandra's. "We like smoked turkey sandwiches."

"On Thanksgiving?" Leandra couldn't hide the shock in her voice. "What about dressing and gravy, pumpkin pie and cranberry sauce, all the trimmings?"

"We don't got trimmings," Brittney said, twisting to hug her father close. "We only got bread and turkey, and a bag of cookies."

"I'm not much of a cook," Nate said on a sheepish note. "Except with a barbecue grill, of course."

Leandra didn't know how the next words came out of her mouth, but somehow they popped out before she could think it through. "Then you can all come to my house for Thanksgiving. We'll surely have more than bread and turkey. And I know my parents would love to have you."

Amid the cheers and high fives of his children, Nate gave her a look caught somewhere between panic and pleasure.

"Are you sure about this?"

"I'm not so sure about this," Leandra told her mother early the next morning. "I should have asked you first, Mom."

"Don't be silly, honey." Colleen moved around her big kitchen with the efficiency of years of putting on big spreads for her family. "We have plenty of food, more than enough, and you couldn't very well let that adorable family have sandwiches on Thanksgiving, now could you?"

"I didn't want that," Leandra said, shaking her head. "I guess I forgot how lucky we are, to be such a close-knit clan. Even when we fight, we've still got each other. The Welbys don't have anybody, really."

"Well, now they have us, thanks to your kindness," Colleen replied as she handed Leandra a dozen boiled eggs. "Make the deviled eggs for me, honey. You should be safe with that project."

Leandra made a face. "I guess I need to learn to cook."

"Might come in handy one day," her mother teased.

Leandra watched as Colleen mixed the ingredients for her famous corn bread dressing. She loved watching her mother in the kitchen. Colleen always had a peaceful smile centered on her face when she was cooking.

Leandra longed for that kind of serenity, wished she could be more like her mother, but it just wasn't in her nature to be…serene. She'd always been scattered, anxious, in a hurry. And for what?

What was she searching for?

"How are the eggs coming?" Colleen asked with a mother's knowing grin. "Now, don't worry about your brothers, Lea. This is my house and if I say we're having company for Thanksgiving dinner, then that's the final word on the subject."

"If you say so," Leandra replied, cracking and peeling eggs in a hurry. "But we both know they'll resent this—they do like to be clannish at times."

"Well, they can get glad in the same boots they got mad," Colleen said. "I'll have no fighting and squabbling on Thanksgiving."

"Who's squabbling?" Jack came in from the den, carrying a baking dish. "Here's the macaroni and cheese. Now what's up? You two fighting over deviled eggs?"

"No, we were just discussing dinner," Colleen told him as Margaret came through the arched doorway. "We're having guests."

"Oh?" Margaret gave her mother-in-law a questioning look. "Anyone we know?"

"I believe you do know them," Colleen replied, an impish spark in her eyes. "The Welby family."

Margaret's smile turned as sour as the pickle relish Leandra was dumping into the deviled egg mix. "What? Surely you're joking?"

"I don't joke about dinner," Colleen replied, her smile intact. "Leandra invited the Welby family here for Thanksgiving dinner, so Margaret, be a dear and set four extra plates—one at the main table and three at the children's table, please."

"You're putting those three heathens with my little Philip and Corey, and Michael's Cameron? They'll ruin the boys' dinner."

"How so?" Colleen said, her dark brows lifting.

"Well, I don't know. They'll probably throw food and…they might not have the best of manners. They are just so…rowdy."

"Then we'll just have ourselves a rowdy Thanksgiving this year," Colleen said. "Set the table, Margaret. Time is ticking away."

"Well, I never." Margaret slammed the dinner rolls she'd baked from scratch down on the counter. "Leandra, I don't know what's gotten into you. First, giving that little girl the best angel part, now this. What's next—you going out to their house to hang Christmas decorations?"

"Now there's a thought," Leandra replied dryly, amused at her sister-in-law's antics. "Margaret, they were all alone and planning on having sandwiches. How would you feel if that were your situation?"

Margaret held the plates she'd grabbed from the

cabinet to her chest. "Well, I'd be sad and lonely, of course. Oh, all right, I guess what's done is done. We can't uninvite them, after all. But I'm going to keep my eye on those three."

"That's the giving spirit," Colleen said, all the while stirring the big pot of dressing mix. "Now, troops, let's get this together."

With that, she started issuing orders to everyone who happened to walk in the door. "Howard, honey, could you make sure there's enough wood for a fire? And Michael, make sure we have enough chairs—get some of those foldable chairs from the garage, dear. Kim, you can mix the tea and make sure we have enough juice for the children. Jack, don't sit down just yet. We need you to check on the turkeys—they've been in the cooker since dawn— just about time to pull them off to cool down. Richard—now where is Richard?—he needs to put the ice in the coolers and get the drinking glasses lined up. Oh, and everyone, we're having four more for dinner. The Welbys are joining us, and I'll hear no protests, whines, moans, nor will I tolerate any rude, unneighborly behavior. Is that clear?"

Amid the nods, surprised looks, and "Yes, ma'ams" Colleen called out, "Oh, and whose turn is it to carve?"

"Mine, I believe," Mark said as he entered the kitchen and let out a long sigh. "Ah, the smells of home and hearth. Mom, you've done it again."

"What's that, son?"

"Made me glad to be a Flanagan," Mark said as he managed to sidestep several fast-moving bodies to give his mother a peck on the cheek. "Happy Thanksgiving, Mom."

Leandra stood back, in awe of the organized chaos surrounding her. At one time, she'd hated this—hated the house full of people, talking and walking all at the same time, hated being shoved here and there by too many brothers and too much commotion, hated not having a private moment to herself. But today, today, she was so very glad to be right in the middle of the Flanagan clan. Safe at home. Loved. Centered.

How had she walked away from all of this? And why?

She watched as her father held little Carissa and made the baby bubble over with laughter. Watched as Cameron and Philip ran through the den, little Corey right behind them, chasing a remote control car that threatened to uproot anyone who got in its path. Watched as Margaret and Jack chuckled and whispered husband-and-wife nothings to each other as they set the table together. Watched as Michael leaned over to kiss Kim, a special quietness in the look meant only for his wife. Watched as Mark recited horrible on-the-spot poetry out loud—"Ode to Giblets"—while he polished the carving knives.

Her family was quirky, unpredictable, clannish—

and so special to her. And yet, she still felt set apart, detached almost, from the close-knit group. Where was the missing link?

Then she looked up to find Nathan Welby and his three children, huddled in the middle of the big den with confused, afraid looks on their faces.

"Nate," she said as she rushed toward them, so glad to see them here.

He looked directly at Leandra, then smiled that lazy smile. "We knocked," he said, "but I guess no one heard us. Can we come in?"

"Of course," Leandra said, smiling as she took the platter of turkey Nate had brought.

"Since we had it anyway…" he explained, shrugging as he handed her the heavy foil-wrapped plate.

"It smells wonderful," she told him. "C'mon in."

Layla and Matt hung back, shy, while Brittney rushed forth to get involved with the remote control car race. Philip immediately grinned at her and sent the car crashing against her white tights.

"Wanna pway?" he asked while he rammed the revving vehicle against her black Mary Jane shoes.

"Can I?" Brittney asked, her little hands on her hips. "Can I have a turn steering?"

"Guess so." Philip shrugged, then handed her the controls.

Nate smiled as they took off together. "Your nephew's a cuteypie."

"And walking trouble," Leandra said in a low whisper, a grin covering her face. "But I think Brittney can handle him."

"She can hold her own, that's for sure," Nate replied.

Wanting to make them feel comfortable, Leandra urged Matt and Layla into the kitchen. "Mom, look who's here."

"Well, hello there," Colleen said, wiping her hands on her Kiss the Cook apron as she came around the long counter. "Nathan, it's good to see you again. It's been a while."

"Yes, ma'am." Nate extended his hand to Colleen's.

"And Layla, how are you, darling?"

"Fine," Layla replied, a shy smile turning her face from pouty to pretty. At Nate's pointed look, she added, "Do you need some help, Mrs. Flanagan?"

"How nice of you to offer." Colleen glanced around. "You can fold the napkins and help Margaret put them around the tables."

Layla nodded, then took the white paper napkins Colleen offered.

"And Mr. Matt? What would you like to do?"

Matt shrugged, then tucked his hands in the pockets of his baggy jeans. "I don't know."

Just then Richard came in, carrying pies and soft drinks. "Hello, everyone." If he was surprised to find Nathan Welby and his children standing in his mother's kitchen, he didn't let on. "Hey, Matt, Nate. How's it going?"

"Fine." Nate shook Richard's hand. "Need help there?"

"I sure do," Richard said, handing Nate a box. "I bake these pies at my grocery store and so I brought two to help Mom out. We need to pop them in the refrigerator." He turned to Matt then. "And buddy, I think you can set these colas on the counter then help me check on the turkey and ham—see if they need to come off the grill?"

"Sure," Matt said. "I love ham."

Much later, after all the greetings and small talk, Howard said grace, then the dinner progressed with lots of conversation and eating, one small food fight between Brittney and Philip, and then a whole lot of groaning from overstuffed tummies. When they were finished eating, Colleen gathered the older children up and took them for a nature walk in the big backyard, while Margaret and Kim got the little ones settled down for their afternoon naps. As everyone else gathered around the big television in the den to watch football, Leandra found herself alone with Nate in the kitchen.

"I'm glad you came," she said, then laughed. "Did I already say that?"

"It's nice to hear it again," he replied. "It's good to be around a big family. I—I never had that."

"Really?" Wanting to know more, she handed him

a slice of pecan pie and a fresh cup of coffee, then led him to a quiet corner of the breakfast nook where a small built-in storage seat was nestled underneath the bay window. "Where is your family, anyway?"

"I never really had one," he told her as he gazed into the leaping flames of the big kitchen fireplace, the music of a half-time show on the nearby television blaring in the background. "I—I lived in a children's home most of my life."

Not understanding at first, Leandra stared over at him. "You—"

"I was an orphan. The Children's Home took care of me until I was old enough to get out on my own."

Leandra felt that little warm spot in her heart growing to a fiery heat inside her very soul. "I can't imagine," she said, wishing there was something better to say.

"No, I don't suppose you can," Nate replied, looking back into the den where her relatives sat around in complacent camaraderie. "You're lucky to have such a big, loving family."

"I was thinking the same thing earlier today, but I didn't always think that," she admitted, mortified that she'd often wished to be an only child. "But I'm learning to appreciate them."

"That's good." He glanced back at the fire. "I used to dream of a family like this. Loud, noisy, pushy, fun. I guess that's why I don't always discipline the children the way I should. I like having them in the house, like the noise and shouting. And I like knowing they will always have a home. At least, I'm trying to give them one."

"You're doing a pretty good job," Leandra said, proud of his quiet strength. "Underneath all their bluster, they really are sweet children."

"All things considered, I reckon so," he replied. Then he said, "Hey, don't go feeling sorry for me. I'm okay. The people at the home were good to me until it was time for me to move on. I had some rough years as a teenager, but then I grew up and tried to be responsible, and for a while, I knew what it meant to have a real home."

"You mean Alicia?"

"Yes. She was my heart, my home."

He grew quiet then.

"Well, you still have your children," Leandra said. "They are so beautiful, Nate. And they are a part of you and Alicia."

Just then a loud crash from the front hallway, followed by a wail of childlike pain, brought them both to their feet.

"I have a bad feeling about this," Nate said as he urged Leandra toward the noise. "I think one of my beautiful little angels just destroyed something."

Chapter Six

"Well, we almost made it through the day without any catastrophes," Nate told Leandra an hour later as he headed his family toward his waiting truck. "And I mean it, Leandra. I'm going to replace your mother's vase."

She waved a hand in the air. "I told you, it was old."

He glanced up at the well-maintained white two-storied house. "Yeah, and probably priceless."

Leandra didn't miss Nate's wistful look or the resignation in his words. Based on what he'd told her earlier, he'd never had a home of his own until now. With a little fixing up, his home could be every bit as lovely and traditional as her parents' one-hundred-year-old rambling house, but Nate probably still wouldn't feel the kind of security her family had always taken for granted. That chance had been snatched from him when Alicia had died. It would be hard to make him see that most of her family wouldn't judge him as harshly as he seemed to be judging himself.

Trying to reassure him, she said, "No, it held more of a sentimental value. She got it from the local discount mart years ago."

Leandra didn't have the heart to tell him that she'd given the white ceramic vase to her mother for Christmas when Leandra was around twelve years old, or that it had been bought and paid for with ten dollars of hard-earned allowance money. That didn't really matter right now.

But it mattered to Nate.

He lowered his head, then kicked a cowboy boot in the dirt. "I don't know if I can find one exactly like it, but I'll come up with something."

"That's not necessary."

"I insist."

Leandra knew he'd make good on his promise, too. Nate had been embarrassed to find Brittney standing in the front hallway, holding the pieces of what had once been a white vase full of silk mums and fall leaves.

Before Brittney could stop crying and explain, Margaret had rushed into the foyer to grab little Philip, who lay kicking and screaming on the floor as he held a hand to the goose egg on his forehead.

After they'd all calmed down, Brittney had explained between hiccuping sobs that they'd finished their walk and decided to play hide-and-seek, and she'd accidentally bumped into Philip as he'd rounded the corner by the stairs. Philip had somehow been propelled into the round walnut pedestal table centered in the big hallway, and in an effort to stop himself, he'd grabbed at air. Instead, his hand had hit the tall vase, causing it to topple over and fall to the tiled floor.

Colleen had come up on the whole scene, explaining that Philip had run ahead of them, hoping to hide. But when he'd come around the corner, he hadn't known they'd be just opening the front door.

"You really don't have to leave," Leandra told Nate now, wishing Margaret hadn't made such a scene about the tiny bump on Philip's head. "Philip is all right. He's had worse scrapes."

Nate turned, a smirk on his handsome face. "Yeah, but your sister-in-law doesn't think too highly of me and my brood right now, so I think it's best we head on back home. It's getting late and I've got some work to finish up anyway."

"You said you weren't going to work today," Layla told him before stomping toward the truck.

Before Nate could reply, Brittney tugged at his jeans. "I'm sorry, Daddy. I didn't mean to bump into him. It was an…accee-dent."

Layla opened the passenger side door. "Yeah,

and you're an *accident* waiting to happen. Get in, Brittney."

Brittney's blue eyes teared up yet again. "I said I was sorry."

"Brittney, honey, it wasn't your fault," Leandra said, rushing around the truck to take the little girl in her arms. "Philip said you were both running and that you just bumped together. You can't help it if he hit the table with his head."

"And knocked the vase over with his hand," Matt reminded them, clearly glad he wasn't the one in trouble this time.

Leandra remembered after the walk, Matt had stayed out in the backyard, talking to Howard. The two had hit it off immediately, since they both had a passion for fishing.

"I fell down, too," Brittney replied, her big eyes solemn. "But then I got up to pick up the vase parts."

"Are you okay?" Leandra asked, her eyes scanning the child for any signs of bleeding or bruises.

"Just hurt my bottom," Brittney admitted, her cherubic lips turned down. "I don't want to go home, though."

"We have to leave, sunshine. It's late and everyone's a little tired," Nate told her. "Now let Miss Leandra buckle you in tight. And tell her you had a very good time."

"I had a very good time," Brittney echoed. "And I still don't want to go home."

"Will you come and see me again?" Leandra asked, giving the child a peck on the cheek.

Brittney smiled, then giggled. "Can I?"

"Why sure you can."

"Nate?"

Both Nate and Leandra turned to find Colleen and Howard coming down the steps.

"Wait. I have some leftovers for you," Colleen told him.

Nate herded Matt into the truck, then turned to Leandra's parents. "That's mighty nice, Mrs. Flanagan. But I don't think I could eat another bite."

He rubbed his completely flat stomach, causing Leandra to wonder how the man could pack away so much food and still look fit as a fiddle.

"Then save it for tomorrow," Colleen said, handing him a grocery bag filled with plastic containers of food. "We sure did enjoy having you and the children over."

Nate nodded, shifted his feet, then said, "We had a nice time, too. And I do apologize for the broken vase."

"It can be replaced," Colleen said. She glanced at Leandra with her own apologetic smile. The vase had been one of her mother's favorite things, but Leandra knew that her mother put people and their feelings ahead of material things. "Besides, my grandson is just as responsible for breaking it, even though his mother might not see it that way. But I was there and one child was coming from one way and the other from another way and they collided. It was an accident, plain and simple."

Nate shifted his feet again, then nodded. "Well, I still feel bad about the vase. But I appreciate the dinner and the leftovers."

"Y'all come back any time," Howard said, shaking Nate's hand. "And don't worry about the vase or Philip. His head is as hard as a fence post."

"Is his mama calmer now?" Nate said, a hesitant grin splitting his face.

"Margaret's a bit high-strung, but she'll be okay. She's rocking Philip to sleep in one of the bedrooms. Too much excitement." Howard winked then. "And I think my grandson has a crush on your Brittney."

"She's a heartbreaker," Nate admitted, smiling over at his youngest daughter.

And so is her father, Leandra thought. Every time Nate smiled, the whole world seemed to turn golden and sunny. He should smile more often. *And I should quit acting like a silly schoolgirl.*

Howard laughed, then leaned into the truck. "Matt, son, I meant what I said. Just give me a call and we'll go down to the pond and do a little fishing."

"Okay," Matt said, a shy smile cresting his face. "Thank you for showing me your boat and fishing reels."

After a wave goodbye, Leandra's parents went

back inside. And Nate was still smiling that lazy, knowing smile. It was a mixture of embarrassed pride and sincere gratitude.

The late-afternoon air was crisp on Leandra's flushed cheeks as she gazed up at Nate. "They really are glad you came."

"Oh, they're just being polite. You have a very nice family."

"And we're working on Margaret," Leandra teased, poking at his arm. "Guess I'll see you Monday."

"After work," he reminded her. "It might be seven before I can get there."

"No problem. We'll be rehearsing every night between now and the week before Christmas. So you can finish up the set and work around us, if you don't mind."

"I don't mind at all."

"And I'll have your check waiting for you tomorrow night," Leandra told him. "We appreciate you helping us out on your week off, Nate."

They stood silent for a minute, until Layla moaned and groaned inside the truck. "Can we just go home now?"

"She's pouting," Nate said underneath his breath. "Her siblings always embarrass her one way or another."

"She's at that age," Leandra reminded him. "My brothers used to embarrass me in the worst kinds of ways, too."

"They teased you a bit today, if I recall."

Leandra recalled, too. Somehow, her four brothers had managed to get in digs about her single status, her inability to cook, and the fact that she was very cranky in the morning. She'd be surprised if Nate ever talked to her again.

"Hey, I didn't believe a word they said," he told her now, his smile so sparkling and sure that she had to grin right back.

"Well, they were telling the truth—to a point. I like being single and I don't like to cook, but they exaggerated my shortcomings just a tad. I'm not too cranky after I have a cup of coffee."

"But you are a real city girl, aren't you?"

The question seemed so serious, she wasn't sure how to answer it. Maybe because right now, she didn't know the answer. She wasn't so sure about what she wanted from life anymore.

So she nodded. "Or so I thought."

He gave her a long stare, his bemused expression belying the serious gaze centered in his topaz eyes. "Right now, you look like you belong right here."

Leandra felt the heat rising to her skin, in spite of the cold November afternoon. "Do you think so?"

Nate leaned around the open truck door, close enough for her ears only. "Yep. You're all fresh-faced and dewy, like you've been on a long winter walk. You look like you're just waiting for someone to snuggle with on that window seat in your mama's kitchen."

Leandra became frozen to the spot, acutely aware of his eyes on her, of his gentle smile, of his lips, his hand stretched across the door handle.

To break the magnetic pull that seemed to be bringing him ever closer to her, she laughed and tossed a curl off her face. "It *is* chilly out here. The fire will feel good when I go back in."

"Then don't let me keep you," he replied, standing back as if he'd just now realized he'd been flirting shamelessly with her. "Go on inside and get warm."

Leandra *was* warm, too warm. But she shivered anyway and wrapped her arms across her midsection. "Well, goodbye then. See you later."

"Later." Nate gave her a reluctant look, then slid into the truck with his children.

Leandra watched as they took off up the highway, headed toward home and what looked to be a glittering winter sunset.

And she knew she'd never look at the window seat in her mother's kitchen in quite the same way.

Nate looked at the birdhouse one more time. He'd finished it late last night, and he had to admit, it had turned out better than he'd imagined. But would it be good enough for Leandra?

He wanted it to be pretty—for Leandra and her mother. It was a gift to thank them for their kindness last week at Thanksgiving, and to replace the broken vase.

And a good excuse to see Leandra again.

Who was he kidding, anyway? Nate tossed down the paintbrush he'd used to put the finishing touches on the birdhouse. He wasn't in the same league with Leandra Flanagan and her family, not by a long shot. Being around her and her prominent, well-mannered family only reminded Nate of all of his miseries and shortcomings. Reminded him too much of Alicia's family and their disdain for their son-in-law. That disdain now separated his children from their own grandfather, Davis Montgomery.

He'd never been good enough for Alicia's father, especially since her death. Then after Mrs. Montgomery had died, too…well, the old man hadn't made much effort to keep in touch. Which just proved Nate surely wasn't good enough to become involved with Leandra, either.

And yet…

The door to the old barn creaked open then. Layla stomped in, slamming the door shut behind her. "I figured you'd be out here."

"Hello, sunshine," Nate said, feeling a little more than guilty for daydreaming about a woman he couldn't have. He placed the birdhouse back amid the clutter of his worktable. "What's up?"

"Matt needs help with his math and Brittney's been coughing and sneezing. I think she's getting a cold, not that *you'd* care."

"Hey, wait a minute there." Nate turned to face

his hostile daughter. "Layla, want to tell me what's eating at you? You've had a burr in your bonnet for weeks now."

Layla's sigh shuddered all the way down her slender body. "Daddy, why do you stay cooped up out here all the time?"

Nate glanced around, then back to his daughter. "I work out here, honey. You know that."

"You work at your regular job, during the day," she retorted. "Then you head out here as soon as we're finished with supper."

"I—I like working with my hands," Nate said, hating himself for the weak excuse.

Layla moaned, then turned to leave. "Well, it sure would be nice if you'd come in the house every now and then to check on your younger children. I get tired of having to be their keeper."

Nate halted her with a shout. "Stop right there. Young lady, you are not going to talk to me in that tone."

Layla looked down at the dirt floor. "I'm sorry, Daddy, but…it's the only way to get your attention sometimes. I'll go check on Britt, give her some cough syrup."

Nate stared at her for a minute, hoping to decipher all the hostility he saw on her frowning face.

"Thanks, honey," he finally said on a softer voice. "I'll be in soon, I promise." He looked up at her then. "And Layla, I'm sorry, too."

She closed the door and left him standing there amid wood shavings and power saws. But he knew she was right. He needed to learn how to just sit still and listen to the sounds of his children. He'd tried so hard to do just that, but somehow he always wound up out here, or worse—taking on extra projects that kept him busy at least two or three nights a week.

He'd been depending on Layla too much lately. Making her watch her younger brother and sister, making her do housework, probably making her life miserable in the bargain.

Now that he stopped to think about it, she really didn't get out much and do the things most teenage girls did, such as go to the movies or the mall, or have sleepovers. No wonder she was sullen and pouting all the time.

"I'll make it better, Lord," he promised. "Somehow."

Maybe Leandra could help him there. She knew about girls. He'd ask her about taking Layla on a shopping trip, let Layla pick out a special Christmas present for herself.

But ultimately, Nate knew the task of seeing about his oldest daughter fell to him. If he started depending on Leandra and then she up and went back to Houston, that would only make matters worse for Layla.

Which only reinforced everything he'd been thinking about earlier. He had no business pursuing a relationship with Leandra right now. Maybe ever.

Especially since he'd made a big fool of himself on Thanksgiving by coming very close to kissing Leandra Flanagan right there by the truck. But she'd sure looked tempting, standing there in her baggy sweater and jeans, her wind-tossed hair falling across her freckled face.

He had to get over this need, this temptation to take things further with her. The woman had made it clear from the time she'd set foot on his property that she wasn't interested.

Yet…he sensed something there. It was in her eyes when she looked at him, in her smile when he walked into a room, in her every action. Was she fighting against this as much as he was?

And what was she really fighting? Leandra hadn't told him much about her big-city life or why she'd suddenly left it all to come home. Whatever had happened had apparently left a bitter taste in her mouth and given her cold feet about any new relationships.

He had to know. Wanted to know.

Maybe he'd just up and ask her.

Or maybe he'd just mind his own business and try to be a better father.

He looked down at the wooden birdhouse, thinking it wasn't good enough. Nothing he'd ever done had been good enough.

But right now, it was all he had to give.

* * *

"Can you stop by my truck?" Nate asked Leandra the next night after rehearsal. "I have something for you."

Leandra swallowed back the surprise she felt. He'd been avoiding her since Thanksgiving. And now he had something to give her.

"What is it?" she asked, wondering why Nate had seemed so distant over the past few days.

They'd worked together, getting the set ready for dress rehearsals. The props looked great and Nate had just about finished designing the entire set. After Nate was done with his official chores each night, he'd sit and watch the production, or sometimes he'd wander off into the night. Several times, she'd found him outside, gazing at the stars. Sometimes she'd find him talking quietly to Reverend Powell.

That, of course, was a good sign and might explain his distance and quiet aloofness. Maybe Nate was wrestling with his faith; maybe he was quietly coming to a change in his life. And maybe that meant he didn't want any distractions from her.

"Nate," she said now, "what do you have for me? Another prop? Another complaint from Margaret? Or did you ride your horse to work again?"

"Nope, I didn't bring Honeyboy this time." His smile broke the tension lining his face. "I've finished most of the props and thankfully, Margaret hasn't had one complaint tonight, but hey, the night's young, right?"

Leandra laughed. His sense of humor might be dry and unexpected, but Nate got in his own zingers when he wanted to. And he was obviously beginning to understand that her high-strung, well-meaning sister-in-law would probably never be satisfied with anything in life.

"Margaret would complain if the moon shifted," Leandra said in a whisper, "but some people are happy even when they whine their way through life."

Nate nodded. "I know. And she was as cute as a button when she stomped that little foot the other night and demanded to know who stole Philip's angel wings."

"We had to break it to her gently that the angel himself left his wings in the little boys' room." Leandra grinned, then shook her head. "Even angels have to go to the bathroom sometimes."

Changing the subject, she poked at Nate's arm. "Okay, so what's this big surprise in your truck?"

"C'mon and I'll show you," he told her as he took her by the hand. "And hurry before my kids come charging out the door."

Realizing they'd be alone near the moonlit prayer garden, Leandra had to take a deep, calming breath. She'd never been alone in the dark with Nate, but she sure had thought about being alone with him. A lot.

"They're having cookies and hot chocolate,"

she managed to pant out. "They should be out in a few minutes."

"This won't take long," he said as they reached the truck. "I made you and your mama a little something, just to replace the vase."

Leandra watched as he hauled a bag out of the back of the pickup. "Nate, I told you—"

Whatever protest she'd been about to mount ended when she saw the object he offered over to her.

It was the most beautiful birdhouse she'd ever seen.

Chapter Seven

Leandra took the delicate wooden birdhouse in her hands, holding it up to the nearby streetlight so she could see the intricate design better.

"Nate, this is so pretty. Where did you get it?"

When he looked down, then shifted his booted feet, she suddenly realized he hadn't bought it.

"You made this?"

He nodded, still looking at the ground. "It's not a vase, but I thought it might be pretty sitting on your mama's hall table during Christmas."

"Absolutely," she replied, silly tears springing to her eyes. "She's going to love this."

"It's no big deal," he said, looking up at her at last. "I just wanted to do something to thank you both for your kindness."

Leandra turned the birdhouse around in her hands so she could again hold it up to the streetlight just over their heads, careful not to drop it on the concrete. It was about a foot wide at the top and just as tall, made of what looked like pinewood. The roof slanted down in an inverted V-shape to cover the square base. The whole thing had been varnished and lacquered until it shined, but what really caught her attention was the detailing.

The slanted roof was shingled with dainty little wood cutouts tipped in white paint that sparkled like freshly fallen snow. The door and two side windows held intricately designed wooden shutters also touched with brilliant white icicles. There was even a smaller window just below the roof, right above the little open door, which had a small window box complete with flowing ivy. And all around the roof, the snow-tipped eaves had been painted with tiny red poinsettias and holly berries, set against little green magnolia leaves.

It was exquisite.

"It reminds me of a cuckoo clock," she said.

"Without the cuckoo," Nate replied, smiling sheepishly. "I'm glad you like it."

"I love it," Leandra said, a catch in her voice. "How did you make all the little curlicues and swirls around the openings and roof? And the snow and flowers—they look so real."

"I have all kinds of jigsaws and sometimes I carve pieces by hand. I paint the designs on."

"Amazing. Sounds as if this isn't your first effort."

"I've made a few," he admitted. "It's just a hobby. Something to pass the time. I'm working on a version for each season of the year."

Leandra carefully placed the delicate house back in the bag. "This is much prettier than that old vase. My mother will be thrilled. I'll go put it in my car right now."

Nate took the bag from her. "Here, let's put it back in the truck for now." He placed the bag inside on the driver's seat. "Want to go for a walk?"

Caught completely off guard, Leandra didn't have time to come up with all the excuses she needed to refuse. "Sure."

He took her to the prayer garden in the church-yard just opposite the civic center.

But then, she'd known that's where he was going to take her, at least had hoped he'd do so.

"It's a pretty night," Nate said as he pulled her to a wooden bench with a tall, spindled back. "I like the quiet…sometimes."

"Me, too," she said, wondering what the "sometimes" meant. "These rehearsals sure do get noisy and disorganized. It's nice to find a moment to just sit."

"You're doing a good job, bringing all these folks together."

"I've had a lot of help," she told him. Sensing his need to talk, she prattled on herself. "You know, this production started as a small play in the church fellowship hall. But it became so popular, with so many people coming, they had to add extra performances and move it to the civic center."

"Well, the Wonderland of Lights sure brings in a lot of tourists."

Leandra looked down the street where millions of tiny white lights blinked and twinkled on the old courthouse centered in the middle of town. The Wonderland of Lights brought in thousands of people each year from Thanksgiving until New Year's Eve, and this year had been no exception. Already, Leandra had seen the buses and cars full of people coming each night to see the awesome Christmas decorations.

Not only was the courthouse strung with over 250 thousand lights, but just about every other building in Marshall, both commercial and residential, was also decorated. The civic center was decked in bright colorful lighted cutouts, and the church held a breathtaking lighted cross. There was also a lighted star over a nativity scene made completely from white wire figurines covered with the same tiny white lights that were hanging all over town. It was a Marshall tradition that had made the city famous throughout the world. Even the trees glistened with starlike white lights.

"It's impressive," Leandra said, remembering how she'd always enjoyed the lighted city during the Christmas season each year. "Have you and the children taken the official sightseeing tour yet?"

"No. I've been so busy—" He stopped, looked at the lights. "Guess I'll have to make time."

Leandra shivered as a cold night wind whipped around the corner. "The temperature's dropping."

Nate took off his lightweight denim barn jacket and wrapped it around her. "How's that?"

"Better," she said as she looked up at him. Even better than better, she thought to herself. The jacket still held his body warmth and the clean, woodsy scent of whatever soap he had used that day. She'd like to buy a gallon of the stuff, whatever it was.

Nate glanced over at her, his catlike eyes appraising her with that lazy, I'm-taking-my-own-sweet-time way. "You're almost lost in there."

"You're a lot taller than me," she said by way of explanation. "Thanks, though."

"You're welcome—though."

His eyes held hers, shimmering as brightly as any Christmas lights she'd seen. Mercy, when Nate Welby set his mind on flirting, it made her insides curl into ribbons of fire. She was very glad she was sitting down.

Then he tilted his head, his eyes centered on her face.

"You didn't thank me properly for the bird-house," he said, his voice as gravelly as the pebbles beneath their feet.

"I didn't say thank you?" she asked, acutely

aware of how he'd managed to wrap a long arm around her neck.

"You might have, but I was kinda hoping for a hug or maybe a peck on the cheek."

"Really?"

"Really."

"Is that why you brought me to this secluded bench?"

"Maybe." He shrugged, turning serious. "Or maybe I just wanted some peace and quiet."

"It's up to you," Leandra said, meaning it.

If Nate Welby wanted to kiss her, she wouldn't stop him, couldn't if her heart depended on it. But she wouldn't push him into something he might regret either. Because her heart also depended on that not happening. She couldn't bear his regrets.

"I reckon you're right there," he said. "Maybe I won't find any peace until I have kissed you."

Then he pulled her head around, his fingers gentle on her cheekbone, and touched his lips to hers, tentatively at first. After lifting his head to gauge her reaction, he kissed her again. This one took a little longer.

"You're welcome," he said as he let her go, his eyes holding hers in the glittering moonlight.

Leandra felt as if she'd been in a snowstorm and was now melting in a puddle of heat like Frosty the Snowman. Nate's kiss had dissolved her completely, making her a pile of helpless mush.

But apparently it hadn't brought him that peace he was seeking.

"I shouldn't have done that," he said as he stood up and pulled her with him. "I told myself not to do that, and look at me. I went and did it anyway."

Confused and hurt, Leandra asked, "Was kissing me that painful?"

He turned then, taking her back in his arms. "No, Leandra, it was that good. Too good."

"You're afraid of me, aren't you?" she asked, her tone full of disappointment.

"Yes, I guess I am," he admitted, his hand coming up to cup her chin. "But more than that, I'm afraid of myself. I don't want to mislead you, and I sure don't want to hurt you."

"Because you're not over Alicia?"

"Because I never did right by Alicia, and I don't know if I could do right by you."

Leandra's frustration brought her back to reality.

"That's ridiculous. You have to stop blaming yourself, Nate. If you don't, you'll never find any peace, any happiness."

"Maybe that's my punishment."

"Only if you let it be."

Then he turned the tables on her. "Yeah, well, what's your excuse? You left Houston for some reason. Want to tell me about that?"

"No, I don't," she said, thinking he sure would

go to any lengths to take the attention away from his own problems.

Then he surprised her yet again. "I'd really like to know."

The soft edge in his husky voice almost did her in. But she wasn't ready to tell him the whole sordid story. "Let's just say that I had no choice."

Leandra could see the determination in his eyes, even in the muted moonlight. Nate wasn't going to let this go so easily.

"You left a high-paying job to come back home. That right there shows it must have been pretty bad. What with you being such a gung ho city girl and all."

Now he was becoming downright sarcastic. "Nate, I didn't just leave a job," she blurted out. "I left a bad relationship with an older man who happened to be my boss."

He didn't say a word. He just stared down at her.

Mortified, Leandra hung her head, refusing to look at him. "Satisfied?" she asked in a quiet whisper.

"Not nearly enough," he replied just as quietly.

With that, he let her go, then turned to head back to the truck. Leandra followed, emerging from the shadowy garden just as the Welby children came running toward their father. She quickly shoved Nate's jacket into his hands, thinking he'd never want to kiss her again. He'd looked both shocked and appalled by her revelation.

"What were you doing in the garden?" Layla asked, suspicion in every word.

"Were you kissing?" Matt chimed in, grinning from ear to ear.

"Does this mean Miss Leandra might be my new mommy?" Brittney shouted as she hopped from foot to foot. "I knew it, I just knew it."

"Hey, hey," Nate said, embarrassment making his voice shaky, "you three need to mind your own business and quit trying to rule my private life. To question number one, we were just talking. To question number two, Miss Leandra was thanking me for the birdhouse, and to question number three—Britt, Miss Leandra can't be your mother. We've talked about this, honey."

Brittney stopped hopping and glared up at the two adults standing stiffly in front of her. "But you said you liked her."

Nate sighed, then ran a hand across his chin. "I do like her." He turned to Leandra then. "A lot."

Leandra quickly quelled the relief flooding through her system. Maybe Nate wouldn't judge her as harshly as she tended to judge herself— something she realized they had in common at least—but that didn't mean he'd try kissing her again, either. She'd have to settle for being liked. A lot.

"Then what's the holdup?" Brittney asked.

Layla moaned and turned to stare at her sister.

"The holdup, dummy, is that our daddy still loves our mama and that Miss Leandra doesn't want to be stuck with the three of us and that old, falling-down house we live in. Now, can we please go home? I've got to study for a spelling test."

"Layla, I think you owe Miss Leandra an apology," Nate said as he stomped after his retreating daughter.

"For what?" Layla asked in defiance. "It's the truth, isn't it?" She looked from her father to Leandra, hope warring with despair in her blue eyes.

Nate lifted his head toward the stars, as if asking for God's wisdom and guidance. "I will always love your mother, no matter what happens, sunshine," he said. "And Miss Leandra will be going back to Houston after Christmas."

"So it is the truth?" Matt glanced at Leandra, his gaze accusing. "I thought you liked us, too."

Leandra didn't know how to deal with this, especially after the exchange Nate and she had just had. Bending down, she said, "Matt, I do care about all of you, but, honey, being an adult is complicated. Your father is a wonderful man, but he still misses your mother. And I don't know what I'm going to do after Christmas. But we both want what's best for all of you."

"You being my mama would be the bestest," Brittney said with a pout as she twisted a thick blond curl around her chubby finger. "Can't you please just think about it, Miss Lea?"

"It's Miss Leandra," Nate said, correcting her.

"Lea is fine," Leandra replied, turning to scoop Brittney up in her arms. "All of my friends call me Lea."

"And we are her friends," Nate told his children. "Let's just leave it at that for now, okay?"

Layla hurried to get inside the truck, slamming the door behind her. Matt gave Leandra another inquisitive look, then followed his sister. But Brittney held on to Leandra's neck and hugged her long and hard.

"I'm gonna talk to God one more time."

Leandra returned the hug, wishing with all her heart she could make this sweet child understand that she was asking too much—of both her father and Leandra.

"We can all talk to God, Brittney," she said. "Maybe He'll provide us with the answers we need."

Nate took the child from her, his eyes meeting Leandra's over Brittney's head. "Don't forget your birdhouse."

Leandra followed him to the truck, then took the bag from him, lowering her head to avoid his gaze. "Thank you. It really is beautiful."

Nate tugged at her chin so she had to look him in the eyes, his expression full of remorse and pain. "I hope it makes up for...for everything."

"It does," she said. The birdhouse made up for everything except the great pain centered in her heart. "Thank you again, Nate. Good night."

Then she turned and walked back to her own car, the memory of his kiss still as fresh as the cold wind blowing across her face.

And just as elusive.

"It's one of the most beautiful things I've ever seen," Colleen told Leandra later as they stood in the kitchen admiring the birdhouse. "And Nate made this?"

"Yes," Leandra said, her hands wrapped around the mug of hot chocolate her mother had offered her the minute she walked in the door. "Amazing, isn't it?"

"Very," Colleen said, her attention turning from the birdhouse sitting on the counter to her daughter. "What's wrong, sweetheart? Hard rehearsal tonight?"

Leandra took a long sip of the creamy liquid, marveling at her mother's ability to make it just right every time. The taste of rich chocolate milk laced with vanilla and cinnamon only made Leandra want to cry for some strange reason.

"No, rehearsal went well, actually. Everyone is getting settled into their parts and, for once, Margaret didn't make any demands. She was quite pleasant tonight for some reason."

Colleen laughed, then patted Leandra's hand. "I

think Margaret's in good spirits these days because she has wonderful news to share with the rest of us."

Leandra glanced up to see the maternal pride on her mother's face. "Another baby?"

"Exactly," Colleen replied. Then she placed a finger to her lips. "But keep it quiet. She wants to announce it at Sunday dinner. You know how she likes to make a big production." Colleen smiled again, then tugged at Leandra's hand. "Now tell me, what's bothering *you?*"

But Leandra's melancholy mood had just gone two shades darker. "First Kim has another baby and now Margaret again. Those two sure are fertile."

"They're married women," her mother pointed out, her eyebrows lifting. "And most married women like to have children."

"Not like me, I suppose," Leandra couldn't help but spout back. "Single and without a maternal bone in my body, right?"

A frown skittered across her mother's face. "I didn't mean to imply—"

"Oh, Mama, I'm sorry," Leandra said, pulling her mother's hands into hers. "It's just been a long day and I guess I'm worried about the future. Christmas will be here in less than three weeks, and then my work here will be over. I don't know what to do with my life after that."

Colleen pulled up a bar stool and indicated to

Leandra to do the same. "Are you having second thoughts about returning to Houston?"

"Yes, I think I am," Leandra had to admit. "At first, I told myself I had to go back—you know, to face the music, to get back on that ol' horse. But now…" She shrugged, tried to smile, then looked toward the window seat across the kitchen. "I just don't know."

Colleen looked at her daughter, her face once again as serene as always. "God has a plan for you, Lea. You know that, right?"

"Yes, I believe that with all my heart, Mama. It's just hard to sit back and wait for Him to reveal that plan. Why does He have to be so slow sometimes?"

Colleen laughed again. "Oh, you always were the impatient one. You couldn't wait to get out of Marshall and get on with your life."

Leandra nodded. "I thought my plan had been formed already. But I guess even the best laid plans change, right?"

"They sure do. And we can't blame God for that, or cast doubt about it. We just have to come up with a new plan, with His guidance."

"I'm trying," Leandra said. Then she looked down at the birdhouse. "It was so sweet of Nate to build this for us, don't you think?"

Colleen touched a hand to one of the tiny open windows on the little house. "Yes, very considerate. But then, Nathan Welby is a considerate man." Mimicking Leandra, she added, "Don't you think?"

Leandra saw the inquisitive look centered on her mother's face. "Yes, Mama. I think he's considerate, interesting, and…off-limits."

"Oh, really?"

"Really. Nate has made it very clear he's not ready for anything beyond friendship."

"Oh, and what about you?"

Leandra shook her head. "I'm not ready either. I have to get my life back on track before I can even consider having a relationship with someone again. William's betrayal left a distinct fear in my heart."

"William Myers wasn't worth your time or effort, darling. And I'm glad you got rid of him."

"More like, he got rid of me."

Colleen leaned forward. "Did you love William?"

Leandra thought about that long and hard, fighting the image of Nate's disgust when she'd told him about her past. That led to a comparison of her feelings for William with how she now felt about Nate.

But there was no comparison. The little bit of something she felt for Nate right now, this very minute, far surpassed anything she'd believed she'd felt for William.

"No, I don't think I loved him at all. I was enamored of his image, of what I thought he could do. I thought I was happy with William, and I was content to keep things on an even level, without any further commitment. I felt safe with William. There were no hassles or demands."

But all of that had changed, she remembered, the thoughts of their last days together turning her hot chocolate to a bitter taste in her mouth.

"William was exciting, dashing, wealthy, powerful. All the things I had always dreamed about in a man. But, you know, those were the very things that turned me against him in the end."

Colleen let out a long sigh. "Well, good. Because what that man expected from you could only have led to heartache and regret." Colleen got up to come around the counter. Putting a hand on each of Leandra's shoulders, she said, "You did the right thing, walking away. You stuck to your morals and the upbringing your father and I tried to instill in you. And that makes me so proud."

"Thanks, Mom," Leandra said, hugging her mother close. If only *she* could find some pride in herself again.

They both heard footsteps on the tiled floor, then parted to find Howard standing there with a questioning smile on his face. "Everything okay in here, ladies?"

"Everything is more than okay," Colleen said. "Since you both worked late tonight, I held dinner—red beans and rice."

"That sure sounds good," Howard said as he came to stand by Leandra. "I'm a starving man."

"We can't have that, now can we?" Colleen said as she took his hand across the counter.

Howard's gaze moved from his wife's face to the birdhouse. "What's this? It looks like a little Christmas cottage."

"It's a birdhouse," Colleen explained, turning it to admire it all over again. "Nathan Welby made it for Leandra and me."

"Well, how about that." Howard whistled low, then stood back to admire the ornamental little house. Then he put a finger to his chin. "Seems to me I remember Nate and Alicia coming in to the bank a few years back to talk about this very subject."

"Birdhouses?" Leandra asked, surprised. "I got the impression this was a hobby Nate had just taken up."

"No, I'm pretty sure they wanted to talk about a possible loan—to start some sort of craft business. Alicia went on and on about how Nate could create anything from wood."

Leandra looked down at the lovely house. So, Alicia had been in on this dream, this design, too. Somehow, that rubbed salt in her already wounded heart. She'd believed Nate had created this just for her.

Turning back to her father, she asked, "What happened? Why didn't they start the business?"

"She died a little while after that, honey. Guess Nate didn't have the heart after that." He went to the refrigerator to take out the tea pitcher. "I was prepared to give them the loan, too. It would have been risky, but they seemed so excited and happy.... Of course, you are not to repeat that, understand?"

Leandra nodded absently, then sat still as her father's voice trailed off. So Nate had had a dream of creating these beautiful houses, of turning it into a business. And yet, that dream had crashed right along with his wife's plane.

Dead. Put aside in a cloud of grief.

Until now.

Suddenly, her heart soared with renewed hope. Regardless of Alicia's influence, Nate had designed this house for her, for her family.

For Leandra.

Maybe he was beginning to work through his grief. Maybe he did feel something besides friendship for her, after all.

And maybe there was a way she could show him that she supported him and believed in him.

A lot.

Chapter Eight

"Daddy's not home yet," Layla told Leandra two days later.

Leandra stood on the porch of the big house with Mutt sniffing at her long trouser skirt. She wondered why she'd acted on impulse and decided to ride out to the Welby place. She had tons of extra work to do—Chet thought she'd make a great marketing director for the city—and apparently in his mind, had already hired her for the job.

Standing here now, she thought burying herself in work would be the perfect solution to keeping her mind off Nate Welby and his children. And yet, here she was at their front door.

"Well, can I come in anyway?" Leandra asked, hoping she could at least have a talk with Layla while she was here. The girl was obviously in need of some feminine attention, but all that attitude got in the way.

"I don't know—"

Before Layla could finish the sentence, Brittney came bouncing down the stairs. "Miss Lea! I'm so glad you're here. We need help with the Christmas decorations."

Layla gave her young sister a warning look. "Dad said we have to wait until he gets home, remember."

Brittney shook her head, causing her two long pigtails to swing from side to side over her shoulders. "Uh-uh. He said we needed adult superfision."

"Adult super*vision,* squirt," Layla corrected. "And you need a speech therapist."

"Do not.

"Do, too."

"Girls, girls," Leandra said, still waiting on the porch, still petting the overly friendly dog, "please don't fight. I'd be glad to help, as long as Layla thinks it's okay for me to come inside."

Layla looked back at Leandra, her expression changing from concerned to resigned. "Well, you aren't a stranger and you are an adult. Yeah, sure. I guess Daddy won't mind. He's working late *as usual.*"

She backed up to open the big door wide. Mutt took that as his cue to come in. He pranced ahead of Leandra and headed up the wide wooden staircase, barking, his shaggy tail wagging. She heard Matt calling out to the dog upstairs.

Leandra stepped into the foyer, her eyes scanning the large, spacious rooms. "Wow, this place is incredible. It's so big and airy."

"And drafty," Layla said, pulling her zippered fleece jacket tighter around her midsection as she looked longingly at the empty fireplace. "We aren't allowed to start a fire when Daddy's not here. He's worked on the furnace, but sometimes it still goes out. We're supposed to get a new one after Christmas."

Brittney nodded, then took Leandra by the hand. "Yeah, cause Daddy's getting a big bonus check from his boss. That's how he's gonna fix the furnace. And we get presents, too."

"That's good," Leandra replied as she allowed the child to guide her into what looked like the den off to the right. On the left, a matching room held a huge battered antique dining table and eight matching chairs.

"Twin parlors," Leandra said, marveling at the potential of the house. "That dining table is beautiful."

"My mama bought it at a garage sale," Layla said. "She'd planned on redoing it, but…"

Her voice trailed off, causing Leandra to glance over at her. "Your mother sounds like a wonderful person."

"That's her picture," Brittney said, pointing to a brass-framed print over the fireplace mantel.

Leandra didn't have to see a picture of Alicia Welby to know the woman was perfect in every way. Long blond hair, big blue eyes, a smile that would light up any summer meadow. She could just imagine Nate and Alicia, running through a field of wildflowers together, falling down in the grass, laughing, loving.

Shaking away the image, Leandra decided she'd made a big mistake, coming out here. She wanted to see the rest of Nate's designs, talk to him about producing them for the public. But now, she wasn't so sure Nate would be ready for that.

But she'd already talked to Richard about the possibility of Nate displaying some of his bird-houses in Richard's store out on the highway. Flanagan's Food and General Merchandise would be the perfect place to showcase Nate's work, since the store was designed like an old-fashioned general store and carried art and crafts by several local artisans.

Once Richard had seen the house Nate had made, he agreed Nate had talent and could probably sell lots of the dainty little birdhouses. Especially during Christmas. It made perfect sense to Leandra.

But would it make sense to Nate?

Well, all she could do was ask. If he said no, then that would be that.

In the meantime, she could at least spend some time with his children and help them get this lovely old house ready for the Christmas season. That would save Nate some time and maybe improve his own spirits.

And she'd start by building a fire in the fireplace.

He couldn't make any sense of the way he'd been feeling lately.

Nate turned the pickup off the interstate, taking the highway that would lead him home. Just ahead, the sun was setting over the western sky, and with it that old sense of dread settled around Nate's shoulders like a welcome yoke.

He always dreaded going home. He loved his children, but pulling the truck up that long gravel driveway every night was one of the hardest things he had to do.

Until now.

Lately, Nate hadn't been dreading it as much as he used to. And that had him confused and wondering, and even more determined than ever to hang on to his dread.

If he let go of the dread, of the pain, then he would be dishonoring his wife's memory, wouldn't he?

If he thought about kissing Leandra Flanagan again, as he'd done just about every waking hour over the past couple of days, then he'd be unfaithful to Alicia, wouldn't he?

"Tell me, Lord," he said out loud, beating a hand against the steering wheel. "Tell me how to let go— of both of them."

He longed to be free of the guilt and grief that had colored his world for so long, longed to let go and give his children the love and attention he knew they craved. But if he gave in to this need to be free, that would mean having to finally let go of Alicia, too.

And he wasn't ready to do that.

And yet, Leandra's kiss kept beckoning him.

Her lips had been so soft, so sweet against his. That sweetness had jolted him all the way to his toes.

Which was why nothing made any sense anymore. How could he have feelings for two completely different women—one dead, one very much alive?

His dread was being replaced with a new feeling, one that he really wasn't ready to acknowledge.

And yet it was there, staring him in the face, coloring his melancholy with vivid shades of autumn fire. Liquid brown eyes, flashing. Fiery brunette hair, shining in the sun. A bright smile that seemed to change even the worst winter day to something bright and brilliant. And a big heart, so big it seemed to be trying to burst out of her petite little body.

Leandra.

He didn't want to hope. Couldn't bring himself to put a name to his feelings. He wanted to cling like a desperate, drowning man to his only lifeline.

His dead wife.

One more mile and he'd be home.

Then a voice echoed through the rumbling truck, a voice so clear, so distinct, that Nate thought he'd left the radio on.

But it wasn't the radio.

Alicia's not coming back, Nate. She's gone and she's at peace now. She'd want you to find your own peace. She'd want you to love again.

"No," Nate said, fighting against what he already knew in his heart. "No, I'm not ready yet."

And then he turned the truck off the road, toward his home. And slammed on the brakes so hard, gravel spewed up to hit the driver's side door.

Dusk surrounded the old white house. Dusk, and a thousand twinkling white lights strung around the porch posts, and across the front of the gabled roof. White icicle lights that moved and glittered like golden-white stars.

And on the door, a big evergreen wreath with a red and gold shiny ribbon trailing down from its top.

Somebody had decorated his house for the holidays.

Somebody had dared to disrupt Alicia's memory, her domain, *his* sacred, sad sanctuary.

And he had a pretty good idea just who that somebody was.

The little whisper of hope was gone now. And the dread was back, a welcome ally as Nate prepared to do battle.

"She might be gone," he told the voice he'd heard earlier, "but that doesn't mean I'm ready to have someone come in and take over completely."

It was time he got his head back on straight, then set Leandra Flanagan straight about a few things.

Nate entered the house, ready to roar his outrage. But he stopped just inside the door, his roar turning to a whimper of protest that he couldn't begin to voice.

There was a fire in the fireplace.

The mantel had been decorated with red, glowing candles and magnolia leaves. The den had been cleaned up, the pillows fluffed, the throw rugs straightened and swept. Two bright, fresh poinsettias sat on either side of the huge hearth.

He had to shut his eyes to the sheer beauty of it.

Hearing laughter in the kitchen, he opened his eyes and turned to the big dining room that they never used. It was set for dinner, with the old, chipped china they'd bought secondhand years ago. Another poinsettia graced the center of the table, and on the mismatched buffet, white candles burned in the silver candelabras Alicia had found at a flea market.

Everything looked homey and cozy, like a scene from a spread in a magazine. Everything seemed perfect.

Except for the horrible smell coming from the kitchen.

Determined to nip this intrusion in the bud, Nate

stomped down the hallway to the rear of the house, intent on giving Miss Leandra Flanagan a dressing down she would never forget.

Instead, he came upon a scene he would always remember.

His three children were centered around the butcher block counter he'd build years ago, flour on their hands and all over their faces, their backs to him as they watched Leandra and noisily offered encouraging instructions. Mutt lay by the back door, a dubious expression coloring his dark eyes. When the dog saw Nate, he lifted his head, rolled his doggy eyes, as if to say, "Don't ask," then whimpered and flopped his head down on his paws to stare up at his master.

But the woman standing by the stove really caught Nate's attention. Leandra had more flour all over her than any of the kids. It was in her hair, on her hands, all over her black cashmere sweater, and all the way down her checked trouser skirt. She even had flour dusted across her black loafers.

"What's going on around here?"

At the sound of his voice, the room went silent. Nate's children and Leandra all whirled around at the same time.

"Daddy, you're home!" Brittney said, rushing to fling herself in his arms. "Did you see? Did you see the lights? We did it ourselves. Miss Leandra wouldn't let me get up on the ladder, though. I got to do the short parts."

"I saw, pumpkin," Nate said, giving the child a kiss before he set her down and wiped a dab of flour from his own face. He glanced toward Leandra then. "I've seen all of it. You've been very busy."

Matt pointed at the stove. "And we're making you chicken and dumplings for supper."

Layla shrugged, then wiped her hands down the front of her jeans. "Except, we sorta burned the first batch."

"That explains the smell, at least," Nate replied, his gaze still locked with Leandra's. "I thought I told you kids, no cooking or fires while I'm not here."

"But Miss Leandra's an adult," Brittney pointed out.

"Are you sure about that?" Nate said, then instantly regretted it when he saw the hurt look in her dark eyes.

"I'm sorry," she said at last. "I can't cook. But I wanted—"

"She wanted to make you dinner," Brittney interjected, "and surprise you with the decorations. And tomorrow, we're going to get a tree, right, Miss Leandra?"

"If your father doesn't object," Leandra said, her hurt expression hidden by a slight smile. "Now, I'd better watch this new batch of dumplings. Maybe this time, I'll get it right."

Matt glanced over into the bubbling pot of white mush. "Yeah, cause Mutt wouldn't even eat the last batch and that dog eats anything."

Upon hearing his name, Mutt lifted his head, sniffed, then got up and ran from the room, his tail wagging a hasty farewell.

Leandra's smile turned into a frown. "I *can't* cook. I don't know why I tried. I shouldn't have done this."

Layla shot Nate a warning look, then hurried to the stove. "But these dumplings look okay, Miss Leandra. Really. And they smell good, too."

"Better than the last ones," Matt said, grinning.

Brittney pulled Nate close, tugging at his hand. "See, Daddy, don't them look right?"

"It's those," Layla corrected.

"Okay, okay," Brittney said, moaning. Then she made a dramatic effort to correct herself. "*Those* dumplings look just right."

Some of Nate's initial anger drained away, to be replaced with a teasing tone. "Well, how many poor chickens had to die for this dinner?"

"Only one," Layla told him. "We used canned broth with the chicken broth to make the dumplings, but we got most of the chicken out before the dumplings got scorched. We had more canned broth, so we started another pot with that."

"I'm going to drop the chicken meat in once I see if this batch is edible," Leandra told him. "Honestly,

I don't know what went wrong. This is my mother's recipe and I followed her instructions."

Nate stared over at her, enjoying the skittish way she tried to explain, her hands lifting in the air with each word. Which only made little flour dust balls float out all around her. Then he reminded himself that he was supposed to be angry with her.

"We just forgot to turn the heat down," Matt explained, wiping even more flour across his smudged face.

Leandra checked the burner button, then went to the sink to wash her hands. "Hopefully, this will be ready in about ten minutes." Then she turned to the children. "Let's get this cleaned up, and we'll get the salad and tea out of the refrigerator. I'll drop the chicken back in to heat it up, and Matt, you can pour the milk."

The three children went to work wiping down the flour-dusted counter while Leandra tried to dust herself off with a dish towel.

After the children had gone into the dining room, carrying drinks and condiments for the salad, Nate walked over to Leandra. "Why'd you do all of this?"

She looked up then, into his eyes. With a little shrug, she said, "I'm wondering that same thing myself." Lowering her head, she added, "You're mad."

Nate couldn't deny that. "I *was* good and mad, yeah. When I pulled up and saw all those lights—"

"The children asked me to help, Nate." She gazed up at him then, a pleading look centered in her eyes. "I came by to see you, but you weren't home yet. They wanted to decorate, so I agreed to help. Then we had so much fun, and you were late, and it was dinnertime and they told me you like dumplings—" She stopped, turned back to the sink. "I'm sorry."

Nate tried to find the words he needed to say. He wanted to tell her that this wasn't her house, that she had no right to just come barreling in here and take over, changing things around, trying to make this house something it could never be.

But when she looked up at him, with flour smudged across her cheek, with her heart in her eyes, all he could do was reach out and touch her face. "You've got a glob of flour right there," he said, his fingers brushing away the white specks. Then he smiled. "Actually, you've got flour on just about every part of you."

Leandra let out a little rush of breath. "I think I've got more on me and the kitchen floor than in the dumplings," she said. "We should have just ordered pizza."

"They don't deliver way out here," he replied, his fingers still touching on her face. "And I do like dumplings, even scorched ones."

She reached up to take his hand away. "But you're angry with me. I—I overstepped the bounds, didn't I?"

"Yes, you did," he admitted. "We normally don't go all out for Christmas."

"But why not?"

"It just makes...it makes it harder."

"But the children—"

"My children are just fine. They've been just fine."

"So you *are* angry, and you think I should mind my own business?"

"Something like that."

She pushed past him then. Taking the plate of chopped chicken off the counter, she dumped it into the dumpling pot, stirred it, then turned off the burner. "Well, here's your dinner. And I'll be leaving now."

"Hey, wait just a minute," Nate said, reaching out to catch her by the hand. "Since you cooked it, you have to eat it. Or are you afraid you'll get food poisoning?"

"Don't try to make me feel better, Nate. I messed up and now I don't know how to fix it."

"More flour and a new pot," he replied, his hand in hers. "Don't leave."

"But, I'm so stupid. I thought—"

"You wanted to help my children," he reminded her. "Look, Leandra, I know how persuasive those three can be, especially when they gang up on a person. And they know that you're too nice to turn them down."

She looked down at the floor. "It was hard to say

no, but I enjoyed helping them decorate. They said you hadn't done it in a long time."

"No, and I did promise them," he said, guilt in each word. "It's just hard sometimes."

She glanced back up then, her eyes wide. "But it can get easier, Nate. With time and prayer. That's what my mother always tells me when I'm struggling with a big problem."

"Time and prayer," he repeated. "Seems like I'm all out of both."

"You only have to ask."

He let go of her hand then. "Ask what—that God give me my wife back, that He show me how to give my children the life they deserve? What should I ask for, Leandra?"

"You're mad again."

"I've been mad for the last three years," he retorted, pushing a hand through his hair in frustration.

"Then you need to ask for relief, Nate. You need to find some peace, some closure." She reached a hand to his face, her fingers treading like an angel's wings over his skin. "You need to let go of the past and look toward the future."

The need he felt for her then caused him to back away. He couldn't, wouldn't pull her into his arms and ask God for salvation or peace. He would fight against this, with his every breath. Because he liked being miserable too much.

"I'm not ready to let go," he told her.

"I know," Leandra replied. "And that's why I should just leave right now."

But she didn't get to leave, after all. Brittney bounced into the room, pushing between them. "Can we eat? I'm starving."

Nate picked up his daughter, then tickled her tummy, his smile belying the darkness in his eyes. "I'm hungry myself. And I sure don't want to miss out on those dumplings." Looking at Leandra over Brittney's head, he said, "C'mon, Leandra. You cooked. You get to serve. And then, I'll wash the dishes and clear up everything else."

"Not everything, Nate," Leandra told him as she whirled past him. "There's a lot that needs to be cleared up between us, but I don't think you're ready to admit that just yet."

Chapter Nine

Nate had cleaned the kitchen, all right. After they'd eaten dinner, with the children laughing and talking over the loud silence between the two adults, he'd promptly done his part, then stomped off to the barn to "check on Honeyboy and do some work." That left Leandra with the children. Since tomorrow was Saturday, she'd told them to settle into their pajamas so they could watch a late movie.

Earlier, in the midst of a fit of impulsiveness, she'd promised them hot chocolate and cookies by the fire, to cap off what she had hoped would be a lovely evening. But that had backfired the minute their father had arrived, with a pop every bit as loud as the dry wood now crackling in the fireplace.

Nate did not appreciate any of her efforts.

And to think she'd started out with the best of intentions.

Since they'd had the night off from rehearsals, she'd decided it would be a good time to talk to Nate about mass marketing his birdhouses. Then, suddenly, she'd been up on a ladder stringing Christmas lights—lights that she'd had her brother Richard deliver from his store, along with the poinsettias and candles, and supplies for making dumplings.

"You're turning into a domestic dynamo," Richard had teased on the phone. "What else did you need? A chicken and three cans of chicken broth? Leandra, I'm worried about you—if you're cooking for this man, that means it's serious, and that also means his health is in serious danger."

Although her brother had been joking, his words now rang true. She'd not only ruined dinner, but also any chances of furthering things with Nate.

And since when had she decided to further things, anyway? Since that kiss, dummy, she told herself as she poured hot chocolate into mugs on a big tray next to the cookies. She then carried it into the den where the kids sat already watching the movie.

Seeing the three Welby children all curled up with pillows and blankets by the roaring fire only added to Leandra's misery. She wanted Nate there, too. She wanted to curl up with him by that fire.

But Nate had retreated into his memories and his guilt.

"Does your father work in the barn every night?"

she asked Layla now, concern for the girl motivating her question.

"Just about," Layla replied as she took a mug from Leandra. "He's always taking on extra work, even though he's been promoted at his regular job."

"But surely he spends time with you, right?"

"Only when he's forced to," Layla said, her words low so the younger children wouldn't hear. Then she added, "He's a good daddy, Miss Lea. He just misses our mama, and I guess you figured out I look just like her."

Leandra nodded. "You're just as pretty."

"That's why he hates me," Layla blurted out. Then, clearly mortified, she said, "Don't tell him I said that."

Leandra put her cocoa down on a nearby table. "Honey, you're wrong. Your father loves you. Surely you know that."

"He loves me because he has to—that's his duty as a father. But…" Her voice trailed off, and Leandra watched her swallow back the tears. "I remind him of her and because of that, he hates being around me. That's why he goes out to that old barn every night."

"Oh, baby." Leandra pulled the girl into her arms, rocking her back and forth while silent tears slipped down Layla's face. "Shh. Don't cry now."

"What's the matter?" Brittney asked, ever curious even if she was sleepy-eyed.

"The movie," Leandra said, grabbing the first excuse she could find. "This is the sad part and Layla doesn't want to watch. Better hurry, or you'll miss the ending."

With that, Brittney snuggled back down inside her old quilt. "Don't be sad, sister. It's just a movie."

Leandra wished life could be that way—just like a movie or a book with a happy ending. But life didn't always play out the way people dreamed it would.

"Have you talked to your father about this?" she asked Layla a while later, after the girl had settled down and both Brittney and Matt were snoozing on the floor by the fire.

Pushing Leandra away, Layla fought for the attitude that had kept her true emotions hidden so well. "He's not the talking kind, or haven't you noticed?"

"Yes, I've noticed," Leandra admitted. "But if you went to him, told him how this makes you feel—"

"No," Layla said, jumping up off the couch. "I couldn't do that. He'd just get even more mad at me. He doesn't like to talk about Mama at all. And Brittney is always asking questions—she was too young to even remember Mama. It would just make things worse if he knew I'd said something to you." Grabbing her blanket, she said, "You can't say anything, Miss Lea, please. You can't tell him."

"I won't, I promise," Leandra told the jittery teen. "But he needs to know, honey."

"He knows," Layla said, the wisdom of the two words warring with her youthful expression.

Suddenly, Leandra understood the girl's predicament. Layla and Nate were tiptoeing around each other, each trying hard not to disturb Alicia's memories. And neither of them had even come close to dealing with her death.

That had been obvious tonight.

Nate had been so angry! She'd seen it, felt it, the minute he'd entered the kitchen. And just because his children had wanted the house decorated. But he didn't want anything changed or rearranged. He wanted to keep this house intact, even though it was in obvious need of some tender loving care. He wanted to freeze time, to keep things the way they were when Alicia had lived in this house.

"Well, she wouldn't want this," Leandra told herself a few minutes later as she rinsed their cups and put away the cookies. "She would want her children to be happy and healthy. She'd want them to celebrate life, not preserve it in a time warp. And she'd want you to be happy, too, Nate."

But would she want you to be with someone like me?

Leandra finally got the children off to bed, then turned to go out to the barn. "I'm going to tell him I'm leaving now," she said to Mutt. "And while I'm at it, I just might give the man a piece of my mind, too."

Mutt whimpered his response to that suggestion, then wagged his tail in anticipation.

Nate moved the tiny piece of wood back and forth through his fingers, trying to decide if he wanted to carve it into a leaf or a flower.

Then again, maybe he'd just leave it the way it was. Why couldn't people leave well enough alone, anyway?

He thought of Leandra, standing in the middle of his kitchen, standing in the very spot where Alicia had stood so many nights. He could still hear Leandra's laughter as he'd entered the front door tonight.

But he couldn't remember Alicia's laugh.

And that hurt so much.

Throwing the wood down, Nate stood there staring at his workbench. He couldn't even hide behind his work tonight. Couldn't even think beyond Leandra trying to make dumplings.

Dumplings!

He'd eaten them, scorched parts and all, just to please his children, just to be polite to her, and actually, the food hadn't been half bad. And all the while, he'd noticed her hair, shining softly in the candlelight, her laughter echoing across the table at him, calling out to him, her eyes, beseeching and encouraging, glancing his way as she chattered away with his children.

Her lips.

"How can I feel this way, Lord? How can I want to be with another woman? A completely different woman?"

Different in so many ways.

Yet, so like his Alicia in other ways.

Leandra had once again been kind to his children. She'd once again taken over where no one else had bothered to even lend a hand. She'd put their needs, their requests, above her own comfort. She'd made them happy, laughing and carefree again.

And that, he had to admit, had been her saving grace.

Suddenly, all the anger drained out of Nate, leaving him with a fatigue so great, he swayed against the sturdy workbench. "I need some help here, God."

"You sure do," Leandra said from the open doorway.

Nate whirled to find her standing there, staring at him, her hands in the big pockets of her wool overcoat. He didn't miss the pain etched across her face. He could see it clearly from the dim overhead light.

"Go ahead," she said as she walked closer. "Tell Him your troubles. Don't let me interfere."

Nate shuffled his feet, looked down at the sawdust covered floor. "Can't a man have a private moment to pray around here, at least?"

"I'm sorry," Leandra said, backing out of the barn. "I just wanted you to know the children are in bed and I'm going home."

"Wait," he said, turning around. "We need to talk about a few things. You said we needed to clear the air."

Leandra stopped just outside the door. "I came out here to do that very thing, but now I think the air is completely clear, and so are your feelings toward me and my…intrusion. Again, I am so sorry."

Nate let out an irritated sigh, then in two long strides had her by the arm, pulling her back inside the barn. "Would you just quit apologizing? You haven't done anything wrong."

She scoffed, glanced away. "Oh, except decorate a house you didn't want to decorate in the first place, no matter what you promised your children. Except cook a meal that turned out to be a fiasco even on the second try, and make myself a general all-around nuisance. I'd say that's a lot to be sorry about."

Nate stared down at her, hoping to make her understand everything that was troubling his tired heart.

"It's not you," he told her, his hands on her arms. "It's me, Leandra. It's my bad attitude, my problems, me and my pain and guilt, and my lack of faith."

"Oh, I understand," she told him, her eyes glistening in a pool of unshed tears. "And that's why I came to say good-night. I won't push myself off on you again, Nate. It was foolish, considering that I've already been through one bad relationship. I should have learned from that, but no, I had to come home, take on this job just to tell myself I'm still worthy of some kind of work, then just like that, I saw you standing by that pasture, with your dog and your horse and your three adorable children, and I got this funny notion all the way down to my toes."

"Leandra—"

"No," she said, pushing him away as she turned her back to him. "I guess I was on the rebound, you know. Same old tired reasoning. I took all the signals the wrong way, wanted more from you than you were willing to give. But, I can see it all so plainly now. You don't want my help, don't need me in your life. You've got it all planned out, exactly the way you want it."

She whirled then. "Except that your children are suffering because you are so lost in the past, you can't even begin to see that they need their father."

"I'm a good father," he said, anger clouding his better judgment.

"Yes, you are," she replied. "You are a good, dutiful father. You do all the things that are expected of you. But what about the unexpected, Nate? What about that?"

The anger was back, refreshing and nurturing, and so welcome he almost cried out with relief. "You have no right to come into my home like this and tell me how to raise my children. You don't know the first thing about children, and from everything I've seen, you don't even want to have any of your own."

She stood there in the moonlight, her hands shoved in the pockets of her coat, shivering. Silent. But her eyes, oh, he'd never forget the pain in her eyes. That pain shouted a message, a warning, to him.

He wanted to take back what he'd just said, but the words were still echoing out over the night. Never to be taken back.

"Leandra," he said, reaching for her.

"No," she said again, her voice strained and husky. "You're absolutely right, Nate. I don't know anything about raising children. I never thought I'd want children. I thought I had my life all mapped out and then everything changed. Everything turned ugly and I came home, a complete and utter failure."

She shrugged, her laughter brittle with a bitterness that tore through his hard heart and made his anger feel like a brick pressing against his windpipe. "I guess you and the children were just a distraction, a way to prove to myself that I had a heart, and some maternal qualities, after all. But, hey, I even failed at that, too, didn't I?"

He tried to reach out to her again, and again, she pushed him away, her hand flying out in defense.

"No, it's all right. I understand what you're trying to say to me. We weren't meant for each other, and it's silly and a waste of time for us to pretend. So…let's just keep this as business. You're just about finished with the set and the props and I've got your check all ready down at city hall. Two more weeks and I'll be on my way back to Houston." She whirled and started toward her car. "And then, I guess I'll see what else I can do to make my life a total mess."

Nathan stood there, stunned, as she got in her car and backed it around. And then she was gone, leaving him to stare off into the night.

Mutt came running up, whimpering for attention. But Nate couldn't give the dog the attention he craved.

Maybe Leandra was right, he thought as he locked up the barn and made his way to the house. Maybe he was making all the right moves, but would he ever be able to really love anyone again?

Would he ever be able to give his children the one thing they needed the most—his heart?

That heart hurt tonight, hurt from the cold wind on his back, from the cruel words he'd flung out at Leandra, and mostly, it hurt from her response, her own self-condemning speech.

He'd caused her pain, the one thing he'd hoped to avoid. He'd turned things around, blamed her for his own inconsistencies, his own failures.

"I shouldn't have let things go this far," he reasoned

as Mutt hit the porch ahead of him. "I shouldn't have flirted with her, teased her. And I surely shouldn't have kissed her there in the prayer garden."

But you did, Nate. Now what are you gonna do about it?

"Mutt, did you learn how to speak?" Nate asked, glancing around.

But Nate knew that what he'd just heard had come somewhere from deep inside himself. His conscience was arguing with him.

His conscience was telling him to go after Leandra and ask her for another chance.

"I'm not going to listen, not tonight," he said out loud. "I've already hurt her enough."

Mutt groaned, then barked to be let inside where it was warm, where his bed waited just inside the pantry doorway.

"I hear you, boy," Nate told the dog. "It's gonna be a long, cold night, that's for sure."

Especially with the scent of Leandra's perfume, and a faint whiff of scorched dumplings, still lingering in his mind.

Chapter Ten

The next Monday night was hard for Leandra. They would rehearse early in the afternoon and on some nights this week, to accommodate everyone's work schedules. Now that the children were out of school for the holidays, everyone was more able to go through a full-scale dress rehearsal. Soon though, it would be the real thing in front of a sold-out audience each night.

Next week, the pageant would have a four-day run with the last performance ending on Christmas Eve, just before the annual candlelight service at the church across the street. The service was every bit as popular and anticipated as the pageant. Leandra expected a big crowd there, too.

Now that the pageant was becoming a reality, it seemed almost anticlimactic. She should be excited. The rehearsals were going well. The stage decorations and props were incredible, and everything was moving along right on schedule. She'd worked so hard, such long hours, not only on the pageant but on several other projects Chet had dropped in her lap, and becoming involved with Nate and his children had only added to both the stress and the joy of this whole production. What would she do once this was all over?

Things were already over, she told herself. At least as far as Nate was concerned.

All weekend, she'd dreaded tonight, dreaded seeing Nate's face, the memory of his words forever etched in her being as a reminder of her utter failure.

"You don't know the first thing about raising children. You don't even want children."

He had been so right. And so wrong.

Because she'd changed over the past few weeks.

Now, Leandra's heart was playing tricks on her. Now, each time she thought about being in that drafty old house with the three Welby children, drinking hot chocolate and eating cookies by the fire, she only longed to have that chance again. Over and over again.

All day Saturday, she'd moped around until her mother had put her to work wrapping Christmas gifts. Sunday, she'd gone to church, hoping to find some solace in Reverend Powell's powerful words. But even the scriptures leading up to the birth of Jesus couldn't bring her any joy.

Sunday afternoon, she'd gone for a long walk in the cold, praying, listening, hoping to find some answers in her silent meditations.

But now, as she sat here watching people file in for the rehearsal, she knew there was only one answer.

She couldn't fall in love with Nathan Welby.

She wouldn't fall in love with Nathan Welby.

She'd certainly never set out to do that.

Quickly, she made a mental inventory of why she'd been thrown into this situation in the first place.

I quit my job. I came home. Wanted to stay busy, so took job as pageant coordinator. Had to hire a carpenter. Children wanted me to be their mommy. Couldn't do that, so decided to be a good friend, even though I'm terribly attracted to their daddy.

It should have ended there, except that she'd rushed headlong into asking Nate and the children to Thanksgiving dinner.

That dinner, at least, had been nice. Wonderful, except that her mother's vase had been broken.

Nate gave me a birdhouse. *For my mother.*

Nate kissed me.

I got this crazy notion to help him sell birdhouses. So I went out to house. Got talked into building a fire, decorating for Christmas, and cooking dinner. Ruined dinner. Ruined our friendship. Ruined everything.

Fools rush in where angels fear to tread.

And now I am utterly confused and miserable.

End of list. End of story.

Now, she had to muster up the courage to face him. She didn't have any choice. She had to get through this week, then the performances next week, and then it would be over.

"I can do that," she said out loud. "I have to finish what I started."

"You're talking to yourself," Margaret told her as she sat down in the seat beside Leandra. Then she took one look at Leandra's face and groaned.

"My, what's wrong with you? Are you coming down with the flu? I don't want the baby exposed—"

Leandra took Margaret's hand away from her stomach. "I don't have the flu, so stop worrying. I'm just in a mood. Tired, I guess."

Margaret grinned knowingly then poked Leandra on the arm with a slim finger, her diamond solitaire shining in the muted auditorium light. "Richard told Jack and me about your dinner with the Welbys. No wonder you're exhausted. Cooking for those three children and that man—"

"I'd rather not talk about that," Leandra said, her tone dismissive. "And Richard shouldn't have told you, either."

Margaret twisted around to stare at her. "Oh, he just thought it was so sweet. Face it, Leandra, you've never gone to this much trouble for a man before. We're all dying to hear the details."

Leandra got up, her clipboard and papers clutched to her chest. "Look, there are no details." Then glaring down at the dubious expression on Margaret's face, she added, "And just for the record, I *did* cook for William every now and then."

"But mostly, according to what little you've told me about the time you spent with William, you ate just about every meal out," Margaret interjected. "You told me that. Told me he took you to fancy restaurants all over Houston."

"Well, that's over and so is any more attempts to cook for the Welbys," Leandra said, her patience snapping.

Margaret got up, too, then placed a hand on Leandra's arm, the teasing lilt in her voice gone. "Are you okay?"

Leandra saw the concern in her sister-in-law's eyes, and instantly regretted her outburst. "I'm fine, Margaret. Just stressed about this production. I'm sorry I took it out on you."

Margaret patted her arm. "You know you can tell me anything, and I won't blab like Richard did. Not if you really don't want me to—just say so."

"Thanks," Leandra told her, appreciative of Margaret's rare show of discretion. She felt sure she *could* trust Margaret if she really needed to confide in her, but Leandra wasn't ready for that. "It's nothing, honestly. I just overstepped my place with Nathan and now I feel awful about it. I shouldn't have cooked dinner at all. And I intend to keep my distance from now on." Then she glanced around and whispered low, "He's not over Alicia."

Understanding colored Margaret's big eyes. "Oh, I see. You know, Lea, it's hard to lose someone we love. Friends and family try to bring us comfort, but it takes a long time to accept. Death is so final, and the answers aren't easy. Maybe Nate's just not ready to take that next step." She shrugged then shook her head. "And…I'd sure be hesitant about stepping in to fill Alicia's shoes. How she put up with those children—"

Leandra held out a hand to quiet her, almost glad Margaret had stopped philosophizing and was now back to her old snobbish self. "I know. But believe me, the children aren't the problem. I've figured it all out in my head. I was on the rebound from breaking up with William. I needed to feel needed, and the children pulled me into this relationship. Nate is a kind, wonderful man, but I'm pulling myself out. As of now."

"Oh, really?" Margaret sounded doubtful. "Well, I hope for your sake, that's true." She placed her hands on Leandra's shoulder, then leaned close. "'Cause Nate and the children just walked through the back door."

He tried not to look for her. But Nate couldn't help himself. His gaze automatically searched the crowd gathered in the auditorium, looking for Leandra.

Then he saw her, standing on the other side near the stage with her back to him, talking to Margaret.

This was going to be hard.

All weekend, he'd cursed himself for a fool. He shouldn't have treated her so callously after she'd been so nice and helpful to his children.

His children, he reminded himself now. Leandra had tried to tell him how to take care of his own children. That wasn't right.

But she'd been right about him. And so very wrong, too.

He loved his children. Yet he knew he'd been avoiding them, letting them drift along on the coattails of that love. He'd only been mad because Leandra had pointed out the obvious. Yet, he wasn't ready to let someone else in on his misery. He wasn't ready to relinquish paternal rights to another woman besides their mother.

He'd just have to do better at being their father. Having thought about this all weekend, he'd made good on his promise by taking the children to a movie, then Christmas shopping. He'd even toyed with the idea of taking them to church on Sunday, but a million excuses clouded that promise right out of the way. He had stayed away from the barn, at least. They'd put up a Christmas tree on Sunday afternoon.

And he could still remember Brittney's words.

"I thought Miss Lea was going to help us decorate the tree, Daddy."

"She couldn't make it, honeypie. But we'll get the job done."

And he would get the job done. Alone. He didn't need some city woman telling him how to raise his children, how to decorate his house, how to…smile again, laugh again, feel again.

He didn't need Leandra Flanagan.

So here he stood, trying hard to be a good father, trying hard to live up to the pressure, the pain, hoping he could make it through this next week of staying here in the same room with her to watch his children rehearse. He'd promised them he wouldn't leave. He was going to keep that promise, no matter how much he wanted to go to Leandra and beg her to come back and make more dumplings.

"We have a major problem," Chet Reynolds told Leandra a few minutes later.

Everyone was settled into the seats directly below the stage to go over last minute business items. Leandra intended to make a few suggestions when Chet came rushing in the back door, his hands waving, his big feet flapping against the concrete floor.

"What's the matter, Chet?" she asked, concerned for the man's health. His face was red and he was breathing heavy from rushing up the aisle.

"It's the lion," Chet began, then took a long

calming breath, his Adam's apple bobbing. "And the lamb."

Leandra glanced around. "Where is Mr. Emory anyway? He's our lion and he gets to try on his costume tonight."

"Was our lion," Chet said, waving his hands again. "He had a heart attack about two hours ago. He's in the hospital."

"Oh, my." Leandra hated hearing bad news such as this. Mr. Emory was a sweet old man and he loved being a part of the theater since he'd done some acting in his younger days. He wouldn't want to miss out on being the lion in this production. "I hope he's going to be all right," she said above the murmur of concern moving through the crowd.

"He's fine," Chet told her, his sentences choppy and breathless. "Lucky it was mild. Rest and therapy. But he can't be in the pageant. Doctor's orders."

"I understand," Leandra said. "And I sure hope Mr. Emory recovers soon. Luckily, we still have time to find another lion. Someone tall and willing to roar a bit now and then."

"My Daddy'd be perfect for that," Matt shouted, grinning from ear to ear. "He roars at us all the time."

Leandra's gaze instantly connected with Nate's. He was sitting at the back of the crowd, slightly away from the main players. After hearing Matt's rather loud suggestion, Nate slouched down in his seat and ran a hand over his chin in agitation.

Before Leandra could say anything, Chet spoke up. "Nate, you would make a good lion. You got the right coloring and everything."

Nate stood up, then shook his head. "Nah. I'm only here to help with the set. I work behind the scenes."

"But Daddy, we need you," Layla said, twisting in her seat to stare at her father. "We don't have much time and all you have to do is march out when we're singing the animal song."

"And he gets to roar really loud," Matt reminded her.

After the laughter had settled down, Nate stood there with his hands in the pockets of his jeans, a distressed look covering his face. "Oh, all right," he said at last, defeat in every word. "I guess I can do that much, at least." Then he looked directly at Leandra. "It'll give me a chance to spend some time with my children."

"Yea! My daddy's the lion," Brittney said, rushing headlong into Nate's arms. "Now you get to rehearse with us every day."

"I sure do," Nate said, his eyes still on Leandra.

She could read that expression well enough to know he was only doing this to show her he could be a good father. Well, she was glad for that, at least.

Chet tugged at her sleeve, bringing her back to reality. "And what about the lamb?"

"What about the lamb?" she asked, wondering what else could go wrong.

"Thelma Nesmith," Chet said, his eyebrows shooting up like bird's wings.

"Yes, Thelma is our lamb. Don't tell me she dropped out of the production, too?"

"Got a cruise for Christmas from her rich son over in Dallas. She'll be leaving in two days. Saw her at the post office today. Said she was gonna call you tomorrow. Might as well tell you tonight, though. We need a new lamb."

Leandra smiled, took a long breath, then nodded. "I'll go through the directory and find someone tomorrow, Chet. No problem."

"You could be the lamb," Brittney said, smiling at Leandra. "My Daddy said you're as pretty as a lamb, 'member?"

Leandra groaned silently while the flush of embarrassment went up her neck and face. "Uh—"

Margaret raised her hand then. "You would make a lovely lamb, Leandra. That has a nice ring— Leandra the lovely lamb. And you have to be nice to the lion."

Making a mental note to seriously strangle her sister-in-law later, Leandra shook her head. "I have enough to do without wearing a lamb's costume."

"But Miss Lea, we need someone tonight to

practice," Matt said. "C'mon. You're the same height as Miss Thelma anyway. We won't even have to make another costume."

"I…" Leandra stopped to find too many hopeful gazes all staring directly at her. She'd asked all of them to give of their time and talent, so how could she refuse at this late date? "I guess I could fill in," she said at last, "since we don't have much time and I won't have to learn too many lines."

Chet beamed. "Shucks, all you have to do is sit with the lion and let there be peace on earth, goodwill to men."

"Is that all?" Leandra said, her chuckle just as shaky as her heart felt right now. "A piece of cake."

"This production just got a whole lot more interesting," Margaret said, grinning from ear to ear.

"I'll deal with you later," Leandra told her under her breath as everyone headed to find their costumes for the first dress rehearsal. Then, pulling Margaret to the side, she added, "I thought you wanted me to stay away from Nate Welby and his children."

Margaret glanced around to make sure no one could hear them, then turned back to Leandra, smiling. "That was before I realized you're in love with the man."

"I am not."

"Oh, Leandra, you'd better practice in front of the mirror before you become that little lamb.

'Cause that big, bad lion has a thing for you, and I think you feel the same way about him—and it's not my place to interfere with that, what with peace on earth riding on this entire relationship."

"I'm glad you find this so funny, Margaret."

"It's just good to see you in love at last, even if it is with that cowboy and his brood—better you than me," Margaret told her before she scooted away, her grin still intact.

What does she know? Leandra silently asked herself. Margaret was so shallow and snobbish, she was probably just enjoying Leandra's discomfort. Yet, in her heart, Leandra knew even Margaret wasn't that rotten. Margaret had good qualities, and she had been concerned earlier. It must be the hormones from the new pregnancy making her act and sound crazy.

I am not in love with Nate Welby, Leandra told herself.

Then she looked up and saw Nate standing there, watching her, his eyes that golden, hazel shade of wonder, his hair curling around his face like a lion's mane, his lips twisted in a wry, resigned expression. The man didn't have to roar; she could read him loud and clear.

"I certainly feel like a lamb," she said as she headed to find her own costume. "A lamb about to go to the slaughter."

Mr. Tuttle came up to her then, already dressed

as Santa Claus. "The lion and the lamb—Nate and you," he said, his chuckle moving down his big belly. "Now that's worth the price of a ticket."

When Leandra gave him a mock-mean glare, he only winked and smiled, as if he knew exactly what she wanted for Christmas.

Suddenly, this production had taken a new twist.

But Leandra couldn't be sure it would be for the better since she knew in her heart there would be no peace between her and Nate Welby, at Christmas or any time soon.

Chapter Eleven

"And so, right there in front of everyone, Leandra and Nathan both agreed to being the lamb and the lion in the production. It was so funny." Margaret gave a dainty little shrug and giggled behind her hand. "Especially the look on Leandra's face."

Everyone around the dinner table was now looking at Leandra in hopes of a repeat of her shocked expression, no doubt. Well, she wasn't going to give them one. "Margaret, I can't understand why you're so fascinated with all of this. To hear you talk, you'd rather eat nails than be seen in the same room with the Welbys."

Margaret stopped giggling to glance over at Jack for support. "Well, I wouldn't exactly put it that way, Lea. I just had some legitimate concerns about the man and those ragamuffin children, but I have to admit since I've been working with them on this production, I've kinda gotten used to them."

Colleen smiled, then passed the barbecue sauce to Howard. "Thanks for bringing dinner, Richard. I was afraid with all the last-minute work on the pageant, I'd have to serve grilled cheese sandwiches for dinner."

The pageant rehearsal had been early today, so they were having a casual midweek family dinner consisting of barbecue and all the trimmings from Richard's store. He cooked and smoked his own meat on a huge grill out back. His barbecue, baked beans and potato salad were all famous for miles around. As were his homemade pies.

Taking the hint to change the subject, Richard grinned and saluted his mother. "My pleasure. But I think next week we ought to let Leandra whip up some of her famous dumplings. From what I hear, they keep you full for days to come."

Leandra threw down her napkin. "Okay, that does it. Does anyone else want to tell a cute joke about my personal life? Since it's open season on Leandra, let's hear it. C'mon, don't be shy." She moved her head from side to side, waiting.

The room was suddenly quiet.

Then Mark spoke up. "I'm glad it's you and not me, Sis. When you were away, I was the one who got all the teasing remarks. Seems if you're single and a Flanagan, you don't stand a chance of getting any peace around here."

"Amen to that," Leandra said, Mark's words calming her down a bit. "How did you deal with it, Mark?" she asked him, ignoring Jack's smirk and Richard's grin.

Mark winked, then said, "I just kept right on eating my dinner, and as you know, I always carry some ready reading material. It tends to drown out the superficial small talk."

Michael spoke up then. "We gave up on you long ago, Mark. You're a lost cause. But we're still holding out for little Lea here. *If* she can learn to cook."

"Now, boys," Howard said, his tone soft but firm. "There's no law that says a woman has to know how to cook to get a man. There's more to love than fried chicken and turnip greens."

"Maybe," Richard replied as he stabbed another slice of brisket, "but it sure doesn't hurt."

"What are you worried about, little brother?" Jack asked Richard, laughing. "You can outcook any woman around here—except Mom, of course."

"You saved yourself there, Jack," Colleen replied, one hand on the high chair to hold Philip in and the other on the windup swing right by her chair, where baby Carissa snoozed away to a soft lullaby. Little Corey was in another high chair beside his parents. "And Richard, you're engaged, so you don't count."

Richard chewed his meat, then nodded. "Yeah, and I miss Sheila. I'll be glad when she's done with medical school in Dallas. I'll see her during Christmas, at least."

Leandra groaned. "So *I'm* the center of speculation these days. How did y'all find out about my dumplings, anyway?"

Everyone spoke at once, each blaming the other.

"Richard told me."

"Well, Michael told me."

"Kim called me."

"Jack told Margaret and—"

"That explains it," Mark shouted over the fray. "Margaret can't keep a secret."

Kim spoke up then. "She kept her pregnancy a secret for four whole weeks."

Margaret glared around the room, her tiny hands on the table. "I didn't want to spoil *your* being the one with the new baby," she said to Kim. "Even though you're ahead of me in the girl department."

"Sorry." Kim stuck out her tongue, then smiled over at her baby daughter. "There's enough joy for both of us, though—boy or girl."

Margaret nodded to that. "And—I can keep a secret. It wasn't me," she told the group. "Richard got the whole thing started about Leandra cooking for the Welbys. It was just so funny, picturing Leandra stringing lights and cooking dumplings. Dumplings, of all things? Lea, why didn't you start with something simple like canned soup?"

Leandra slapped a hand on the table, her patience

growing thin. "Okay, okay. I'm trying not to lose my temper, since you are all family and some of you are in a delicate way. But that's enough. Can we change the subject, please?"

Sensing that her daughter was about to cause a scene, Colleen nodded. "Leandra's right. This is none of our business."

"Good," Leandra replied, taking a piece of Texas Toast to sop up barbecue sauce. "I'm glad someone in this room can be tactful."

"Let's change the subject then," Richard replied. "Let's talk about…oh…say…birdhouses. I was expecting to have at least half a dozen to sell before Christmas."

"Birdhouses?" Margaret perked up again. "You mean, like the one on the table in the front hallway. Didn't Nate—"

Leandra stood up then. "Yes, Nate made the birdhouse, for Mama, as a means of repaying *her* for Thanksgiving."

"That was nice," Mark said, a hand on his sister's arm. "Sit down and tell us about it, Lea."

Leandra saw the warning look in Mark's eyes. Ever the calm, detached professor, he was telling her to let it go. If she lost her cool, they would just suspect that she really did have feelings for Nate. But Mark looked as if he already knew that, too.

She sank back down in her chair, defeated. "Yes, Nate makes birdhouses in a little workshop out in his barn. I was impressed with the craftsmanship, so I told Richard about them, hoping that he would display some of them in the store."

"Which I agreed to do," Richard said, his tone serious at last. "Only I have yet to receive any. Did you talk to Nate about bringing them by?"

"Not really," Leandra admitted. "We didn't get around to discussing it."

"Better things to do," Michael said, giving his wife a knowing look.

Leandra gritted her teeth, then asked God for patience. "I was getting the children to bed and cleaning up the kitchen."

"Dumplings everywhere—" Jack began, but his mother's hand on his arm stopped him. "Oh, back to the birdhouses—do you think Richard could actually sell some of them? I mean, are they that good?"

Richard pointed toward the front hallway. "Have you looked at the one up front? It's truly the work of an artist. I think Nate has real talent."

"So do I," Leandra said, glad to be focusing on something besides her personal feelings for Nate. "I had hoped to convince him to turn it into a business. He could market them and sell them on a regular basis. The money would make a nice nest egg for his children's education."

"He'd need start-up funding, honey," Howard reminded her. "Did you talk to him about that?"

"No," she said. "But I'm glad you're willing to consider lending him the money."

"I told you, we'd already agreed to that years ago," Howard said. "Just too bad he never came back in to secure the loan."

Jack spoke up then. "Lea, I had doubts about Nate, but if Dad thinks it's worth a shot, then I'm behind it. I wish him luck." He smiled over at her then. "And you, too."

"Thank you," Leandra said, feeling better. "Nate would appreciate that. He told me he grew up in an orphanage—he's not used to accepting help from others. He'd want to do this on his own, his way, I'm sure."

Which is why she'd been hesitant about approaching him. He'd probably just turn her down flat. Especially now, when she'd already interfered in his personal life.

Howard gave her a reassuring look. "Nate has a good credit record and he pays his bills. He could get the loan on his own merit, so don't worry about that." Then he pointed a finger around the room. "And of course, this information shouldn't leave this room."

"Of course." Jack nodded, then gave his wife a meaningful look.

"I know the rules," Margaret said, rolling her eyes. "We don't discuss bank customers' finances."

"Even if we are a talkative, informative bunch," Mark teased.

"So when are you going to talk to him, get this thing rolling?" Richard looked at Leandra across the table.

"I don't know," she said, aware that everyone was staring at her. "We've both been so busy."

"Well, don't waste too much time," Richard replied. "We've only got a few days before Christmas and this Saturday will be my busiest day. We could use a good, quality product—people love unique handmade things to give for Christmas. Then after the rush, he can see about turning this into a full-fledged business venture."

"I'll try to talk to him soon," Leandra said.

Finally, the conversation drifted to other things. An hour later, dinner was over, leaving Leandra to do the dishes and wonder just when she'd find a chance to talk to Nate. They'd managed to be civil to each other over the last couple of rehearsals, in spite of being thrown together as the lion and the lamb. But it was easy to stand quietly like a demure lamb when you were actually wearing fleece. And she had to admit, Nate made a formidable lion, tall and golden, and almost savage-looking in spite of the cute costume.

The hard part was trying to avoid Nate when they weren't in costume. The man seemed to be everywhere at once. Whereas before, she could usually find him away from the crowd, now he was right in the center of things.

Was it all an act for her benefit, or was Nate beginning to see that he needed to spend more time with his children? Was he actually enjoying himself?

He'd helped with the set, just as he'd promised. He'd nailed his lion's roar on the first try, causing everyone to clap and laugh. He even seemed more comfortable around the members of the troupe, most of whom belonged to Leandra's church. And she'd seen him talking quietly to Reverend Powell on several occasions. He'd even donated his check back to the church, as a means of thanking the Reverend for being so kind to his family.

She'd had to find this out from Margaret of all people!

Because Nate didn't speak to Leandra unless it was absolutely necessary. That made having to stand by him, knowing he was right behind her onstage, even harder to bear. She could sense his presence as surely as she could smell his clean, woodsy soap. She could hear him breathing when the music ended and everything grew quiet.

She could easily reach out and touch him, given how Mr. Crawford had positioned them at the right side of the manger scene, set apart from the donkeys and camels, since they represented peace on earth.

Peace on earth. But no peace in her heart. Not as long as Nate was around.

And not as long as her well-meaning family continued to tease her and question her about her relationship with Nate and his children. She still needed to ask him about those beautiful birdhouses, but Leandra couldn't find the nerve to approach him.

As she climbed in to bed that night, snuggled underneath her mother's old quilt, birdhouses were the last thing on Leandra's mind. That little idea would have to be put on the back burner. Nate wouldn't listen to her idea, not now. Maybe not ever.

And she wouldn't interfere again, no matter how much she longed to be snuggled with him on the couch in front of the fire.

Two days later, Leandra was working at city hall, doing the final paperwork on expenses for the Christmas pageant, when the phone rang.

The receptionist told her, "It's Layla Welby. She sounds really upset."

Wondering what was wrong, Leandra remembered the children had left today's early rehearsal with Mr. Tuttle. Since Nate hadn't been able to get away from work, the kindly old man had promised to see them home safely.

"I'll talk to her," Leandra said, a million worries flowing through her head. While the fourteen-year-old was more than capable of taking care of her younger siblings, Leandra still worried about the children when they were home alone after school, and now all day because of the winter break. Taking a deep breath, she waited for the connection. After getting the go-ahead from the receptionist, she said, "Layla, it's Leandra. Is everything all right?"

"Miss Lea, you've got to come quick. Daddy's at work, but I called his cell phone and I can't reach him. I left a message with the dispatcher, but Daddy hasn't called back. I didn't know who else to call."

Leandra's heart stopped in her chest, then took up a fast-paced beat. "What is it, honey? Are you hurt? Are Brittney and Matt okay?"

"We're fine, but there's a strange woman knocking at the door. She wants us to let her in but I don't know if I should let her come in the house. She says she's our Aunt Helen."

"Then what's the matter?" Leandra asked, confused. "Surely if she's your aunt—"

Layla gulped, then raised her voice for emphasis. "Miss Lea, you don't get it. We don't have an Aunt Helen."

Chapter Twelve

Leandra tried not to break the speed limit on the way out of town, but the need to get to the Welby place made her push her car to the limit. Trying to think back, she remembered that Nate didn't know his parents or any family, so this woman couldn't be any relation to him.

But what about Alicia's parents? Her mother was dead, but what about her father?

Nate never mentioned his father-in-law. He'd said Alicia's folks were just starting to come around, had just reconciled things with Alicia when she'd been killed. And then her mother had died. Had they tried to made amends with her husband and their grandchildren before that death? Nate hadn't shared much about that with her. And she'd never heard him mention an Aunt Helen.

There was a lot Nate hadn't shared. The man was

locked up as tight as a jar of pickled peaches. Sealed. Not to be opened until he was good and ready. And Leandra was beginning to think Nate might not ever be ready to open himself to the world, or God, ever again.

Lord, we need you right now. I need you to help me. I promised I wouldn't interfere again but I have to help Layla. I can't ignore the plea of a child.

She wouldn't ignore Layla's call for help. No matter how mad it might make Nate later. But how could he be mad at her for this? If his children were in danger, he'd want someone to come. Even Leandra.

Bearing that in mind, she pulled the car up to the house, noticing the rented sedan parked in the driveway.

Leandra stopped her own car behind the big sedan. And that's when she noticed the woman pacing back and forth on the front porch.

No wonder Layla refused to let the woman in the house.

Aunt Helen, or whoever she was, was wearing a bright-red Christmas sweater. Rudolph the Red-Nosed Reindeer was plastered across the front in vivid brown and white sequins, and each time the woman moved, Rudolph's shiny red nose blinked brightly. Underneath the thick sweater, she wore black wool pants, impeccably cut, over three-inch-heeled black patent pumps. She had a ring on every finger, in every color of jewel imaginable. Each time she moved her hands, her long red fingernails warred for attention along with her diamonds, emeralds and rubies. Her hair was a silvery-gray and her lips were the same striking red as her sweater. When she heard Leandra's car pull up, she picked up an expensive-looking black patent leather purse that looked more like a suitcase and whirled around, one hand on her tiny hip, to stare down at Leandra.

"And who are you?" the woman asked, looking through her dark sunglasses at Leandra.

Leandra took another calming breath. Up close, the woman was really beautiful. And well preserved. Her makeup was minimal, except for the bright lipstick, and her dark eyebrows arched out over her big eyes in perfect symmetry. She had an air of wealth about her in spite of the fluffy, big hair and the ridiculous sweater. She also held an air of intimidation, as if she were used to giving orders and expecting them to be followed precisely.

"I'm Leandra Flanagan, a friend of the Welbys," Leandra told the woman as she walked slowly up the steps. "And I don't think we've met."

Inside the house, Mutt barked loudly at this intrusion. At least the children had a capable watchdog.

The woman took off her dark shades and shoved them into the bottomless purse, then put out a hand to Leandra. "Well, I'll be. You're a tiny little thing, ain't you? I'm Helen Montgomery."

Leandra took her hand, noted the firm handshake, then gave the woman a slight smile. "Can I help you, Mrs. Montgomery?"

"It's Miss, honey. Never married, never wanted to. But I would like to see my nieces and my nephew in there before I die. If that's all right with *everybody* here." She glared toward the front door, where all three Welby children were peeking out from behind the glass panes, and Mutt's shaggy face could be seen peering over the window seal. "Stubborn lot, ain't they? Got that naturally, I reckon."

Leandra immediately liked Aunt Helen, even if she wasn't quite sure if she could trust her. "I'm sorry. They're just following their father's orders. He's at work and they've been told never to open the door to strangers. That's why they called me."

"But I ain't no stranger," Aunt Helen said, clearly appalled. "I'm a Montgomery, honey." When Leandra could only stand there with a questioning look, the woman added, "Of the *Kentucky* Montgomerys. Land sakes, girl, I'm their grandfather's sister."

Realization dawned on Leandra. "Their grandfather—you mean, Alicia's father?"

"The very one," Helen Montgomery said, bobbing her head. To her hairdresser's credit, not one hair moved when she did it. "Davis Montgomery is my brother."

"I see," Leandra replied, clearly caught between

a rock and a hard place. "Well, it's nice to meet you, but I don't know if Nate—"

Aunt Helen threw up her bejeweled hands, causing the gold coin bracelet looped around her tiny wrist to jingle against her aged skin. "Look, Leandra is it? I've been all the way around the world, been traveling for years, moving here and there. Well, I'm tired of traveling. When I got home to Kentucky and asked my brother about these three children— children I've haven't seen in years—I knew I had to come here. My brother is a stubborn old cuss, but I'm even more stubborn than him. And I want to get to know my kinfolk hiding behind that door."

Leandra could feel for the woman. And for the children behind the door, too. Why on earth hadn't Nate and Mr. Montgomery tried to work things out between the two of them, for the sake of those three precious children?

She looked heavenward, thinking, *What should I do, Lord?*

Helen watched Leandra, her intense blue eyes moving over Leandra's face with all the bearing of a hawk. "Look, honey, I don't blame you for worrying. I guess I am a sight, standing here stomping my feet in the cold." Then she reached over to take Leandra's hand in hers. "I'm a churchgoing, God-fearing woman, believe it or not. And I have to do right by those children in there, since my brother hasn't bothered to make amends." She held tight to Leandra's hand, then leaned close. "I don't have any younguns of my own, and my brother is like a brick wall, hard as stone. I'm hoping I can bridge the gap between him and Nate."

When Leandra saw the genuine concern, coupled with real tears, in the woman's eyes, she knew she couldn't turn her away. "Nate won't like this," she said, thinking he'd blame her for interfering again. But what choice did she have?

"Suga', you let me handle Nathan Welby," Helen Montgomery told her, patting her hand. "Now, can we please go inside out of this cold? I'm gonna take a chill, standing here without my coat on."

Leandra finally motioned to the children. "You can open the door, Layla. It's all right."

The teenager unlocked the big door, then opened it slightly, her gaze traveling over Aunt Helen in a mixture of awe and fear while Mutt tried to claw his way through the crack. "Are you sure, Miss Lea?"

"Positive," Leandra told her, hoping she'd made the right decision. "Hold Mutt off her, okay?"

Layla opened the door, then told Mutt to get. The dog sniffed Helen a couple of times, but when she growled at him with arching eyebrows and an amused expression on her porcelain face, he took off running out into the yard.

Leandra guided Helen inside, then turned to the three wide-eyed children standing in a circle in the hallway. "This is Helen Montgomery—your mother's aunt, which makes her your great-aunt."

"So you really are our Aunt Helen?" Brittney asked shyly, her little hands covering her face.

"That I am, suga'," Aunt Helen said as she dropped down on her knees right there on the floor. "Can Aunt Helen have a big ol' hug?"

Brittney glanced up at Leandra for direction. Leandra smiled and nodded. "It's okay, honey."

Brittney rushed into the woman's open arms then, hugging her as if she'd known her all her life. "I never had an aunt before."

"Yes, you did," Aunt Helen replied, looking up at Leandra. "You had me all the time. You just didn't know it. And bless your hearts, you don't remember me, do you?"

The children stood there with blank expressions on their faces.

"My hair's gone more gray since they last saw me," she explained to Leandra with a hand over her mouth.

"No, we don't remember." Layla stood back, still wary, but when Helen rose to give her an unnerving head-to-toe appraisal, she shrugged. "I'm sorry I wouldn't let you in."

"That's all right by me," Helen told her. "You were just doing what your Daddy taught you. And you did a mighty good job of it, too."

Leandra noticed she didn't push for a hug from

Layla. Instead, she just reached out and touched a gnarled hand to the girl's cheek. "So like your mother."

Then she turned to Matt. "And you, young man. From what I can tell—and if my memory serves me correctly—you look a whole lot like your papa—handsome fellow."

"How'd you know that?" Matt questioned.

Helen gave him a bittersweet smile. "I was at your mama's—" She stopped, then quickly changed her story. "Your lovely mama, bless her, sent me a picture of the two of them on their wedding day. They sure looked happy." She brightened, then touched a finger to his nose. "And you sure look like Nathan."

"Everybody tells me that," Matt said, his blue eyes big with wonder. "Where'd you get all those rings and bracelets?"

Aunt Helen hooted with laughter, then grabbed Matt to hug him close, the rings and bracelets sparkling and clanking as she did so. "I got them here and there, all over the place. Italy, Morocco, Greece, Japan. I been everywhere and then some. 'Course you'd never know that from this Southern drawl, would you now?" She stood back then, her gaze moving over the three awestruck children. "But let me tell you something right now—there is no place like home. And there is nothing like having family."

"Is that why you came to see us, 'cause we're

family?" Brittney asked, her finger reaching out to touch a dangling bracelet.

"Certainly," Aunt Helen replied, taking the colorful beaded bracelet off to drape it around Brittney's tiny arm. "Hold on to that for me, will you? And don't lose it. It was handmade by my Native American friend in Oklahoma—a full-blooded Caddo."

"You know Indians?" Matt asked, fascinated.

"I know *Native Americans,*" Aunt Helen gently corrected. "In fact, I'm a walking history lesson. Betcha didn't know you had such a smart ol' aunt, did you?"

"We didn't know we had you at all," Brittney said by way of an apology. "Or we woulda let you in."

"That's okay," Helen said. "I'm in now, darlin'. And I ain't going anywhere for a good long while."

Leandra felt tears pricking at her eyes. That might be good news to the children and good for Aunt Helen's sense of family obligation. But she knew one person who might not like having a long-lost relative coming for a holiday visit.

Nate Welby did not like surprises.

And he especially wouldn't like *her* being involved in this one.

Not one little bit.

A little bit further and he'd be home.

Nate pushed the old truck up the highway,

looking forward to a hot meal and maybe a warm fire in the fireplace. His pledge to be a better father was actually turning into a real commitment. Maybe prayer really did work.

Except that today, he hadn't been able to take a break from work to attend the rehearsals, and to top things off, the batteries on his cell phone needed recharging. He'd forgotten to charge the thing last night. Too many distractions. Well, he'd make up for those slipups by spending the evening with his children.

He had dinner in the take-out bag next to him in the truck—good food—fresh cooked vegetables and baked chicken from one of his favorite diners out on the highway. He'd make a fire—that had been the ritual since Leandra had started that first one the other night—then he'd read Brittney the Christmas story she'd been begging him to read to her for weeks now. And while the children were out of school for the Christmas holidays, he also planned to help Matt with his math, put in some overtime so his son would be up to speed once school started back up. Adding and subtracting sure had changed since Nate's school days.

But a father could change and adjust with the times, too, he guessed.

It was amazing how he *had managed* to change his schedule, change his whole mind-set, so he could spend more time with his children. It hadn't been as hard as he'd envisioned.

He just had to take it one step at a time, the same way he'd been doing everything since Alicia had died. The dread of coming home each night was slowly being replaced with the need to see his children, to know they were safe and happy, something he'd only monitored from a distance until now.

And he had to admit, it was good to find the house all aglow with holiday lights each night. The bright lights and Christmas decorations chased away the gloom, the bad memories. And maybe this spring, he'd start on that remodeling project he and Alicia had always talked about. He could handle that, if he just took things slow.

Start off slow, work your way up to it.

That's how he viewed everything in life and now his own philosophy was working fine. Except when it came to his feelings about Leandra.

One whole week and he missed her already.

One whole week of being in that huge auditorium with her, with other people all around. And yet, sometimes it felt as if he and Leandra were the only two people in the room. He'd get a whiff of her perfume before she rounded the corner. He'd see her in that funny lamb's costume, white fleece from head to toe, and remember the way she felt in his arms. Then he'd remember the pain in her eyes when he'd accused her of not knowing anything about being a mother.

Lord, I wish I could take that back, he thought now.

But it was too late. Too late for him to admit that Leandra had been a kind, considerate friend to his children, even if she'd never been a mother to anyone before.

"She has the right instincts," he said out loud, the country tune on the radio echoing in his head. "And I shouldn't have been so cruel to her."

If only he could have another chance. He wouldn't rush headlong into it this time around. He wouldn't give her a birdhouse and a kiss. He'd just take things slow, nice and easy, to be sure he knew what he was doing.

Nate turned the truck into the yard, then stopped at the mailbox. Leandra's car was parked at his front door, beside another car he didn't recognize.

Nate shook his head, then slapped a hand on the steering wheel. "I hear you talking, Lord. And I guess You're answering my prayer." A little hesitant, he had to wonder what Leandra was up to now.

And maybe now was his chance to make amends with Leandra, to take things slow and win her over with a steady, sure heart. If only he could be so sure.

One way to find out.

He grinned then. "Please, Lord, all I ask is no more dumplings. A man's stomach can only take so much."

Chapter Thirteen

Standing back to admire the set dinner table, Leandra laughed at how Helen Montgomery had performed her culinary wizardry and kept the children entertained all at the same time. She had produced an exotic pasta dish from a few noodles and some butter, milk and cheese, complete with steamed vegetables and colorful chopped peppers. And she'd let the children help with each step, guiding them, coaxing them, telling them stories every bit as colorful as the food. She also taught them words in several foreign languages as she went along from the main course to some sort of poached dessert involving apples and cinnamon.

For someone who'd never had children of her own, Aunt Helen sure knew a lot about how to control and entertain them.

Much more than I'll ever know.

That thought made Leandra wince, but she tried to keep her own smile intact while she glanced at the clock. Nate was late and she was worried. Dreading the moment he arrived, she was still concerned that he hadn't called to check on the children. Maybe his promise to do better had all been an act, after all.

"And maybe I should have gone home for dinner," she mumbled to herself as she poured milk for the children and iced tea—Aunt Helen's own spiced recipe—for the adults.

She'd planned to do just that—go on home. But Layla had seemed shy and nervous around bubbly Helen. When Leandra had announced she was about to leave, the child had stopped her with an imploring look.

"Can't you stay with us, Miss Lea? You don't have to cook this time."

Aunt Helen immediately picked up on that little tidbit. "Oh, you *are* a close friend, then? Do you cook for Nathan and the children often?"

"I've only know the Welbys a short time," Leandra explained. "They're all involved in the Christmas pageant—"

"And Miss Lea is in charge of everything," Brittney added, grinning. "She says this is going to be the best Christmas pageant the town of Marshall has ever seen."

"Really?" Aunt Helen's perfectly arched brows

shot up at that declaration. "I'm thinking I'd better stick around and find out for myself." Her sharp gaze centered on Leandra. "And what about you and Nate?"

Brittney looked up, mouth opened to reply to that particular question, but Leandra shook her head at the little girl and gave her a mock-stern look. Which caused Brittney's bottom lip to jut out in a pout.

"We're friends," Leandra hurriedly explained, then before the children could give their own definitions of what that meant, she shooed them into the kitchen to finish their chores—with Brittney glaring at her the whole time.

But she hadn't fooled Aunt Helen. "Friends, huh? I'm sure Nathan could use a *friend.* The poor man's been out here on his own for too long, from everything I've seen and heard—which hasn't been much since I've been out of the country for months on end. I should have kept in touch more."

Curious, Leandra asked, "What *do* you know about Nathan? Does Mr. Montgomery ever mention Nate and the children at all?"

"Stay for dinner and we'll talk," Helen had replied, her gaze both knowing and understanding.

So now here Leandra stood two hours later, waiting and watching, hoping for answers to all her burning questions, hoping to find some way of understanding Nate and his pain and his anger. She and Helen hadn't had that talk yet. The older woman had somehow managed to keep too busy with cooking and cuddling the children to answer Leandra's earlier question.

Of course, Helen had been more willing to answer all the questions the kids asked—mostly about their beautiful mother. After hearing the tidbits of information and anecdotes Helen dispensed so clearly and lovingly, Leandra felt as if she'd never live up to the image of Alicia Montgomery Welby.

And yet she had so many questions.

Why am I here, Lord? What am I searching for? Why does this family seem to draw me? Why does Nate seem to be the one?

That thought stopped her. The one? *The one for me? The one I could so easily love? Am I crazy?*

"No," Leandra said to herself. "No. I'm just concerned for this family, for these children and their plight." And she did care about Nate. But she wouldn't let her feelings develop into anything other than those of a concerned friend.

She only wanted to help, not hinder.

But would Nate see that, understand when he came home to find a strange woman in his kitchen and Leandra supervising the whole thing?

She heard the front door opening, then whirled to face him. "Nate, hello."

He filled the doorway in his battered leather jacket and worn jeans, a big man with a wavy tawny-colored mane and eyes that seemed to see right through her denials as their depths changed from golden to bronze.

"Hello, yourself," he replied, a bemused smile on his face. Then he sniffed. "That sure smells good, but I brought dinner." He held up the two white take-out bags he balanced in one hand. "If I'd known—"

Leandra didn't miss the implication. She should have called him. "The children couldn't reach you," she tried to explain. "So Layla called me at work."

Nate's expression shifted from a smile to a frown. "The batteries went out on my cell phone and I was away from the site office. I didn't get any messages." Then he continued, "Is everything all right?"

"Yes—no." Seeing the fear and concern in his eyes, Leandra held up a hand. "Everything's fine, Nate. It's just that…the children had a visitor—"

"Who?" At the sound of voices in the kitchen, Nate slammed the door shut with his booted foot, then headed down the hall, past where Leandra stood in the formal dining room. Taking a deep breath, she hurried around the long table to head him off in the kitchen.

But she was too late. By the time she got around the corner, Nate was standing there on the other side of the big kitchen, the take-out bags still in his hand, a look of utter shock and confusion coloring his face. "Helen?"

Helen Montgomery turned around from the stove, the Rudolph nose on her sweater blinking at Nate just over the ruffles of the white apron she'd donned early. "Hello there, Nathan. How are you?"

Nate stood there, his mouth dropping open as memories assaulted his senses. Alicia had loved her Aunt Helen.

"She's like Mary Poppins," Alicia had told him. "She drops in with all her tales of traveling the world, brings me all sorts of fun gifts and treasures, makes life so much fun, then she leaves again. And I always miss her so much. She'll understand, Nate. She'll understand about us and how much we love each other. She'll come to our wedding. I know she will."

And she had.

Nate closed his eyes to the pain and the memory of Alicia's words. Helen Montgomery had understood almost too well just exactly how much he had loved her niece. Which meant she now knew exactly how much he was hurting. And he didn't want or need the pity he thought he saw in her crystal-blue eyes.

"Well, don't just stand there with your chin on the floor, boy. C'mere and give me a hug."

"She likes to hug," Matt warned his daddy as Nate somehow managed to set the bags on the counter. In two strides, he was across the room, enveloped in Helen's arms.

"Ah, it sure is good to see you again," Helen told him. "It's been too long."

He remembered a big car pulling up to the gravesite. He remembered a petite woman swathed in fur and jewels getting out of the car. She had stood apart from the rest, watching and listening as the minister said one more prayer over Alicia's grave. And she had stayed at the gravesite long after everyone else had left. Nate knew this because he'd found Helen there when he'd gone back later that day. She'd given him a calm pep talk—something about remembering all the good in life—then after a brief, silent hug, she'd climbed in the big car and…left.

And now, here she stood in his kitchen.

"Over three years since the…funeral," Nate said now, conscious of the children watching him. They probably expected him to rant and rave, to throw one of his fits. Truth told, that's exactly what he wanted to do. Then he looked over at Leandra and saw that same expectation in her dark eyes, too.

Well, he'd just have to show them, all of them, that he was trying to change. So he pushed back the dark memories swirling like a wintry fog around his head and mustered up a smile that felt like plastic pulling at his skin.

"What brings you to Marshall, anyway?" he asked Helen as he stood back to look down at her. Even in her high heels, she was still a petite woman.

But what she lacked in size Helen made up for in integrity and determination.

Nate *was* glad to see her.

"I came to see my nieces and that handsome nephew," she said, waving a hand at Matt. Then she looked back up at Nathan. "I had no idea things weren't good between you and Davis...I wish I'd known."

"He doesn't discuss us," Nate said, pulling away.

And *he* never talked about Davis Montgomery. What was the point? They'd both made a feeble attempt, while Mrs. Montgomery was still alive, but once she'd passed on things had changed and Davis had stopped calling. The man had long ago washed his hands of Nate and his own grandchildren.

"Davis is a bitter, self-centered old man," Helen replied, nodding her understanding as she untied her apron.

"Who's Davis?" Matt asked, curiosity widening his blue eyes.

Helen's gaze flew to Nate's face. "You mean to tell me these children don't even *know* about their grandfather?"

Layla glared at Nate then. "We're not allowed to talk about him, or our mother, either."

Nate ran a hand over the five o'clock shadow of his beard, figuring it was payback time and Layla had a lot of resentment stacked against him. "Now, Layla, that's not entirely true—"

"Yes, it is," she replied, capitalizing on having someone's attention at last. "Every time I ask you something about Mama, or our grandfather in Kentucky, you change the subject or tell me you don't want to talk about that right now." Then she lowered her head, breaking Nate's heart with her soft-spoken plea. "We need to know, Daddy. Can we ask Aunt Helen...let her tell us some more stories about Mama and...and our granddaddy?"

"We have a granddaddy?" Brittney asked, her eyes wide, her little hands on her hips. "Nobody *never* tells me anything."

And nobody tried to correct her grammar this time, either.

Nate glanced around to find every eye in the room centered on him. Waves of guilt and remorse washed over him, beating him back even as they cleansed him. How could he have been so blind, so stupid? Why had he denied his children this one thing—the legacy of their mother's memory?

Because he was bitter and unforgiving, pure and simple.

Looking toward Layla for understanding, he nodded. "Honey, you can ask Aunt Helen anything you'd like, okay?"

Surprisingly, the room stayed quiet. Where Nate had expected the three children to bombard their great-aunt with questions, instead they all just stood there, staring at him as if he'd actually changed into the lion they'd forced him to play in the pageant.

Then Layla walked over to him and put her arms around his midsection to give him a hug. "Thank you, Daddy," she said before backing up, her head down. "Supper's ready."

He watched as Helen gave him a quiet, questioning look before she herded the kids through the wide doorway leading to the dining room. Then he turned to Leandra. "I've still got a long way to go, don't I?"

She glanced up at him, pride evident in her eyes. "That was a first step, Nate."

Nate pulled her close then, fighting the need to hug her tight. "I am trying, you know. And I—I need to apologize for the things I said the other night—"

"You don't have to do that," Leandra replied. "I'm just glad you're not angry with me for being here tonight. I didn't want you to think I was interfering again."

He brushed a wayward curl off her cheek. "How could I think that? You came when my children needed you. I'm grateful for that."

She relaxed then, her smile reminding him of how pretty she really was. She was wearing a long, cream-colored sweater over a floral skirt in shades of rich brown and stark gold with a little red mixed in. His autumn woman.

When had he decided she was *his?* he wondered.

He couldn't lay claim to her. It wouldn't be fair to either of them. But he sure liked having her in his arms.

Oblivious to Nate's inner turmoil, Leandra laid her head against his chest then looked up with a little chuckle.

"Aunt Helen gave us quite a scare," she said with a shrug and a shake of her head, making her hair fall back across her face. "She is…a very interesting woman."

"She doesn't suffer fools," Nate replied, grinning. "It was just such a surprise."

"I hope you don't mind that I let her in—after giving her the third degree, of course."

"No, I don't mind. It's kinda nice, having her here again." *And having you to come home to,* he thought. Maybe he *could* ease into being with Leandra. He'd been thinking about her all day and now here she was. Just like everything else, if he took things slow…

Leandra laughed then. "And…guess what?"

Nate quirked a brow, enjoying this intimacy, this brief stolen time with her, and wanting badly to kiss that laugh on her beautiful lips. But that wouldn't be taking it slow. That would be another hasty mistake. So instead, he said, "What?"

"I didn't cook dinner."

"Well, amen to that."

When she playfully hit him on the arm, he

grabbed her hand. "May I escort you to the table, Miss Flan-again?"

"I'd be delighted, Mr. Welby."

Nate guided her into the dining room, a sense of peace settling over his shoulders. But when he glanced down the table to find Helen's cool blue gaze on him, he instantly regretted that sense of peace.

Alicia's aunt was here for a rare visit, and he'd just been standing in the next room, longing to kiss another woman. What had he been thinking?

And what was Helen Montgomery thinking about him right now?

"I'm thinking out Nate likes you," Helen told Leandra later as they cleared the kitchen. Nate was in the den playing a video game with Matt. Every now and then, they could hear a groan of frustration from the father as his child scored yet another baseball victory.

Leandra glanced over at Helen, trying to decide if the woman was for her or against her. All through dinner, Helen had laughed and chattered away in her rich drawl, mostly talking to the children. But Leandra hadn't missed the keen, interested looks or the knowing expressions Helen had sent toward her and Nate.

Deciding she had nothing to hide or be ashamed of, Leandra nodded, then faced the other woman. "He does like me. We're good friends."

"So, you feel the same about him?"

Leandra focused on the constantly blinking Rudolph nose centered on Helen's left shoulder. "Yes, I do. I like Nate a lot and I adore the children."

Helen stood there, staring, those perfectly sculptured brows lifted in two highly feminine arches. "I see."

"Does that bother you?" Leandra asked, her hands on the counter.

"Should that bother me, honey?" Helen retorted, the keen stare intact.

Leandra knew she was being studied and dissected. "Alicia was a special person," she said, groping for the right words. "Anyone who enters this house can see that. I'm not trying to take her place."

"And anyone who comes here can also see that Nate's let time come to a standstill," Helen replied. "Alicia had such high hopes for this old house. She woulda fixed it up into a showplace."

"But now—"

Helen turned to face Leandra, interrupting her with a hand on her arm. "But now, it's time for Nathan to get on with his life. Is that what you were going to say?"

Leandra faced her squarely, with a clear determination. "No, actually I was going to say that I hope Nate can pour the love he felt for Alicia into raising their children. That should be his top priority. They need their father, to guide them in life and in their faith."

Helen dropped her hand away from Leandra's arm. "And they need their grandfather, too."

Surprised, Leandra lifted her own brows. "Do you think Nate and Mr. Montgomery will ever be able to get past their resentment and anger?"

"Only one way to find out," Helen replied in a low voice. "Get them together."

"Is that why you came here?" Leandra asked, dread in her heart.

"Yes, it is," Helen told her. "And now, I'm even more sure I'm doing the right thing."

"Oh, and why is that?"

"Because of you, young lady. I had my doubts at first, but now I know. I was hoping someone around here would help me bring Nate and my stubborn brother together, and I do believe you're perfect for the job."

Chapter Fourteen

Leandra opened her mouth to speak, then stood there staring across the kitchen counter at Helen Montgomery. "You can't be serious?"

"As serious as cactus thorns," Helen replied, her gaze steady and level. "Now don't tell me you ain't up to the challenge. I thought I had you pegged for a fighter."

Leandra didn't know whether to be flattered or on full alert. "I fight for what I believe in—"

"And don't you believe those children need some attention and love from their grandfather?"

"Of course I'd like to see that happen, but—"

"But what? Afraid Nate will pout and fume? I don't doubt he'll throw a good and mighty fit. But we can't let Davis and him keep us from doing what's right." Helen let out a deep breath. "The good Lord knows those two are as stubborn as the day is long. When I last talked to Davis, he told me he was going to try hard to reconcile things with Nate—"

"How long ago was that?" Leandra interrupted, wondering if Nate had turned the man away.

"About two years," Helen admitted. "I'm as guilty of neglecting them as anyone," she added, shaking her head. "But I had some wanderlust left in my soul. Didn't think I had to worry, since Davis promised me." She stopped, banged a hand against the counter. "I could just shake both of 'em."

Leandra understood completely, but she had to make Helen see that she wasn't the one to help bridge this gap. "I don't think Nate would appreciate me being involved in this. He's already made it clear that I should let him raise his children the way he sees fit."

"He can't see past his grief and his love for Alicia, honey," Helen returned. Then the fire in her crystal-blue eyes softened at the expression of pain and discomfort Leandra couldn't hide. "'Course, you know all about that, don't you?"

"Yes, I do," Leandra said. "I care about Nate, but I've accepted that we can't be anything more than just friends. And I have to tell you, I'll be leaving Marshall right after Christmas."

Helen's pout was pure disapproval. "And why's that?"

"I have to go back to Houston. I've got to find

another job or I'll have to give up my apartment, my life back there."

"Are you so sure you want to go back?" Helen asked, her brows arching in that disconcerting way again. "Honey, we just met and I don't know all the details, but the way you look at Nathan Welby— well, I get the impression you'd like things around here to change in a positive way, with you being part of the positive. Am I wrong?"

Leandra couldn't answer that. If she spoke the words out loud, she'd melt into a helpless puddle of defeat. Instead, she said, "As I told you, Nate and I have agreed to be friends. And...I have to make some decisions regarding my future. I've held off long enough."

Helen lifted her chin, then gave Leandra a sideways glance. "Sometimes, we just have to trust in the Lord and let things take place in a natural kind of way."

"You sound like my mother."

"We're older, wiser, and we've got the blessed assurance of God's wisdom," Helen replied. "Now, can I count on you?"

"Count on her for what?" Nate asked from the hallway. He strolled into the kitchen, a slight smile on his face. "The munchkins and the Mutt are all in bed at last, but what are you two up to?"

Helen gave Leandra a warning look. "I want to get to know Leandra a little better and I'm counting on her to come around more while I'm visiting," Helen said. "To help me adjust."

"Just how long are you planning on staying?" Nate asked, a teasing light in his eyes.

"Oh, you know what they say," Helen countered. "After three days…"

Nate grinned, then put an arm around her shoulders. "You can stay as long as you want, you know that."

"Mighty generous of you," Helen said, hugging him close. "How about through next week—at least till Christmas?"

Nate glanced over at Leandra. "That'll be just fine. We could use some cheerful company around here for the holidays."

"Then it's settled," Helen said, lifting her arm away. "And on that note, I'm going to bed. Layla said I could bunk with her."

"She's up there getting your spot ready right now," Nate told her. "Sleep tight."

"Don't let the bedbugs bite," Helen finished. Then to Leandra, "It was good to meet you, suga'. Hope to see you soon." She leaned close. "And don't worry about that other. I'll take care of it."

"What other?" Nate asked, a mock frown on his face.

Helen handled him with a wave of the hand. "Just Christmas surprises—nothing for you to be concerned about just yet."

"Thanks," Leandra told the other woman, relief flooding her senses. "I'm sure we'll see each other again."

After Helen went upstairs, Nate turned to Leandra. "Wanna walk out to the barn with me? I need to check on Honeyboy, make sure he's all warm and toasty in his stall."

Surprised at the invitation, Leandra told her heart to slow down. It took off so fast, she was sure it skipped a few beats. "Sure," she said, a little breathless. "Let me get my coat."

The night was clear and cold, with a full glowing moon and a million silver-blue stars hanging against a velvet-soft sky.

Nate took her hand to help her down the steps. "Watch that rotten board," he said, grinning up at her.

"I remember it well," she replied, her hand in his. His fingers felt so strong, so sure wrapped around hers.

Together, they slowly made their way down the sloping yard toward the big barn.

"I'm glad you stayed for supper," Nate said. "I didn't like how we left things the other night."

"I shouldn't have been so pushy," she replied. Hoping to make him understand, she added, "You're a very good father—I didn't mean to imply otherwise."

They reached the barn door and Nate turned to

face her. "But you were right about a lot of things. I just didn't want to hear the truth."

Longing to ask him what really *was* the truth, Leandra kept her mouth shut. It was enough that they'd formed a tentative bond for now. She didn't want to ruin another evening with Nate. And she reminded herself, now might be the perfect time to bring up the possibility of showcasing some of his birdhouses at Richard's general store. That was a safe, businesslike topic, at least.

She waited as Nate turned on the dim overhead light then tugged her toward Honeyboy's stall in the back.

The big horse snorted hello then pushed his nose over the stall to get a closer look at them.

"He's a beautiful animal, Nate," Leandra said, coming close to let the horse nuzzle her hand. "I think he wants a late-night snack."

Nate obliged by giving Honeyboy a handful of grain. "Not too much now, fellow."

After making sure the horse was comfortable and warm, Nate started back toward the front of the barn.

But Leandra held back. "Nate, could I see some of your work? Maybe some of the birdhouses?"

Giving her a sly grin, he teased. "Want to see my etchings, huh?"

Leandra's blush of warmth sent the chill in the old barn right out the door with her good sense. Ignoring the tingling sensations racing down her spine, she tried to remain serious. "I want to see what you do out here every night. What you've created."

He glanced around, hesitant. "Oh, I don't know about that. There isn't much to see, really."

Leandra pushed ever so gently, determined to show him that his talent shouldn't be hidden away. "C'mon, if all of your designs look like the one you gave my mother, then I'd say there's a lot to see."

"It's just a hobby," he told her. But he took her by the hand even as he said the words. "I don't expect to make anything out of it."

Sensing an opportunity, Leandra said, "Richard was really impressed with our birdhouse. He said he could probably sell dozens of them in his store— what with the Christmas rush and everything."

"Is that a fact?" He grinned, then took her over to the workshop area. He stood silent for a minute, as if remembering, then said, "I don't know if that's possible."

"But wouldn't you like to see?"

Nate turned to face her again. "What's cooking in that pretty head of yours, Leandra?"

She smiled, her eyes widening, her tone hopeful. "I really think you have talent and I also think you should try to promote that talent. I should know. This is what I did for a living back in Houston."

Nate put his hands in the pockets of his leather jacket. "Now *there's* something *I'm* curious about. Tell me about Houston. What happened back there?"

So Nate had found an opportunity to seize the moment, too, Leandra mused. Well, maybe it *was* time she told him the truth. Maybe if he could see that she trusted him enough to let him in on her own failings, he'd learn to trust her in return.

"It's not a pretty story," she said in a low voice.

He reached out to touch her cheek, the warmth of his fingers gliding over her skin making her feel all flush inside. "I want to know."

Deciding to push one more time, she said, "If I tell you all about it, will you show me the rest of your birdhouses?"

"You drive a hard bargain," he replied. Then he nodded and lifted her chin with the pad of his thumb. "Start talking."

Leandra swallowed, suddenly aware that the old barn had become silent and still, waiting. An occasional creak and Honeyboy's contented snort now and then finally broke the silence, but Nate's warm gaze on her kept Leandra from hearing anything over the beating of her pulse.

"I worked for a large advertising firm," she began, her hands in the pockets of her black wool topper. "I did a good job and soon I was promoted to senior account executive."

"What does a senior account executive do exactly?" he asked in that teasing drawl.

She smiled, tried to relax. "I solicited major companies to advertise through us. We designed their ad campaigns and took care of all their public relations and marketing, working with their in-house departments, of course."

He stepped closer. "Of course."

Trying hard not to be distracted by his ever-changing eyes or his intense expression, Leandra continued. "As I said, I was very good at my job and soon, I was making more money than I ever dreamed possible."

"And you became that city woman you always wanted to be."

She didn't miss his frown.

"Yes, that was me." She shook her head, turned to lean against a large support post. "And I made so many mistakes." She let out a sigh, wishing she could just go back and change things. But it was too late for that. And she needed to get this out in the open. "My boss—the president and owner of the company—was an older man named William Myers—" She stopped, remembering that just a few days ago, she'd let it slip to Nate that she'd been involved with her boss. Now she was mortified that he wanted to hear the whole story.

"Go on," Nate said, his gaze level, his expression neither condemning nor questioning.

"We worked together on one of the major campaigns and after that...we started dating." She shrugged, tossed her hair off her face. "At first, it was just platonic—someone to be seen around town with—companionship. He'd never been married and he was content to remain a bachelor. I was convenient, since I didn't make demands on him. And I wasn't ready for marriage or children either, so our relationship worked for both of us."

"What a perfect setup."

She gave him a wry smile. "Or so it seemed." Pushing hair off her face, she began again. "We went along like that for a while. Then something changed in William. He started wanting more and I thought I might be ready to give it, but I wasn't sure if I loved him enough to make such a commitment. I thought he wanted to get married."

Shaking her head, she added, "I got this silly notion that I'd be the wife of a successful executive. I'd live in the big mansion on the hill, have fancy cars, eat at the finest restaurants—all the things I'd dreamed about growing up. But suddenly, having a family *did* seem important. And yet, part of me kept saying, 'But you don't want to get married. You don't want children. You want to enjoy life, stay single.'"

He stopped her there. "Why was that so important, staying single, not having children?"

Letting out a sigh, she replied, "Because I grew up in this large, loud family. I watched my mother always cooking and cleaning, and doing the car pool thing, the volunteer work with the PTA and the church. I guess I just needed some space, away from all the commotion, away from my overbearing, lovable brothers." Shaking her head, she laughed. "I don't know how my mother does it. I only knew I didn't want to find out."

She paused, took another breath. "So what you said the other night—"

"I was wrong to assume that about you," Nate interrupted, anger clouding his face in the moonlight from the partially open door. "You'd make a great mother."

Leandra almost bolted then. The soft, husky catch in his voice only made her want to give in and fall into his arms. She wanted *him* to give her that chance to prove she could be a good mother.

Holding on to the pole behind her, she pushed back the need to be consoled and reassured. "It doesn't matter. You were right. At one time, I only wanted wealth and success. I thought those things would fulfill me, make me complete, give me the world I'd always thought I was missing living here in this small town." She let go of the pole, dropping her hands at her sides. "But I was so wrong. And soon, all my big, shallow dreams were thrown right back in my face."

"What happened?" Nate asked, frustration playing across his face. "I can't stand this—just spit it out."

She had to smile at his impatience, but she dreaded telling him the truth. Finally, after a long deafening silence and the intensity of his unwavering gaze, she blurted the truth. "William didn't ask me to marry him, Nate. He asked me to move in with him, to live with him."

She watched Nate's face for his reaction. Would he turn away from her, disgusted with her superficial whinings?

"Let me get this straight," he said, his voice quiet. "The man didn't want to marry you, yet he wanted to…to…"

"As my mother would say, he wanted me to live in sin with him."

"And you turned him down flat."

Yet again, he'd somehow managed to make her smile in spite of her misgivings. It had been a statement, not a question. Nate somehow knew exactly what she'd done, which meant he thought she had *some* good qualities, at least.

"Yes, I did. Because I realized that contrary to all my sophisticated pretentious thinking, I was really a country girl at heart. And a Christian. I couldn't do something that went against my moral fiber."

"So you quit."

Another statement. Another sweet assumption.

"No." She actually managed a chuckle. "I broke things off and concentrated on my work. But William couldn't take rejection, especially from someone he considered an underling. So…he started harassing me at work, making demands on me, criticizing everything I did. I was still the same—still hardworking, dedicated. I handled several exclusive accounts but one by one, they were snatched from me and handed over to some-one else."

Nate groaned. "What did you see in this weasel, anyway?"

"I started asking myself that same question," she replied. "I had been so blinded by ambition, by success, that I'd almost thrown away everything I believed in, just to say I'd made it in the world. I actually might have married William without loving him, if only he'd asked me."

"You can do much better than that kind of creep," he said, anger justifying his words.

Nate's self-righteous defense of her only endeared him to Leandra even more. "Yes, I know that now," she admitted. "And each time he punished me, I saw more and more that I didn't really belong in that kind of world. A world where money and power are put ahead of people and in-tegrity. The final straw came when he gave me my annual evaluation. I didn't get a promised raise, and two of my best accounts were handed to another woman in the office—a woman he'd just started dating a few weeks before that."

"Scum," Nate mumbled under his breath.

"Exactly," Leandra replied. "I saw the pattern,

realized I'd been a complete idiot, and understood that he'd only wanted me as a decoration. He never really cared about me." She dropped her head then. "I felt so used, so dirty.

"But the worst of it was—I'd been using him too, for my own purposes. When I stopped to analyze my own motives, I felt empty, sick at heart. I'd been so selfish, trying to control my life, fighting against the very instincts that make me who I am inside. I'd turned away from God, turned away from the love and support of my family, neglected my own soul's nurturing, and I came very close to making a big mistake. William and I had treated what should have been a deep and abiding love and respect between a man and a woman with little more than a casual passing. When I thought of the love my parents feel for each other, even after all these years, well…I knew I'd been so wrong.

"I went home one night, stood in the middle of my upscale, ritzy apartment, and saw the emptiness all around me. I realized I was just as bad as William. So I did some heavy praying and after pacing the floor all night, I reached a decision."

Drained and exhausted, tears misting her eyes, she looked up at Nate. "The next morning, I turned in my resignation and…I came home."

Nate pulled her into his arms, hugging her with such a fierce warmth and strength, Leandra knew at that moment that she had indeed come home. At last.

Nate stroked her hair gently. "No matter what you think you did, the man had no reason to ruin your career or treat you that way. You should sue him."

"Sure I could sue him for harassment, and bring out the fact that I had been dating him." Leandra stood back and shook her head. "He'd make mince-meat of me, convince people that I'm just a woman scorned. I won't put my family through that kind of pain. I just want to forget the whole thing, get on with my life."

Nate stepped close again, his hands still caught in her hair. "So what are you going to do now?"

Leandra's heart knew the answer, but she couldn't voice what her heart was shouting at her. "I don't know. I only know that…I've changed in the last few months. I *do* want the simple, basic things—a home to come to whether I'm hurting or happy, and a family that loves me, no matter what, and no matter the size of that family."

"Anything else?" he asked, so close now she could see the tiny flecks of brown and green in his cat eyes. And a gentle yearning.

Did she dare tell him her sweet dream? Her fragile hope?

"I'd like to have a family of my own someday," she said, thinking that would cover everything without revealing anything.

But Nate had a determined, awe-filled look on

his face, a look that matched her own hope even while it scared her. "What made you change your mind, city woman?"

Hesitant, she said, "I told you—I realized that William and I had been—"

"All wrong," he interrupted, his face lined and shadowed from the muted overhead light, his big hands pushing through her hair so she couldn't look away. "I understand that, but I think there's more. So I'll ask you again. What made you change your mind, Lea?"

He'd called her Lea. The intimacy of that, the gentle way he'd said it, brought her a kind of joy she'd never experienced before with any man.

"I think you know the answer to that," she whispered as she reached her arms around his shoulders.

He tugged at her hair, urging her to him. "I want to hear you say it."

Leandra looked up at him, a thousand wishes merging into a silkened thread of need in her heart. "You," she said at last, breathless. "*You* changed my mind, Nate."

His expression shifted from determined to doubtful, and yet he held her there. For a long time, Nate just stared down at her, his gaze traveling like a whisper over her face, finally touching on her lips.

And Leandra held her breath, waiting for the war inside him to end. Waiting for him to find some sort of peace.

"*I'm* no good for you," he said even as he pulled her close. "Maybe you *do* belong in that big mansion on the hill."

Leandra could almost read his mind. He was afraid, because Alicia had given up everything to be with him, and to his way of thinking, she'd paid dearly for that choice. Could he risk that again with Leandra? Could he ask her to do the very same?

Yes, she would risk a lot by falling in love with Nathan Welby. This wasn't safe or shallow. This was very real, more deep and abiding than any form of friendship. And Nate knew that better than anyone. Was he testing her? Giving her one last chance to walk away?

She didn't want to walk away. She wanted... *Oh, Lord,* she prayed, *give me the strength to be worthy of this man. And please, give him some peace, some comfort.*

"I belong right here," she told him, a hand touching his cheek. "If only you'd let me in."

Nate closed his eyes, kissed her hand, then moved close to kiss her lips, testing her, demanding proof and draining her of all willpower. Leandra pushed a hand through his thick, wavy hair, savoring the coarse feel of it, savoring the sweet taste of his lips. This couldn't be wrong, not when it felt ten times more right than anything she'd had with William.

And yet, she could still sense the hesitancy in

Nate. As much as he needed her, he didn't want to let go completely.

Leandra pulled away to give him a beseeching look. "What can I do to convince you?"

He looked down at her, the tenderness and doubt in his eyes only adding to her own fears and needs. She wanted so much to wipe away all his pain.

"Just keep kissing me," he finally said, his mouth capturing hers again.

The kiss was long and sweet, filled with a thousand sensations and a thousand hopes. Leandra could feel the shift in Nate as he slowly gave in to what they both felt so strongly. With a deep longing, she returned his kiss, hoping this tender thread that had somehow bonded them wouldn't be broken again.

When he finally lifted his head, Nate took a breath and grinned, sighing as he managed to regain control. "I think I'd better show you those birdhouses."

Leandra's heart glowed with a warm fire and a burst of white-hot joy. Nate trusted her, at last.

Chapter Fifteen

❧

"This is amazing," Leandra told him much later as
she stood admiring the rows and rows of birdhouses
Nate had made. He'd hidden them away on a high
shelf underneath a canvas tarp. But they needed to be
out in the world. Quickly, she counted at least
twenty tiny houses of various shapes and sizes, some
made out of pine, some made out of oak. A cypress
one here, complete with Spanish moss, a pirogue—
a boat draped in fishing net—and a tiny Cajun sign
that read *laissez les bons temps rouler*—let the good
times roll—hanging over the door. A cedar one over
there, rustic and fresh smelling, the tiny trees surrounding it a miniature of the tree from which he'd
built the house. Each house had its own distinctive
character. Each looked like a home. The careful
details, the ornamentation, all spoke of a gifted hand.

She whirled around, dancing toward him. "Nate,

we have to show these to someone. You—you have such talent."

He shook his head. "I told you, it's just a hobby. Something to pass the time away."

Something to keep the memories away, too, Leandra thought. This man, this gentle, sweet, sad man, built miniature houses for God's small creatures, to replace the real home he thought he'd lost when his wife died.

And yet, his own house sat crumbling around him.

She had to make him see the connection, the correlation between the two. She had to make him let this go, give this gift to others, so that he could find the gift of forgiveness and grace that God readily offered to him.

"Nate, please," she began, asking God to help her do this the right way, "let me display some of these in Richard's store, just to see."

He shook his head again. "I don't think I'm ready for that."

She watched his face, saw the pain centered there in the lines of fatigue around his eyes. His smile didn't reach into those golden eyes. And he refused to look at her.

"And why not?" she finally asked, needing to hear what was in his heart. "Why would you want to keep making these wonderful houses and not show them off to the world?"

He stalked around the workbench, a dark frown

marring his face. "I don't think people would be interested. They're just birdhouses, Leandra."

"They're art," she replied, determined to make him open up, one way or another. It would be the only way he'd ever come to her, and back home to God, completely.

"I don't know about art," he said, lowering his head to gaze at her, a stubborn, proud expression giving him the lionlike quality she'd seen in him when they'd first met. "I just know I like to stay busy, work with my hands. It's doodling, playacting, something to do."

"Playacting," she repeated. "Building little homes, beautiful little objects with such exquisite detailing. Why wouldn't you want to share that gift with others?" Then she tossed him the one question he wasn't ready to answer. "You gave *my* family one. Why did you do that, if you don't want anyone to see them?"

Nate stared at the woman across from him, his heart near bursting with the need to pull her back into his arms. But his whole body was stiff with resistance. So he told her a lie. "I was just returning a kindness, nothing more."

Why *had* he given Leandra and her mother the birdhouse? He'd wanted her to have something beautiful from him, something that was a part of his heart, his past, his dreams. He hadn't been able to give that gift to anyone, until now. And he still wasn't sure why he'd done it for Leandra, except that it had seemed important at the time.

Oh, Lord, what's happening to me? Is this Your answer, Your way of telling me to snap out of it?

Well, he didn't want to snap out of it. He'd taken this too far, way too far with his gifts and his kisses. But earlier, Leandra had felt so good, so right, in his arms. Earlier, he'd told himself it was okay to hold her, to kiss her, to listen to her innermost secrets. He'd asked her to tell him everything. He'd needed to know.

He'd given in to this—this opening up of his own wounds, his own festering regrets and secret yearnings. He had no one to blame but himself.

And yet, he wanted to lay blame at God's door, just as he'd done for so long. That was so easy, so simple. It took all the responsibility away from Nate's own shoulders.

And he wanted to be angry again, to hide the hurting need inside his heart. To hide the truth.

"What are you trying to say, Leandra?" he asked now, a cold shield of frustration making the question edgy and sharp. *Please, God, give me something to be angry about.*

She looked as frustrated as Nate felt. "I'm trying to make you see that you have a gift, a talent. Why are you letting it go to waste? Why are you hiding it away underneath a dirty canvas? Why don't you open it up and let it out in the world? Is it because Alicia's not here to share it with you?"

His head came up then, but he couldn't begin to speak. But Leandra had a lot more to say.

She stopped long enough to take a breath, then said, "I know about the loan, Nate. You and Alicia came to my father—I know this was your dream. It can still happen. My father will help you in any way he can—"

"No."

Okay, he had something to be angry about now. It should feel good, but instead he felt miserable, alone, suffering. At least *that* was familiar.

"How dare you?" he said, halting her with a shaking hand up in the air between them.

With each question she'd hurled across the workbench at him, Nate's anger had grown until all he could see was the red pain of grief—his old friend—there in the muted light of the barn. But now, oh now, blessed, welcome rage replaced the grief. This time, she'd gone too far.

"What do you mean?" Leandra asked, going quiet. "I was just trying to explain, to help—"

"I don't want your help," he told her, shouting so loudly the rafters shook and Honeyboy let out a whinny of protest. Pointing toward the birdhouses, he said, "That was *our* dream—Alicia's and mine. How dare you—you discussed it with your father? He had no right to tell you anything about what Alicia and I wanted, no right."

"He only told me when I insisted—about the

birdhouses," she tried to explain. "He…we want to help you, Nate."

The anger flared like a torch in the night, burning at the emotions he'd tried to deny. "I don't need your help. Can't you understand that? Can't you see that I loved my wife and no woman can ever replace her?"

No matter how that woman makes me feel!

And then he knew, he'd succeeded once and for all. He'd hurt Leandra beyond repair. Yet, he felt no victory. The anger, the grief, felt as dry and bitter as dust and dead leaves in his mouth. It cut to his very core as he watched her face, saw the pain there, saw the hurt, the shock, the realization.

"Yes, I can see that," she said, her voice so quiet, so raw he had to strain to hear her. "I see everything, Nate. It's all very clear to me." She waved her hands toward the tarp, then turned and yanked it down, away from the clutter of the birdhouses. "I can see that you want to hide away here in this old barn, away from your pain, your regrets, away from the knowing faces of your own children. And I feel so sorry for you, so sorry."

"I don't need your pity—"

Leandra pivoted, her eyes all fire and flash now. "Oh, it's not pity. It's…a sad kind of acceptance. You don't want to be happy, really happy, ever again. You want to stay hidden away, covered up, like your precious designs, because if you come out into the light, if you ask me, or my family, or God Himself, for help, then you'll be betraying Alicia. But worse, you'll be tearing down that big wall of grief you're hiding behind."

She came around the table then, her hands at her side, her expression calm and rigid. "If you let go of that grief, you'll have to come clean. You'll have to let go of Alicia's memory and actually forgive yourself. But you can't do that. You can't accept that you're really worthy of forgiveness."

The silence encrusted them in a cold, brisk snap, like a branch caught in a frozen wind.

Then finally Leandra spoke again. "But you're so wrong, Nate. Your children think you're worth forgiving. They just don't know if you can ever forgive *them* for being a part of their mother. Do you know that Layla thinks you hate her? Do you?"

His heart caught in his chest, weighing him down so he had to catch his breath. "Stop it—"

"No," she shouted. "I won't stop it. I won't let you continue to punish yourself this way. Forget the artwork, this goes deeper. You need help, Nate. But then, I've tried to help you, haven't I?"

When he didn't answer, she said, "Well, it's your turn. Now it's all up to you. *You* have to find the strength to help yourself. And…*you* have to ask God, really ask Him from your heart, to give you grace. You have to learn to love yourself again, before you can love your children…or…me."

"I don't love you," he shouted, wagging a finger at her, denial his last true weapon. "I don't...love you."

"I know that," Leandra said, simply, quietly. Then she turned away and headed for the door.

Nate watched her go, his heart calling for her to come back, come back.

A still, silent emptiness penetrated the old barn. The building was full of clutter, full of colorful, decorative little houses.

Empty houses.

Just like his soul.

Was this how Leandra had felt that night, standing all alone in her apartment? He remembered what she had told him, and then he remembered how she'd handled her failings. She'd come home to her family and her Heavenly Father, seeking solace, seeking grace.

But Leandra had much more courage than he could ever possess. He stood there, paralyzed, afraid of his own emotions, and wondered what to do next. He wanted Leandra, but he couldn't have her.

"I don't deserve to be happy again," he said into the stillness.

Then a piercing shard of moonlight from the partially opened door shot through the night, coloring Nate's creations in a glow of pure translucent beauty. He looked up, his gaze never wavering from that one bright spot. Standing there, he remembered Leandra's words earlier about coming out into the light. But he was so afraid, so afraid.

Then suddenly, he understood. He'd been praying, but not with his whole heart. He hadn't let go; he'd wanted to control the blessings God gave out to him. Nate had been in charge, so sure he didn't need anyone, so sure he could never love another woman again. So sure he didn't need God's help or guidance in raising his children. And he'd failed miserably.

"God, dear Lord, help me, help me," he said at last. Then he fell to his knees and cried the tears of the weary.

"I do love you," he finally said, the confession cutting through his throat like bramble as he fought against both it and his tears. "I do love you." He was not only talking to God, but he was telling Leandra the truth at last.

Realization and acceptance poured over Nate like baptism water, drenching him, cleansing him, purging him of all the hostility, all the blame and guilt, all the self-hatred and self-denial.

He wiped his face and got up, then rushed to the door. "Leandra, come back—I do love you."

But she was already gone.

Christmas Eve. Leandra glanced out the kitchen window, wondering if the predictions of snow the weatherman had hinted at would come true. It rarely snowed in East Texas, but the weather had been bitterly cold and icy all week and a huge winter storm was bearing down on them from the northwest. Would they have a white Christmas?

"Honey, do you want some hot chocolate?" Colleen asked as she walked into the kitchen. "Before you head out for the pageant?"

Leandra turned to face her mother, hoping the drained, tired expression she'd seen in the mirror just minutes before was well hidden behind the smile she tried to muster. "Sure, Mom. That sounds great."

"The last performance," Colleen said as she automatically measured milk, cocoa, cinnamon, sugar and vanilla into a big pot on the stove. "Sit down while I stir. I'll be done soon."

Like a sleepwalker, Leandra obeyed her mother. One more night, and then it would all be over. The strain of the last few days was catching up with her. Only through sheer determination and constant prayer had she made it through the first couple of performances.

But her heart wasn't in the program. She kept remembering how angry Nate had been, how he'd declared he only loved Alicia. Leandra had rushed out of that old barn, determined to never set foot on the Welby property again. But when she'd reached her car, she'd fallen against the cold steel and metal, her head in her hands, and cried tears of frustration and anger.

The night had been so cold. And she'd felt so alone. She'd actually thought she'd heard Nate calling to her just as she opened the car door. But it had only been the wind, moaning a forlorn, lonely whine.

Now, she was sleepwalking. Was this how Nate felt each day as he pined away for Alicia? Only half alive, only going through the duties and motions of each day, his soul lost in the past, lost in what might have been?

The production had been a success, with each actor playing his part, each song right on key, each drama clear and deeply moving. Everyone had complimented Leandra on doing a good job.

But she had to wonder, could they all see the pain, the heartbreak in her eyes, in her gestures, in her movements? Did they know that each night as she stood there beside Nate, both of them in their costumes, that he had broken her heart beyond repair? Had anyone noticed how she avoided Nate's gaze, how she managed to ignore him when he called her name, how she managed to stay on the other side of the stage until it was time for them to play their parts?

Did anyone notice that she was so in love with him she could barely breathe?

Someone had noticed.

"Lea, we need to talk," Colleen said in a quiet firm tone. "Here's your cocoa."

Leandra glanced up, completely unaware that her mother had even finished making the hot drink. "What is it, Mom?"

"Sweetie, I'm worried about you. You haven't been yourself over the last few days. Are you worried about going back to Houston?"

Leandra shook her head, the effort of moving almost too much to bear. "No. I'm ready to go back. I need to get back to my life." *Except that I don't have a life anymore.*

Colleen settled on a stool across from her daughter. "I had so hoped you'd decide to stay here. Chet could use your help down at city hall—said he'd ask the city council to give you a raise and make you marketing and public relations director for the city. Have you thought about that?"

Leandra nodded, tried to muster up a smile. "Chet's mentioned it a few times. He wants an answer, but I don't think—"

"It's Nate, isn't it?" Colleen asked, her hand falling across Leandra's. "Honey, tell me what happened."

Leandra knew she could pour her heart out to her mother, just as she'd done when she'd first come home from Houston, and Colleen would listen and try to advise her, without condemnation, without judgment, but always with a mother's strong, fierce love. But where to begin?

"Mom, how do you know when it's real?"

Colleen looked confused for a minute, then said, "You mean love?"

Leandra nodded, unable to say more.

Colleen smiled, patted her hand, then let out a long sigh. "Love is hard to explain, honey. It's a kind of magic, but not like that in a fairy tale or like a magician pulling flowers out of a hat. Love, true love, involves the magic of faith, in knowing that this was part of God's plan. It comes from the heart, and it's more powerful than anything on earth."

Leandra looked up then, tears streaming down her face. "More powerful than a man's love for his dead wife?"

"Oh, honey." Colleen came around the counter to take Leandra in her arms. "I thought as much. You're in love with Nate, aren't you?"

Leandra nodded against the sweet warmth of her mother's old wool cardigan. "But he says he doesn't love me."

"Do you believe him?"

Leandra pulled away, wiped her eyes. "No. I think he does love me, but he's too afraid to admit it. He thinks he'll mess things up, the way he believes he did with Alicia. He feels so much guilt."

Colleen pushed a strand of damp hair off Leandra's face. "You know, honey, it's Christmas. A time of miracles and love. Give Nate some time to settle things with God. If he cares about you, he won't let you go back to Houston." She stood back then, her smile reassuring. "And something tells me he does love you, very much. I had that figured the day you brought that beautiful little birdhouse home."

"I wish I felt as sure as you do," Leandra said.

Because time was running out.

Chapter Sixteen

He didn't have much time left. Nate pushed the old pickup up the highway, headed for town. It was Christmas Eve and he wanted to spend it with his children and the woman he loved.

Leandra.

Would she ever be able to forgive him?

He'd sent Layla and the young ones on with Mr. Tuttle and Aunt Helen—those two had sure become fast friends—so they could get ready for the last performance of the pageant. But not before Helen had come out to the barn to give him a good talking-to.

"How come you stay cooped up out here so much?"

Not wanting to go into detail, Nate grunted. "I work out here."

"Yeah, so I hear. Every night, it seems." When

he didn't respond, she asked, "So what are you doing out here on Christmas Eve?"

"I'm working on something—a Christmas gift for a friend."

"And would that friend happen to be named Leandra Flanagan?"

Nate had given up trying to hide his feelings. If he'd learned one thing since falling for Leandra, it was that the truth would come out, one way or another. "Yes, it's for Leandra. And Helen, I'm sorry if you don't approve, but—"

"But what? Who said I didn't approve? I like that girl. She's pretty, honest, and...she loves your children. What more could I ask?"

Surprised, Nate smiled for the first time since he and Leandra had parted. "You never cease to amaze me, Helen."

"Are you in love again, Nathan?"

"Yes," he told Helen. Then he showed her what he was making.

Helen nodded her approval, a smile gentling the frown that had her eyebrows standing straight up on her face. "Well, she hasn't been around since the other night, and she sure keeps her distance at the Christmas pageant. You two been fighting?"

"Something like that."

"You're a stubborn one, Nate Welby."

"Too stubborn for my own good." He looked up then, the honesty making him feel edgy, almost dizzy. "I don't want to lose her."

Helen punched the sleeve of his denim jacket. "Well, when are you gonna give this to her, and for land sakes, when are you gonna tell her you love her?"

"Tonight," he replied. "Tonight, after the Christmas pageant."

Helen had given him a secretive, knowing smile. "I think tonight is gonna be chock-full of surprises. I love Christmas."

"It's the Christmas Eve performance and Heather Samuels comes down with bronchitis," Chet said, one hand on his head and the other on his stomach. "What are we gonna do, Leandra? We gotta have a solo of 'Silent Night.' It's a tradition."

They were at the civic center, getting ready for tonight's sold-out performance. Leandra didn't think she could take much more.

"I know, I know," she replied, looking down at her watch. Thirty minutes until production and now this. Heather Samuels had the voice of a pop diva and was every bit as pretty. "Is there anyone else who could possibly do it?"

"I can," a small voice said from behind her.

Leandra whirled to find Layla standing there, her big blue eyes filled with hope. "I can sing the solo, if that's okay with y'all."

"Are you sure, honey?" Chet asked, shrugging as he glanced over at Leandra. "Heather's hard to beat, what with her winning all them contests and titles and such."

"I can do it," Layla said, her voice gaining strength. "Mrs. Flanagan—Colleen—says I have a natural talent for singing. Not that anybody at my house would notice."

Leandra knew the girl was referring to her father. She'd already heard Layla complaining that he'd stayed out in the barn most of last night. And now he was late again. Had he just gone back into his self-imposed exile rather than face the truth?

"Okay, Layla," she said, instinct telling her to give Layla a chance. "You will sing the final solo—'Silent Night.' Do you need a warm-up practice?"

Layla's smile was sheepish and shy. "I've been practicing in the bathroom already." Then she looked up at Leandra.

Leandra saw the doubt and sadness in the girl's eyes.

"What's wrong?"

Instead of answering her, Layla rushed to hug Leandra close. "We all wanted you to be our new mother. I'm sorry it didn't work out."

Leandra told herself she wouldn't cry. Yet tears pricked her eyes. "Me, too, honey."

Nate reached the auditorium a few minutes before the time for the production to start. After hurrying to get into the lion costume, he saw Leandra backstage.

The look she cast toward him told him she wasn't too pleased with his being late.

And maybe he was too late. Too late to make amends with his children. Too late to heal the rift with their grandfather, something Helen had been urging him to do. And way too late to make Leandra see that he'd been the biggest kind of fool.

He just wanted to get through this, so he could make Leandra see reason. So he could tell her that he loved her.

But right now, all he could do was wait for his cue.

An hour later, Nate came back out on the stage along with all the other players. Taking his position as lion, he watched Leandra's face underneath the white fleece of her own costume. The lamb didn't look peaceful. And the lion felt like roaring his own discontent. It was time for the last solo, and Nate couldn't wait for it to be over.

"Silent Night."

As the choir off to the right hummed and swayed, the audience members each lit their own thin white candles, passing the flame until the darkness flared brightly with hundreds of tiny beacons. Those beacons seemed to be calling to Nate.

Then with the candlelight to guide them, the angels came to watch over baby Jesus. Little Brittney sure made a beautiful angel. Even rambunctious little Philip looked angelic as he strolled onto the stage. And his own Matthew stood straight and tall, a true shepherd.

Unlike during the other performances, tonight, Nate's impatient, bruised heart seemed to fill with a joy he'd never experienced before. Alicia would be so proud of their children. And he was proud of them, too. Yet it had been a long time since he'd told them that.

Just one more thing he needed to do, to set things right again. If he could just get through this night.

Where was Heather, anyway? It was time for the solo.

And then the entire building seemed to hold its breath as one beautiful angel walked out onto the stage. Nate waited, expecting the local beauty queen to sing as she had during the other productions. But when he instead saw a beautiful blond-haired girl, dressed in flowing pink, his heart stopped.

Layla.

He must have gasped, because Leandra turned to look up at him. Nate didn't even realize he'd reached up to grasp both of Leandra's arms until he looked down and saw he was clinging to her as she stood in front of him. But he couldn't let go.

And then he heard Layla's soft sweet voice and wondered if the angels were indeed singing tonight.

As his oldest daughter sang this most holy of songs, Nate's heart let go of the last of its bitterness.

All was calm, all was bright. He had a future filled with hope, and…his heart was filled with a heavenly peace.

He could almost hear Alicia's sweet words echoing in his daughter's beautiful voice.

Nate, be happy. Be strong. Be at peace. It's all right now, darling. Everything is as it should be.

When Layla finished the song, Nate fought against the tears falling down his face. He leaned toward Leandra then, his hands still gripping her arms.

"I didn't know," he said, the whisper full of an urgent tenderness. "I didn't know."

To his great relief, Leandra didn't pull away—they were onstage after all. Instead, she turned to glance up at him, her own eyes misty and brimming with tears. Then she placed a hand on his arm. "Now you do."

"That was the most beautiful—" Helen stopped, dabbing at her eyes with a tissue, her expensive white wool suit smeared with tear streaks. "Layla, darling, you are blessed with an incredible voice. What a songbird!"

Nate, still in costume, stood with his family in the hallway just beyond the stage. Pulling Layla close, he said, "Honey, I am so proud of you. Why didn't you tell me you could sing like that?"

"I tried," Layla replied, hugging him tightly.

"But I never listened, did I?"

At her muffled "No," he lifted her chin with a thumb. "Well, from now on, things are gonna be different. I'm going to be a better father, to all of you."

"That's a start," a gruff voice said from behind him. "And I'm going to join in that promise by being a better grandfather."

Nate turned to find Davis Montgomery standing there in an expensive wool overcoat and tailored business suit.

"Hello, Nate."

Nate glanced over at Helen. "You called him."

"I surely did. Merry Christmas, Nathan."

Davis came closer, then smiled down at the three wide-eyed children standing with Nate and Helen. "Layla, I'm your grandfather Montgomery. And I just have to say that you have the voice of an angel."

"You heard me?" Layla asked, a smile brightening her face.

"I heard you." Davis extended his hand to Nate. "And if your father doesn't mind, I'd love to follow y'all home for a Christmas Eve visit."

Nate looked down at the hopeful, expectant faces of his children, then reached out to shake the other man's hand. He had to start living up to his promises and tonight was as good a time as any. "I don't mind at all. We'd be glad to have you."

"Then we'll just go on home and get the coffee started and the pecan pie cut," Helen said, grabbing

Nate by his lion's mane to turn him around. "While you take care of that…unfinished business."

Nate followed the direction of her gaze.

Leandra was watching them from the other door.

Leandra told herself to just go. Get out of this silly costume and go on home. But her family was waiting for her at the church across the street. She couldn't skip the Christmas Eve service. She needed to be with her family, now more than ever.

But Nate was waiting for her at the end of the hall.

At least, he looked like he wanted to tell her something. But then, he'd had plenty of time, all week, to talk to her.

You avoided him, remember?

She watched as he kissed his children and sent them off with Helen and their grandfather. She'd figured out the tall, distinguished-looking man must be Davis Montgomery. Would Nate turn him away, too?

It didn't look that way. Davis was laughing and talking, with Brittney up in his arms and Matt right at his heels asking questions as they left the building with Helen.

The now quiet, deserted building.

Leandra stood at one door, and Nate stood at the other.

Then he motioned for her.

And she went to him.

"Can you come out to the prayer garden with me?" he asked.

Her heart tapped at her chest like a bare branch hitting a window. "Nate, I—"

"Please?" he asked, his gaze never wavering.

In spite of the agony she felt deep inside, Leandra saw something there in his eyes. Something firm and sure. And complete.

"Let me go change," she replied, not willing to have a serious conversation in a lamb's suit.

He looked down at his own outfit. "Yeah, I guess I'd better do that myself. I'll meet you there in about five minutes."

A short time later, Leandra was dressed in her best burgundy wool Christmas dress, her black wool topper keeping the chill of the icy wind off her as she made her way over to the prayer garden. It was nearly dusk, and the church service would be starting soon, *but Nate wanted to see her.*

She kept telling herself not to get excited. *Don't let your heart do this.* He just wants to say goodbye.

That's all.

But when she looked up and saw him coming toward her in his jeans and worn leather jacket, her heart got the better of her. He was carrying a large, gift-wrapped box. And he was smiling.

"What's this?" she asked when he handed her the box. The shiny Christmas paper felt cool against her hands as she took the package.

And then it started to snow, the shimmering flakes falling like crystallized teardrops all around them.

She held a hand up to catch a delicate snowflake. "Maybe we'd better—"

"Open it, Leandra. Before I lose my nerve."

She looked up at him, watching the tiny perfectly formed snowflakes as they hit his thick, wavy hair and settled on his bronze face. Nate ignored the snow, his gaze locked with hers, and in the silence of the white cadence, Leandra saw hope there in his eyes.

She sat down on the bench—the same bench where he'd first kissed her. With shaking hands, she tugged at the colorful holiday paper, then tried to get the box open.

"Let me help," Nate said. Bending down on one knee, he kneeled in front of her to hold the square box while she reached inside to claim her prize.

And then she saw it. A small, Victorian house. Another birdhouse. Though the churchyard lights were muted because of the falling snow, Leandra could tell this was an exact replica of his own house.

Except this one wasn't rundown or forlorn looking.

And over the doorway, there was a small gold-etched sign that read Lea's House.

"Nate," she said as she held the dainty white-and-blue house on her lap, "it's so…perfect."

"It can be," he said, still on bent knee. "If you'll still have me."

"What do you mean?"

"I mean," he said, reaching up a hand to crush her hair against her face, "that I was wrong. And I'm asking you to forgive me. I didn't tell you the truth the other night."

She leaned her head into his open hand, pressing her cheek against the warmth of his palm. Then she closed her eyes. "What is the truth, Nate?"

He urged her head up. "Look at me."

She opened her eyes then, to find him so close, his gaze holding her there.

"I love you," he said. "And…I want you to be my wife." When she tried to speak, he quieted her with a finger to her lips. "And I want you to live in a house just like this one. My house. Our house. I'm going to remodel it from basement to turret, rebuild it like I built this little house, just for you, Lea. Only you."

Leandra couldn't stop the tears from falling. Nor could she stop her next words. "But…it was Alicia's—"

"Was," he said, the one word filled with so much pain and despair, she wondered if he still had doubts himself. *"Was,"* he repeated, stronger now, his finger still brushing her lips. "But I'm okay with that—I've made my peace with the Lord. And I'm willing to show off those birdhouses, if you still have a hankering to be my marketing manager." He moved his fingers over her face, touching on teardrops and snowflakes alike, then leaned close to give her a quick kiss. "I'm a changed man, thanks to you."

"Nate, I didn't mean to change you."

"Ah, but you did. You did. And I thank God for it. And...I want you in my life now and forever." Taking the little house from her, he placed it back in the box. "Now, what do you say? I can't offer you fancy cars and city lights, but I can offer you this love I feel with all my heart. Will you marry me?"

Before she could answer, they heard running feet moving across the parking lot. Leandra looked up to see three children barreling down on them. Three happy, grinning, blond-haired children.

"Did she say yes? Did she?" Brittney asked as she slammed into her father and sent him sprawling in the newly formed snow. "Aunt Helen told us you were gonna ask her. Can we watch?"

Matt and Layla reached them then, their faces cherry-red from the cold and their own excitement.

Layla, as usual, stood back, waiting. And behind her, Helen and Davis huddled together, brother and sister alike as their wing-tipped brows shot up in a questioning expression.

"They insisted on finding you," Helen explained with a shrug.

"Well?" Matt asked, his hands on his hips, his head slanted at a sideways angle. "Are y'all really getting married?"

Nate, on the ground with Brittney glued to his neck, lifted his face toward Leandra. "That all depends on Leandra. Will you marry us, Miss Flan-again?"

Leandra looked down at the man at her feet, her breath catching in her throat. He sat there in the snow, with a child on his lap, looking so lovable, so honest, that she knew she couldn't ever leave his side again.

"Yes, I will marry you—y'all," she said, tears streaming down her face. "Yes."

Nate lifted himself up, holding Brittney tightly in one arm as he placed the other around Leandra and kissed her firmly.

"Thank you."

"For what?" she asked, her lips inches from his.

"For believing in me, for agreeing to be my wife. For forgiving me."

"I love you," she said.

Brittney giggled as Nate stood and held her high in the air, swinging her around in the soft, silent snowfall. "She loves us, sunshine. What do you say about that?"

Brittney smiled her delight as her father whirled her around and around. "I'm glad," she called out, enjoying the echo of her words as she flew through the air. "But I told you she was perfect, didn't I?"

"You sure did," Nate said, lifting her out over his head.

"I'm a snow angel," Brittney said, squealing in

delight as she held her arms out, the snowfall hitting her face. "And I've finally got a new mommy."

"That's good enough for me," Helen said, grabbing children in both hands. "Now, Nate put that child down before you both throw up. Why don't we head back to the house for a real celebration?"

Nate dropped Brittney to her feet, caught his breath, then pulled Leandra up off the bench. He took Leandra's hand on one side and Layla's on the other. Looking back at Matt, Helen and Davis, he said, "I've got a better idea. Let's go to church."

And that's exactly what they did. As a family.

Epilogue

The next Thanksgiving…

"Leandra, thank you so much for inviting us to your home for Thanksgiving." Colleen looked down the long table at her daughter, her words lifting over the drone of many voices talking all at once.

Leandra smiled at her mother, then glanced at her husband. "Thank Nate, Mom. He's the one who insisted it was our turn to play host. I think he just wanted to show off the house."

Jack held up his tea glass. "Well, the house *is* beautiful, but I'd like to especially thank him for keeping *you* out of the kitchen. Nate, the smoked turkey and baked ham sure do look good."

Nate laughed while Leandra wagged a finger at her brother then said, "I made the fruit salad, thank you."

Margaret bobbed her head. "I watched her. She knew exactly what she was doing."

"Just so she didn't make any of her famous dumplings," Richard said, grinning from ear to ear.

Davis Montgomery, sitting by Aunt Helen, lifted a brow. "I don't think I've ever had your dumplings, Leandra. Maybe you can whip up a batch while I'm here."

Helen, resplendent in a dark-brown sweater with a happy, grinning gold-and-orange turkey embroidered across the front, winked at Leandra, then slapped her brother on the back. "I'm sure she'd be glad to do just that, right, Lea?"

Nate smiled, then leaned over to kiss his frowning wife. "Everyone should experience your dumplings at least once, honey."

When her brothers all started snickering and hiding their grins behind their white linen napkins, Leandra couldn't resist her own smile. "Okay, enough," she replied, slamming a hand down on the Battenburg lace tablecloth. "Everyone contributed to *this* meal, and I'm just thankful that we're all here together."

"Me, too," Nate said, taking his wife's hand. "And I'd like to say grace now."

While everyone held hands around the table, and the children—Cameron and Philip, Corey, Brittney and Matt sitting at the smaller children's table, and his all-grown-up Layla sitting quietly by Mark—all closed their eyes to give thanks, Nate took a moment to reflect on the past year.

He still couldn't believe how good his life was now. He had three wonderful, healthy children and he'd inherited a large, loud, pushy, nosy, loving family when he'd married Leandra back in the spring. As he looked around at the people gathered at his dining table, Nate once again thanked God for giving him a second chance to be happy.

His children now had their Aunt Helen and their grandfather Montgomery in their lives on a regular basis. He was glad they'd come to be here today, too.

Jack and Margaret sat together by Leandra's parents. Those two had taken some time to get used to, but they'd turned out to be his closest friends. And now they had a brand-new baby daughter, Emily. Michael and Kim had accepted Nate right away. He watched as they fussed over their toddler, Carissa. Mark was still the quiet, observant one, but he'd been the best man at their wedding, and he was a good listener—and still very much single.

And Richard—Richard had helped Nate to launch Welby Woodworks by pushing Nate's designs in his store and setting up a Web site on the Internet. Now, it seemed everybody wanted a Welby birdhouse in their own home. He had orders well into next year.

Nate also owed a big thanks to Howard and

Colleen Flanagan. They'd accepted his children as their own grandchildren by offering advice, baby-sitting and carpooling whenever he and Leandra were busy.

And they stayed very busy these days, what with his regular job as construction foreman and his business on the side, and her work at city hall. But they were never too busy for family. Now, Nate's after-hours work was scheduled with family in mind—the children and Leandra pitched in and helped, and kept him company while he worked. The barn was now a place for all of them to be together, not just a retreat for a man with a broken heart.

And Leandra.

Thanks to Leandra, his heart was full and happy again. And his house was built on a strong foundation of faith. Leandra had made this place a home by working tirelessly to redecorate and refurbish each and every room. Today, the whole house shined and glistened with all the colors of fall—pumpkins on the porch, gold, orange, and burgundy colored mums growing in the many flower beds and sitting in clay pots and brightly painted containers all over every available surface of the house. The Welby home was full of so much bounty—more than he ever dreamed possible.

Nate finished the prayer, then smiled at the people, the family, that filled his home on this special day. But he had one more thing to be grateful for on this Thanksgiving. Giving Leandra a questioning look, he whispered, "Can I tell them?"

"Tell us what, Daddy?" Brittney said from her spot at the children's table.

Philip grinned and swiped her roll while she wasn't looking, but a frown from his grandfather made him put it right back down.

"You've sure got big ears," Nate told his youngest daughter. "But your mom and I do have a surprise." He sent Layla a special, secret look. She already knew—they'd had a long talk last night. Her smile told him she couldn't wait to share the news with the rest of the family.

"What? What?" Brittney asked, jumping up in her chair.

"Don't knock your milk over," Nate warned. Then he turned to Leandra. The tears in her eyes only added to the glow on her face. His wife had never looked more beautiful.

"Tell them," she said, her eyes bright.

Taking her hand in his, Nate looked out over the table, took a deep breath, then said, "We're going to have a baby."

Everyone started talking at once. Margaret and Kim both got up to hug Leandra, while Howard and Colleen hugged each other and grinned. Davis and Helen gave each other a long, meaningful look, then shook hands with Leandra's parents. Brittney danced around the table, clapping her hands and squealing her delight.

"I hope it's a boy," Matt said, rolling his eyes at his sister's embarrassing display of pride.

Leandra's four brothers gave each other high fives and hooted with laughter. "She finally did it," Richard said.

"That's great," Mark added, his gaze centered on Leandra. "I'm happy for you, Sis."

Leandra wiped the tears from her eyes, then glanced out the window to the big, sunny side porch just off the dining room. "Look, Nate. The cardinals are in their house. Maybe they'll have babies soon, too."

Nate watched as the birds fussed and played on the tiny porch of the Victorian birdhouse he'd built for Leandra last Christmas. Like a beam straight from heaven, rays of noonday sunshine poured a bright golden light over the dainty little house.

Lea's house.

He'd never seen a more beautiful sight.

* * * * *

Dear Reader,

We've all made plans for ourselves only to have those plans change through circumstance. Sometimes it's hard to understand why life doesn't turn out the way we wanted. And sometimes, we find strength through adversity.

When Leandra found Nathan, he was broken in spirit and shut off from what mattered most in life—his home, his family and his faith. Leandra was beginning to discover these things were important to her. Now she had to show Nate he was still worthy of a happy home and strong faith in God.

It was wonderful to bring these two very different people together with those basic principles we all seek in our plan for life—home and family, faith and love.

God does have a plan for each of us, but we have to step out into the light and ask for his help in order to see that plan. I'm so glad Nate took that step and made a home with Leandra. Maybe you've lost your way, lost sight of God's plan for your life. If so, turn to the light and ask God to guide your way. He will direct your steps. I hope this story comforts you in your own faith journey.

Until next time, may the angels watch over you while you sleep.

Lenora Worth

LARGER-PRINT BOOKS!

GET 2 FREE LARGER-PRINT NOVELS PLUS 2 FREE MYSTERY GIFTS

Love Inspired®

Larger-print novels are now available...

YES! Please send me 2 FREE LARGER-PRINT Love Inspired® novels and my 2 FREE mystery gifts (gifts are worth about $10). After receiving them, if I don't wish to receive any more books, I can return the shipping statement marked "cancel". If I don't cancel, I will receive 4 brand-new novels every month and be billed just $4.49 per book in the U.S. or $4.99 per book in Canada. That's a savings of over 30% off the cover price. It's quite a bargain! Shipping and handling is just 50¢ per book.* I understand that accepting the 2 free books and gifts places me under no obligation to buy anything. I can always return a shipment and cancel at any time. Even if I never buy another book, the two free books and gifts are mine to keep forever.

121 IDN EYLZ 321 IDN EYME

Name	(PLEASE PRINT)	
Address		Apt. #
City	State/Prov.	Zip/Postal Code

Signature (if under 18, a parent or guardian must sign)

Mail to Steeple Hill Reader Service:
IN U.S.A.: P.O. Box 1867, Buffalo, NY 14240-1867
IN CANADA: P.O. Box 609, Fort Erie, Ontario L2A 5X3

Are you a current subscriber of Love Inspired books and want to receive the larger-print edition?
Call 1-800-873-8635 or visit www.morefreebooks.com.

* Terms and prices subject to change without notice. Prices do not include applicable taxes. Sales tax applicable in N.Y. Canadian residents will be charged applicable provincial taxes and GST. Offer not valid in Quebec. This offer is limited to one order per household. All orders subject to approval. Credit or debit balances in a customer's account(s) may be offset by any other outstanding balance owed by or to the customer. Please allow 4 to 6 weeks for delivery. Offer available while quantities last.

Your Privacy: Steeple Hill Books is committed to protecting your privacy. Our Privacy Policy is available online at www.SteepleHill.com or upon request from the Reader Service. From time to time we make our lists of customers available to reputable third parties who may have a product or service of interest to you. If you would prefer we not share your name and address, please check here. ☐

LILP09

Love Inspired® SUSPENSE

RIVETING INSPIRATIONAL ROMANCE

PROTECTING *the* WITNESSES

*New identities, looming danger and forever love
in the Witness Protection Program.*

TWIN TARGETS BY MARTA PERRY
JANUARY 2010

KILLER HEADLINE BY DEBBY GIUSTI
FEBRUARY 2010

COWBOY PROTECTOR
BY MARGARET DALEY
MARCH 2010

DEADLY VOWS BY SHIRLEE MCCOY
APRIL 2010

FATAL SECRETS BY BARBARA PHINNEY
MAY 2010

RISKY REUNION BY LENORA WORTH
JUNE 2010

*Available wherever books are sold, including most
bookstores, supermarkets, drugstores and discount stores.*

www.SteepleHill.com

Steeple
Hill®

LISPTW10LIST